Zieglitz's Blessing

Zieglitz's Blessing

A Novel

by

MICHAEL GOLDBERG

CASCADE *Books* • Eugene, Oregon

ZIEGLITZ'S BLESSING
A Novel

Cascade Books
An Imprint of Wipf and Stock Publishers
199 W. 8th Ave., Suite 3
Eugene, OR 97401

www.wipfandstock.com

PAPERBACK ISBN: 978-1-6667-4006-6
HARDCOVER ISBN: 978-1-6667-4007-3
EBOOK ISBN: 978-1-6667-4008-0

Cataloguing-in-Publication data:

Names: Goldberg, Michael, author.

Title: Zieglitz's blessing : a novel / Michael Goldberg.

Description: Eugene, OR: Cascade Books, 2023.

Identifiers: ISBN 978-1-6667-4006-6 (paperback) | ISBN 978-1-6667-4007-3 (hardcover) | ISBN 978-1-6667-4008-0 (ebook)

Subjects: LCSH: Jews—Fiction. | Jewish families—Fiction. | Fathers and sons—Fiction.

Classification: PS3608.O633 Z45 2023 (paperback) | PS3608.O633 (ebook)

VERSION NUMBER 070522

To Cissie and Lou

"Why don't You come down and fight like a man!"

—Professional golfer Tommy Bolt shaking his fist at the heavens
after lipping the cup on six straight holes

Acknowledgments

I once heard the writer Isabel Allende tell the story of visiting her dentist for a checkup and having him say to her, "You know, when I retire, I'm going to be a novelist." Allende replied, "You know, when I retire, I'm going to be a dentist."

I suspect Allende knows from experience the truth of the old adage, "There's no such thing as good writing—only good rewriting." Whatever quality my writing has achieved in this book comes from the rewriting I've done thanks to the prompting of what I've always cherished: intelligent readers. When I first started writing *Zieglitz's Blessing* over a dozen years ago, no reader's insights could have been more helpful than Phyllis Gorfain's. Later on, the astute comments of her brother, Louis Gorfain, were invaluable as well. I'm also indebted to Randy Auerbach, Chris Brewster, and Jack Sammons, who read earlier drafts of the book. My son, Matthew, another early reader, additionally contributed, with his brother Nathaniel, to the book's cover design. As the project moved toward completion, I never could have done without the sharp-eyed edits of Rodney Clapp.

I'd especially like to thank the novelists, Scott Guild, who quite correctly pushed me to change the book's title, and Elizabeth McCracken, who encouraged me to keep writing and even more important, put me in contact with Catherine Nichols, without whose perceptive editorial suggestions this book, quite simply, would never have come to be.

Finally, I am grateful to my mother Edye and to my love Stephanie, both of whose patience and support have been this Zieglitz's constant blessing.

I

He lifted his hospital sheets and peered down at its stump with disgust.

From the time he was eight days old, it had identified him. It had marked his belonging to them. It had signified his belonging to Him. Now, its disfigurement served as a repugnant reminder of what he and God each had become. A prick.

Not that things had started out that way.

"Our God and God of our ancestors, sustain this child. Let him be known among the Jewish People as 'Yerachmiel ben Baruch.'"

Zieglitz had no actual memory of the event, nor, given his own recent experience, could he conceive of a male of any age wanting to summon up the image of a blade's slicing off part of his penis. The first he'd heard of his initial maiming had come from his father eight years later, and then, only in passing.

"Look, Ricky," he could still hear Daddy saying, "I had a *bar mitzvah* at the *shul*, and so did your Grandpa Irv. It's a big step in your life, a sign of your becoming a man. But to get ready for it, you have to go to Hebrew school. It's totally up to you. Do you want to get *bar mitzvah*ed or not?"

Ricky was flabbergasted. Mommy hadn't left brushing his teeth or getting his shots up to him, and she'd given him no say in taking the swimming lessons in which she'd enrolled him to "get you away from your books for once." Daddy had never given him much leeway, either, except for where to move next in checkers, something he'd invariably get wrong. Why, then, he wondered, had his father given him a say now in something so important?

"It's like this, Ricky," Daddy began, seeing his blank stare. "I want you to have more choices about what happens in your life than I've had in mine. If you decide against having a *bar mitzvah*, I know there'll be people who'll go along with your mother and accuse me of being cheap, of wanting to dodge the *shul*'s dues and the Hebrew school's tuition. But I don't care what any of them thinks—not even Pop!"

Ricky realized what a big deal it'd be for Daddy to stand up to his father, Grandpa Irv, who could read Hebrew faster than anybody else at their seders. He never stopped for any English, not for so much as a "Blessed art Thou, O Lord," which the rabbi Ricky would later become knew was the Haggadah's rendering of its most recurrent Hebrew phrase, "*Baruch atah Adonai*." The way Grandpa Irv whizzed through those words, they sounded like "Broke Otto Adenoid."

"I guess it all boils down to this, pal," Daddy said, placing his hands on Ricky's shoulders. "Do you want a *bar mitzvah*? Are you willing to go to Hebrew school to have one?"

Ricky didn't need to think twice. "Can't wait!"

"All right, then," Daddy replied, "you need to know what your Hebrew name is. It's the first thing they'll ask you in class."

"What do you mean, my 'Hebrew name'?"

"That's the name you got at your *bris*—"

"What's a '*bris*'?"

Daddy took a deep breath; it wasn't a topic he'd planned on addressing. "When you were eight days old," he explained, "a rabbi came to the house to perform a ceremony called a '*bris*'—what's known in English as a 'circumcision.' It's something we Jews have been doing for thousands of years . . ." It took several minutes before Daddy got around to the part about the knife and Ricky's *schmeckle*.

"But why *there*?" Ricky gasped in disbelief.

"Because that's where God told Abraham to do it," Daddy responded.

Daddy had just told Ricky the scariest story he'd ever heard: from the beginning, God, being Jewish, and pain had been inextricably bound up together.

Seeing that the appeal to Tradition had gotten him nowhere, Daddy invoked Science. "You know what happens if you don't get circumcised, Ricky?" he said. "Your foreskin, the penis flap Jews cut away, gets *schmutz* trapped beneath it. Lots of studies say that's why *goyim* get so much cancer down there."

Ricky's face said it all: clinical research was no match for how icky circumcision still seemed.

"Enough about your *bris*," Daddy gave up, returning to his original point. "All you need to know for now is that you got your Hebrew name then. When they ask you for it at Hebrew school, tell them it's 'Yerachmiel ben Baruch.'"

"So my middle name in Hebrew is 'Ben'?"

"No," Daddy answered, "'ben' is Hebrew for 'son of.' So you're 'Yerachmiel son of Baruch,' who's me."

At that precise moment, his spouse walked in. "Bernie, I heard what you just told Ricky. It's bad enough I had to give up my maiden name when I married you, but why shouldn't Ricky's Hebrew name include mine, too? Last time I checked, there was only one Jew in history with only one human parent, and look how he ended up!"

"What were they going to call him—'Yerachmiel, son of Baruch and *Madge*'?" Bernie retorted. "At least I've got a Hebrew name. Nobody from your family has one!" He turned back to Ricky and said in a much softer voice, "You see, pal, 'Yerachmiel' is the same Hebrew name your great-grandfather had. Ever since I was your age, Pop's told me how some Cossack bastard in the old country killed him."

"Thank goodness, Ricky," Mommy threw up her hands, "I was the one who picked what you'd be called in English."

"What's so hot about 'Roderick'?" Bernie rejoined.

"It's a strong, masculine name."

"If it's such a great choice, then why didn't we nickname him 'Roddy'? You know the reason. Other kids would've made fun of him and said he was a *feigele* like that actor, Roddy McDowall. Nobody'll tease him about 'Ricky.'"

Madge wasn't about to let Bernie have the last word. "Have you told Ricky how many years of Hebrew school it'll take him to have a *bar mitzvah*? Have you mentioned how many days and hours he'll have to spend there each week?"

And that was his introduction to what it meant to be Jewish. According to his father and mother, it was being heir to one long saga of suffering.

Ricky already knew something about suffering. He thought back to the first event he could recall. Having barely turned two, he was staring up at a car frame so close it had scraped his face. A year or so later, he learned how he'd wound up there when, getting ready for bed, he said to Mommy concerning his favorite toy, "Who gave me my fire truck? Was it you and Daddy?"

"No, it wasn't us."

"*Who then?*"

"It's a long story," she said, trying to slip away so she could catch a TV show that she loved.

"Does everybody live happily ever after?" he asked, scootching under his covers.

"Hardly," she snorted, glancing at her wristwatch. "Even before you were born, this little town of Huppertsville had been home to our family for a long time. It's where your father and I grew up—both sets of your grandparents had businesses here. There was 'Mr. Z's Women's Apparel,' which your Grandpa Irv and Grandma Thelma, the Zieglitzes, started and 'Apters' Market,' which my folks, Jack and Dina, owned. Mother ran the register while Dad stocked the shelves. We were so poor then we had to live in the attic over the grocery. It wasn't until Prohibition—"

"What's that?" Ricky said.

"When it was against the law to sell liquor. It wasn't until Prohibition that we had enough cash to move out of the attic and into a boarding house. We rented three rooms there: one for me, one for my parents, and one for visitors who'd drop by to discuss 'expanding the business'—or so Mother told me. Once Prohibition ended, Mother and Dad somehow managed to get liquor licenses before anybody else in the county. In no time flat, they'd opened two bars, and all the hard times were over. I can still see Dad driving up in our first new Chrysler Imperial and hollering, 'No more ridin' around in the same goddam truck we use to haul produce!' Not long after that, Mother and I got an even bigger surprise when he bought *Casa Futura*."

Ricky couldn't imagine anywhere grander. The largest house in Huppertsville, none of the aluminum-sided bungalows flecking the Midwestern hamlet could touch it. Surrounded by acres of dense woods with sprawling lawns and gardens, the fifteen-room mansion was built in a classic Spanish style. It had cream, stucco walls, a terra-cotta-tiled roof, and black iron grillwork around its balconies and atop the walls of its serpentine driveway. The ironwork formed arabesques at the gates opening onto the estate.

The grounds also encompassed a cottage that, in miniature, mirrored the manor above it. Ricky lived in it until he was five, and he loved living there because of who lived in the great house just up the way—Dina, whom he called "Dee-Dee" and her husband, whom he called "Jack," though either would have been fine with whatever he called them so long as it wasn't "Grandpa" and "Grandma," or "Grandad" and "Granny," or anything else that made them seem *old*. "So this cottage where we live," Mommy went on, "used to be the home of Mother and Dad's gardener, Judd, and his wife, Essie, who was their maid. When you were born, Mother and Dad set them up someplace else and let us move down here. Like now, your father didn't have much money, and I guess they thought being near them again would help cheer me up."

"Are Jack and Dee-Dee rich, Mommy?"

"Let's just say they don't have to pinch pennies anymore. Not that your father's parents don't have money, too," she added resentfully. "They just won't spend it!"

"Mommy, tell me how I got my truck!"

"Let me finish!" she snapped as she glanced again at her watch. "You know Jack and Dee-Dee's garage, where they've got their two cars and the grocery truck? Since it's by the widest part of their driveway, we used to keep your tricycle in it so you could ride around up there whenever you wanted. One afternoon, Dee-Dee was backing out her Chrysler to go to the grocery when you pedaled in right behind her. She didn't see you. How could she? The car was so big, and you were so little! The only thing that made Mother stop was the sound of metal grinding on metal. She says she's never forgotten that noise—it's why she doesn't drive anymore."

Ricky's memories hadn't left him, either. He could still feel the blood oozing down his forehead and the tricycle's nickel-plated handlebars pinning his chest beneath something dark and enormous above him. Out of the corner of one eye, he could see a fireman talking to Dee-Dee, perhaps telling her, "If it weren't for that trike frame, Dina, the boy would have been crushed." He couldn't hear the fireman's actual words, though. They were drowned out by his screams of "Where are my mommy and daddy?!"

Out having a swell time as it so happened.

"I'd had it up to here looking after you, Ricky, and I needed a day off," Mommy said without any thought about the impact her words might have on him. "So I had your father drive us to the state capital in Excelsior. It's only forty miles away, but when you're stuck here in the boondocks, it might as well be four hundred. It's where I always have to go to get the newest fashions—I swear, they never have anything at Mr. Z's! Anyway, we didn't find out about your getting run over until we got back that night. I know it must have been awful for you, dear, but," she paused before saying wistfully, "it was one of the best days I've ever had!" She'd forgotten all about Ricky's truck. It didn't bother him, though. He was fast asleep.

As Ricky got older, his parents' absences grew more frequent, but he didn't mind them. He no longer missed either one of them, because Dee-Dee and Jack would never miss a chance to be with him. Whenever his mother would frantically call *Casa Futura*, complaining, "I've had it with Ricky! You need to come get him! I have to get out!" Jack would arrive within minutes. Ricky would follow him up the flagstone path from the cottage to the mansion with the fire truck Jack had bought him tucked under his arm. Dee-Dee would give him the run of the house, and, if that didn't seem sufficient—not to Ricky, but to her—she'd have Jack drive them to the small-town pleasures Huppertsville had for a child to enjoy: its park where Dee-Dee would push him to and fro on a swing; its tractor lot where Jack would hoist him onto a green-and-yellow John Deere; its Dairy Queen where they'd buy him a soft-serve vanilla cone crowned with a butterscotch glaze.

Something else made Ricky feel good about being with Jack and Dee-Dee; unlike his father and mother, they always got along. One night, after his parents had been fighting again, he asked Daddy, "Why did you and Mommy get married?"

"Simple," Daddy said. "Your mother was the only Jewish girl in town, and I was the only Jewish boy."

Daddy's explanation struck five-year-old Ricky as a powerful reason not to marry somebody Jewish.

"There was a little more to it than that!" Mommy huffed, in no mood for a cease-fire. "I was a few years behind your father in high school, where all the girls had crushes on him. He had such gorgeous blond hair and blue eyes, he could have passed for a Gentile."

"And was Mommy the prettiest girl, Daddy?"

"Not exactly," Madge said bitterly before Bernie could answer. "I was chubby like you, Ricky, and besides wearing braces, I had the Apter nose. Before I got it fixed later on, I'd look at that eagle beak in the mirror sometimes and think it could open beer cans!"

"But you were still smart, right, Mommy?"

"Not like your father," she said grudgingly. "He won the state high school debate tournament and then the nationals in Washington. College was a snap for him. Just like high school, he graduated near the top of his class."

"Were you in college together?"

"No, Mother and Dad sent me to a private, out-of-state school. Your other grandparents, true to form, had your father go to State U., where it was a whole lot less pricey."

"Did you do good in college like Daddy?"

"The only thing I was good at," she said ruefully, "was sitting around and playing bridge for two years. Mother and Dad really wanted a grand-child, and when they saw that I wasn't much interested in studying, they said they'd throw me a big, fancy wedding if I'd come home and marry your father. What a mistake that was! I shouldn't have fallen for his uniform when he came back from the war."

"Tell me what you did in the war, Daddy!" Ricky shouted.

"There's not much to tell," Daddy said with a shrug. "The war started just as I was finishing college. I volunteered for the Navy, they commissioned me as a second lieutenant and sent me to the Pacific, where I was assigned to a destroyer. The captain made me the ship's antiaircraft officer.

I had to make split-second decisions before opening fire whether incoming planes were the enemy's or ours. I was also the guy charged with unjamming the guns anytime they got shells stuck inside them."

"It sounds really exciting!"

"Stressful's more like it . . . ," Daddy said quietly. "Before the war, I'd planned on going to law school after college. With my debate experience, I thought I'd be right at home in a courtroom. But after three years on that destroyer, I couldn't take any more pressure. So it didn't take much to convince me to stick around here and take the job at Mr. Z's." Daddy stopped and shook his head. "So, Ricky," he said dolefully, "look what's happened to your war hero father: he's a *schlepper* who sells *shmata*s for his parents and who lives in his in-laws' old servants' quarters."

"Look, Bernie," Mommy barged in, "it hasn't been easy for me, either! If your parents weren't so chintzy, and this town weren't so tiny, there'd be more opportunities for us all!"

Bernie didn't even try to rebut her. "Fine, Madge, fine," he said, worn down. "I'll see what I can do."

Three days later, he arrived home early yelling, "Madge! Ricky!"

Alarmed, Madge came running. "Bernie, what's wrong?!"

"Nothing!" he responded with a broad grin. "We're gonna move to Medina!"

"What's 'Medina'?" Ricky asked.

Beaming down, Daddy answered, "It's the biggest city in the state just north of us. Unlike this burg, it's got plenty to do!"

Even though Ricky thought Huppertsville had plenty to do—the park, the tractor lot, the DQ—he didn't say anything. His parents for once seemed happy.

"It couldn't have gone any better," Bernie told Madge. "When I called Aileen, in Medina, I was a little nervous about asking that sister of mine to get her SOB husband on the phone to see if he'd give me some leads. I was floored when Ernest picked up and said he'd be more than glad to show me the ins and outs of becoming a developer like him. Do you remember when we visited him, Aileen, and their four boys at the huge home he built them in the middle of Greenlawn, the city's ritziest area? How do you think he got the dough to do it? By being so successful at putting up cookie-cutter tract houses all over Medina! I can't wait to for Ernest to give me some tips. —And get this, Madge! Right across the street from him and Aileen, he's going to erect a roomy split-level for Mom and Pop. That'll make it a whole lot easier for me to tell them I'm leaving the store."

Ricky couldn't have felt worse about Daddy's news. It meant moving far away from Dee-Dee and Jack and *Casa Futura*. At least, he consoled himself, Mommy and Daddy wouldn't argue anymore. And who knew? Maybe he'd like the new house in Greenlawn, where he'd have cousins nearby to play with, especially Jimmy, the youngest of the four, who, like him, hadn't yet turned six.

His family didn't wind up in Greenlawn, though; Daddy couldn't afford it. Instead, they had to settle for an older home in the working-class neighborhood of Graceland. "Aileen says there aren't many Jews here," Daddy remarked, driving through it.

"Maybe we'd have been better off staying in Huppertsville after all," Mommy said.

When Ricky saw their new home, he wished more than ever that they had. Unlike the bright, cream-colored stucco of the Huppertsville cottage, the Medina house had flaking, gray shingles that melded into the gunmetal skies the city's belching steel mills produced. His parents' ongoing clashes only intensified the gloom all around him.

"This place is so awful, Bernie!" Madge groaned one night at dinner after they'd lived there a few months. "Why can't you ask that brother-in-law of yours for some pointers about selling more houses? For that matter, why can't you just ask your parents for the money to move out to Greenlawn like the rest of your family?"

"Goddammit, Madge, I don't need this!" Bernie exploded. "I'm sure as hell not going to talk to Ernest. Every time I reach out to him for a piece of advice, he acts like I'm trying to snatch his right nut! And asking Mom and Pop for money—are you kidding? They're still mad at me for calling it quits with the store."

When his parents started going at it like that, Ricky would retreat up to his room. He'd climb in his rocker and, cradling his knees tight under his chin, he'd begin rocking slowly backwards and forwards, futilely seeking the comfort he'd found in the chair's gentle swaying as Dee-Dee sang him to sleep with "Lullaby and Goodnight."

With the start of third grade, when he'd just turned eight, the sense of dread that dogged him at home began stalking him on the way back from school. Every day, two older boys, Nick and Dirk Kyrchyk, would lie in wait to attack him. Regardless of how he changed his route, the Kyrchyks would still find him, ambushing him from behind some bush, hedge, or tree. As one of them pinned him, the other would pummel him. Though he'd flail back, he'd always lose, one against two, stubby against strapping. He didn't know why the brothers bullied him. Maybe it was because he was like his father, brainy. Or maybe it was because he was like his mother, pudgy. Or perhaps, the notion more than once flashed through his mind as the

Kyrchyks rained down their blows on him, it was because he was like his Cossack-killed namesake, Jewish.

When he finally told his mother and father about the Kyrchyks beating him up, Mommy said, "Bernie, why don't you call those boys' parents?" to which Daddy responded, "Why don't *you*, Madge? My plate's full. What do you do except lounge around here all day? You sure as hell could pick Ricky up after school if you wanted!" Mommy wheeled around, went up to her room, and slammed the door behind her as Daddy stalked out the back door. Left all alone, Ricky thought of the Britannica film his class had seen the day before about wolves. "I wish I'd been born a wolf pup," he said under his breath. "Their mommies and daddies protect them."

So when Daddy asked whether he'd be willing to go to Hebrew school so he could get *bar mitzvah*ed, making his mind up was easy. Twice a week, a bus would pick him up after his last class and whisk him past the Kyrchyks to sanctuary at the *shul*. Besides, if the Kyrchyks hated him like the Cossacks hated the Yerachmiel before him, he might as well learn why.

II

"Quite quiet, class, or I'll get quite cross with you!" said Mr. Galston, or, as he'd told his Hebrew school students to address him, "*Mar*" Galston. A rabbinical student at Medina's world-renowned seminary, he'd informed them that "*Mar* is a term of respect in Judaism for one's teacher," a title that he'd emphasized was "age-old."

To Ricky, *Mar* Galston didn't look age-old with his peach fuzz goatee and gangly frame. If anything struck him as old about *Mar* Galston, it was the way that he spoke using old-timey words pronounced with an accent that Ricky, a fan of *The Adventures of Robin Hood* on TV, pegged as coming from "Merry Olde England." But even if he'd never watched a single episode of the series, Ricky still would have nailed *Mar* Galston as English because of a comment he'd heard Mommy make to Daddy after she'd switched off a radio program called *The Goon Show*. "I don't know why they'd take something like that from the BBC and broadcast it here! Everybody knows you have to be English to understand their humor." Ricky figured that was the reason nobody but *Mar* Galston was laughing after he'd said to the class, "If your parents inquire as to my rationale for agreeing to undertake your tutelage, apprise them it couldn't be simpler: the position pays the rent on my flat!" Later that first day of Hebrew school, Ricky learned just how unfunny *Mar* Galston could be.

Class had pretty much begun the way Daddy predicted. "As I recognize you," *Mar* Galston instructed the eight-year-olds seated before him, "you shall proceed to recite your Hebrew name." He nodded to the bucktoothed, bespectacled little girl perched front and center among the five rows of desks crammed into the dingy-green, cinder block classroom.

"'My Hebrew name's 'Esther'!" chirped Emily Funkelbush, clearly pleased to have been called on before anyone else.

"Excellent, young lady!" *Mar* Galston said. "'Esther' is a name esteemed by the Jewish people for more than two thousand years!"

Mar Galston turned his attention to the red-haired boy sitting beside her. "And you, sir, what's your Hebrew name?"

"Aryeh!" declared Louis Chazen, Ricky's best friend since first grade when Louis, seeing that Ricky's pencil had broken, offered one of his own. "It's a little small," Louis had said, "but it's there if you need it." As Ricky got to know Louis better, he discovered that Louis could have been describing himself.

Mar Galston congratulated Louis with a hearty "Well done, Aryeh! Your name in Hebrew means 'lion.' We Jews have always had lions amongst us!"

Mar Galston came last to Ricky, who, having been dropped off by his bus only a minute before class, had had to take a seat in the back. The second *Mar* Galston looked over his way, he sang out, "Yerachmiel ben Baruch!" Beaming, Ricky waited to be complimented for being the only student to have included his father's name, too. "*Yerachmiel*?" said *Mar* Galston. "Where on earth did you ever get *that* name?"

". . . At my *bris*."

"Did your family have the foggiest notion of what that name actually means?"

Shrinking down in his seat, Ricky shrugged as *Mar* Galston peered down at him over his horn-rims. "Let me enlighten you then! Your name means 'May God have mercy!'—I can't think of one more pathetic."

Ricky replied quietly, "It's the same name my great-grandfather had . . . he got killed by the Cossacks."

"So a fat lot of good it did *him*!" *Mar* Galston cackled as his English sense of humor had Ricky, who'd never felt so stupid, bordering on tears.

In the classes that followed, *Mar* Galston made sure Ricky had plenty of company. He'd randomly call on students to read some piece of Hebrew aloud and then stand back as they stumbled all over themselves trying to decipher letters that not only looked nothing like English but ran in the opposite direction across the page, right to left. Worse yet, they weren't being tripped up by long paragraphs, drawn out sentences, or even individual words—just strings of meaningless sounds. "Unless you master the phonetics of Hebrew's consonants and vowels," said *Mar* Galston, "you shan't ever become proficient enough to lead the congregation in prayer." Ricky wasn't persuaded, muttering under his breath, "Ba, bee, boo. At this rate, I'll be doing my *bar mitzvah* in baby talk!"

Similarly frustrated by *Mar* Galston's slow pace, a number of parents *kvetched* to the Hebrew school's principal as well as to the *shul*'s board of directors. In the end, *Mar* Galston was forced to relent. "Over my objections, you'll be reading Hebrew henceforth from the prayer book—or as we shall be referring to it here, 'the *siddur.*' As I place a stack of *siddurim* at the end of your row, take one, and pass the rest on."

No sooner had *Mar* Galston finished speaking than a loud thud made him flinch. Louis, pivoting to slide his row's stack of *siddurim* to the next student, had accidentally brushed his elbow against his own book and sent it crashing down on the classroom's linoleum floor.

"*Aryeh!*" shouted *Mar* Galston. "Pick up that *siddur* this instant and kiss it!"

Ricky asked himself why the *siddur* needed kissing. Had it been hurt? Would kissing the *siddur* make it feel better like he did when he was little and Dee-Dee had kissed him after he'd fallen down?

Mar Galston glared at Louis. "Under no circumstances do we leave our *siddurim* lying on the ground without immediately retrieving them and lifting them up to our lips. The same holds true for every book Jewish tradition deems holy."

"What if the book's holes are tiny?" Ricky blurted out. "Do you still have to kiss it?"

Mar Galston slammed his fist on his desk. "Don't be smart with me, Zieglitz! You know perfectly well what I mean." He snatched a piece of chalk and with a series of scratches so squeaky they made Ricky wince, he scrawled on the blackboard, "H-O-L-Y!" Wheeling around, he stared at Ricky and growled, "Clear enough now for you, Zieglitz?"

Ricky wished *Mar* Galston would treat him the same as the other kids and call him by his Hebrew name. But he'd have to bring it up later—he didn't want to make *Mar* Galston madder. So he asked him, as politely as possible, "*Mar* Galston, what makes a book holy?"

Mar Galston glowered at him, seething with resentment that he'd been reduced to teaching such an ignorant blockhead. "Even Gentiles know what makes a book holy! It's got God's name inside it!"

Now Ricky was more confused than ever. He remembered the time Timmy Brewster had invited him over at Christmas. They were fiddling around in the living room with Timmy's new toys when his grandma shuffled in with her red-tipped, white cane. Making her way to the sofa, she bumped into a small occasional table Timmy's mother had set out for the holidays. A bowl of peppermints on it went cascading down on the carpet along with a big, thick book that had gold-stamped on its black leather cover "Holy Bible."

"Oh, my!" was all Grandma Brewster said, cupping her hands to her mouth.

"Don't worry about it, Ma," was all Timmy's mother said, running in from the kitchen.

"I'll scoop 'em up!" was all Timmy said, shoveling the candy back in the bowl.

But picking the Holy Bible up off the rug, nobody in Timmy's family said, "Kiss it!"

Looking back, Ricky couldn't figure out why—the Brewsters' Holy Bible must have had God's name in it, too. As *Mar* Galston announced "Class dismissed!" and Ricky leaned over to close his *siddur*, the solution leapt off the page: in their Bible, God's name wasn't in Hebrew! But that only raised another, more troubling problem for Ricky. If a Jew's holy book hit the ground and he didn't kiss it, would God hit him with something bad in return? Ricky could still picture Grandpa Irv at *shul* on the High Holy Days praying—or as his grandfather had put it, "*davening*." He'd never forget how Grandpa Irv kept bowing up and down as he *davened*. He'd called it "*shuckling*," and he did it so fast, he made it look like he couldn't tell God quickly enough, "Yes! Yes! Yes! —Whatever you say, I'll do!" God seemed to scare Grandpa Irv, Ricky thought, as much as the Kyrchyks terrified him.

The next class only made God more frightening.

"This afternoon," proclaimed *Mar* Galston as the session began, "there'll be no Hebrew recitation."

Ricky had to stop himself from whooping out, "Great—today, no baby talk Hebrew!"

"For the next two hours," *Mar* Galston continued, "we'll be exploring one of the Bible's best-known stories."

From Grandpa Irv's seders, Ricky already knew the one about the Jews leaving Egypt, but he'd never heard a story even close to *Mar* Galston's.

"However much I may beg to differ," *Mar* Galston said to the class, "the tradition presumes that you're approaching adulthood. Hence, it's only fitting that you're exposed to a story meant for adults. It's about a non-Jew named Job. As you say farewell to childhood, you'll likely learn the same two hard lessons Job does—I know I most certainly have! First, you'll come to see that life can be painfully difficult, and thus, second, insufferably unjust. If your Hebrew were up to snuff—and you knew even the slightest bit of Aramaic—we'd examine the book of Job in its original languages. In light of your limitations, however, I've prepared an English adaptation. It's a summary, actually, that not only reflects the text's turning points but also respects the lesson's regrettable time constraints. I know it's too much to ask you to retain what we cover in one session until the next."

After each student had received a copy of *Mar* Galston's version of Job, they took turns reading aloud, with Emily, of course, going first. As Ricky heard his classmates read the story, he learned that Job was a very good man who was richer than anybody else around him. All of a sudden, things changed, because Satan—"the Devil," according to *Mar* Galston—bet God that if He let Satan hurt Job enough, Job wouldn't stay loyal to God anymore. When God took Satan up on his bet, Ricky couldn't understand why God would do such a thing. (Was it a slow day in the universe, he wondered? Hadn't Mommy always told him he got into trouble when he had too much time on his hands?) Having got God's permission, Satan had men carry off all Job's daughters and kill all his sons. Next, lightning struck all Job's animals and after that, Job got a bad case of boils. (Ricky could still hear Daddy yowling at Mommy when he'd had a boil, "Madge, call the doctor! —This goddam thing hurts like hell!") Eventually, Job's friends stopped by, supposedly to make him feel better. But they only made him feel worse, first by pestering him to admit that everything awful that had happened to him was his own fault and then by nagging him to pray to God for forgiveness. (Once again, Ricky was at a loss to make sense of the story; why, at that point, didn't God just fess up to Job about His bet with the Devil? Maybe God was ashamed of Himself—Ricky knew what a hard time he had coming clean to Mommy or Daddy after he'd done something he shouldn't have.) Finally, when Job couldn't take any more and complained to God it just wasn't fair, God thundered at him, "Who are *you* to challenge *Me*?" (Ricky couldn't help but notice that in the story, God sounded a lot like *Mar* Galston.)

Mar Galston looked at his watch and said, "Since our time's almost up, allow me to sum up the story's finale." He paused and then said with a flourish, "As the Bard so well put it, 'All's well that ends well!' Ultimately, God, in His goodness, made Job whole again, replacing what he'd lost with new children and livestock."

"Big deal," Ricky muttered. "Did anybody ask Job's dead kids or animals how *they* felt?"

Mar Galston was about to let everybody go home when Louis's hand popped up.

"Yes, Aryeh?" *Mar* Galston replied, raising his own hand to have the class remain seated.

"Is there really a Devil?"

"For Jews, Satan doesn't exist. We're not superstitious like Gentiles! To us, Satan is merely a metaphor for temptation."

Still puzzled, Louis asked, "What's a metaphor?

"A comparison. For instance, I'd be employing a metaphor were I to say to a lady wearing stunning millinery, 'Madam, your hat's the Taj Mahal!'"

"What's the Taj Mahal?" Louis responded.

"A grand tomb in India!" snapped *Mar* Galston.

"But *Mar* Galston, why would a lady wear a tomb on her head?"

"Don't be so obtuse, Mr. Chazen!" *Mar* Galston erupted, making it clear not only to Louis but the whole class that he was in no mood for more questions about Job.

But Ricky couldn't let go of Job's story. He decided he'd ask Grandpa Irv about it when he went with Mommy and Daddy to the split-level in Greenlawn for their weekly *Shabbos* evening dinner, the only time they were invited over even though Aunt Aileen and her family were welcome whenever they wanted.

"Grandpa Irv," Ricky buttonholed him after dessert, "something came up at Hebrew school . . ."

"—Not 'Hebrew school'!" Grandpa Irv corrected him. "That's *goyisch.* Jews call it '*cheder.*'"

"Okay, at *cheder*," Ricky started over, "our teacher *Mar* Galston . . ."

"—You mean your *melamed*," Grandpa Irv interrupted him again.

"Okay, at *cheder*, our *melamed*, had us read about Job."

"Ah! Job's one of the most profound books in the *Tanach.*"

"What does 'profound' mean?" Ricky asked timidly, embarrassed to show his learned grandfather how little he knew.

"Profound means very deep—*very wise!*"

Ricky, seeing he had come to the right person, said, "Grandpa Irv, here's the part about Job I don't get: why would God make a bet with the Devil to let bad things happen to a good man?"

"As I said, the *Tanach*'s account of Job is very profound."

"Grandpa Irv, there's nobody else I know who can help me!" Ricky pressed him. "I'm going to Hebrew school—to *cheder*—so I can get up at my *bar mitzvah* and lead the *davening*—you know, the prayers. But if God's so mean, even to good people, why should we pray to Him at all?"

The Sage of Greenlawn, brow furrowed, closed his eyes for a while. Opening them, he craned forward toward Ricky and dispensed his advice: "God, shmod—*daven!*" Ricky, like Job, had gotten his answer. When it came to questioning God, the wise thing to do was shut up.

Meanwhile, at Hebrew school, Ricky and his classmates did anything but keep quiet. As bored with *Mar* Galston as he was with them, they grew ever noisier and more rambunctious, yammering at first in loud whispers, then in unrestrained yapping, before moving on to shooting rubber bands at each other until someone yelled, "Stop it!" When *Mar* Galston inevitably fell back on his overused threat, "Quite quiet, or I'll get quite cross!" they screeched back like so many parrots, "Quite quiet! Quite cross!"

One afternoon, right before class, *Mar* Galston walked into the Hebrew school principal's office and resigned in a huff—"I find such impertinence intolerable!" Although that day's session was cancelled for lack of a teacher, by the next time the class met, the *shul* had found a replacement. "I just know we're going to have fun!" trilled Mrs. Rosenfeld, an elderly sisterhood volunteer. But Ricky and his classmates, having tasted blood with *Mar* Galston's departure, quickly turned on Mrs. Rosenfeld, too, as well as on her two successors. For the children, it developed into a game: how soon after getting another unfortunate instructor into their classroom, could they get their *melamed* out?

At the head of every uprising was Aryeh the Lion. Despite being small for his age, Louis was fierce, even brazen, never backing down, whether in Hebrew school or anywhere else. His fearlessness was a magnet to Ricky and Graceland's other four Jewish boys, who weren't nearly as brave. In a neighborhood where along with the Kyrchyks, most kids, thanks to their parents, despised them, they clustered around Louis as much for self-defense as for friendship

By banding together, they gained more than a sense of security: they acquired a reputation as the worst nightmare of any non-Jewish boy unlucky enough to cross their path all alone. One day, as they were playing a makeshift game of baseball near Louis's house (three on a team with the batter calling which side of the diamond he'd hit to), Dirk, the younger Kyrchyk, cut through left field on his way home. When Louis, who was pitching, spotted him mid-windup, he called out to the others, "Get him!" In no time, they had Dirk surrounded. Stepping to within an inch of Dirk's nose, Louis snarled, "What d'ya think you're doin' on our field?!"

"Hey, Shorty, who says it's *yours*?" Dirk snarled back, pushing Louis away.

Louis, turning crimson, lunged forward and knocked Dirk off his feet. The next moment he was on Dirk's chest, landing one punch after another. Joining in, the rest of Louis's gang began kicking Dirk over and over. Ricky merely looked on. The consequences of hitting a Kyrchyk worried him much more than the prospect of his buddies calling him "Chicken!"

Louis finally called off the attack when Dirk, curling up in a ball, began whimpering, "I give, I give." As Dirk struggled up off the ground, Louis kicked him once more for good measure and roared, "Don't let me ever catch you on *our* field again!" Dirk sidled away like some wounded animal, glancing behind him every so often to make sure Louis's pack wasn't stalking him. He had nothing to fear, though. The boys had gone back to playing baseball.

Two hours later, they were in the final inning with Louis's team, as usual, ahead, and with Louis, as always, the captain. He never failed to pick Ricky for his side, for which Ricky couldn't have been more grateful—he knew what a bad player he was. "I want somebody as smart as I am," Louis had explained, "—somebody who knows how to run bases." While Louis's father coached him in Little League, and while the other Graceland dads practiced hitting and pitching with their sons, Ricky's lacked the patience to work with him for long.

When Ricky's turn at the plate rolled around, he dug his Keds into the dirt, choked up on his bat, and bore down, hoping that even if he didn't get a hit, he wouldn't strike out. Just then, a voice boomed, "*Is that them?!*" Ricky whipped around to see where the holler had come from. Across the street from left field, Dirk stood alongside a bigger and brawnier look-alike, a teenager Ricky didn't know.

Racing ahead of Dirk, the teenager tore through the infield, reached home plate and pushed Ricky aside before heading toward the on-deck circle and Louis. "You carrottop kike! My kid brother said you and your Yids beat him up!"

"That's right, Roman!" Dirk cried out, drawing up behind him.

"So, what of it?" Louis sneered.

Out of nowhere, a switchblade appeared as Roman advanced slowly toward Louis, menacingly waving the knife back and forth. Louis held his ground, though, until, at the last possible second, he called out to his troops, "Scatter!" As the boys dispersed in every direction, Roman, temporarily distracted, made the mistake of taking his eyes off Louis, who shot forward and socked him in the stomach before dashing away toward home.

Meanwhile, his comrades in arms, after initially splitting up, regrouped behind him. Ricky, the baseball bat still clutched in his hand, brought up the rear as everyone made for the Chazens'. As soon as they got there, Louis slammed the front door behind them. Hearing it bang shut, Mr. Chazen rushed in from the den where he'd been going over some papers he'd brought home from his law office. He took one look at Louis bent over, gasping for air, and burst out, "Son, what's the matter?!"

"We were just playing ball, Dad," Louis said innocently, "when some big kids started chasing us with a knife."

"It's them!" yelped Jeffey Blumberg, peeping out from behind a curtain. There, on the Chazens' lawn, stood the Kyrchyks, not only Roman and Dirk now, but Nick joining them, too.

Mr. Chazen, every bit as fiery as Louis, bolted out the door, snatching the bat from a startled Ricky. On top of the Kyrchyks before they realized what was happening, he poked the bat barrel in Roman's belly. "Raise a finger to my son again, and I promise you'll be sorry." Roman backed away, as did his brothers. Retreating from the lawn to the street, they departed, eyes fixed on the pavement.

Lying in bed that night, Ricky couldn't get over Mr. Chazen's going out and facing down the Kyrchyks when, as a lawyer, he didn't have to. He could have simply stayed inside and called out that if they didn't clear off his property, he'd have them arrested and then sue the pants off their parents. Ricky couldn't imagine Daddy doing anything close to that, even if he'd gone to law school like he'd wanted. What, Ricky kept asking himself, gave Mr. Chazen the guts Daddy lacked?

After a phone call to Louis the next Saturday morning, he thought he'd found out.

"It's Ricky," he said when Louis picked up. "Wanna mess around at my house?"

"Wish I could, Ricky, but we always go to services *Shabbos* morning. It's why my dad got all our Little League games moved to Sunday—sorry, got to go!"

As Ricky put down the receiver, he recalled all the times he'd heard Mommy and Daddy call the Chazens "good Jews." Could that have been why God had been so good about shielding Louis and Mr. Chazen from the Kyrchyks? All at once, Ricky's questions about Job vanished. Though Job had been good, he hadn't been Jewish—no wonder God had let bad things happen to him! For Ricky, that left only one option: he'd become as good a Jew as the Chazens. Like them, he'd go to *shul* and latch on to God's protection.

III

———

Saturday morning, 7:30, and Ricky was racing to get ready for *shul*—underwear, white shirt, gray wool slacks, navy blue blazer, black socks, cordovan slip-ons, and the tan-strapped, silver-plated Timex Dee-Dee had given him for special occasions. He still hadn't finished dressing.

A maroon tie flung over his neck, he flew downstairs to the kitchen. "Daddy," he said, out of breath, "I can't tie this."

"Come on over, and we'll have you fixed up with a Windsor in no time."

"God, Bernie!" Madge exclaimed after he'd done it. "That knot's so big—it makes Ricky look like he's got a goiter!"

"It's a *man's* knot, Madge!"

"In case you haven't noticed, Bernie, Ricky's a little *boy*! Can't you tie something smaller?"

As Daddy undid the Windsor and tied a four-in-hand, Mommy told Ricky, "Honey, I'm glad you have Jewish friends here—it's one of the reasons we moved to Medina. Just don't get *too* Jewish on me. I mean, I wouldn't want you to go to Israel and become a *kibbutznik*."

Bernie rolled his eyes. "Whaddya think, Madge—they're on those communal farms playing bridge?!"

"Okay, Mr. Know-It-All, if you're so Jewish, why don't *you* take Ricky to services and sit with him? I was embarrassed to have to ask the Chazens if they'd give him a ride and help him get settled."

"Don't start, Madge! If I don't go out to the job today to keep an eye on the painters, they won't do jack shit."

Today of all days, his parents' squabbling irritated Ricky as much as the scratchy wool pants chafing his thighs. "Shouldn't we leave, Mommy?" he pressed her. To keep *schmutz* off his dress clothes, she'd said she'd drive

him to Louis's—meaning no Kyrchyk could jump him. Becoming a better
Jew had already begun to pay off!

Once he and Mommy arrived at the Chazens', Louis's mother invited
them in. "I'm so glad Ricky's joining us!"

"—And right on time!" Mr. Chazen added, rushing into the living
room while buttoning his jacket. "Kids—let's get going!" he called to the
back of the house.

A few seconds later, Louis traipsed in with his teenage big sister Sonya,
who fumbled in her purse for a brush to comb her frizzy brown hair.

"When should I pick Ricky up?" Mommy asked.

Mr. Chazen shook his head. "No need—we'll drop him off." Before
going, Mommy gave Ricky a perfunctory peck on the cheek.

Shortly before 8:30, Mr. Chazen pulled up to the *shul* with his family
and Ricky. As they stepped inside the lobby, Mr. Chazen plucked a black,
rayon *yarmulke* from a basket. "Here, Ricky, have a *kippah*," Mr. Chazen
said, using the same word that *Mar* Galston, a stickler for Hebrew, had insisted his students call it in class. After getting another for Louis and one
for himself, Mr. Chazen took a blue-and-white prayer shawl from a wooden
rack and held it taut in front of his face. He softly recited the Hebrew stitched
on its collar, which he kissed at each end before draping the *tallit* over his
shoulders and adjusting its tasseled four corners to hang evenly. When
Ricky reached for a shawl of his own, Louis grabbed his wrist. "We don't get
to wear one till we're *bar mitzvah*ed. They probably think we'll get the *tzitzit*
all tangled." As Ricky stood blushing, Louis took down two *siddurim* from a
bookshelf, handing one to Ricky and keeping the other.

Mr. Chazen held the sanctuary door open while everyone walked in.
Ricky had been in the sanctuary before on *Rosh Hashannah* when all the
children were briefly brought up from the dreary kids' service in the basement to hear the *shofar* being blown. Even so, the massive hall still left him
wide-eyed. He gaped at the blue-and-cream–checkered dome spanning its
ceiling and the three aisles of burgundy runners trisecting its rows upon
rows of only slightly less crimson seats. He almost walked into Louis as he
ogled the sanctuary's twelve stained-glass windows. Each pane depicted a
biblical figure, some of whom Ricky recognized from what little Hebrew
school he'd had. To him, they and the others looked like they were standing
sentry, guarding the Jews gathered below.

Mr. and Mrs. Chazen took seats in the front among the two dozen
people who, like them, had come early. Sonya sat down a little farther back
next to some other girls and, taking out her lipstick and compact, promptly
began primping with them.

Ricky felt a tug on his sleeve. "Over there!" Louis said, pointing to the last row on the opposite side. Ricky trailed after him until Louis, having scootched in from the aisle, nodded "Here's good" as he pushed down on a seat's spring-loaded cushion. To his right sat another boy who, catching sight of Ricky, gave him a look even darker than the corner they sat in.

"Y. H.," Louis whispered, "this is Ricky. It's the first *Shabbos* morning he's come here."

"What the hell made you do something stupid like that?" Y. H. responded, his own voice anything but hushed.

". . . It's hard to explain," Ricky hesitated. If he hadn't let his best friend in on why he'd started coming to *shul*, he sure wasn't going to open up to some guy he'd just met. What could he say? —That it was his insurance under "God's Good-Jew Protection Plan"?

Just then, an old man in the first row doddered up the four steps to the sanctuary's raised stage and shambled over to the smaller of the two reading stands on it.

Ricky leaned over and quietly asked Louis, "Is that the rabbi?" During the *shofar* blowing, he'd never been able to see him, because his family always sat so far back. "The only thing your parents really take religiously, Bernie," Mommy had sniped, "is holding on to their last nickel. If they'd just shelled out a little more for our seats, we wouldn't be stuck in the boonies!" Ricky still didn't understand why, if you were willing to pay more, you got to pray more up front. Was it like buying a box seat at a ball game so you got a better view of your team's best hitter? —And did that make the rabbi the synagogue's star player?

"Nah, that's just some old guy," Louis replied. "It'll be a while before the rabbi's up on the *bimah*."

The old man produced a big, black book from underneath his lectern, and, peering over the rims of his glasses, rasped out, "Page 42." As the people down below rifled through the pages of their *siddurim*, the old man began rapidly mumbling Hebrew like Grandpa Irv at the seder. At brief intervals, he'd raise his voice, then lower it again while in between, the congregants, whose numbers had steadily increased, droned on. They reminded Ricky of the sound flies made when they buzzed around something dead under his house.

A half hour passed before the old man finished and stepped off the *bimah*. He was replaced at the lectern by a middle-aged man who'd been seated on the stage all along. His body was shrouded in a long, black robe while his head was capped by a *kippah* of the same color, though not like the flat, round ones worn by the other men there, but about three inches tall and pinched at each of its four corners.

Cupping his hand to his mouth, Ricky slouched over toward Louis and once again asked, "Is *that* the rabbi?"

"Uh-uh—it's the cantor. The rabbi isn't even here yet."

"If the rabbi doesn't need to show up early," Ricky thought to himself, "how come the rest of us do?"

The cantor hooked his thumbs under his *tallit*'s embroidered, gold collar. He cast his eyes down at the oversized *siddur* on the stand and grunted, "Page 86."

Unlike the speed demon before him, the cantor couldn't have gone slower, like he was singing opera. At least with opera on the radio, Ricky could change channels. Now, he'd just have to sit there as the cantor dragged on syllable by syllable.

An hour later, as the cantor trilled his aria's last note, another man, outfitted just like him—black robe, gold-embroidered *tallit*, pastry-puff *kippah*—entered through a door at the rear of the stage and sat down on an ornately carved mahogany chair with ruby-red padding.

Louis nudged Ricky's elbow. "*There's* the rabbi!"

Ricky prepared himself to hear something special.

The rabbi got up and walked over to the other, much larger rostrum, on which lay open another outsized *siddur*. "Page 117," he said and sat down.

An elderly couple tottered up to the *bimah* with a beefy young man behind them. Once there, the rabbi and cantor joined them in front of the ark, which Ricky remembered *Mar* Galston calling "the most sacred spot in the *shul*." As the aged spouses wrested open the ark's heavy bronze doors, the congregation stood up and broke into song. In spite of the huddle on stage partially blocking his view, Ricky could still see the ark's three tiers of Torah scrolls, each swaddled in bright blue velvet and gleaming with a silver pointer, breastplate, and crown.

The brawny young man lifted out the ark's largest Torah and, as the congregation continued singing, carried it down off the *bimah* followed by the rabbi, cantor, and halting husband and wife. As Ricky watched, every row emptied out, its Jews straining to touch the scroll with their fringes or prayer books, which they afterwards swiftly drew up to their lips. To Ricky, it was obvious why. Since the Torah had God's name in it, people were trying to get a taste of His power! Ricky couldn't wait any longer. Jostling past clusters of grown-ups to the *shul*'s other side, he brushed his *siddur* against the scroll as soon as it got close. Then he kissed the prayer book as hard as he could, just like the love scenes in movies.

The Torah moved on, but the rabbi and cantor, some distance behind, slowed by congregants shaking their hands and wishing them "Good *Shabbos*," hadn't yet got to where Ricky was standing. Unsure what to do, he didn't move a muscle, afraid they might scold him for pushing past the adults and cutting to the head of the line. But he needn't have worried. Visibly irked that the Torah had gone on without them, they walked right by him. He might as well have been as invisible as the God they professed to worship.

When the Torah got back to the *bimah*, it was laid on a low, wide table between the two lecterns. Yet another senior citizen wobbled up on the stage. But this one, in Ricky's eyes, wasn't just old—he was *ancient*. Looking up at the sanctuary's windows, Ricky muttered under his breath, "I'll bet he knew all of those guys."

Once more, the rabbi walked up to his rostrum. "This week's portion is *Lech L'cha*. Following its reading, I shall address my remarks to a passage of particular relevance wherein Abraham, as a sign of God's everlasting covenant, circumcises himself along with the other males in his household."

"Abraham *bris*sed himself!" Ricky almost burst out. What Daddy had told him about his own circumcision didn't seem nearly so bad now.

Glancing at a note card on his podium, the rabbi said, "The Torah reading commences in our *chumashim*—page 45."

Ushers began distributing big, blue books to each row. By the time Ricky got his, he was already squirming as he pictured Abraham slitting his own wee-wee. Meanwhile, up on the *bimah*, the rabbi whizzed through another Hebrew prayer, after which somebody else ripped through some more. Ricky couldn't help thinking that the faster you read Hebrew, the more points you scored with God. Hebrew school, he concluded, might not be such a waste after all.

The Torah reader inched up to the table, so hunchbacked his nose came close to grazing the scroll. He took a long, wheezy breath, then coughed and brayed out, "*VaYOYmehr AhdoNoy el AvROYM . . .*"

Ricky cringed—he'd never heard singing so screechy! With its nasal, high-pitched quaver, it sounded like somebody yodeling Chinese. He uncovered his ears long enough to flip ahead in the *chumash* in search of the part about Abraham's *bris*. First, he came to a section that told how God changed Abraham's name:

> . . . And God talked with him saying, "As for Me, behold, My covenant is with thee, and thou shalt be the father of a multitude of nations. Neither shall thy name any more be called Abram, but thy name shall be Abraham . . ."

Ricky didn't care what a multitude was, or how many of them Abram played papa for. The only thing he wanted to know was whether Abram detested his new name as much as he despised Yerachmiel, the one that had been tacked onto him. Why couldn't God, *why couldn't Daddy*, have left well enough alone?

Troubled more and more by the minute, Ricky frantically turned the book's pages until he found what he wanted. In sheer disbelief, he read about Abraham's *briss*ing, his son Ishmael's, as well as every other man's who lived with him:

> God further said to Abraham, "You shall circumcise the flesh of your foreskin." . . . Abraham was ninety-nine years old when he circumcised the flesh of his foreskin, and his son Ishmael was thirteen years old when he was circumcised. . . . Thus Abraham and his son . . . and all his household . . . were circumcised with him.

"Are you kidding me?" Ricky said to himself. He couldn't imagine somebody Abraham's age going through with a *bris*, especially in olden times when, he'd learned in some book, they didn't have medicine to put people to sleep. Besides, what thirteen-year-old would hold still to be *briss*ed? Ricky decided Ishmael must have been held down by Abraham's servants—who hadn't figured out yet that they'd be next in line for the knife. The thought crossed Ricky's mind that being around the Kyrchyks might be lots safer than being near God.

Another hour went by before the old man's caterwauling stopped and the rabbi returned to his podium. "This morning's *haftarah* can be found on page 60," he said before walking back to his seat.

Another graybeard trundled up to the *bimah*. Shuffling to the Torah table, he opened his *chumash* and immediately began singing off-key. Increasingly restless, Ricky didn't even try lowering his voice: "*Jeez!* Can't anybody here carry a tune?" Twenty more minutes ticked by before the *haftarah*'s yowling came to a close.

The rabbi stepped to his rostrum again. Fidgeting, Ricky hoped he'd finally say something worth hearing, but instead, he just stood there, staring out over the sanctuary without saying a word. For a moment, Ricky thought the rabbi might have forgotten how his talk was supposed to begin. Hadn't that happened to him when he'd drawn a blank giving a book report in front of his second-grade class? The rabbi, though, didn't look rattled. Out of the corner of his eye, Ricky spied Louis and Y. H., who, for the first time that morning, were sitting perfectly still. Taking a few furtive peeks at the grown-ups, he noticed that they, too, sat motionless and mum. All of a sudden he got it: the rabbi wouldn't say anything until he had absolute silence. And why not? Nothing could be more important than explaining how Abraham could have carried out God's gory commands without thinking twice.

The rabbi, at last satisfied his voice alone would be heard, began speaking. "In today's *parasha*," he said, "you may have observed that in chapter 17, verse 11, the Lord enjoins Abraham our Father to 'circumcise the flesh of his foreskin.' And yet, you may also have noted that, according to verse 24 of that selfsame chapter, Abraham 'was circumcised in the flesh of his foreskin.'"

Ricky wasn't sure that he followed.

"Thus," the rabbi continued, "we have an apparent contradiction between the two verses. Whereas the former mandates that Abraham should circumcise himself, the latter implies that Abraham was circumcised by others. How are we to reconcile this seeming textual discrepancy?"

Ricky was still in the dark. But what did he know? He was just a kid while the rabbi was "a scholar"—or so Grandpa Irv had said at a Friday night dinner. Ricky felt certain the rabbi's talk would set to rest everything about the first *brisses* that gave him the creeps.

"As always," the rabbi went on, "the best place to start is with Rashi, who points out the different *binyanim* of the Hebrew verbs used in the respective verses."

"Rashi"? "*Binyanim*"? Ricky was lost. He glanced at the adults around him. Apparently, the rabbi's words had also gone over their heads, many of which had dropped onto their chests, slowly rising and fallen. Five minutes later, Ricky was sound asleep, too. A thunderous "*Whop!*" jarred him and his fellow slumberers awake as the rabbi, having slammed his fist on his lectern, raised his voice for effect. "In summation," he expounded, "this week's *sedrah* raises a *halachic* question of timely importance: may a non-Jew perform a circumcision? You are invited to join me in my office following the *kiddush* to review the traditional commentaries on this critical issue." Done, the rabbi proceeded back to his throne.

"That's it?!" Ricky nearly blurt out. Wasn't the rabbi going to talk about what happened to Ishmael? —Or about a dad who'd do it and a god who'd command it?

The bullnecked young man, still up on the *bimah*, tramped to the table where the Torah lay, rewrapped. Taking his *siddur*, he said in a deep, booming voice, "We read together in English the prayers for the congregation, the government, and the State of Israel—page 128." Although Ricky could finally follow along, the prayers still left him cold, making him even antsier for the service to be over. But once the Torah's porter wound up the English, he started jabbering more Hebrew. Another quarter hour elapsed before he shouldered the scroll and, with the rabbi and cantor in tow, transported it down off the stage. This time, nobody lurched forward to stroke it, instead half-heartedly gesturing at it with their fringes and prayer books as it went by. Despite Ricky's being as worn out as everyone else, he wasn't about to pass up another chance to score more points with God. Summoning all the strength he had left, he lunged at the Torah with his *siddur*, tagged it, and then shoveled the book up to his mouth like he was somebody starving. Which he was. He didn't need his Timex to tell him it was well past noon; his grumbling stomach, which had missed breakfast and now hadn't had lunch, let him know it. Seeing the ark's doors close on the Torah, he thought the service would end any minute and he'd soon get something to eat.

He couldn't have been more wrong.

"The service continues," said the rabbi, "with *Musaph*—page 137."

"What's *Musaph*?" Ricky anxiously asked Louis.

"It's the additional service," yawned Louis.

"'*Additional*,' Louis? Haven't we sat here long enough as it is?"

"We won't be sitting, because most of *Musaph*'s said standing. To make it go by faster, do what I do—read the English."

But the translation only made Ricky feel worse as he read how God, "Who hath prescribed the sacrifices," wanted two sheep barbecued for Him each *Shabbos*. To take his mind off the charred little lambs, Ricky for once started reading the Hebrew. The very first word transfixed him: it was *Baruch*—Daddy's Hebrew name! The English on the opposite page said it meant "blessed," which Ricky knew had to be something good, since Ba-ruch, he saw looking back at the Hebrew, was used in the rest of the prayers alongside most mentions of God. His own Hebrew name, he realized, hadn't been used in a prayer even once.

Musaph ended slightly past one, but, by now no surprise to Ricky, the services kept going. First, the synagogue's president recited a long list of the congregation's upcoming events. Next, the cantor and rabbi alternated singing and reading—what else?—more Hebrew prayers. As the cantor finished leading another down-tempo hymn, the rabbi stretched his arms and intoned, "We rise for the closing benediction." Like so many other words that morning, "benediction" left Ricky stumped. "Closing," though, didn't. Still, he'd been fooled often enough already that he wouldn't believe services were over until he heard somebody on the *bimah* actually say so. For once, he wasn't let down. The rabbi babbled a little more Hebrew, culminating with a solemn "Amen."

"—C'mon!" Y. H. roared, shoving past Ricky and Louis. "Let's get up to the *kiddush*!"

Y. H. sped out the exits to the lobby and, grasping a banister, practically launched himself to the social hall upstairs. Louis followed close on his heels with Ricky lagging well behind, too polite—and too petered out—to be pushy. By the time he'd trudged up the stairs, Y. H. and Louis were nowhere in sight. Looking around, he saw five long tables arranged in a horseshoe, a white tablecloth covering each one. Mrs. Chazen and several other women were busy setting out foil trays arrayed with cakes and pastries. Meanwhile, some men, two to a table, were filling tiny, plastic cups with red wine for adults and grape juice for children. At the top of the horseshoe, the cantor stood lifting a large, silver goblet with wine up to its brim. When he began singing another Hebrew solo, Ricky thought that he'd scream. To his relief, the cantor, who was as famished as he was, wrapped up in less than a minute.

"*L'chaim!*" the throngs around the tables cried out as they hoisted their cups and swooped down on the platters.

"Hey, kid!" Ricky heard Y. H. hollering to him. "If you don't move fast, the old people will cram all the good stuff in their *tallis* bags and pocketbooks to take home. Just don't get whacked by their elbows!"

Y. H. started wedging his way forward. Whenever he stepped on somebody's foot, they'd look down, at first scowling, then seeing who it was, they'd smile and pat him on the head. For Ricky, there was only one explanation: Y. H. had racked up so many hours in services that God had no choice but to shield him from getting walloped!

Ricky held back, though, knowing he hadn't logged nearly as much time at *shul* as Y. H. When he'd finally got to the tables after squeezing past knots of adults while continually stammering "Excuse me," he heard Y. H.'s voice yelling, "Over here!" Spinning around, he spotted Y. H. waving at him to join him and Louis. Walking toward them, Ricky saw that Y. H.'s cheeks were as puffed out as a squirrel's jam-packed with acorns.

"So, Wicky," Y. H. said, spewing out a mouthful of crumbs, "wad'ya dink 'bout all dis?"

"Huh?"

"I asked you," Y. H. said, wiping his mouth on his sleeve, "what you thought about services."

"I thought they were boring, but you come here so often, you probably don't."

"You're joking, right?"

"So what makes *you* come, then?" The moment Ricky said it, he regretted it, assuming from what the way Y. H. had spoken so far he was someone who didn't like being challenged.

Y. H.'s response surprised him. "Well, what do you know? Somebody who's got a mouth on him like me! We're on the same side, kid—no easy answers. But why you haven't you gotten something to eat? Christ, you sat through all that crap! You deserve whatever you want."

"I would've liked some strudel, but I couldn't get by the old people."

"You mean the *AKs*?"

"The '*AKs*'?"

"The *alte kokkers*—the old farts. Don't go anywhere! I'll be right back!"

As Ricky looked on, Y. H. waded into the sea of codgers engulfing the tables. At his approach, they cleared a path, forming a wall to his right and his left. Ricky couldn't believe it. It was like Moses splitting the sea!

"Eat up!" Y. H. said, returning with a plate piled high with strudels.

"Thanks, but this is way too many."

"—Do what you want with them. Take them home with you like the *AKs*, or leave them here in the garbage."

Ravenous, Ricky wolfed down the strudels while Y. H. and Louis threw back cup after cup of grape juice, with Y. H. even sneaking some wine on the side.

"Louis, Ricky!" Mrs. Chazen's voice rang out. "Time to go!"

Without so much as a "See ya," Y. H. walked away.

"What's with that guy?" Ricky asked Louis on their way to the lobby.

Louis smiled. "If it weren't for Y. H., there's no way I'd be here."

"Okay, but what gives with his name? Just what does 'Y. H.' stand for?"

"Best not to ask," Louis said darkly.

When Mr. Chazen pulled up in front of Ricky's house, Ricky thanked him and Mrs. Chazen and told Louis and Sonya goodbye. He ran up the sidewalk and knocked on the front door. "So how was it?" Mommy asked him the instant she opened it.

Seeing his father sprawled out on the sofa, just back from the job, Ricky said, "Daddy, know what? Your Hebrew name means 'blessed.'"

"I could have told you that," Mommy jumped in. "Every time your father smacks his thumb with a hammer, he shouts, '*God blessit!*'"

Unwilling to hang around for his parents to start trading zingers, Ricky headed upstairs. "These pants are really itching me—I got to go change."

Once safely up in his room, Ricky let out a sigh, grateful Mommy and Daddy hadn't questioned him more about *shul*. As much as he'd hated it, he knew he had to spend more time there. —Look how it'd worked for Y. H.! —Look how it'd worked for Louis and his dad! Even though getting God to watch out for him, too, was going to be tougher than he'd thought, he was more determined than ever to get on God's good side, no matter what.

IV

———

"Heads up—ball's coming your way!" yelled Ricky's Little League coach, Mr. Chazen, who, at his wife's prodding, had put the nine-year-old on his team when the season began. "Please, Norman," she'd urged him, "Ricky's such a good influence on Louis. So polite and considerate—not at all like Y. H."

"Mom's wrong about Y. H.," Louis spoke up, "but she's right about Ricky's being a really nice guy. —Sure, Dad, he's not much of a ballplayer. If you were his coach, though, I think he'd get better."

Mr. Chazen's shout interrupted Ricky's gazing down at his left shoe as it idly arced back and forth across the grass in right field where he'd been relegated for his team's sake as well as his own. He hadn't had a ball hit to him all year. Now he looked up and searched wildly for the fly hurtling toward him. Too late—the ball bonked his temple. Fortunately, the ball's descent had stripped it of most of its velocity and, with it, its sting. Ricky fell to the ground anyway, not only to draw sympathy but to deflect catcalls for letting in the two winning runs.

"Walk it off, Ricky," said Mr. Chazen, who'd jogged out from the bench. Still feigning injury, Ricky let Mr. Chazen help him up and then slowly limped toward the foul line. He'd almost crossed it when, behind him, somebody sneered, "Nice going, *Dickee*."

Turning around, Ricky saw it was the team's starting pitcher, Rollie Jaffe. A blimp of a boy who'd been held back in fourth grade at his school in Greenlawn, Rollie's head-high fastballs at batting practice, along with his low blow put-downs in between throws, always made Ricky flinch. "You little *Dickee*, I had the game put away, and you blew it. Just wait till the next time you face me!"

Dinner that evening didn't make Ricky any less anxious. Daddy's houses hadn't been selling, and night after night, his frustration was an un-welcome guest at the table.

"Goddammit, Madge, you need to cut back!"

"I have, Bernie, but there's still not enough!"

"Well, don't go calling your parents again!"

"Please, then, Bernie, I know it would be hard, but could you try yours one more time?"

"Don't start Madge, or I swear to God, you'll regret it!"

The phone suddenly rang in the kitchen. "I'll get it!" Ricky said, re-lieved to have an excuse to slip out.

"Zieglitz's residence, who is this, please?" he answered the way Mom-my had taught him.

"It's Louis's dad, Ricky," the voice on the other end said. "How are you feeling?"

". . . Fine," Ricky spluttered, surprised by the call.

"Glad to hear it! —Say, is your father around?"

"Wait just a second," Ricky replied as he covered the receiver with his hand and called Daddy.

"Who is it?" Daddy called back.

"Mr. Chazen."

"What the hell does he want?" Daddy said, storming in. As always, his temper terrified Ricky. ". . . I'm not sure," he mumbled.

Daddy snatched the phone from his hand and began talking as though he were telling off a salesman who'd interrupted his meal. "Okay, Chazen, what's so damn important you had to speak with me *now*?!" A few seconds later, he erupted, "Whaddya mean, 'Where'd my son learn to play baseball?' —Where the hell did you learn to coach?!" With that, Daddy slammed down the receiver and snarled at Ricky, "*Satisfied*? As if I didn't have enough on my plate—just one more damn thing for me to do!"

Late afternoon the next day, Ricky was busy with his homework when Daddy barged into his room. "Grab your mitt and hardball," Daddy ordered him. "We're going out back to practice."

"But, Daddy, it's getting dark."

"Don't be a baby!"

Cowed, Ricky went to his closet and took down the cheap glove and ball Daddy had bought him at Woolworth's. Once in the backyard, where more weeds grew than grass in between the splotches of dirt, Daddy grabbed hold of Ricky's shoulders and positioned him ten yards away. While Bernie would have liked to put more distance between them, he didn't want Ricky standing too close to his late-model Chevy, which he kept parked in the driveway rather than in their dilapidated garage with Madge's old Ford.

"Catch this, then throw it back!" Daddy barked, smoking the ball at Ricky.

Ricky's mitt snapped backwards, its five-and-dime padding no protection against the lightning strike that surged through his hand. "Not so hard, Daddy!" he squealed.

"Stop whining! Throw it!"

Because Daddy wasn't wearing a glove, and Ricky didn't want to hurt him, he lobbed the ball to him underhanded.

"No—not like that! Like *this*!" Daddy roared, zipping the ball back even harder than before.

A split second later, another fireball seared Ricky's hand. He flung down his mitt and started frantically rubbing his palm.

Daddy angrily stomped the length of the yard and glowered, "You think the ball's hard? Try life! —Start being a man." Wheeling around, he marched back to his spot by the house. "This time," he hollered at Ricky, "put some heat on it!"

Ricky wound up and heaved the ball as hard as he could, only to see it sail over Daddy's head and rattle an upstairs window.

"Dammit! Concentrate!" Daddy screamed as he scooped up the ball, reared back, and unleashed it. Ricky jumped out of the way. The ball pasted the Chevy.

While the likeliness of hurting his son hadn't bothered Bernie one bit, the mere thought of damaging his car unhinged him. Barreling past Ricky, he sprinted to the driveway, where he inspected the Chevy bumper to bumper. After determining it hadn't been dented, scratched, or otherwise marred, he thundered at Ricky, "Next time, stop the damn ball!" He stepped off ten paces and began throwing again, letting up some, though more out of concern for the Chevy than Ricky. Still, before long, he was rocketing pitches at Ricky once more.

"Please, Daddy," Ricky begged, "don't burn it in!"

He might as well have been pleading with the Chevy. Daddy uncorked the next pitch and drilled him right in the eye. Ricky crumpled to his knees and cupped his hand over the socket, sure that if he took it away, his eyeball would be in it. Mommy, hearing him wailing, charged out of the house. "*Bernie*! What did you do?" she demanded. Before he could answer, she was at Ricky's side, lifting his hand from his face. "Let's go in and put some ice on that eye before it swells up even more." As she walked Ricky back to the house, she shot Daddy a look that was a beanball of her own.

Drained by the day's ordeal, Ricky slept so soundly that night, he almost overslept *shul*. Afraid he might miss his ride with the Chazens, he threw on his dress clothes, including his tie, which by now, he could knot for himself.

Mommy met him at the foot of the stairs. "I tried calling the Chazens to tell them we're running late, but nobody answered. I'll just have to take you myself. As usual, your father's out with his houses."

When Ricky walked into services half an hour later, he didn't need anybody to tell him where he'd come in. Over the past year, he'd gone to *shul* often enough that he knew they'd be taking the Torah out any minute. He started heading toward Louis and Y. H., but as he got closer, he saw another kid occupying his seat, yakking with them and horsing around. The only places left were up front. As Ricky sidled through the thicket of adults in the third row, he recalled how Y. H. had wisecracked after he'd come to *shul* a few times, "You gotta get here early for a good seat in the back."

Not long afterwards, the ark's doors were opened, and Ricky, along with the grown-ups around him, rose to his feet. Bored as always by the incessant string of introductory prayers, he shifted his weight back and forth from one to the other. But as the scroll was removed and people broke into song, he unexpectedly found himself caught up with them, the singing no longer alien, outside him, but *in* him. As the melody billowed up to the sanctuary's domed ceiling, his own voice buoyed by the rest, Ricky, for the first time in his life, felt part of something bigger than he was. He hadn't experienced anything like it before, but whatever it was, he loved it. He didn't feel all alone anymore—not with Rollie, not with the Kyrchyks, not even with Daddy.

He skipped the *kiddush*, where a potshot from Y. H. or a poke from an *AK* might end up breaking the spell. Instead, he went out to the parking lot to wait quietly for Mommy. After forty-five minutes, the Chevy rolled up. Daddy pushed the passenger door open and said, "Get in." He didn't say anything else until he pulled in the driveway. "Your mother said you were late this morning, and since she had to take you, I had to pick you up—Christ, can't you do anything right?" But for once, Daddy's rage just washed over Ricky. Sheathed in his newfound sense of security, it left him unscathed.

Monday came, and Ricky fairly skipped to school; he hadn't felt this good since moving to Medina. He'd almost made it the whole way when he spotted Nick and Dirk Kyrchyk half a block ahead of him. He held back, hoping they wouldn't see him, but it was too late. Dirk, turning around to pick up some change that had dropped out of his pocket, called to his brother, "Hey, Nick—it's Zieglitz!"

"Aww, poor guy," Dirk mocked Ricky after they'd caught him while he was running away. "Just look at that shiner!"

Stroking his chin, Nick said, "Gee, it looks kinda lonely. Why don't we give it some company?" Without warning, he hammered Ricky's good eye.

Dirk clapped his brother on the back and hooted, "Nice goin'! We better scoot if we want to make the first bell."

Ricky missed the first bell as well as the second; half blind, he could scarcely see the sidewalk. When he finally staggered in the school's main doors, he was met by the principal, who'd posted himself there to catch latecomers. He was about to reprimand Ricky for being so tardy, but once he saw how he looked, he sent him straight to the nurse.

"Gracious, dear! What happened to *you*?" the nurse asked the moment Ricky stepped in her office. Ricky didn't say anything, too ashamed of himself to explain—and too afraid of the Kyrchyks to snitch.

When the nurse finished looking at Ricky's eye, she said, "I think it'd be best, dear, if you went home and rested. Give me your number, and I'll call your mother to come get you." But after several attempts, the nurse gave up and sighed, "Sorry, dear, it appears you'll just have to stay here."

She bandaged Ricky's latest black eye with some gauze and wrote him a hall pass. When he entered his classroom, some of the children, seeing his eyepatch, began squawking "Aargh!" Except for the teacher, only Louis seemed to care how he was, whispering to him as he walked by, "Gosh, Ricky, what happened?!" Once more, Ricky stayed silent, still too humiliated to answer and still too in fear of the Kyrchyks. —What if his hotheaded friend went after them in revenge, and then they came back at him again to get even?

When school ended that afternoon, Ricky froze at the doors before stepping outside. He looked one way, then the other for Nick and Dirk, like a rabbit twitching on the lookout for a fox or a weasel.

"Need a lift, Ricky?" Louis asked, tapping his shoulder. "My mom's coming for me, and she can drop you off at your house, or, if you want, you can come over to mine."

Ricky felt like hugging Louis. "Your house sounds great!" he exclaimed.

When Mrs. Chazen drove up, Louis, with Ricky beside him, leaned his head in the window and asked, "Mom, can Ricky go home with us?"

Mrs. Chazen took one look at Ricky and said, "Certainly! In fact, if you'd like to, you can join us for dinner."

"Thanks, but I probably ought to check with my mom."

"You can do it first thing when we get to the house," replied Mrs. Chazen.

But Ricky had no better luck than the nurse, and so, at six, after Mr. Chazen got home, everybody sat down for supper. For Ricky, dinner with the Chazens was everything that dinner with his own family wasn't. No bickering, no wrangling, no brawling. Why, Ricky thought to himself, couldn't he have been born a Chazen?

As they cleared the table after dessert, Mrs. Chazen told Ricky, "I'm going to try your house again. Your parents must be worried sick."

After somebody finally answered, Mrs. Chazen said, "No, no, Ricky's been no trouble. It's just he looks like he's been in a scrape—nothing serious, mind you—but when he couldn't reach you, I had him eat with us. I'm sure you'd do the same for Louis—" Cut off, she came back to the table visibly shaken, turning to Ricky as she said softly, "Your father's coming to get you."

When the bell rang, Louis went to answer it. Daddy walked in, saw Ricky's eye, and burst out, "What the hell happened to you?!"

"—My money's on those thug Kyrchyks," Mr. Chazen broke in.

Daddy shook his head in disgust. Bad enough his boy couldn't catch a pitch, he couldn't throw a punch, but now, even worse, he'd mortified him twice in front of Norman Chazen. Muttering "Thanks" to no one in particular, he hustled Ricky out the door. Once he got him in the car, he exploded, "God—what a fucking embarrassment you are!"

When they got home, Daddy, still seething, shoved Ricky into the kitchen. As soon as Mommy saw him, she rushed over to cradle his head. "Go get ready for bed, darling," she said so only he could hear her, "and when you're done, I'll tuck you in."

After Ricky finished brushing his teeth, he went to Mommy's bedroom to have her come tell him good night. Peeking in, he saw her talking on the phone. 'Thanks bunches. See you tomorrow!" she cooed into the receiver. Ricky assumed she was speaking to one of her bridge ladies. When she'd put down the receiver, he went in, looked around, and becoming a skittish rabbit again, asked her, "Where's Daddy?"

"Out," Mommy responded, her voice flat. She took Ricky's hand, led him to his bed, and pulled the covers snugly up to his neck. "Sweet dreams," she said, kissing his forehead.

When Ricky awoke and there was still no sign of his father, he figured Daddy had already gone to work. But at breakfast, he couldn't come up with a reason for Mommy's offering to drive him to school. He didn't spend any time, though, trying to work out one, because what did it matter? —No Kyrchyk would be able to touch him. "It's a deal, Mommy!" he whooped.

"First, let's have a look at your eye." After Mommy peeled back the bandage, she told him, "It's not nearly as bad as I thought! Do you want me to tape on another gauze pad, or should I just leave it off?"

"Leave it off!" he answered at once. He didn't need any more teasing about being a pirate.

The school day began normally enough—arithmetic followed by reading, then social studies and recess. As Ricky got near the glass doors leading onto the playground, he saw two silhouettes framed by the sunlight. When the pair walked in out of the sunshine, Ricky couldn't believe his eyes. "Dee-Dee and Jack! What are you doing here?"

"We've come to take you back to *Casa Futura* for a while," Dee-Dee said, bending down to embrace him.

"But what about my clothes? . . . What about my schoolwork?"

Putting his arm around Ricky's shoulder, Jack said, "It's all taken care of! We bought you some new duds, and we got them in the trunk. Your schoolbooks and lessons ain't gonna' be a problem, either. Madge said she'd get them from your teacher and mail them. So the only thing we need now is you! What do you say we hit the road?"

Jack took Ricky's hand, and together with Dee-Dee, headed out to the fresh-off-the-showroom, baby-blue Imperial parked at the curb. Sliding into its sprawling back seat, Ricky scrunched himself up against Dee-Dee. Meanwhile, Jack jumped in the driver's seat, turned the ignition key, and stepped on the gas. Speeding away from all the terrors of Medina, Ricky smiled. Maybe God had started to keep an eye out for him at last.

V

———

A gentle tap on the shoulder woke Ricky.

"Rise and shine!" said Hazel, the cheerful round woman who, when she wasn't minding the register at the grocery, cooked for the Apters on holidays and other times they had people over. "I've brought up your breakfast," she added, setting a silver tray on the nightstand.

At first, Ricky wasn't sure where he was. The big bed wasn't his, and neither was the cherrywood dresser, nor the big-screen TV in the corner. As Hazel drew back the room's gold satin curtains, his head cleared: he was at *Casa Futura*.

Hazel moved the tray to the bed and said, "I made you French toast. If memory serves, it's your favorite. There's a glass of fresh-squeezed orange juice and some fruit salad, too—we don't want you getting plugged up!"

As Ricky watched Hazel pour syrup on the French toast, he was glad she'd made it and not Dee-Dee. "Mother could burn corn flakes," Mommy had joked. Ricky knew it wasn't Dee-Dee's fault, though. Her own mother, he'd learned from Jack, had died when Dee-Dee was just eleven and hadn't been taught how to cook yet. "Besides," Jack had told him, "it wouldn't have made no difference. Dina and her two little brothers couldn't afford anything but baloney sandwiches thanks to their old man who threw away all their dough at the track."

Hazel patted Ricky's hand. "It was good seeing you, but I've got to get going. You remember my husband, Wayne? He's waiting downstairs to take me and Dina to the grocery. Don't think for a minute, though, that you'll be all by your lonesome. Jack says he's staying behind to take you some place special."

After Hazel closed the door behind her, Ricky gobbled up his breakfast, eager to get down to Jack. He sprang out of bed and hustled to the dresser,

36

where he threw on some of the new clothes—underwear, socks, jeans, and a T-shirt—Dee-Dee and Jack had bought him in Medina. Next, he flung open the closet and knotted the shoestrings of his old Keds. As he looked up, he glimpsed his face in the full-length mirror on the door: the black-and-blue eyes staring back made him cringe. Only Jack's abruptly calling up, "Hey, kiddo, are you ready?" made him remember there weren't any beanballs or Kyrchyks within a hundred miles. He loped down the brick-red tile steps to the foot of the stairs where Jack met him, grinning. "Thought we'd take a ride to Excelsior. Ever been there?"

"I don't think so."

"Well, what are we waiting for? Let's get going!"

Walking briskly as always, he led Ricky to the mansion's three-car garage where the Imperial sat between his pickup and riding mower. After Ricky hopped in the front seat beside him, he backed out, before heading down the serpentine driveway past the wrought-iron gates toward Huppertsville's Main Street. Passing by Bud's Auto Shop, Citizens' State Bank, and the boarded-up Mr. Z's, he came to the outskirts of town where he turned on to Route 3, let out the car's V-8 engine, and covered the forty miles to Excelsior in just over twenty-five minutes. As he drove along the capital's broad boulevards, Ricky gaped at the immense homes, some of which, like the governor's, were even more dazzling than *Casa Futura*. When they'd reached the heart of downtown, Jack stopped in front of a store above whose two sets of double doors, ten-feet high red-white-and-blue letters proclaimed, "Lapides's Sporting Goods." Turning off the ignition, he told Ricky, "Everybody out, kiddo—we're here!"

The moment Ricky walked into Lapides's, what he saw staggered him: fishing rods, golf clubs, tennis rackets, hockey sticks, and skis as well as all the attire to go with them. Over his shoulder, he heard Jack say to someone, "I'm looking for Sol."

"I think he's in the stockroom," the salesman replied. "I'll page him."

A little while later, a man about Jack's age appeared who, like him, was broad shouldered and, except for a slight paunch, well built. "Hey, Jack, good to see you! It's been way too long. How's Dina?"

"We're both doing fine, Sol."

"And who's this with you?"

"This here's my grandson, Ricky!"

Sol squatted down beside Ricky and said, "You know, Ricky, Jack and I played semipro ball together. I was just a so-so catcher. But your granddad! He could do it all—pitch, hit, and field. All the big-league teams sent around their scouts to watch him."

Ricky was wide-eyed; Jack had never said a word about his ball-playing days. "What happened, Jack? Did you get hurt before you got to the majors?"

Sol jumped in before Jack could answer. "—Yeah, he got heart-struck! Before your gramma, he had a girl in every town. But once he met her, that was it for his life on the road."

Shaking his head, Jack said, "That's all in the past, Sol. Today's about Ricky. Where do you keep your mitts?"

Ricky panicked. Was Jack going to buy him a new glove so when he returned to Medina, he could practice more with Daddy and get walloped again? As Sol walked ahead of them, Ricky tugged on Jack's sleeve and said in a low voice, "But my dad already bought me a glove."

"Your ma told me all about that piece of crap!" Jack retorted.

Sol stopped beside shelves stocked with gloves for every position and sized hand, whether lefty or righty. "How about this, Jack? Take a mitt home with you for Ricky to try out, and if he decides he doesn't like it, bring it back and exchange it, no questions asked."

"You got a deal!"

"Always happy to help an old friend," Sol said as he was paged to somewhere else in the store.

After Sol departed, Jack walked over to a bin full of baseballs farther down the aisle. Plucking one out, he returned and held up Ricky's right hand, then reached for some gloves he thought might fit it. "Feel all right?" he asked after Ricky tried each one on. If Ricky answered, "Yes," he'd plop the ball in the glove's pocket and say, "Can you squeeze the mitt so's the ball don't fall out?" If Ricky responded with "Yes" again, Jack would plunk the ball in the glove's webbing. "What about now, kiddo?" he'd ask. "Can you still hold it?" At last, they came to a glove where all of Jack's questions met with nothing but yeses from Ricky.

Nodding his approval, Jack said, "Good choice—it's a 'Duke Snider.' He's a pretty fair fielder. Lots better hitter, though. Which reminds me, you need a bat. Think I saw some on the aisle before this one."

Ricky's heart raced. Did Jack think that buying him his own bat would stop Rollie beaning him? He tried to distract Jack by saying, "Why don't we go look at basketballs? I'd like to get better shooting." He wasn't any better at basketball than baseball, but at least when he'd played in Greenlawn with his cousins, he'd never been conked.

"In a minute," Jack said as he tucked the glove under his armpit, the baseball secure in the mitt's webbing, and walked Ricky to the bat display around the corner. "See the number burned in the bottom of the handle?" he said. "That's how many ounces the bat weighs." Sliding one out of the rack, he told Ricky, "I think this one will be light enough for you. Go ahead and take a couple of rips." Once Ricky had swung the bat a few times, Jack asked, "So how's it feel to you, kiddo?"

"It's okay," Ricky answered quietly, still uneasy as he thought about batting against Rollie.

"Let's go take a look at their basketballs," Jack said.

"No, I don't want one anymore," Ricky said now that his stalling tactic had failed. Jack paid the cashier, making sure she'd give Sol his thanks once again. Out in the car, he looked over at Ricky and said, clicking his tongue, "Betcha I can get us home faster than we got here. There'll be plenty of daylight left for us to practice!"

Practice with Jack? Ricky could only imagine what his face would look like after that! In a desperate attempt to slow Jack down and eat up some time, he said when they rolled up to Huppertsville's lone stoplight, "I could use a Dairy Queen. How about you?"

"Sure thing!" Jack responded. "We'll still have an hour or two to practice."

As Jack started the car after they'd finished, Ricky, full of ice cream, dozed off on the way home. Pulling into the garage, Jack gave Ricky's elbow a nudge. "Time to break in your new mitt!"

Ricky wished he hadn't had the ice cream cone as his stomach began churning. If his father burned the ball in, what would happen when Jack, a former semipro, threw it to him? He slowly got out of the car and silently followed Jack along the edge of the driveway. Midway down it, Jack stopped and pushed away some vines that had overgrown a small gap in the ironwork fence. As Ricky walked through, he saw a broad, open meadow. He was astonished that in all the time he'd spent at *Casa Futura*, no one had ever taken him to it. Dee-Dee must not have wanted him wandering down there on the driveway alone after his accident. Seeing the meadow now, he knew her fears hadn't been unfounded. Its emerald-green grass beckoned him, its thick stands of sycamores on three sides drew him in, and its flagstone wall on the fourth summoned up images of the winding path from the great house to the little cottage where he'd been happy.

For Jack, the wall evoked a sentiment that was entirely different. "Built that damn thing myself," he said as he caught Ricky eyeing it. "Every year, I make it higher."

"What's on the other side, Jack?"

"—Graveyard. Hate those goddam places, and I sure as hell don't want to see one when I go walking around my yard. —Let's start throwing! How far away do you want me to stand?"

"Farther back," Ricky said, wary of Jack's arm. He put on the new mitt from Sol's. Unlike his old one, it felt soft and supple.

After Jack had moved off some distance toward the wall, he went into a small windup and said, "Here it comes!"

Ricky braced himself, but he needn't have: Jack floated the ball to him in a slow arc.

"Now it's your turn," Jack told him. "Throw it back!"

Ricky's return was off-target, but Jack nabbed it easily. After several throws, he began pitching the ball harder. Even so, Ricky never flinched; the Excelsior glove, with its deep, padded pocket, swallowed up the ball's bite.

"You're doing real good catching, kiddo, but let's work on your pitching. You can't just throw with your arm. You got to put your shoulder and legs in it, too!"

An instant later, Ricky's pitch spanked Jack's palms. "Way to put some heat on the ball, kiddo! Might have to get a mitt for myself!"

Next Jack walked in and picked up the bat. "I'm going to hit some balls so we can practice your fielding. It's a game called 'Fungo.' Dunno why it's called that—maybe short for 'I'll have *fun* hittin' the balls while you *go* after them.' But that ain't important, because here's all you need to remember: keep your eye on the ball. Now go out about halfway to the wall, and I'll swat you some grounders like you was playing infield."

Infield! Mr. Chazen had never let Ricky do that, and Daddy wouldn't think of it—what if a grounder got by him and dinged the Chevy?

Jack's first grounders were like his first pitches, slow and easy for Ricky to catch. "Since you seem to be getting it down pretty good," Jack said twenty minutes later, "I'm going to spray it around." Regardless of where he hit them, though, Ricky still scooped most of them up.

"Okay, time to shag some flies," Jack said, motioning him farther away with the bat. After Ricky jogged out nearer the wall and signaled Jack he was ready, Jack flipped the ball up in front of him and took a smooth swing with the bat. Ricky never took his eyes off the long, lazy fly, tracking the ball into his glove until it jerked backwards. Jack called out, "Nice going, kiddo! Now let's see you run to get them." No matter where Jack lofted them, though, Ricky usually caught them. After a while, Jack finally said, "This time, I'm going to hit you a high one, and I want you to pretend there's a runner rounding third who you have to nail at the plate." He flicked the ball up and banged out a towering fly. For a moment, Ricky lost it in the sun, but unlike Little League, he didn't duck out of the way. Shielding his eyes with the mitt, he located the ball plummeting toward him, and, once it dropped in the glove's pocket, nimbly dug it out and drilled it to Jack. As the ball slapped against Jack's hands, Ricky, hearing Jack scream "Ow!" thought he might have hurt him. But Jack wasn't yelping, "Ouch!"—he was yelling, "*Out!*"

Beaming, he cried to Ricky, "Know what, kiddo? You got what it takes to play ball!"

Nobody had ever said that to Ricky before, certainly not Rollie, definitely not Daddy, not even Mr. Chazen. But their encouragement couldn't have matched Jack's, which cheered on Ricky's resolve to become as good as he was—and not just at baseball.

"Get ready!" Jack sang out as he sent another fly soaring. Ricky kept running back, his eyes locked on the ball, until, bumping into the wall, he watched it sail over his head.

Jack bellowed at him, "Stay put! I don't want you going into a graveyard until you have to."

That was just fine with Ricky: he wasn't about to go traipsing around in a cemetery—who knew what might reach up and grab him? As the sun started setting, he only got more anxious when Jack, having hoisted himself over the wall, still hadn't climbed back out. At last, Jack emerged victorious, holding the ball up for Ricky to see. "Lucky it's still light! Never would've found the damn thing in the dark. We still got some time before dinner, though. It's your turn to bat."

Ricky froze. Running around to catch Jack's pitches was one thing. Standing in to hit them was another.

Jack stepped off fifty paces from where he'd been standing. "I read somewhere that in Little League, this is about the distance between the mound and the plate. Seem right to you?"

". . . Guess so," Ricky mumbled as he slowly walked in with visions of Rollie's high, hard ones hurtling at him.

But Jack didn't throw anything like Rollie. His pitch came in slow and straight down the middle. Ricky still backed away.

Jack told him to relax. "Honest—I ain't going to hurt you."

Ricky let out a deep breath. Jack threw him another perfect strike. This time, he hung in; he took a big swing at the ball—and whiffed.

"Kiddo, keep your eye on the ball! And remember, you don't have to kill it. You just have to kiss it to give it a ride."

As the ball left Jack's hand, Ricky never took his eyes off it, waiting until the last possible moment to make contact.

Crack!

Ricky watched the ball fly over Jack's head, gaining almost enough altitude to clear the flagstone wall.

"That's the way to do it, slugger!" Jack shouted.

Ricky had never come close to hitting a ball like that; the feel of the bat striking it thrilled him as much as the sight of it taking off up and away. "Throw me another, Jack!" he whooped with delight.

Noticing the sun sinking on the horizon, Jack said, "We're losing the light, so we probably ought to get back to the house. What do you think?"

Ricky didn't need any persuading; he still sported a black eye from the last time he'd kept practicing despite the sun's going down. "Fine with me, Jack," he answered.

When he walked in the front door, Dee-Dee, who'd arrived home a bit earlier, told him, "Got a surprise for you—Hazel's come made us dinner! It's what she used to cook us at Thanksgiving from turkey and dressing to yams and pecan pie. By the time you and Jack wash up, she'll have the food on the table."

Ricky was so excited, he kept his fingers under the faucet mere seconds before sprinting into the dining room. He stopped beside the ornately carved, high-back chair that was always his on Thanksgiving, one of twelve surrounding the oblong, custom-made mahogany table. As he sat down, he took in everything he loved about the room: its walls with their ebony inlaid panels; its midnight-blue oriental carpet filled with intricate curlicues in deep crimsons and swirls in soft tans; its walnut-beamed ceiling from which hung a crystal chandelier that, together with the room's latticed windows, bent the dimming daylight into rainbows. Seeing the meal Hazel had set out on Dee-Dee's finest china, he smiled to himself knowing that even if he'd gorged himself on the Dairy Queen only half an hour before or hadn't run it off playing ball in the meadow, he still wouldn't pass up Hazel's cooking, right down to the last bite of her pie.

"Well, how was it?" said Hazel, walking in from the kitchen to clear off the dishes.

"Jim-dandy as always," Jack answered.

"That goes for me, too," said Dee-Dee.

"Me, three!" Ricky joined in. "You're the best cook ever!"

"That's because you're one of my best eaters!" chortled Hazel. Ricky got up to help her take the plates to the kitchen, where, after she'd washed them off, he dried them. Removing her apron, Hazel tousled his hair and told him, "Hope I get to see you again before you go home."

Ricky wondered how long that would be. How many days before he'd have to go back to Medina, Daddy, and the Kyrchyks? Once his head hit the pillow, though, he fell fast asleep. Snug in the big bed, he'd never felt safer.

When he awoke the next morning, he glanced at the Westclox on the nightstand and saw it was well past ten. He jumped out of bed, hurriedly got dressed, and galloped down to the kitchen, hoping to catch Dee-Dee and Jack. Instead, he found a note on the table:

Dear Ricky,

There's the kind of cereal you like in the pantry, and there's fresh milk in the fridge. Meanwhile, the mailman just dropped off a package your mother sent special delivery. I think it's your lessons and schoolbooks. Jack put them on the desk in the library. —He'll be back for you by noon.

Love,
Dee-Dee

Ricky took out the cereal and milk and, after he'd eaten, went to the study where books lined the shelves floor to ceiling. He spread his homework over the solid oak desk and sat down in its overstuffed, brown leather chair, quickly becoming so absorbed in his assignments that even when the hall clock chimed one, he didn't notice that Jack still hadn't come home. Around half past, Jack finally returned.

"Didn't want to disturb you," Jack said when Ricky spied him standing silently at the doorway of the study. "But I have to tell you that seeing you here in this library makes me want to bust my buttons. The books on the shelves came with the house, but I couldn't read them if I had to. Didn't have much education and neither did Dina, and your ma, well, she was never one for reading. Seeing you, though, hunched over studying like that makes me believe that one day, somebody from our side of the family will put books to good use. For now, let's get you some lunch. I expect you built up an appetite working so hard."

"Not really, I got up kind of late and had two bowls of cereal. —What I'd really like to do is go practice some more."

". . . Well, I'm supposed to stop by the other bar this afternoon . . . ," Jack hesitated, before saying, "Ah, what the hell! It ain't every day that you're here!"

As they walked down the driveway to the meadow, Ricky asked Jack, "Can I bat some more?"

For the next hour, Jack kept pitching and, like the previous day, each pitch he threw came in slightly faster. More often than not, though, Ricky smacked a sailing fly, a crisp line drive, or a sizzling grounder. He'd forgotten all about Rollie until, without warning, a fastball flew dead at him. He spun out of the way in plenty of time.

"See?" Jack said. "Just keep your eye on the ball, and everything'll be fine."

Ricky stepped back up and dug in his Keds. But because Jack's previous pitch had thrown off his timing, he got way out in front of the next one and pulled it into the sycamores. "I'll get it, Jack," he said, scampering toward the trees. "Stay put!" Jack bellowed at him, but Ricky had already vanished into the woods. Chasing the ball down a slope, he didn't see a root sticking up and tumbled all the way to the bottom, where he came to rest in a tiny clearing. His gaze fell on a small gazebo whose style, with it stucco walls and terra-cotta roof, mimicked the mansion's. "Wait!" Jack barked from behind him, but once more, he kept going. He stepped inside the gazebo, where his eyes fixed on the mosaic adorning its floor: bone-white tiles ringing bright blue ones that formed a Star of David.

Catching up, Jack said, "Sorry, Ricky, I didn't mean to holler at you like that. It's just I ain't sure I want you to see this place."

"Why not, Jack? And why's there a Jewish star here?"

Jack sighed, "It's a long story. There used to be this real tough guy in town named Mackey Teeter, and him and me occasionally did business together. Now Mackey had a wife, Rose, and the two of them lived at *Casa Futura* before me and Dina. While Mackey was an SOB, Rose was one fine person. She'd come to Huppertsville from New Orleans, where she'd been brought up a lady. Living here was rough on her, there not being much around to occupy her. You know those books in the library? They're all hers. Some of them she brought with her; the others she sent away for after she got here. Reading them was how she passed the time. But you know what was really hard on Rose? She was Jewish, and like you know from having to move to Medina, there ain't hardly any Jews around here. For once, though, Mackey did something thoughtful. He built Rose this gazebo—he said it'd be her 'chapel' where she could pray any time she'd want to. Of course that's a bunch of hooey. Know where I learned that? Right before Madge and Bernie got hitched, Irv and Thelma wanted me and Dina to go to Excelsior to have your folks get blessed by the rabbi. So I put in my two cents and said, 'Let the rabbi come here, and we'll throw a party after.' But then Irv said, 'Nothing doing! A *shul*'s where Jews go to pray.' Well, I'll never forget what happened once I got there. The rabbi came over and said to me that with my being Madge's father, I ought to have what he called 'an honor.' But seeing as I can't read any Hebrew—hell, I have enough trouble with English!—he gave me an honor that wasn't a speaking part. 'Hagbah' he called it. I just had to lift up the scroll when he gave me the high sign. Damn thing was pretty heavy, and right in the middle of my lifting it up, he leans over and warns me not to drop it. 'It's got God's name in it!' he tells me. Anyway, getting back to this gazebo, it must have suited Rose fine, because she stayed here and put up with Mackey."

Jack took a deep breath. "This is where the story gets real sad, Ricky. One winter, Rose came down with something, a couple of days later it turned into pneumonia, and three days after that, she was dead. Mackey was never himself again. He couldn't have cared less about our business. But it wasn't like he was just sitting home grieving. Truth was, he couldn't stand being anywhere near *Casa Futura*, since everything there reminded him of Rose. He even tried moving down to the cottage, which back then, like now, was empty. Didn't do any good, either. So one day, he up and says to me, 'Jack, I know I owe you some dough. Why don't I just give you the house and call it even?' And that's how Dina and me came to live here. What Mackey did might have seemed strange to lots of folks, but not me. I can understand how bad he felt . . . ," Jack's voice drifted off, "losing somebody you love."

Ricky didn't say anything, because he didn't know what to say. He stepped past Jack and retrieved the ball, which he'd spotted lying in some underbrush near the edge of the clearing. He marched up the slope to the meadow, where Jack joined him several minutes later. After handing Jack the ball, he walked in toward the plate, assuming Jack would go back to the mound. When he turned around, though, Jack was at the base of the wall. "Aren't you going to keep pitching to me, Jack?" Ricky yelled.

"Yeah . . . sure," Jack faltered. He trudged in and, all his gracefulness suddenly gone, mechanically chucked the ball at the plate. It fell short, bounced up, and split Ricky's lip.

Ricky's howl brought Jack's mind back to the meadow. Dashing in, he lifted Ricky's chin and, seeing the blood dribbling down it, cursed, "Dammit! What the hell was I thinking? Let's get you back to the house."

Leaving the baseball gear behind them, Jack put his arm around Ricky and shepherded him up the driveway. When they got home, Dee-Dee, who'd beaten them just by a few minutes, heard Ricky sobbing and rushed to the hallway to see what was wrong. "My fault, Dina," Jack told her.

"Am I going to have to get stitches?"

Jack smiled. "Not if I got anythin' to do with it! I just need some stuff from the bathroom." He came back with a jar of Vaseline and a Q-tip. Dabbing the swab in the jelly, he carefully daubed Ricky's lip, which, in less than a minute, stopped bleeding.

"Where'd you learn to do that?" Ricky asked, in awe of Jack more than ever.

"Picked it up when I was boxing."

"That's even neater than baseball!"

"I don't know about that! I got knocked around plenty. Lucky I had a good cut man to stop my bleeding when some palooka slit open my eye. Without that guy—his name was Angie—there'd have been lots of fights I would have lost instead of winning."

"Did you get to be champ?" Ricky said, his lip completely forgotten.

"Well, I was moving up the ladder, and my manager said I had a shot at the title."

"What stopped you?"

"Simple—Dina! She'd get so worried before one of my fights, she couldn't eat or sleep. One day, she laid down the law: 'You either give up the boxing ring or I'm giving your engagement ring back!'"

"Weren't you sad?" Ricky asked, recalling how Daddy had sounded about having to give up his hopes of becoming a lawyer.

"Hell, no! I cared a lot more about Dina than boxing. And anyway, it was a damn good thing she got me out of the ring. If she hadn't, I probably would have ended up punch drunk with even less brains than I got now." Coming closer, he cupped Ricky's cheek in his palm. "You've got brains, Ricky, and that's a helluva lot better than having a haymaker."

That night, Ricky slept in the big bed even more soundly than before.

The next day when he got up, he took his time dressing, figuring he'd have a few hours until Jack came home to get him. He shambled down the stairs to the kitchen for breakfast. Dee-Dee and Jack were still there.

"Your ma called," Jack said, his voice flat. "I got to take you home."

"*Why?*" Ricky yowled.

Dee-Dee replied, "Better if she tells you. I'd come along with you if I could, but I've got produce orders arriving today."

Trying to lift Ricky's spirits, Jack said, "We're going to stop for breakfast at a place you ain't been to before. I already got your bat, ball, and mitt from the meadow, and they're stowed in the trunk. As soon as Dina packs the duds that she bought you, we can get going."

Ricky was too disappointed to answer. Not long afterwards, Dina brought down his bag, and as he was about to give her a perfunctory kiss goodbye on the way out, she hugged him and whispered, "I love you."

When Ricky got in the car, he sat in the back instead of the front. Jack drove down the driveway, then along Main Street, and except for its purr, the Imperial was silent. After they'd gone about five miles on Route 3, Jack turned in to Oscar's Country Diner. As Ricky plodded behind him into the restaurant, a balding, barrel-chested man in an orange plaid shirt and lime pants welcomed them at the door. "Glad to see you, Jack! How are you, and how's the missus? —And who's this you got with you?"

"Me and Dina are in the pink, Oscar—thanks for asking. And this here's my grandson, Ricky."

"Pleased to make your acquaintance, Ricky," said Oscar.

Ricky, still moping, didn't respond. Oscar mistook it for shyness. "Why don't we get you two seated?" he said, taking them to a corner booth, where they sank down in its turquoise Naugahyde cushions as he laid out silverware and napkins on its tabletop's pale yellow Formica. "The usual?" he asked Jack.

"Can't resist. Like always, steak and eggs and a cup of coffee, black."

"Coming right up! And for you, young fella?"

Ricky hadn't stopped sulking, and when he didn't respond once again, Jack ordered for him. "French toast, Oscar, a large juice and a glass of milk." But after the food came, Ricky scarcely touched it.

After a while, Jack said, "Look, kiddo, Dina and me don't like you going home, either. But I'm thinking there's another reason you don't want to go back—on account of being bullied, I mean. Even if your ma hadn't told me, I could have figured it out because of those shiners you've got."

The shame was too much; Ricky broke out in tears. How could a chicken like him be Jack's grandson?

Jack told him, "Ain't nothing to be embarrassed about. Almost everybody's been bullied at one time or another."

"Not you, I bet," Ricky sniffled.

"How do you think I got so good at fighting? Tell you what. I'll get the bill and then, we'll go out to the parking lot. There's some stuff I want to show you. We're going to put a stop to those bullies beating you up." He paid the check, thanked Oscar, and took Ricky to an empty space next to the Imperial. Ricky couldn't imagine what Jack had in mind, but after everything he'd taught him about baseball, how could he not trust him about learning to fight?

Jack looked at him and said, "Okay, kiddo, make me a fist."

Ricky balled up his hand. "Not that way, kiddo," Jack said, prying it open. "Hit somebody hard enough with your thumb stuck between your fingers like that, and you'll break it. If you wrap it around them instead, the other guy will get nothing but a fistful of knuckles." He refolded Ricky's hand and then told him, "Now punch me in the gut as hard as you can."

Ricky held back. "What if I hurt you?"

"That'll be my problem. You just take your best shot!"

Ricky swung with all his of might, but Jack didn't budge—Ricky might as well have given him a poke with his pinky.

"You know, kiddo, when I started out, I was terrible at throwing a punch till I learned it was like throwing a baseball. —You have to get your shoulder and legs in it, too. Go ahead and belt me again!"

Ricky reared back, and like he'd pitched in the meadow, propelled his arm forward with his shoulder and legs. Jack bent over and let out an "Oof!" After he caught his breath, he said, "That's the stuff, champ. Let's get back in the car before you lay me down for the count. There's some other tips I want to give you."

Once they were on the road again, Ricky stopped wondering about why he'd been called home; all his thoughts revolved around getting more pointers from Jack on how to punch out the Kyrchyks. Jack began, though, in a way he hadn't expected. "You already know a little about my time prize-fighting. But before that, I did some fighting I ain't proud of. When I was going on eighteen, I got thrown out of school for hitting a teacher."

Ricky was speechless. He couldn't believe anybody would hit a teacher, least of all Jack, his idol.

"After that, kiddo, I began hanging out with what you'd call a bad crowd. The government had just outlawed booze, and the easiest way to begin making money—and making it quick—was to start selling hootch as a bootlegger. Most times, I wasn't worried about the cops—hell, lots of them were on the take and in on it, too. It was other bootleggers I had to keep an eye on, because sometimes they'd try to heist my whiskey along with my dough. When they were packing guns, there wasn't anything I could do about it, since after I got married to Dina, she wouldn't let me carry one of my own. But when those other mugs didn't have any guns, using my fists was the way I hung on to my loot. Now I'm going to let you in on a se-cret: street fighting's tougher than prizefighting. In the ring, it's just one guy against another. But in street fighting, there's usually two, three, sometimes even more guys coming at you. They can still be whupped, though, and it's the same way you handle bullies."

"What is it, Jack?"

"Hold your horses! I'm getting to that. What you've got to remember is that most bullies are yellow—it's why they always got a gang with them or at least a sidekick. Once you understand that bullies are lily-livered, the way to deal with them ain't a mystery: when one starts pushing you around, you push him right back a lot harder. Now I won't lie to you—after you pop the bully one, he might hit you back. Sure as hell, though, it'll be the last time he'll come after you because next time he'll go after somebody who won't put up any fight at all—somebody who won't cost him anything. So with those two brothers who have been bullying you, give the bigger one a fist right in the belly just like you did me. Remember, don't punch him in the face! You could get in a heap of trouble for breaking his jaw or nose or messing up his eye. But like I said, slug him right in the breadbasket so's you double him up. His brother won't know what the hell to do—he'll be scared stiff. I promise you that neither of them will ever bother you again. You get what I'm saying?"

"Uh-huh," Ricky answered quietly. While what Jack had told him seemed to make sense, he couldn't picture himself making Nick Kyrchyk keel over. And what about Roman and his knife?

Around three, Jack pulled up in the middle of the Zieglitzes' driveway. The garage door was open, and Ricky wondered why the Chevy was inside with the Ford. He was about to lift up the door handle when Jack took out a notepad from his shirt pocket and tore off a page. "Look, kiddo, these here are the phone numbers for the house, the grocery, and the bars. You need me or Dina, call us collect." Pressing the scrap of paper in Ricky's hand, he told him, "Hang on to this like it's got God's name!"

Ricky nodded, got out, and as Jack trailed behind him with the suitcase and baseball equipment, walked to the back door. Mommy opened it and took him in her arms. "I'm sorry you had to come home, but your father wants to see you."

Ricky clutched the paper tight in his fist.

VI

————

What Daddy wanted to see him about, Mommy didn't say, not because she wouldn't, but because she couldn't. The only thing Ricky knew for certain was that Daddy still wasn't home by bedtime. He patted the pocket of his pajama top. The slip of paper Jack had left to keep him safe was working.

The next day, he had his doubts. At first, the paper still seemed to be watching over him when Mommy peeked in and said, "I just phoned the Chazens and let them know you wouldn't be going to *shul* today." His belief wavered once she added, "I'm taking you to the hospital to visit your father."

"Is Daddy dying?" Ricky asked, fingers crossed in his robe, hoping the next father Mommy got him would be better.

"Oh, honey, Daddy's not going to die!" Mommy answered, cradling Ricky's head. "He just needs a little rest."

". . . So, maybe, we shouldn't disturb him?" Ricky volunteered, glancing at his Timex and figuring he could still catch the Chazens if he hurried. —An hour of *Musaph* sounded more appealing than fifteen minutes with Daddy.

Mommy held him tighter. "I don't know what we did," she said, "to deserve a child as sweet as you. But we won't be bothering Daddy. Every time I call him, he never lets me go without asking, 'When can I see Ricky?' Don't worry—it'll be just fine." Ricky wasn't persuaded. Even though he'd waffled on how he felt about the paper, he made sure as he got dressed to transfer it from his pj's to his pants.

On the way over, Mommy tried to get him to relax by distracting him with questions about his time in Huppertsville. "What did you do each day?" she asked.

"Stuff," he muttered.

"So, honey," she said, "where did you get that new glove and bat of yours?"

"Excelsior," he murmured.

"And how did you like it?" she inquired.

Ricky made no response except for a mumbled, "I don't feel like talking."

When they arrived at the hospital, they took an elevator to a ward where they had to knock on the door before an attendant let them in. "We're here to see Bernie Zieglitz," Mommy told him. Pulling the door fast behind them, he mutely pointed to a glass cubicle in the middle of the corridor.

"Where can we find Bernie Zieglitz, please?" Mommy asked the nurse inside the booth. "Room 5," she replied indifferently without looking up from her gossip magazine. Mommy clutched Ricky's hand as she led him past several patients blankly staring into space opposite another jabbering about aliens invading earth. By the time they got to Daddy's room, Ricky's hand had broken free of Mommy's to take hold of the scrap of paper in his jeans.

"Bernie," she said, gently trying to wake him, "it's Madge and Ricky."

". . . What?" responded Daddy, struggling to open his eyes.

"It's Madge and Ricky, Bernie," she repeated quietly.

"Sorry, Madge," he said, propping himself on his elbows. "It must be the drugs they gave me. . . . Thanks for coming and bringing Ricky."

"Have you heard from your folks or Aileen?" she asked.

"Not a word," he said glumly. "I'd hoped Ernest would offer to look in on my houses. I don't know . . . maybe they're all embarrassed that I'm here."

"I'm sure that's not it, Bernie," Madge responded, smiling wanly. "They probably just want to wait till the doctors say you're stronger."

"Who knows when that'll be?" he sighed. "All they tell me is that they want to keep me for at least another week or two. But we can't afford it, Madge. It'd cost too much, and besides, I have to get back to work."

"Let's talk about that later," Madge said as she stroked his hand. "For now, though, wouldn't you like to talk with Ricky?"

". . . Yeah . . . sure, Madge," he answered. ". . . Would you mind giving us some time alone?"

She saw the panic on Ricky's face and said, "I'll be right outside the door."

"Ricky, it's important to me that you understand," Daddy began once Mommy stepped out, "why I had myself admitted."

Hearing Daddy say he'd gone on his own to the loony bin only made Ricky more uncomfortable. He wished he'd left with Mommy.

"You must think," Daddy said, "that you're living with an ogre, what with my blowing up over every little thing. I want to stop it, but somehow I just can't. Before the war, I never used to have nerves like this. Maybe all those years of enemy planes and jammed guns were too much for me—and now, I'm stuck with those unsold houses! Christ, what made me think I could take the pressure of the building business? I should never have given up selling *shmatas* . . ."

Ricky waited for Daddy to go on. But he only turned away, pulling his blankets above his head. Ricky supposed that meant their talk was over. He walked out to the hall convinced of the paper's power.

That night, his faith in it only deepened. As he was about to fall asleep, Mommy came in and nuzzled his face with hers. "Ricky," she said softly, "your father's wanting to speak to you this morning made me think it's time I had a conversation of my own with you . . ." She pulled back and dabbed away tears from her eyes. "You remember," she continued, drawing close to him again, "my telling you that Dee-Dee didn't know how to cook because she didn't have a mother to learn from? Me, neither. When I was your age, Dee-Dee had to work so hard, I barely saw her, and so, the first year I was married to your poor father, all I knew how to make was tuna casserole. If it hadn't been for a *Betty Crocker Cookbook*, I wouldn't have known how to make even that! But, honey, there's no recipe for making a good mother . . ." By now, Ricky could feel the tears streaming down her cheeks. ". . . Can you forgive me for how I've hurt you?" she asked him, sobbing.

Ricky had never seen his mother cry, much less sorry, and as he shushed her, he was sorry he'd ever questioned the slip of paper tucked beneath his pillow.

Sunday, Mommy couldn't have been nicer: she let Ricky sleep late, have Sugar Smacks for breakfast, watch all the TV he wanted, and go to bed without a bath. Then, on Monday morning, as he was leaving to walk to school, she called after him, "Just give me a minute, honey, and I'll drive you."

Before his trip to Huppertsville, Ricky would have been headed for the garage. With the paper on him, though, he felt like a superhero who had secret powers. "Thanks, Mommy," he said, "but you don't have to."

"Well, what about my picking you up in the afternoon?" she asked.

"I've got Hebrew school," he reminded her.

"I told them you wouldn't be coming in this week. I want things to be easier on you for a while. —And that includes your getting home in one piece!"

"I'll be all right, Mommy," he replied, his hand in his pocket. "No more black eyes—I promise!"

Even in class, Jack's note shielded him. As he was daydreaming about playing ball in the meadow, his teacher abruptly raised her voice, and he thought she was going to scold him. Instead, she was merely trying to be heard above the kindergartners outside for recess.

At breakfast Tuesday, Mommy again said she'd be happy to give Ricky a ride to school. When he turned her down once more, she told him, "Okay, but you're not getting rid of me that fast. I've arranged to take you and Louis to baseball. His mother says it's a real game today, and, considering how many times the Chazens have given you a lift to services, it's the least I can do. Go put your glove and bat in the car, and I'll get Louis's at his house later."

When school let out, Ricky ran to the curb, expecting to see Mommy's Ford. Waiting for him, though, was the Chevy. He groped in his pocket for the paper.

"I only got home about an hour ago," Daddy told him. "Get in, or we'll be late!" Nobody spoke until Daddy pulled up to the ball field and said, "Thought I'd stick around for the game."

"—You should go home and get some rest!" Ricky bleated. As much as he'd improved, he still might muff one or strike out. At least when Daddy had called him a "fucking embarrassment" before, no one else had been there to hear it.

"Resting is all I've been doing!" Daddy snapped.

Ricky got out and grimly trudged to the diamond, where he was met with a jeer from the bench. "Miss me, *Dickee*?" hooted Rollie. Ricky kicked the dirt: why hadn't they kept Daddy locked up in the nuthouse?

"Batting practice!" yelled Mr. Chazen.

As usual, Ricky went last. Since he hadn't had a hit all season, his coach as well as his teammates thought there wasn't much point giving him more than one or two swings. He hoisted his Excelsior bat, and after he'd taken his stance at the plate, Rollie let loose with a pitch that raced toward his head. But the same as he'd handled Jack's chin-high throw, Ricky spun out of the way. "Just like old times, eh *Dickee*?" Rollie sneered.

"Hey, fatso," Ricky heckled back, "when's the last time you got one over?"

"Oh yeah, *Dickee*?!" Rollie retorted, flinging the ball before Ricky had dug in. But this time, the pitch came in waist-high, and Ricky slapped a stinging line drive that smacked Rollie in the belly. He fell to his knees while Mr. Chazen ran to the mound, barking at the boys who'd already surrounded it, "Give Rollie air!" Eventually, Rollie got to his feet and hobbled off the field toward the drinking fountain behind the backstop. As he passed by home plate, Ricky took hold of his sleeve and whispered, "Hope you feel better, *Roly Poly*."

Once the game started, Rollie was so erratic that practically everybody in the other team's lineup bailed out the instant the ball left his hand. Occasionally, a batter would hang in long enough to flail at a pitch and poke it feebly to one of the infielders. Meanwhile, Ricky, who'd lost interest midway through the second inning, idly scuffed the right-field grass with his Keds.

"Coming your way, Ricky!" Mr. Chazen suddenly called to him as the ball veered toward the foul line. A week before, he would have run in the opposite direction, but now he sprinted toward it and, diving, made a circus catch. As he stood up holding the ball triumphantly over his head, Mr. Chazen and all his teammates (except Rollie) began cheering.

"Okay, Ricky, it's your turn to bat," Mr. Chazen said, still clapping, as he jogged in once the inning ended. Despite how he'd hit in batting practice, he knew Mr. Chazen still wasn't expecting much—as always, he was last in the order. At this stage of the game, though, Mr. Chazen wasn't optimistic about any of his other players getting on base, either: the opposing pitcher had retired eight of them in a row on strikes.

As Ricky got set, his teammates picked up their gloves, ready to take the field again, especially after Ricky watched the first two pitches nick the corners of the strike zone with the bat still perched on his shoulder. Up two strikes and no balls, the pitcher likewise assumed Ricky would be an easy out and threw the next one straight down the pipe. It was the pitch Ricky had been waiting for: he blasted it to deep right-center and loped into second, standing up. The team was still whooping it up for him even after the side was retired when the following batter struck out.

As he trotted in to get his mitt before he went back to right field, Mr. Chazen grabbed his jersey and said, "Hold up, Ricky. After that catch you made, I'm moving you to shortstop."

Ricky snatched his glove and strolled out between second base and third. With Jack's coaching and note backing him up, he was confident no ball would get by him.

Rollie's control hadn't gotten any better, but since Jeffey Blumberg (who was almost as tubby) was home with a bug, Mr. Chazen couldn't bring him in from the bullpen. "Just get it over the plate!" Mr. Chazen hollered after Rollie walked the first two batters and fell behind on the next one. Rollie took a deep breath and, without any windup, virtually lobbed the ball to the hitter, who promptly rapped it back at the mound. Still smarting from batting practice, Rollie instinctively covered his gut with his glove while the sizzler ricocheted to the left side of the infield. Springing to his right, Ricky snared it backhanded, and flipped it to the second baseman, who turned the double play. "Way to go, boys, two down!" cried Mr. Chazen. "Ignore the runner on third, and get the out at first." But a play at first seemed unlikely when Rollie quickly ran the count to 3–0. Even so, the other side's coach gave the "hit away" sign to try and bring his runner home. The batter nodded and though Rollie's pitch was low and outside, he lunged at it anyhow, getting just enough wood on the ball to tap a dribbler to Ricky, who scooped it up one-handed, and having no play at first, sidearmed it to the catcher. "*Out!*" roared the umpire the way Jack had in the meadow. But there, on the diamond, others screamed, too, as Ricky's teammates wildly shouted his name.

The game remained scoreless going into the bottom of the ninth when Ricky's team came up to bat. After the first two hitters struck out on six straight fastballs, the pitcher bore down even harder on Ricky, the only one who'd tagged him. He fired a bullet: Ricky swung and whiffed. He followed with a changeup: Ricky swung too soon. He went with another hummer: Ricky belted it over the fence.

As Ricky touched home plate, his team ran out and swarmed him. Even Rollie was pounding him on the back and jumping up and down. "Ricky, who got you playing like that?" Mr. Chazen burst out, straining to be heard. "My Grandpa Jack!" Ricky yipped over the din. He immediately regretted saying it so loud when he glimpsed Daddy rushing toward him, waving his hands like mad.

But Daddy wasn't worked up about Jack. Squeezing through the crowd, he slung his arm around Ricky and exclaimed, "I couldn't be prouder of you, son!"

Chills ran up Ricky's spine. He couldn't recall Daddy's taking pride in anything he'd done—or claiming him as *his*.

While Daddy and Mr. Chazen made up ("Norm, I was a jerk with what I said about your coaching"; "Same here, Bernie, for what I said about yours"), Ricky dusted himself off and felt his pocket crinkle. Jack had told him to hang on to the paper like it was something holy; now, there was nothing he held more sacred. He'd give up a prayer book, a Bible—even a Torah!—before he'd let go of the note.

When they got home, Mommy had supper on the table. She'd made fried chicken and mashed potatoes, which, though they were Daddy's favorite, she seldom cooked, still worried that despite being a size six, she'd backslide into the overweight teenage girl she'd once been. Over dinner, she called Daddy "Sweetheart" and he called her "Baby," and Ricky, for the first time he could remember, was glad to be part of the family.

On Saturday morning, Ricky took his time getting out of bed; blessed with the paper, he thought about staying home from *shul.* In the end, he decided against it—he knew from Hebrew school that Jews weren't supposed to put their trust in anything but God. Just in case, though, he folded the note in his blazer.

"Doesn't Ricky look handsome, Bernie?" Mommy said when he came into the kitchen. "He'll sweep those little girls at *shul* off their feet!"

"Madge, let the boy enjoy his breakfast," Bernie replied, seeing Ricky blush. "When he's finished eating, I'll take him to the Chazens. On second thought, I'll drive him to *shul* myself."

"You don't have to, Daddy—see you later!" Ricky said as pushed open the back door and set off for Louis's. He had the paper, and besides, he wanted to speak to Mr. Chazen about taking over for Rollie at starter.

Outside, Medina's skies for once were blue, and soon, he was whistling a melody from services. All of a sudden, his collarbone throbbed with pain. Turning around, he saw a rock lying on the sidewalk and the two younger Kyrchyks charging toward him.

"Hey, kid, where you going all dolled up like that?" Nick smirked, running up.

"To *shul*," Ricky answered, feeling invincible in his armored blazer.

"You dummy—there's no school on Saturday," Dirk scoffed.

"You stupid *goyim*! —*You're* the dummies!" Ricky fired back.

"What did you call us?!" Dirk screeched putting Ricky in a bear hug.

"I'll bet he's got some cash on him," Nick said as he reached in Ricky's jacket. "What's this?" he taunted Ricky, waggling the note in his face. "Phone numbers to call in case of an emergency—like bumping into me and my brother?" Nick ripped the paper into shreds, and, as they fluttered to the ground, he snorted, "Lotta good they'll do you now!"

Thinking the fun was over, Dirk let Ricky go. But *this* Ricky, rather than cower or slink away, made a fist the way Jack had shown him and launched it full force at the bigger bully's stomach. As Nick lurched backward to dodge it, his pelvis arced forward. "My nuts! My nuts!" he howled as Ricky's punch crumpled him to the street among the note's remnants.

Ricky turned to take on Dirk, but as Jack had predicted, Nick's sidekick was too scared to touch him. While Dirk scuttled over to his brother, Ricky ambled away, guessing that he'd seen the last of the Kyrchyks, Roman included. Even if he hadn't, what difference did it make? He realized he didn't need to rely on the power of some paper to protect him. Now he knew he carried that power inside him. Whether it came from Jack, who'd taught him how to fight, or from God, who'd sent Jack to teach him, didn't much matter. What counted was getting more.

VII

Ordinarily, Ricky would have counted *two* good things having happened that morning: whipping the Kyrchyks, and, because of it, delaying the Chazens enough to miss the first part of the service.

Yet surprisingly, as the service dragged on, instead of being tempted to talk with Y. H. and Louis, he ached to speak to God. "I want You to know I'm really grateful," he whispered during the *Amidah*, the congregation's hushed, standing prayer, "for how You helped me lick the Kyrchyks today. I aimed at Nick's belly, but You made my punch land someplace better, and probably, because of You, my whole week went better with baseball and Daddy. I can't thank You enough!" As he looked back at his *siddur*, for once its unceasing praises made sense.

"Hey! What was going on with you?" Y. H. said, grabbing Ricky's elbow at the *kiddush*. "You actually seemed to be enjoying yourself!"

Ricky wasn't about to give Y. H. a chance to make fun of him and ruin his day. "*Nothing's* going on with me!" he responded, yanking his arm away while accidentally planting it in the chest of a lady who'd walked up behind him. ". . . I . . . I'm sorry," he stammered.

Regaining her composure, the lady replied, "No damage done, and it's always a pleasure to meet a courteous young man." She turned to Y. H. and said, "Won't you introduce us, Yoey?"

Y. H.'s face became as crimson as the sanctuary's carpet. ". . . This is Ricky, Imma."

"'Yoey'? 'Imma'?" Ricky wondered.

"Shabbat Shalom, Ricky—I'm Yoey's mother," said the woman. "I'm always so pleased when he has new friends at *shul*. Are your parents here? Maybe I know them!"

"I don't think so—their names are Madge and Bernie, and our last name's Zieglitz."

". . . It sounds familiar, but I'm not sure from where. I may have heard my abba—Yoey's grandfather—say it once or twice. At any rate, it's very nice to meet you, and I hope you'll keep coming to services."

Y. H. rolled his eyes and walked away.

When Ricky got home, he didn't mention Y. H.'s mother; he didn't know her English name, and he couldn't remember ever hearing Y. H.'s last. As dinner ended that night, he learned them both.

During dessert, the telephone rang in the kitchen. "It's all right, Madge, I'll get it," said Daddy.

"I'll answer it, Bernie—you just enjoy your ice cream before it all melts."

Ricky thought of a third thing to be grateful for, something which he shared with his parents: Daddy and Mommy weren't quarreling anymore, especially about money. Ricky had overheard them say that while Daddy was hospitalized, Jack had paid his construction crews to finish his houses, which, for once, were selling.

Mommy returned to the table with a broad grin on her face. "Bernie, we've got another 'Mr. Popularity' in the family! That was the mother of one of Ricky's friends from synagogue—I think she said her name was Malka Blustein—and she called to see if Ricky could come home with them after services next Saturday to spend the afternoon."

Wide-eyed, Daddy exclaimed, "Malka! Ricky, do you have any idea who that is?"

". . . I think she's the mom of a kid Louis and I sit with at *shul*."

"What's she look like?"

"She's got dark brown hair and brown eyes."

"Anything else you can tell me about her?"

"She's around the same age as Mommy, I think."

Daddy had forgotten all about his ice cream. "Do you know who I bet she is? Rabbi Kimmelman's daughter! Her father *bar mitzvah*ed me at the *shul* thirty years ago! I only met Malka a couple of times, but I met with Rabbi Kimmelman every week when Pop would *schlep* me from Huppertsville for my Hebrew lessons with the other *bar mitzvah* boys. Rabbi Kimmelman seemed larger than life to us, like he was Moses carrying the Ten Commandments. He was more religious than anybody we knew; not only did he keep strictly kosher, but he didn't write or spend money or ride anywhere on *Shabbos* and *yontif*. We were in awe of him—we couldn't have respected or admired him more!"

Ricky felt that way about Jack, but he couldn't imagine anyone having those feelings for the *shul*'s current rabbi. "What made *your* rabbi so special, Daddy?"

"Here's the best example I can give you. Medina used to have a major league team before it moved to a bigger, more prosperous city out west. In those days, the Riveters hadn't had a winning season for a while, but when I was studying for my *bar mitzvah*, they finally made it to the World Series. That year, though, the series coincided with the High Holy Days, and to make things worse, the seventh and deciding game fell on *Yom Kippur*. Even though I begged Pop to let me stay home and listen to it on our radio, he carted me off to *shul*.

"Well, there was no way my buddies and I were going to miss the biggest game of our lives. We knew from our *bar mitzvah* lessons that Rabbi Kimmelman had a radio in his office, which we also knew he never kept locked. So we hatched a plan that while Rabbi Kimmelman was busy with services downstairs in the sanctuary, we'd sneak upstairs to his office, and turn on the radio to listen to the game. It was risky enough leaving services, but because Jews aren't supposed to turn electricity on or off when it's a holy day, let alone the holiest day of the year, we knew we were playing with fire.

"Anyway, we crept upstairs, opened the door, closed it behind us, and put on the radio with the sound down low. We must have been listening to the game for four or five innings with the Riveters leading by a run. That's when, out of nowhere, the office door swung open, and there was Rabbi Kimmelman looming over us!"

"How bad did he yell at you?" Ricky asked, picturing himself getting caught in the rabbi's office red-handed.

Daddy shook his head. "Rabbi Kimmelman didn't raise his voice in the slightest. He just asked what the score was. Once we told him, he thanked us and then politely requested that we go back downstairs to services. As I got up, I reached over to switch off the radio. I'll never forget Rabbi Kimmelman laying his hand on my shoulder and quietly saying, 'Leave it on, Baruch. I don't want you to commit a sin on *Yom Kippur*, especially on my account.'"

"So, Ricky, tell me about this new friend of yours," said Mommy solicitously.

"He's not really my friend," Ricky said, trying to wriggle out of wasting his Saturday on somebody who generally made him feel like a jerk.

"But you still haven't even told us his name."

"It's Y. H."

Mommy replied, "What an odd name! What do those initials stand for?"

"I don't know, but I heard his mom call him 'Yoey.'"

Daddy couldn't contain his excitement. "Let's finish eating, and I'll call Malka to make the arrangements!"

As Ricky and Mommy cleared the table, Daddy hurried to the phone, and after he'd hung up, he all but ran back to tell them what he'd found out. "So Malka really is Rabbi Kimmelman's daughter! And you, Ricky, have become pals with his grandson! They'll take you home with them next *Shabbos* afternoon, and I'll pick you up there later. I can't wait to let Pop know. Maybe it'll get me back in his good graces!"

All the next week, Ricky dreaded going to Y. H.'s almost as much as he'd once fretted about being mauled by the Kyrchyks. But when he sat down at services, Y. H. couldn't have been nicer. "I've really been looking forward to your coming over today. How long do you think you'll be able to stay?"

"I don't know. . . . We'll just have to wait and see," Ricky said, giving his parents' standard answer when they didn't want to be pinned down.

Ricky could tell by the frown on Y. H.'s face that Y. H. didn't like getting that kind of answer any more than he did. Realizing that if he didn't act fast, Y. H. would make his afternoon miserable, he added, "Okay, okay—I can stay as long as you want! It won't be a problem, since my dad knows your mom from when they were kids."

"That's just peachy," Y. H. replied sarcastically, though Ricky couldn't understand why. He only knew that being around Y. H. never was easy.

Y. H. didn't speak again for the rest of the service or even at the *kiddush* until, after nearly everyone had left, he went over to his mother and impatiently asked her, "Can't we go now?" After she'd made sure to wish "Shabbat Shalom" to each of the few people still there, she waved to Ricky and Y. H., saying, "Come, boys, let's begin walking home."

A mile later, Ricky unfastened his dress shirt's starched collar and loosened his tie, but the sweat kept trickling down his neck. He felt like one of the prisoners Daddy had told him the Japanese had put on a death march during the war.

Eventually, after the trek had lumbered on another two miles, Mrs. Blustein announced, "Ricky, we're home!" Looking up, he saw a house under whose front porch awning, a dozen people had sought relief from the heat.

"Shabbat Shalom!" Mrs. Blustein greeted them.

"Shabbat . . . Shalom . . . ," they repeated anemically.

Ricky turned to Y. H. and asked, "Do they all belong to your family? Which one's your dad?"

"None of them—he's at his office! He doesn't believe in this Jewish crap, either, but since he's a doctor, he's always got an out. Meanwhile, I'm stuck here every week with Imma and some new batch of strangers from the *shul.* What does she think? The more of them she has over for *Shabbos,* the more *mitzvah* points she'll get!"

Ricky warily followed Y. H., his mother, and her other guests inside to the dining room where an eggplant-purple taffeta cloth covered the table. At its head was a large, wine-filled silver wine cup with smaller ones at each of its seats while a *challah* occupied its center. After inviting everyone to join in reciting the blessings, Mrs. Blustein served a variety of cold salads, leftover boiled chicken, and a lukewarm stew of potatoes and meat she told them was called *cholent.* Ricky took one taste and, looking around at everybody else, reckoned that, like him, they wouldn't be asking for seconds or sticking around any longer than they had to. As if she shared his assumption, Mrs. Blustein started posing one question after another about that week's *sedrah:* none of her guests dared move for fear they be called on. "How marvelous it's been," she proclaimed after two hours had elapsed, "to have fulfilled the *mitzvah* of studying Torah on Shabbat afternoon!" Ricky started to stand when Y. H. clasped his thigh. "Now, won't you all be so good as to participate with Yoey in the *bentsching?*" his mother respectfully, but emphatically, prodded her company.

Y. H. slunk down in his chair and began spewing out Hebrew faster than Grandpa Irv at Passover. Despite his mother's request, nobody joined him except her, either because, like Ricky, they didn't know the words, or because, even if they did, they couldn't follow Y. H.'s chant, which had little or no tune. At last, Y. H. stopped, and Mrs. Blustein intoned the final "Amen." Ricky let out a deep breath; he'd had enough praying for one day. When, as he folded his napkin and pushed back his chair, Y. H.'s mother said, "You boys are excused to go *daven mincha,*" he was ready to call Daddy to come get him.

After Y. H. led him to his bedroom and locked the door behind them, Ricky said, "Don't you do anything but pray?"

"There's that mouth on you again, kid—it's what I liked about you the first time I met you. Well, I *never* pray except when Imma's around! Why do you think I locked the door?" Y. H. crouched down next to his dresser and pulled out a deck of cards from underneath it. "So what about some poker?"

"I've played a little before with Louis and a few other guys he knows. But I don't have any money on me to bet with."

"I'll take it easy on you—we won't play for money. And besides," Y. H. said wryly, "we wouldn't want to violate *Shabbos,* would we?"

Y. H. dealt the cards, and the two boys played five-card draw followed by seven-card stud and Texas Hold'em as well as a little blackjack. Ricky won the first several games, largely because he could see some of the cards Y. H. was holding. But just because he could read Y. H.'s hand didn't mean he could read Y. H.'s mind to tell whether Y. H. had revealed his cards accidentally or on purpose. As they played on and Ricky kept losing, he got his answer. "I always win in the long run!" Y. H. crowed. Ricky was more suspicious of Y. H. than ever, knowing how fickle he could be and turn on him in an instant. Still, Y. H. seemed in such a good mood that Ricky thought he could risk asking him the question he'd wanted to ever since they met: "So what does 'Y. H.' stand for?"

"Yoav Hirsch—what's it to you?" Y. H. said with an unexpected edge to his voice.

". . . Nothing . . . it's just that I've never known anybody with a name like that," Ricky spluttered.

"Ever hear of King David? Yoav was his hatchet man who rubbed out anyone who got in his way. And don't bother asking why my parents named me after the second-in-command instead of the top banana. Easy! I *was* number two behind my precious older brother, David, their good son, who's off at *yeshiva* studying to be a rabbi."

"Well, what about your middle name, Hirsch?" Ricky pressed.

"He was my mother's little brother, okay? He died before I was born. I don't know how he died, and I don't much care just so long as nobody calls me that name or some other dumb Jewish one like 'Yoav' or 'Yoey.' It's why I began calling myself 'Y. H.' the first week of school. *I am the only one who says who I am!*"

At the sound of a sharp rap on the door, all his defiance vanished as he hastily scooped up the cards, shoved them back under the dresser, and called out, "Just a minute!"

"Yoey, is everything all right?" his mother called back, wiggling the handle.

". . . Yeah, Imma . . . we're fine."

"Please open the door, then. There's someone here to see you."

"Shit!" Y. H. uttered beneath his breath as he slowly unlocked the door. But once he saw the elderly man in the hall, he rushed to hug him, crying, "Zeyde!"

"Yoey, where are your manners?" his mother admonished him.

Beaming, Y. H. said, "Zeyde, this is Ricky, and Ricky, this is my grandfather, Rabbi Kimmelman."

Daddy's description, Ricky thought to himself, fit the old man to a T. Ramrod straight at well over six feet tall, with a long white beard and lively gray eyes, but for the two tablets, he could have been Moses in person.

Rabbi Kimmelman leaned down to pat Ricky's cheek. "Shabbat Shalom, Ricky. The moment Malka informed me of your family's last name, I saw your zeyde bringing your abba to me for his lessons. What a fine boy

Baruch was! So, *nu*, now that you're studying for your own *bar mitzvah*, by what Hebrew name will you be called to the Torah?"

"Yerachmiel," Ricky mumbled, lowering his eyes.

"Ah! Do you know what your name means?"

". . . May God have mercy," Ricky answered even more faintly.

"Who told you that?" Rabbi Kimmelman asked.

"My Hebrew school teacher," Ricky muttered, his gaze still fixed on the floor.

Rabbi Kimmelman gently lifted Ricky's chin till their eyes met and said, "Your *melamed* was wrong, child. Yerachmiel isn't some empty wish for God to show you His mercy. It's a solemn promise He will!"

VIII

———

"Zieglitz! Put your finger here!" said Cantor Pinsky, shoving his pupil's hand to the Hebrew word he wanted chanted in the red *bar mitzvah* primer.

The twelve-year-old grimaced and thought to himself, "Why can't he call me 'Rick' like most everybody else? What makes him so mean?"

Reading the expression on the boy's face, the cantor said, "I know you don't like this, Zieglitz, but this is how I myself was taught as a *bar mitzvoh bucher* in Hungary before the war. I don't want you should get lost doing your *haftorah* in front of the whole congregation. And with the *maftir*, you can lose even easier your place."

"Sure, cantor, anything you say," Rick acquiesced, knowing the next reprimand would be a kick in the shins. While he hadn't thought much of the old cantor, who'd left for better pay at another *shul*, he'd never heard of him laying a hand—or foot—on any of the students he'd had. This cantor had come cheap, or so Louis had said, who'd got it from his father, a synagogue *macher* now, thanks to his burgeoning practice. "The cantor's English isn't that good," Louis told Rick, "so he didn't have many choices. The Board was willing to cut him some slack because of what he'd gone through with the Nazis, but people have started complaining. They're griping that his old-fashioned *davening* makes the service too long, and they're *kvetching* about something else we both know: he's terrible with kids. Dad gives him another year or two at best."

Rick slid down in his chair. He'd seen in a *National Geographic* on Jack's nightstand that the Masai, besides having bare-breasted women, made killing a lion a test of manhood. Rick couldn't get over his tribe making it singing in public just as his voice was changing.

Rick's life was also changing. The junior high he attended was so large that he and Louis had been split into separate classrooms and assigned different lunch periods. They didn't play Little League together anymore, either; their team had been disbanded because Mr. Chazen had gotten too busy to coach it. Practically the only time Rick got to spend with Louis was in services, where the two now sat apart from Y. H., who, on account of Rabbi Kimmelman, had moved up front next to his mother. They were both saying *Kaddish* for his *zeyde*, who'd died the week of Y. H.'s *bar mitzvah* six months before.

As for Rick's own grandparents, Jack and Dee-Dee didn't come to see him nearly so much since they'd purchased a condo in Miami, spending half the year at its nightclubs, spas, and seaside restaurants on Biscayne Bay. Meanwhile, Grandpa Irv and Grandma Thelma were still in Medina, though not in their house in Greenlawn. They'd been moved to a nursing home, he with Parkinson's, she with dementia, their bank accounts emptied to pay for the bleak rooms in which they now lived apart and where their son occasionally visited them. If Bernie had had the heart, he would have gone more. These days, he definitely had the time.

His success as a builder had been short lived. Without Jack's continuing financial support, his cash flow problems returned, and within a year his business went bust. He'd been forced to take a part-time job at a chain store, Full Fashions, which catered to plus-size women. No other employer would hire him, noticing that even the pressure of an interview seemed to unnerve him. As his household's finances became strained, so, too, did his relationship with his wife.

"You mean to say, Bernie, there's nothing else out there that pays more?"

"Name one, Madge, and I'll take it!"

"I don't know—I'm not the one who went to college!"

"Back off, Madge! I'm doing the best I can."

"Can't you ask Aileen and Ernest for money?"

"They're already paying for Mom and Pop at the home. Can't you cut back on the expenses for the *bar mitzvah* reception and party?

"How would that look, Bernie? Like always, I guess I'll have to call *my* family to pitch in!"

"Dammit, Madge, how do you think that'd make me look?"

"*Nu*, Zieglitz? I'm waiting!" said Cantor Pinsky.

"I'm sorry, Cantor," Rick said, stalling. "It's just so hard for me. I don't have a voice like yours, and I sure don't know as much as you do."

"It wasn't that easy for me, either, Zieglitz. God gave me my voice, but even so, I still had to practice to get good."

"Speaking of God . . ." said Rick, still stalling with one eye on the wall clock to see how many minutes were left in that day's ordeal, "what do my *maftir* and *haftarah* have to say about Him?"

"Not my department. When you meet with the rabbi the week before your *bar mitzvoh*, ask him your question. Now back to the *maftir*!"

When the session concluded, Rick went out to the parking lot expecting to see Dad, whose evenings were free since he only worked mornings when the store had less traffic. Instead, Mom was there with the Ford's passenger door open for him. "Hop in! I've got great news—your father's been promoted to full time!"

"That's terrific, Mom—you and Dad won't have to fight about money anymore!" He wasn't sure he should have said what he did, especially when she was so happy. He knew what a sore point money had been for his parents.

"Let's hope those days are over, honey," she said, affectionately cupping his chin in her hand.

Back home, when they walked in the kitchen, Dad was standing over a cutting board, hacking a rack of lamb with a cleaver.

"Tonight's going to be special!" he declared. "In honor of that *shmuck* of a manager Leavitt finally realizing my potential, I'm making us lamb chops for dinner. Bet you didn't know your old man could cook, Rick. Why would you? Haven't done it since your mother and I first got married when I couldn't stand the thought of eating another of her tuna casseroles. I'd cooked all the time for my frat house. God, how the guys loved my lamb chops!"

"That's how we got the cleaver," Mom added. "One of the brothers, Ruby Urblatt, gave it to us as a wedding present. If you look close, you can see where he had our names and the date etched on the blade. Truth to tell, I was ticked off at the time, because I'd always heard that knives given as gifts brought bad luck. But after today, Bernie, we should think of it as a good luck token!"

Up in his room after supper, though, Rick had no luck at all with the cantor's recording; try as he might, he couldn't get the tune. He heard a knock on his door, turned around, and saw Dad poking his head in the room. "Mind if I join you?"

"If you want," Rick said. He chanted the first line, but not one note was right.

"Let me have a crack at it," Dad said as he reset the recording. He played it through once and sang it back note for note. The flawless chanting made Rick suspicious. "Did you have the same *bar mitzvah* portion as me, Dad?"

Dad chuckled. "No, Rick, what I've got is perfect pitch. It makes me a kind of human tape recorder, and it's why they let me join the choir of the First Methodist Church of Huppertsville when I was a teenager, even though I was Jewish."

Rick thought about asking what Grandpa Irv and Grandma Thelma said when they found out, but with his *bar mitzvah* looming as well as his next appointment with the cantor, he had a more immediate question: "Dad, will you help me practice?"

"Glad to!" he responded. Over the next two months, *bar mitzvah* practice went much better than baseball practice ever had. Regardless of how many flubs Rick made, Dad never lost his temper.

Cantor Pinsky kept losing his, though. Seeing Rick's improvement with the *haftarah* (something he never acknowledged), he began devoting more time to the *maftir*, which still gave Rick fits. At his *bar mitzvah*, he'd sing the *haftarah* from the red booklet, where all the Hebrew punctuation, musical notes, and vowels were included, but he'd have to chant the *maftir* from a Torah scroll, where even the letters would look different—some elongated, some squished together, some tipped with tiny coronets. "No more *potchky-ing*, Zieglitz—start singing!" the cantor told him. Rick placed his finger on the mimeographed practice sheet Cantor Pinsky had given him, took a deep breath, and began:

> Ve/av/ro/ham/ben/tish/im/va/say/sha/sha/nah/be/
> hi/mo/lo/be/sar/ar/la/so . . .

"Or-*la-so*!" Cantor Pinsky roared. "How many times I have to tell you, Zieglitz? 'Or-*la-so*'—not 'Ar-*la-so*'!" Furious, he kicked Rick's shin. Rick's hand instinctively balled up in a fist, ready to strike back like the last time he'd been bullied. He remembered, though, what had happened when Jack hit a teacher, so he let his mouth take a swipe at the cantor instead: "Why the hell are you so angry all the time?"

Stunned, Cantor Pinsky spluttered, ". . . I just want your *bar mitzvoh* should have no mistakes."

"Do you really think God cares about that?"

"That's what my teachers told me when I was studying for my *bar mitz-voh*. They said if I chanted everything perfect, God would hear the *shul*'s voice when I led the *davening*, and then we'd hear His voice back when I *leyned* from the Torah."

"But Cantor Pinsky, don't you think that for me to be God's voice, I have to understand what I'm chanting? There's no English translation of my *maftir* on the sheet that you gave me."

The cantor pulled down a copy of the blue *chumash* used at services, opened it, and showed Rick the spot.

Rick clapped his hand to his forehead. It was the same passage that had made him shudder when he'd first come to *shul*—crazy Abraham *brissing* himself, his kid, and all the guys he knew! "Cantor, how could Abraham do something like that?" Rick said.

"Abraham had faith."

"What about you, Cantor? Do you have faith in God no matter what?"

The cantor took a few moments to answer before he said softly, "At your age . . . before the Germans. . . . Would you please try your *maftir* again?" For the rest of the session, he was more patient, and Rick was more relaxed.

That night when Rick stepped in the kitchen, though, his stomach knotted up again. The cleaver was back in Dad's hand, only this time raining down blow after blow on a bare chopping block.

"Bernie, what's wrong?" Mom cried out.

"That SOB Leavitt fired me—said I was too particular with how I did things."

"Bernie, why couldn't you have just done it his way?"

"I might not have known much about building houses, Madge, but I know selling *shmatas* inside out!"

"But Bernie, how are we going to pay for the *bar mitzvah*?"

"I don't want to hear another word about your damn gala!"

"Fine, Bernie—I'll ask my parents for help!"

"Just what I want—their fuckup of a son-in-law on display for all the world to see!"

The next day, like some volcano that had erupted, Bernie cratered. He sank into a depression over the subsequent three weeks, spending all day in bed while at night, his wife slept on the bottom bunk in their son's room. Periodically, Rick would poke his head in and try to get him to come out. "Dad, I could use some help with my *maftir*," he'd say, but Bernie, as if he were back in the psychiatric ward, just looked away.

Meantime, the *bar mitzvah* drew nearer. Rick had made significant progress on his *maftir*, in no small part because Cantor Pinsky had stopped blowing up at him during their lessons. One day as he walked in and started to take out his *haftarah* booklet and *maftir* sheet, the cantor laid some other pages on the desk, saying, "Today, we'll begin with working on your speech."

"But, Cantor Pinsky, I thought the rabbi would be helping me with it. Didn't you tell me I should save my questions about God for him?"

"The rabbi told me when I came here that he's too busy for *bar mitzvoh* speeches. But not to worry—that's another specialty with me. The pages I'm giving you now are the speech I give to all the *bar mitzvoh boychiks* and *bas mitzvoh maideles* who have the same *sedrah* you do. Go home and start memorizing it—at your *bar mitzvoh*, you'll have to say it by heart."

"What's it about?" Rick asked.

"Simple—free will!"

That night, Rick began to read what the cantor had given him. Along with "free will," the speech spoke of "Abraham's obedience," and, of course, his "faith." What it didn't mention, let alone answer, were any of Rick's questions about God. "I need to write my own speech," he groused to himself. All of a sudden, he got a brilliant idea: he'd have Dad help him with it! Hadn't Mom said that he'd won speech contests in high school? When he got to Dad's room, though, he found Mom there on a mission of her own.

"Bernie, you've always been so snazzy. How would you feel about taking Ricky to pick out his *bar mitzvah* suit?"

For the first time in weeks, Dad perked up. "What about Sunday, son? You won't have any school or *bar mitzvah* lessons or services to go to. We'll go to Barnett's, the best men's shop in town!"

When Barnett's opened Sunday at noon, Bernie and Rick were its first customers. Bernie guided Rick to the suits in his size, and Rick quickly pointed to a black one among the pin stripes, windowpanes, and glen plaids hanging on the rack.

"—No," Dad said abruptly.

Rick flushed. ". . . Sorry . . . I'll pick one that's cheaper."

Dad shook his head. "It's not about the money—it's about the color. Black suits are for funerals, not *simchas* like your *bar mitzvah* when we're celebrating your becoming a man."

Rick scanned the rack again and chose a shiny, brown mohair double-breasted. "What about this one? It's the kind rock 'n' rollers wear."

"It's smart!" Dad replied. He waved over a salesman, who snapped his fingers at a tailor, who took Rick's measurements for the alterations to the suit's jacket and pants. After the fitting, Dad steered Rick to other areas of the store, and together, they completed his *bar mitzvah* wardrobe with a new dress shirt, a pair of lustrous brown wing tips and a matching belt, topping the outfit off with a silky yellow tie. "With your good taste, nobody will be sharper than you, son!" Dad told him at the register.

As they drove away with the day's purchases together with the ticket for his suit, Rick said, "I can't wait to show Mom what we got!"

"We're not going straight home, son. I've been feeling so lousy, I haven't been by to see Mom and Pop lately. I think it'd be good for them if you dropped in, too."

"Okay with me," Rick lied. After Barnett's, he couldn't refuse.

Inside the nursing home, he wished that he had. It reeked of ammonia, and as he followed Dad down the hallway to Grandma Thelma's, he had to go through a gauntlet of wheelchair-bound residents, who flailed and squawked at him as he passed by. At the very end of the corridor, Dad entered a room where his mother lay confined to her bed, gazing at a blank TV screen.

He bent down and whispered, "Mom, it's Bernie, and I've brought someone to visit you."

He might as well not have spoken: she kept staring at the television without uttering a word.

Dad gestured Rick toward the bed. "Look, Mom, it's Ricky."

Again, she made no response.

"I guess you're tired, Mom . . . I love you . . ." Bernie said as his voice trailed off. Before leaving, he leaned over to kiss her cheek.

She pushed him away and spoke for the first time. "Don't touch me!—Somebody help!"

Dad whisked Rick out of the room and led him to another wing of the facility before he stopped at a doorway with a nameplate that read "Irving Zieglitz." Keeping his voice down, he told Rick, "Some days, Pop's medicine seems to be working—his tremors aren't nearly so bad. On other days . . . well, let's hope it's a good day."

As Dad took him inside, Rick wasn't prepared for the Grandpa Irv he saw. Although unlike Grandma Thelma, he was alert and sitting in a chair, his head and arms quivered violently while the rest of him looked like it had shrunk. "Hey, Pop, look who's here to see you!" Dad said far too cheerfully. Motioning to Rick, he added, "Come on over, son, and tell your grandpa hello."

With fresh memories of how Grandma Thelma had reacted when Dad got too close, Rick cautiously stepped nearer. ". . . Hi, Grandpa Irv," he stammered.

". . . Hi," a reedy voice answered almost inaudibly.

Dad was desperate, Ricky could see, for the visit with Pop to go better than the one had with Mom. "Say, son, why don't you chant your Torah blessings for Grandpa Irv?"

"Sure!" Rick responded, thankful Dad had given him something to say. While he didn't have his booklet, by now he knew the blessings by heart. As he sang them, he thought he saw a smile flit across his grandfather's face. Dad apparently noticed it, too. Snatching at anything that might keep Pop engaged, he said, "How about telling your grandpa about your *maftir*?"

Once more, Rick gladly complied, recounting how Abraham had performed the first circumcision on himself, the next on Ishmael, and then a string of them on all the other males in his household. This time, though, Grandpa Irv remained expressionless. Rick looked over at Dad, but he was met with a stare as vacant as Grandma Thelma's. Frantic to break the silence, he said, "Grandpa Irv, why would God have Abraham do something so awful?"

Before, when Rick had questioned Grandpa Irv about God's ways, he'd gotten a swift response: "God, shmod—*daven!*" Now, the old man labored to open his mouth and speak, but the Parkinson's, omnipotent and omnipresent, stifled his answer, making it too faint to hear.

The last of Dad's lightheartedness left him. He shuffled over to Pop and listlessly put his arms around him before plodding back to the car with his son. Neither of them spoke on the long ride home.

When they arrived at the house with the packages, Mom said, "That must have been quite a shopping trip! By the way, Bernie, Aileen called right after you left, and I asked her to call back later, but she told me she'd rather leave a message. After making her usual excuses for not visiting your parents, she said she thought it'd be nice if the rabbi would look in on them, especially Pop seeing as how he was so active in the *shul* all those years. Long story short, she wanted you to call the rabbi and ask him, because as she put it, 'You know what a cold fish he is.'"

"For Chrissakes!—Why me?" Bernie howled, storming from the kitchen to the bedroom and slamming the door behind him.

After Mom fed Rick dinner, during which they spoke almost as little as his grandparents had at the home, he went up to bed. Half an hour later, he awoke to his mother's screams down the hall. He sprinted to his parents' room, and when he opened the door, he froze at the sight before him: Dad with a coat hanger twisted around his throat.

"Bernie, *please!*" Madge implored him. "We'll get through this. We'll scale back on the *bar mitzvah*, and I'll call the rabbi myself to have him visit Irv and Thelma. Ricky and I love you. Please, don't do this, please . . ." Bernie collapsed on the bed, sobbing. Mom got some tissues and, after she'd untwisted the wire noose from his neck, blotted up the blood from its gouges.

The next morning, Mom and Dad acted as though the previous night were nothing but a bad dream, calling out to Rick "Have a good day!" as he got on the school bus. That afternoon when it dropped him off at home, he saw a police cruiser parked in front of the house and Mom sitting outside on the steps, bawling.

"Mom, what is it?" he said, running up.

"Ricky . . . it's your father. . . . He's dead."

"*No! What happened?*" Rick cried.

Mom was weeping so hard she could barely speak. "I went to the grocery around two hours ago . . . When I came home a little bit later, he was lying on the kitchen floor, face down. . . . He slashed his throat with the cleaver!"

Rick went numb, lost in a trance for the next three days, through Jack and Dee-Dee's flying up from Florida, Mom's making arrangements for the funeral, and the rabbi's officiating at the burial while perfunctorily reciting the obligatory prayers as Madge stood on one side of the grave with her family while Aileen stood on the opposite side with hers except for Irv and Thelma, whom she hadn't told because "it would have been too hard on them." Every now and then during the steady drizzle, the rabbi mumbled "*Baruch*," sometimes to begin a blessing, at others to insert Dad's Hebrew name in the passage following the place in the service where a eulogy normally would have been given. ("In keeping with Jewish law, the eulogy is omitted for a suicide," the rabbi explained in passing as he skipped it.) Meanwhile, Cantor Pinsky chanted the traditional dirges, his hand never leaving Rick's shoulder. At the service's conclusion, the rabbi pointed to the wet mound of earth beside the open pit and said as he fished in his coat for his car keys, "Yerachmiel, as the son of the deceased, it is your duty according to *halacha* to be the first to assist with his interment by casting a shovelful of dirt on his coffin."

Rick dug some muck from the pile and flung it on the pine box. The sound of it smacking the casket lid snapped him out of his stupor. He looked down and noticed that a few lumps of mud had spattered his new brown *bar mitzvah* suit.

Today, he was a man.

IX

———

"Can she feel the bulge in my pants as much as I do?" Rick asked himself at Louis's *bar mitzvah* party as Andrea Lipsky granted him his one slow dance with her for the evening. Although Andrea didn't have beauty or brains—her face was mostly nose and, despite years of religious school, she still couldn't say whether Abraham was Ishmael's father or the other way around—she possessed two other assets: a pair of blimps for bosoms that made her the object of every boy's desire and the envy of every girl. Besides, the word was she was "fast." Rubbing against her while they swayed back and forth held an additional attraction for Rick. It diverted him from thinking about Dad.

Nowadays, Rick missed him more and more, and although the conversation might have been awkward, he had questions he would have liked to ask him man-to-man: "When you had a wet dream, what did you do with your sheets and pajama bottoms to hide them from Grandma Thelma?"; "Where did you stash your girlie magazines so she wouldn't find them?"; and "What did you tell her after you'd walked in hunched over on account of blue balls from a hot date?" Even so, in the months following Dad's death, other men answered much more important questions for him, the kind which led him to ones he'd have to answer for himself.

"All right, folks, let's take a look at what the Torah says about the tenth plague in Egypt," his Hebrew school teacher, Mr. Weinstock, told the class. "Any volunteers to read Exodus, chapter 12, verse 29 in English? Rick, what about you?" Mr. Weinstock never used his students' Hebrew names, because, as he explained the first time he called the roll, "I don't know any kid who's gone home from Hebrew school and said, 'From now on, just call me Shlomo!'"

The rustle of pages filled the room as Rick and the others leafed through the Hebrew-English Bibles that Mr. Weinstock had persuaded the school to buy them. "The Lord struck down all the firstborn in the land of Egypt," Rick read aloud, "from the firstborn of Pharaoh, who sat on the throne, to the firstborn of the captive, who sat in the dungeon—"

"Thank you, Rick," Mr. Weinstock interrupted. "That's fine."

"But Mr. Weinstock, there's more," Rick objected.

"You're right," Mr. Weinstock said patiently, "but this is the part of the verse I want to focus on now because of an issue it raises. Anyone can see why God would punish Pharaoh. As the king of Egypt, he used all his power to keep the Israelites enslaved! But why punish the prisoner in the dungeon? What power did *he* have to free the Hebrews? —No one? Okay, since it's a toughie, I'll tell you. Even the prisoner in the dungeon wasn't altogether powerless: he still had the power to speak out against what Pharaoh was doing. Staying silent while others were being oppressed made him—like it can make us—as bad as Pharaoh."

"It's what my dad calls being a 'good German'!" Louis yelled out. "That's somebody in Germany who didn't make a peep while Hitler and the other Nazis were killing all the Jews they could get hold of."

"Excellent, Louis!" exclaimed Mr. Weinstock. "But can anybody think of another, more current example?"

"I can!" piped up Emily Funkelbusch, the newly elected president of the Junior Congregation. "A white southerner who doesn't believe in segregation, but who won't speak up against the laws oppressing Negroes, is just like the prisoner in the dungeon." Pausing, she thought for a second and then, pleased with herself, tagged on, "Instead of calling somebody like that a 'good German,' I'd call them a 'good Egyptian'!"

"That works, too," Mr. Weinstock commented, failing to notice how let down Emily looked because he hadn't praised her as much as he had Louis. "So now, gang," he said, glancing at the clock on the wall, "I've got one last question for you—keep your answers to yourselves, though. I don't want anybody to be embarrassed." He turned to the blackboard and wrote: "Are there any good Egyptians in my family?"

Rick thought back to an evening he'd spent at Aunt Aileen's while Dad had been hospitalized and Mom had gone to see him. Cousin Jimmy had lost another round of Scrabble when Uncle Ernest came home griping, "Some *schwartzes* want to buy one of my houses, and I'd like to sell them—a buyer's a buyer!—but I've got to go along with the bankers. If I don't, they won't lend to me, either. Maybe one day things will change for blacks, but until they do, I'm not going to risk my business."

Maybe the good Egyptians were like Uncle Ernest, Rick told himself as Mr. Weinstock dismissed the class. They might have wanted to help the Jews but were afraid to risk crossing Pharaoh. After all, even the prisoner in the dungeon had something to lose: if he spoke out, he might end up not just jailed but dead. There was another question, though, that stumped Rick. Suppose some Egyptian *had* spoken out. What made him do it? His fear of God, his own fearlessness, or something else altogether? Mr. Weinstock hadn't said.

"Did you even study, Mr. Zieglitz?" Mr. Cochran, Rick's junior-high ancient history teacher had jotted across his midterm. "Not much," Rick admitted beneath his breath. He'd figured the course would be a snap given all the ancient history he'd had in Hebrew school, not only about the Egyptians, but also about the others—Philistines, Assyrians, Babylonians, Greeks, and Romans—who'd pummeled the Jews back then. "Listen up, people!" Mr. Cochran said after he'd finished handing back the exams at the end of Friday's class. "You'll have another chance to impress me Monday. There'll be a quiz covering your assignment this weekend on Ramses the Great."

Determined to get an A (or at least a B), Rick opened his textbook the moment he sat down in study hall. He got sidetracked, though, when he got to Ramses's grand building projects and didn't see Israelite slaves mentioned anywhere. Flipping to the index, he looked up "Egyptians," but couldn't find a subheading for either "Israelites" or "Hebrews." He skipped forward to "J," thinking that the book's authors had reckoned Jews deserved their own separate listing. Again, nothing. When he realized there wasn't even an entry for "Judaism," which he'd always heard in Hebrew school was "a major world religion," he made up his mind to let Mr. Cochran know the book's writers were anti-Semites.

But Monday, he wavered. He'd never spoken to a non-Jew about anything Jewish, and after his midterm grade, what was he doing defending his Hebrew school education?

"Mr. Cochran . . ." he faltered when he went up to his desk after class.

"Yes, Mr. Zieglitz?" Mr. Cochran answered, eyes fixed on the quizzes he'd begun marking.

"I just want you to know . . ." Rick stammered, "that I think your class is really . . . interesting."

"I'm glad it meets with your approval," Mr. Cochran said dryly. "No need to brownnose me, though. It won't have any effect on your test score. Anything else?"

"Well . . . ," Rick sputtered, his heart pounding, "when I looked in our book's index . . . there wasn't a single section about the Jews. Doesn't their history count, too?"

Mr. Cochran looked up from the pile of exams. "No, Rick, not like other ancient peoples," he responded, unexpectedly soft-spoken. "That's because most of what he have about the Jews from that time isn't history at all, but a collection of religious fairy tales from the Bible. Same goes for most of early Christianity, too. That's why when we get to the Romans, you won't catch me or your textbook saying a word about Jesus's purported miracles or resurrection. It's like this, Rick—history's about what *actually* happened while religion's about what people *wished* had happened."

Rick knew lots of grown-up Jews who'd agree that Christians' belief in Jesus was just wishful thinking. But what about the *siddur*'s talk of "the Holy One, Israel's Redeemer"? Was Jews' faith in God baloney, too? Rick recalled how Mr. Weinstock had stopped him from reading the last half of the Exodus verse, where it said that in addition to God's striking down the firstborn of Pharaoh and the prisoner, "He smote all the firstborn of the cattle." What just God, Rick wondered, would do that to a bunch of feebleminded animals? And what God of justice—or mercy—would let an out-of-his-mind Dad take his life? Rick's *bar mitzvah* meeting couldn't come soon enough for him: explaining Abraham's antics would be the least of the rabbi's problems.

Mom was all jitters when the day finally arrived. On the way to the *shul*, she chattered nonstop, and when they got to the anteroom of the rabbi's office upstairs, she fidgeted incessantly until the secretary announced them. Walking in, Rick noticed that the door, the same as in Dad's time, didn't have a lock. Long ago, he supposed, it was a sign of Rabbi Kimmelman's trust in his congregation. Now, though, it signified just the opposite, Rick suspected, as he glimpsed the office's bare shelves: for *this* rabbi, no one was above suspicion. The sole costly item in the office was a Danish modern desk that occupied most of its floor space. Like the temple's sacrificial altar, which stood as a sacrosanct boundary between priest and layman, the desktop's massive, glass slab made sure congregants kept their distance from the rabbi.

"Let's start, shall we?" the rabbi said, opening a manila folder, the lone article on the glasstop. "I see, Mrs. Zieglitz, that your son—Roderick, is it?—has been enrolled in our Hebrew school for quite some time now. You can rest assured, therefore, that his ceremony will run smoothly." He plucked another page from the folder and slid it to her across the desk. "You're to fill out this form with the English and Hebrew names—in transliteration if you must—of the men you wish to honor at the service with an *aliyah*. Any questions?"

Madge smiled and shook her head no, relieved that the rabbi hadn't brought up Bernie's suicide.

"I have some questions!" Rick broke in. "Cantor Pinsky said I should ask you about them. To begin with, there's Abraham—"

"Unfortunately," the rabbi cut him off, "I don't have time for that at present. You'll have to arrange another appointment with my secretary, although by now, she's gone for the day. In any event, given how busy I am, she likely won't be able to schedule you until well after your *bar mitzvah*. Before you leave, however, there's one more matter to address." He took the folder's last page and shoved it toward Rick, together with a pen. "By signing this document," he told him, "you commit yourself to our post-*bar* and *bat mitzvah* program, which entails your attending Hebrew school for two more years. I am aware, of course, that in light of your family's recent—how shall I put it?—'mishap,' your continued enrollment might pose something of an economic hardship. That said, as I'm sure we all agree, Judaism often requires us to forgo our own mundane needs in pursuit of its higher ideals." Rick looked to Mom for help; she looked away; he grudgingly picked up the pen and signed. "In Hebrew as well," the rabbi directed him. Seething, he bit his lip and scrawled, "Yerachmiel ben Baruch."

The rabbi retrieved the document and slipped it back in the folder. "And that," he declared, "concludes our business for today."

"Not exactly!" Rick erupted. What got an Egyptian to speak out wasn't a mystery anymore: Pharaoh had pissed him off. Rick decided that if the rabbi was going to hijack his time, he was going to return the favor. "My Grandpa Irv," he told the rabbi, "used to be a member here before he got Parkinson's disease and had to go into a nursing home. My family thinks that if you visited him, it'd cheer him up."

"That's what the Medina Synagogue Council pays a chaplain for," the rabbi answered, peering down at his watch. "Be sure to shut the door on your way out."

"I think that meeting went well," Mom bubbled as they drove home.

"I didn't!" Rick snapped. "Besides being roped into two more years of Hebrew school, I got zero help on my *bar mitzvah* speech."

"Why don't you ask Mr. Weinstock?" Mom suggested, trying to get him to calm down. "You're always raving about what a wonderful teacher he is!"

"I'll think about it," Rick muttered, too sore to admit what a good idea she'd had. The next time Hebrew school met, though, Mrs. Chazen was there instead of Mr. Weinstock.

"What's your mom doing here?" he asked Louis.

"She's subbing," Louis replied.

"Is Mr. Weinstock sick?" said Rick.

"No," Louis answered. "He's fired!"

"*Why*?" Rick blurted out so loud he startled Mrs. Chazen, who, looking around and seeing him, put a finger to her lips to have him lower his voice.

"So what happened, Louis?" he said softly.

"According to my dad," Louis replied, keeping his voice down, too, "Emily's mother hit the ceiling when she told her Weinstock said that if she didn't speak up on civil rights, she was as bad as Pharaoh or Hitler. Myself, I think Emily was trying to get back at him for not kissing her *tuchus* enough in class. Anyhow, her mom got on the horn to every loudmouth she knew. When a mob of them stormed the Board and *kvetched* about Weinstock, it axed him."

At that instant, Rick had his speech.

"That's so sad about Mr. Weinstock," Mom commiserated with him at dinner, "it makes me even sorrier I don't have some better news for you. I know how much you wanted Jack to have an *aliyah*, and I thought lifting the Torah would be perfect for him since it doesn't require any Hebrew. But when I called him this afternoon, he turned me down. Can you believe it? My father who's never backed away from a fight said he doesn't have the nerve to get up on stage at your bar mitzvah! I'm having enough trouble as it is filling the slots on the form the rabbi gave me. Outside of Norman Chazen and some of your other friends' dads, there aren't many Jewish men I'd feel comfortable asking if they'd accept an honor. After supper, I'll phone your Uncle Ernest—I hope he'll take one!"

When she called, though, she never got past Aileen. "What *chutzpah*!" Aileen exploded. "What do you think it meant that none of us came back to your house after the funeral? You killed my brother!"

"But . . . Aileen . . . ," Madge spluttered, "Ricky's not responsible for Bernie's death."

"And don't think for a minute that Pop will be there!" Aileen lashed out, ignoring her. "We still haven't told him what you did to his son. When he asks where Bernie is, we just say he's gone back to Huppertsville to try to reopen Mr. Z's."

As Madge hung up, Rick walked in on her and, seeing how pale she was, asked, "What's wrong, Mom? Who was it?"

". . . Just a crank call," she stumbled. ". . . And shouldn't you be practicing? The service is only a few days away!"

"No sweat," he answered. "I've got my *maftir* and *haftarah* down cold."

"What about your talk, though?"

"It's all done. Just you wait. Dad won't be this family's only standout speaker!"

Not surprisingly, the two of them got to *shul* before nearly anyone else *Shabbos* morning. As they stepped into the vestibule, they were spotted by the *gabbai*, the rabbi's majordomo. "This way!" the stunted old man grunted as he herded them to the front pew reserved for *bar mitzvah* families. "On my signal," he wheezed, "follow me back out to the lobby. I'll tell you what to do when we get there." He hacked a couple of times more before limping off to the *bimah*.

As congregants began arriving, Mrs. Blustein, always among the first to services, sat down in the row behind them. Not long after that, the Chazens took their seats in the pew across the aisle. Meanwhile, the kids from Rick's Hebrew school class began filing in—Emily, Andrea, and, of course, Louis, who, as he used to, sat with Y. H. in the back. Several minutes later, Dee-Dee and Jack came through the sanctuary doors, and Rick, seeing them, started to his feet to go greet them when Mom laid her hand on his thigh, saying, "Better stay put in case the *gabbai* wants us."

"Where's Aunt Aileen?" Rick asked her. "And what about Uncle Ernest and my cousins? Do you think they went to get Grandpa Irv?"

"That's probably it," Mom lied. "Meantime, I've got a surprise for you." She opened her handbag and took out a blue velvet sack that had an amber Jewish star stitched on the side. Unzipping it, she handed him a yellowed silk *yarmulke* and *tallis*. "These were your father's," she said, her voice cracking as she almost broke down. "I know he'd want you to have them—"

"Page 42!" the rabbi cut in. "The introductory service!" On a typical Saturday morning, he wouldn't have appeared on the *bimah* until the start of the Torah reading, but for a *bar* or *bat mitzvah*, he was onstage from the beginning. The *gabbai* led the congregation at an even faster clip than he typically did so there'd be time for a series of elaborate presentations later: a *kiddush* cup for Rick from the Men's Club, a Pentateuch from the Sisterhood, and a lengthy exhortation from the rabbi "to uphold, above all, the *mitzvot* prescribing right conduct toward others."

Once the *gabbai* had whizzed through the opening prayers, he hobbled down the *bimah's* steps and crooked his arm at Rick and Mom, motioning them to the sanctuary's side exit. From there, he hurried them through a long corridor out to the lobby. "When the rabbi says," he rasped, coughing up some phlegm, "'Let us welcome today's *bar mitzvah*,' you go with me back inside. You, lady, return to your seat and *you*, boy," he said, jabbing his finger into Rick's chest, "come sit on the *bimah* where I tell you." Within seconds, the rabbi blared their cue, and the *gabbai* shouldered the sanctuary doors open. When Mom got to her row, she gave Rick a peck on the cheek while the *gabbai* gave him a tug on the sleeve to hustle him up to a chair alongside the rabbi's.

"Page 86!" the rabbi barked from his lectern. The cantor came forward to lead the *davening*, and the rabbi retreated to his throne. As he sat down beside Rick, rather than greet him, "Shabbat Shalom," or "Relax, you'll do fine," he accosted him, "The *aliyah* list—where is it?!" Rick shrugged. "I thought I saw my mom put it in her pocketbook before we left home," he replied. "If you want, I'll get it from her." Scowling, the rabbi growled, "Stay where you are!" and waggled his finger at the *gabbai* to fetch it.

As the service wore on, Rick tried to pay attention to the prayers (or, at least, pretend that he was), but his eyes kept roaming through the congregation. First, they meandered to Louis and Y. H., who made faces at him, then they drifted to Andrea, who had hers glued to a compact mirror, before wandering to Jack's, which displayed an ear-to-ear grin as though his grandson had clinched the World Series with a perfect no-hitter and game-winning home run. Rick's gaze was about to shift someplace else when Cantor Pinsky suddenly trilled, "*Yerachmiel ben Baruch—maftir!*"

Rick stepped to the table where the Torah lay open. His right hand gripped the scroll's corresponding wooden roller while his left curled around the tapered, brass pointer the *gabbai* pressed in his palm. "The little finger at the *yad*'s tip," the cantor had prepared him, "will help keep your place." Rick took a deep breath, then perfectly cantillated the *maftir* together with the blessing before as well as the one after, followed by an equally flawless chanting of the *haftarah* and its benedictions. As the last note left his mouth, a single thought raced through his brain: "*It's over!*" He was about to go back to his seat when the rabbi cuffed his elbow and hissed, "Where's your speech?" Rick tapped his forehead. "In here," he replied coolly. Turning to the congregation, the rabbi said acidly, "Yerachmiel has some thoughts to share about his portion. I, for one, can't wait to hear them."

Rick took a few moments to let the rabbi, cantor, and *gabbai* go back to their places. "First, I appreciate everybody's coming today," he began once they got settled. "It's good to see my friends, along with their parents, especially Mr. and Mrs. Chazen, who've brought me here with them so many times. I'm also really happy to see Dee-Dee and Jack, my Huppertsville family, sitting there down front. I don't know what's happened to my Medina relatives—I hope they're okay. Anyway, I owe a lot to Cantor Pinsky, who never gave up on me, even when my reading and chanting were terrible. I know my voice still isn't that great, but believe me, it's much better than it was." Some people were about to laugh until he added, "I couldn't have done it without my dad, who practiced my singing with me and who I wish could've heard me do my *maftir* and *haftarah* this morning. But my mom heard it, and after all she's done for me my whole life, I can't tell you how much that matters to me or how much I love her. Thanks for everything, Mom.

"I guess some of you probably think that while I'm at it, I ought to thank the *shul*'s Hebrew school, too. But honestly, apart from teaching me how to sound out letters, it didn't do much to get me ready for today. I *still* don't get why God would tell Abraham to circumcise himself, his son Ishmael, and all the other guys around them. And why would Abraham listen?! I mean, if you were ninety-nine years old and had had trouble having a kid, why would you turn around and do something to him that might kill him? Well, since I'm supposed to be a man now, I'll just come out and say it: I'm not sure there really was an Abraham—I'm not even sure there's a God!"

A stillness descended on the sanctuary like when the rabbi came forward to speak.

"I have to admit I learned one valuable thing in Hebrew school, though," Rick started up again, "and I got it from Mr. Weinstock, the only good teacher I had there. He said you have to speak up for people who are powerless. And you know what? The Board fired him for saying that! But while it may have gotten rid of Mr. Weinstock, it can't get rid of what he taught me!

"My Grandpa Irv Zieglitz is somebody who's powerless, because he's stuck in a nursing home with Parkinson's disease. He belonged to this *shul* for a long time, and it always meant a lot to him. But even though my family's wanted the rabbi to visit my grandpa, he hasn't. He acts like his job's just to call out the page numbers in the prayer book. If the Board wants to fire somebody, let them can him! Somewhere, there's got to be a better rabbi."

Rick had barely stopped speaking when the rabbi barged up beside him. "Due to the lateness of the hour," he told the congregation as he jostled Rick out of the way, "the Men's Club and Sisterhood will be mailing their *bar mitzvah* gifts to the Zieglitz home, while I'll be making my remarks to Roderick in private—page 156, the service concludes."

After Cantor Pinsky led the last hymn, he started toward Rick, beaming. The rabbi, though, stepped in between them, shunting Rick off the *bimah* while furiously waving at Mom to join them. "What kind of mother are you," he demanded, "raising such an impudent child?!" Before she could say she was sorry—or Rick could say that he wasn't—a crush of well-wishers overwhelmed them. "*Mazel Tov!*" Jack cried, uttering the only Jewish phrase he knew as Dee-Dee squeezed in and hugged Rick. When Mrs. Chazen's time came, she embraced Rick, too, while Mr. Chazen enthusiastically shook his hand. Next in line was Mrs. Blustein. "Although I might not . . . endorse your views . . . ," she stuttered, fumbling for something complimentary to say, "I suspect my father would have . . . admired your candor." Farther back,

Louis whooped, "I wish I'd given that speech!" just as Y. H. elbowed ahead of him and shouted, "It's about time somebody knocked these jerks on their asses!" Finally, after everyone else had moved on, Andrea cooed in Rick's ear, "I can't wait to see you tonight at your party."

That evening, up in the *shul*'s social hall, she saved all her slow dances for him. "Isn't there someplace we can be more alone?" she whispered as the party wound down.

Rick clasped her hand and guided her along a dark passageway to the rabbi's office. "No way he's going to show up," Rick snorted, opening the door. "There aren't any pages for him to announce." As he kicked the door shut behind them, Andrea grabbed the back of his belt and swirled him around onto the desk. "Touch me! Touch me!" she moaned as she straddled him and thrust his hand in her panties while she plunged hers down his briefs. No girl had ever fondled him there, and he came quickly. Like elderly Abraham, who'd begot a son, he was ecstatic everything worked, and like young Ishmael, who'd also survived a blade-wielding father, he was thrilled to be alive.

X

"What about you and Courtney and me and Clarice double-dating on New Year's Eve?" Rick asked Tom Peterson, his best friend at Huppertsville High and the only guy there more popular than he was. Since moving back to the small town with Mom five years earlier, he'd virtually duplicated Dad's high school career. He had the best grades, all the debate team awards, and having slimmed down during adolescence, Bernie's good looks. Except for Tom's being class president, his senior year would have been a carbon copy of his father's.

"In case you haven't noticed, Rick, this burg shuts down way before midnight," Tom answered.

"Why don't we drive over to the King Cole in Excelsior for dinner?"

"Too rich for my blood, pal. But what if I have everybody over to my house for a party?"

"Good idea—no wonder our class elected you prez!"

Because of Tom and Tom's wider circle of friends who had quickly embraced him, Rick soon stopped missing Louis, with whom he initially corresponded, as well as Y. H., who'd occasionally phoned him to share a dirty joke. But Rick hadn't missed Aunt Aileen at all once Mom let slip why she and her family hadn't come to his *bar mitzvah*. In the intervening years, he'd only heard from them twice, and then merely by mail, first with a clipping of Grandpa Irv's obit and later with Grandma Thelma's, each envelope addressed to him rather than Mom.

His mother's acceptance by the locals, in contrast to her son's, took much longer. Following Bernie's death, she'd been able to manage, thanks to Dina and Jack, the mortgage, utilities, and groceries. She couldn't cope, though, with the stigma of being a suicide's widow whose approach triggered

sudden hushes and whose departure restarted wagging tongues. She'd de-
clined her parents' offer to come live at *Casa Futura*, choosing instead to
move into the cottage again, a sign of her determination to become known
as more than the Apters' pampered daughter.

When she began job hunting, however, prospective employers refused
to see her as anything but a well-off, bored woman out for a lark. Eventually,
she settled for twelve hours a week at Wellington's Shoes on Main Street, a
few doors down from the defunct Mr. Z's, its site now occupied by a second-
hand shop. During her first months there, several female customers dropped
by who in the past would have gotten on their knees to let them ride along
when Jack drove her to an Excelsior movie premiere, but who now jumped
at the chance to have her kneel before them fitting pair after pair of shoes
they had no intention of buying. She nevertheless remained undaunted in
her efforts to earn a new reputation. In time, her persistence paid off as even
the detractors came to appreciate her as Wellington's number one saleslady,
for whom they'd patiently wait until she could assist them.

One morning in late December after a heavy overnight snowfall, a
stranger entered the store. Madge thought he was nice-looking—slender,
dark, and, except for his slush-soaked left shoe, dapper.

"Miss!" he called out to her as he vainly stomped his foot to get rid of
the muck. "Just when I'd thought I'd handled the icy roads from Excelsior—
well, you can see what I stepped in! If you'd get me another pair of black
wing tips, I'll pay you and be on my way. I'm a size—"

"You don't need a new pair," Madge interrupted him. "Let me have the
shoes you're wearing, and I'll get them cleaned up before you know it. Is that
all right with you, Mr. . . . ?"

"Williams—Gene Williams—and your suggestion is better than all
right! Sorry, Miss, but I didn't get your name, either."

"Just call me Madge. Everyone else in town does.'"

Gene gave her his shoes, and less than fifteen minutes later, she brought
them back polished and buffed. Slipping them on, Gene said, "I can't tell you
how grateful I am, Madge. I'm due at your courthouse fifteen minutes from
now, and I can't begin to imagine what the judge assigned to my case will do
if I'm late. How much do I owe you?"

"Not a thing, Mr. Williams. I didn't do all that much."

"'Gene' works, too, Madge, and you're being much too modest. Let
me repay you by taking you out to dinner." Seeing her blush, he did, too.
"Excuse me—I didn't mean to be so forward," he said.

"You weren't!" Madge replied as she hurriedly took a pencil and pad
from the counter. "My last name's Zieglitz, and here's my number."

"I'll phone you tonight!" Gene promised on his way out.

At supper that evening, Rick couldn't recall the last time he'd seen his mother in such high spirits. "You must have made loads of sales today," he remarked between bites of the veal piccata she only made on special occasions.

"Oh, I hardly sold anything."

"Then how come you're smiling so much?"

The phone rang, and Madge raced to the kitchen. "I've got it!" she yelled over her shoulder. Grabbing the receiver and cupping the mouthpiece, she said softly, "Hello, this is Madge."

"Hi, it's Gene—Oh gosh, are you eating dinner? I've lost track of time here at my office. Should I call you back later?"

"No, Gene, now's perfect!"

"I'm serious, Madge, about thanking you for this morning. Saturday night is New Year's Eve. What would you think of having dinner with me at the King Cole here in Excelsior? I could pick you up around six."

"I'd love that! If you come by a bit earlier, I'll make us some *hors d'oeuvres*."

"That'd be great, Madge—See you Saturday evening!"

"Gene, wait— How did your trial go?"

"Would you believe it? Despite my impeccably shined shoes, we still lost! Maybe one day, that judge will decide in our favor. For now, though, I've still got something to celebrate. I met you, didn't I?"

When Madge came back to the dining room, she seemed so lost in thought that Rick asked, "Mom, are you okay? Did that phone call upset you?"

"Just the opposite!" she answered before she told him all about Gene. After Rick greeted her news with silence, she said, "I just know you're going to hit it off with Gene when you meet him Saturday night!"

Mom's announcement took Rick by surprise. He'd never seen her with a man other than Dad, and he wasn't sure he liked it. Despite all that had gone wrong in her and Dad's marriage, her going out with somebody else seemed somehow disloyal. Barely audible, Rick muttered, "I probably won't be here—Tom's invited me to his house for a party."

On New Year's Eve, Rick was showered, shaved, and dressed in what he thought was plenty of time before Gene would arrive. As he finished brushing his hair, though, he heard a knock at the front door.

"Please get that—I'm not ready!" Mom frantically called from her bedroom.

When Gene saw Rick, he was unprepared, too—Madge hadn't mentioned a teenage boy. "Hi, there . . . I'm Gene . . . I'm here for Madge."

"I'm Rick, her son. She'll be down in a minute."

Gene he held up a bottle of champagne and stammered, ". . . This . . . ought to be chilled."

Rick was grateful for the opportunity to step away. "I'll put it in the fridge. If you want, there are some magazines on the coffee table you can look at while you're waiting for my mom." After showing Gene in and getting him situated on the couch, Rick went to the kitchen where he lingered as long as he could. When he returned to the living room, Gene was still there by himself.

"So, Rick, how long have you and your mother lived here?" Gene asked, trying to make conversation.

"About five years."

"And where did you live before this?"

"Medina."

"And what made you move from the big city to a small town?"

From what Mom had told him, Rick knew Gene was a lawyer, and he felt like he was a witness being cross-examined. To his relief, Mom walked in and got him down from the stand.

When Gene glimpsed Madge in her sequined, sapphire gown and satin, cobalt heels, he stood up and cried, "You look utterly marvelous! I was just getting acquainted with Rick, who was about to tell me why you left Medina and—"

"Things just didn't work out there," she cut him off. "Why don't I go get the *hors d'oeuvres*? And, Rick, honey, isn't it time for you to go to your party?"

"A New Year's Eve gala! That ought to be exciting!" Gene said amiably.

"Not a big deal, just going to a friend's house," Rick replied, still ambivalent toward the stranger who'd be taking Mom out. For the past five years, he'd been the man of the house, but now he might be supplanted, and yet, he couldn't remember seeing his mother this happy. He put on his coat, got into the cherry red Chrysler Dee-Dee and Jack had bought him for his sixteenth birthday, and drove to Tom's, where his parents answered the door and directed him to the family room downstairs.

Captain of the school's basketball team, Tom towered over the other kids surrounding him and spotted Rick the second he walked in. "Hey Rick—glad you could make it!" he shouted above the din.

"Me, too!" Rick hollered back. In the corner of his eye, he saw a knot of girls encircled around Tom's girlfriend Courtney, his female counterpart as the school's most popular senior. Just as Tom had his Rick, Courtney had her Clarice, whom Rick would take out, at Courtney's insistence, whenever they double-dated. Like a queen holding an audience, Courtney presided over her ladies in waiting, Clarice chief among them. At precisely eleven,

Courtney summarily dismissed her attendants with a summons to Tom, "Time to take me home!"

"But, Tom, we've got another hour to go before midnight!" Rick said.

"Can't be helped, friend. Her father's a real stickler, and I don't want to cross him, especially now that he's the Board Chair at Hillcrest Country Club. Courtney wants to have this year's senior prom there instead of the school's gym. I honestly don't think the gym would be that terrible—I've got some great memories of games our team won playing in it. Courtney, though, says her dad's gone to a lot of trouble getting everything arranged, and neither of them is about to change their minds now. Would you be a buddy and drop Clarice off at her house? It'll give Courtney and me a chance to be by ourselves on the drive back to her place."

Although Rick and Clarice never had that much to say to one another, he couldn't say no to Tom, and after driving Clarice home and getting a curt good night "Thanks," he headed back to the cottage. "Some New Year's Eve," he groused to himself after he parked in the driveway. As he walked into the darkened front hall and flipped on the light, he dimly made out two figures jumping up from the couch.

". . . We had . . . a change of plans," Mom spluttered, switching on a lamp.

"We had dinner here," Gene added while he hastily tucked in his shirt. "Your mother's quite a . . . cook."

Shocked and embarrassed at having walked in on the two of them, Rick blurted out the first thing that popped into his head, realizing how silly it sounded the moment he said it. "So Gene, which *shul* do you belong to in Excelsior?"

"Beg pardon?" Gene said.

"Which Excelsior synagogue do you go to?"

"Oh, I don't go to any of them."

"—We don't either! There aren't any here, and we've never gone to an Excelsior one."

"My reason's different, Rick—I'm not Jewish. For that matter, though, I also don't attend church. After what happened to my family . . . ," Gene's voice trailed off. He looked over at Madge and said, "I should get going."

"But, Gene, it's not even New Year's yet!" Rick broke in, seeing how disappointed Mom looked. "I'll call my grandparents, Jack and Dee—I mean Dina—to ask if you can spend the night at their house."

"You two are related to Jack and Dina Apter? They're old clients of mine and why I was here this week! The IRS keeps on claiming they're hiding part of their income."

"So you'll stay over?" Rick said. Though he still had misgivings about how fast things were moving between Mom and Gene, the smile which had reappeared on her face made him set them aside for the time being. Before either of them could object, he was on the phone to *Casa Futura*.

"Who the hell is this?" Jack answered, startled awake by the call.

"It's me, Rick."

"What's the trouble?"

"There isn't any. It's just that a friend from Excelsior came for dinner tonight, and it's kind of late for him to be driving back. Would it be all right if he slept at your house?"

"Sure—any friend of yours is a friend of mine."

"Actually, Jack, it's a friend of Mom's and yours—Gene Williams."

"Go ahead and send him up. Tomorrow, you and Madge can explain how you know him."

Back in the living room, Rick told Gene, "It's all set! Now you can stay for New Year's."

"I'll be back in a jiff," Madge said as she dashed off to the kitchen, returning with the remaining *hors d'oeuvres* and champagne along with three glasses, one of which she handed to Rick with a wink. "After what you've just pulled off, I think you're old enough for some bubbly." When the last of the magnum and the appetizers were gone, she turned to Gene and said, "Mom and Dad's is only a short walk from here, but it's so dark now, I think I ought to drive you." Rick's protectiveness towards his mother swept over him again—there'd been a guy at school who'd gotten a girl pregnant in a car's back seat. Before he could say he'd take Gene himself, Mom already had out her car keys. Rick resolved that even so, he'd wait up until she came home. Between the hour and champagne, though, he quickly fell asleep on the couch, which was where Mom found him when she got back well past two. She kissed his forehead, took his arm, and led him shuffling to bed.

When he awoke midmorning, she'd already been up since dawn. Hearing him yawn, she poked her head in his room. "C'mon, sleepyhead, time to get dressed! Mom and Dad have invited us to a New Year's brunch with Gene. Put on that burgundy, cashmere sweater of yours, one of your white, button-down shirts, and your charcoal, wool slacks." Still groggy, he got up, slipped into the clothes she'd chosen for him, and stumbled to the front hall. "Let's walk," she said, flinging open the door. "The cold air will do you good!" As she made her way up the snow-covered path, Rick trudged behind her.

At *Casa Futura*, Jack met them in the foyer. "Wish the brunch was fancier, but me and Dina are heading down to Florida day after tomorrow, so there ain't much left in the house for us to eat. I only had time to grab some stuff off the shelves from our grocery and one of the bars. With it being a holiday, everything's closed."

"Company's what counts!" declared Gene, bounding up behind Jack so fresh and well-groomed that he looked as if he'd brought a change of clothes with him.

"In here, everybody!" Dina called from the kitchen, where she'd set out an assortment of cold cuts, cheeses, and an ice bucket with soda and sparkling wine. "You're the guest, Gene. Take a plate and get something to eat and drink, and have a seat at the table."

"So how long have you known Mom and Dad?" Madge asked Gene after she'd sat down beside him.

Jack answered for him. "Going on ten years now, and I'll tell you this, Madge—Gene's the best lawyer we ever had representing us. He might not win them all, but it ain't his fault when we lose—there's this one sonuvabitch judge who's got it in for us! But you know what? The goddam IRS would've made off with even more of our dough if Gene hadn't—"

"Oh, Daddy, let's talk about something more pleasant!" Madge interrupted. "What *I'm* interested in, Gene, is why you became a lawyer in the first place."

"Simple, Madge—my father! I wanted to grow up to be an attorney like him. In my hometown, which was only slightly larger than this one, everybody looked up to him, not merely his clients, but the other lawyers as well as the judges. I worked as hard as I could to make good grades and ended up going to college and law school back east. After a firm in Excelsior recruited me, I practiced with them for six years before striking out on my own. Luckily, several of my clients went with me, and since then, word of mouth has kept bringing me new ones. Overall, I've been pretty blessed."

Gene's words unexpectedly rubbed Rick the wrong way. Hadn't "blessed" been what his dead father's Hebrew name meant? Before Rick could catch himself, he burst out, "'Pretty blessed'? Sounds like very blessed to me!"

Several seconds ticked by before Gene spoke. "Remember, Rick, when I told you last night I didn't go to church anymore? Well, twelve years ago today, my wife and twin five-year-old girls were driving home from New England where we'd all gone to visit her folks for Christmas. I'd had to fly back early to take care of some last-minute filings for a couple of clients. Ann was about an hour outside of Excelsior when a big rig going the opposite way skidded on a patch of ice and slammed into the car, instantly killing her and our daughters."

For the first time, Rick felt a closeness with Gene. "My dad done in by a cleaver, Gene's family by a semi," he mused. "Pretty blessed, very blessed—what difference does it make if there's no Blesser? —And from the way Mom and Gene look at each other, what difference does it make if somebody's Jewish or not?"

Madge had taken hold of Gene's hand. They'd exchanged stories of loss the night before, and her face flushed with chagrin over Rick's outburst. Gene broke the awkward silence by saying, "So, Rick, your mother tells me you're first in your class. Have you made up your mind where you want to go to college?"

Thankful that Gene had changed the subject, Madge interjected, "I've been pestering him about that. With his grades, I think he should aim high and apply to a private, out-of-state school."

"If that's the case, Madge, Edwards should definitely be on Rick's list! It's my undergrad alma mater, and I'm the regional alumni rep. Let me know, Rick, if I can help."

"Sure, thanks," Rick replied. He knew about Edwards. It was one of the highly selective schools he and Tom had considered, but Tom had rejected it, because he wanted a college with a better basketball team. Besides, Rick knew how little Mom had left over from Dad's life insurance, and it was a real possibility he'd end up at State U., which was fine with him, because not only had Tom said he'd liked what he'd read about its coach, but he'd also told Rick that if it meant their staying together, going there would be okay with him, too.

Brunch ended, as did New Year's and the holidays, but Madge and Gene continued to grow closer while Rick's bond with him likewise grew stronger, if not quite as with a father figure, then as with a big brother whom he could approach for advice. In the spring, as the prom drew nearer, Courtney made it clear to Tom and Clarice—and thus Rick, too—that she expected all of them to come suitably attired for the club. "The stores around here sell clothes that are all right for that smelly old gym, but the shops in Excelsior have what's fashionable for Hillcrest."

"Where's the best place to get a tux in Excelsior?" Rick asked Gene the next time he visited Mom.

"Without a doubt, Rick, it's Arden's. I bought a tuxedo there last year, but I know they also rent them. They're pricey, but worth it."

When Rick travelled to Arden's the next weekend, it reminded him of when he'd shopped for his *bar mitzvah* suit with Dad. The store was not only classy but as Gene had said, expensive as well; the rental deposit alone took all the cash Rick had brought with him. He drove back to Huppertsville at Jack-speed to call Tom and tell him he should go there, too.

There was a long silence before Tom spoke. "There's a glitch, pal. I just hung up with Courtney, and her dad, Judge Hammond, says you can't come."

"Why not, Tom?"

"Because you're Jewish. Turns out Hillcrest doesn't allow Jews."

Rick couldn't believe what he was hearing. "But, Tom, you could change things! You could say that if Hillcrest won't let me come, you won't come, either! I bet *nobody* would go then!"

"And I wouldn't get the judge to write me a recommendation for college! —Without it, I'll wind up at State."

Hanging up, Rick didn't know which hurt worse—being banned from Hillcrest or being abandoned by Tom. He lifted the receiver again and dialed the number Mom had taped by the phone. "Hi, it's Rick," he said when Gene answered. "I need help with Edwards."

XI

"Put down that dogshit, Zieglitz—it's time to strike a blow for the revolution at the Spring Fling!" said Louis, Rick's junior-year roomie at Edwards.

Saturday night and Rick was still stymied writing his term paper for Van den Enden's class, "Three Seventeenth-Century Rationalists: Descartes, Hobbes, and Spinoza," the credit he needed to meet the philosophy major's requirements. Finding the course's subject matter as dull as its instructor, Rick had had a hard time settling on a topic for the assignment that was due Friday. He'd summarily dismissed writing about Descartes, whose mind-body dualism he thought nobody in the last half of the twentieth century could take seriously. Turning next to Hobbes and Spinoza, Rick saw their obvious similarities: each read the Bible unconventionally and took a dim view of human beings ungoverned. And yet, one key difference between them leapt out at Rick. For Hobbes, the state's basic purpose was to suppress the worst instincts in people, while for Spinoza, its ultimate goal was to evoke the best in them. Rick wondered why the two figures differed so much about mankind's potential. Could it be that Hobbes, a Christian, believed Adam and Eve had forever corrupted human nature while the Jewish-born Spinoza didn't subscribe to any doctrine of "original sin"? Rick tossed another notebook sheet into the waste basket, rejecting the sort of facile juxtaposition that the Medina rabbi typically invoked to demonstrate the superiority of Jewish ethics to all others.

Still, Rick was drawn to Spinoza. Though he found Spinoza's prose dense with his talk of "Substance," "Extension," and "*natura naturans*," the man's life had clear parallels to his own. Like Spinoza, who'd been cast out by Amsterdam's rabbis for his thoughts, Rick had become a *persona non grata* with his community's cleric for the ideas he'd expressed. Rick felt another connection with Spinoza, however, that went far beyond their both being alienated Jews. Like Dad, Spinoza had been given the Hebrew name "Baruch," which following his excommunication, Spinoza had changed to "Benedictus," the Latin for "Blessed." Those names, though, hadn't protected either his father or the philosopher from perishing at a mere forty-four years old. The implications nagged at Rick. Since Spinoza was a thoroughgoing determinist, did his philosophy mean that he and Dad were inexorably destined to die at that age? If so, where did human freedom come in?

"Since when you did care about mixers, Louis?" Rick responded, irritated he'd been interrupted.

"Since it's the end of May and my last chance this year as head of the campus SDS to circulate petitions for coeducation at this male chauvinist bastion. Enough with that mental masturbation of yours, and give me some help in the real world!"

"But I have this paper . . ." Rick balked as Louis grabbed his arm and dragged him out the door.

Approaching Edwards's immense commons, they could hear the band's electric guitars blasting out Hendrix's "Foxy Lady." Once inside, Louis, intrepid as always, waded into a phalanx of varsity lettermen carrying beers to their next conquests and launched into a harangue about the evils of sexism. Rick didn't need Van den Enden's essay hanging over him as an excuse to leave—dances brought bitter memories of the Huppertsville prom. As he headed for the exit, he felt a tap on his shoulder. Sure it was Louis about to castigate him for abandoning the cause, he wheeled around ready to bark, "Get away!" Facing him, though, was a petite blonde with deep sea-green eyes, who said impishly, "You're not much for mixers either, I gather—you've been eyeing the doors ever since you got here. Anyway, this is where you offer to get me a beer, after which we can chitchat about what we're studying and our plans for the future—or we could skip all that and go dance." As she walked out on the floor in her blue, Twiggy mini and white, mod boots, she shouted over her shoulder, "My name's Nataliya Lubyatko."

"I'm Rick Zieglitz," he hollered back.

"Is that short for Richard?" she said, turning around.

"No, it's short for Roderick."

"Good—from now on, you're 'Rod.' I once had a boyfriend named 'Richard,' who was all hands." As Nataliya started dancing, newly named Rod joined her. Though he was a fairly good dancer, on account of all the *bar mitzvah* and high school parties he'd gone to, his moves couldn't compare with Nataliya's. Watching her sway and swerve to each beat, he could feel the rhythm, *her* rhythm, surge through him. The two of them continued nonstop until the rock group took a break sometime later.

Gulping for air, Rod asked, "Where'd you learn to dance like that, Nataliya?"

"Dancing like this comes naturally to me, but there's another kind of dancing I take class for six days a week—I'm in ballet at the Institute for the Performing Arts in Manhattan."

Although Rod didn't know much about the Institute, he'd read somewhere that it only admitted the most promising candidates. "I've never met a serious dancer before," he said.

"And what are you serious about, Rod? I do hope it's not something boring," she teased him.

"Philosophy," he muttered under his breath, bracing for a Louis-like barb. To his surprise, Nataliya extended her hand and said, "It's good to meet somebody else who's studying something impractical."

"Would you like to get out of here and go have some coffee?" Rod asked.

"As long as I'm back in time for my train to New York."

"No problem—I've got a car, and I'll drive you to the city if we're late. You'll be home in less than an hour," Rod told her. He walked her to a café around the corner where, after he'd paid, he set down their coffees on one of its abutting, hogshead tables.

"Thank you, Rod," Nataliya said.

"I brought you here so we'd have a chance to talk," he answered.

"That's why I thanked you—I'm grateful for your not taking me some place to have sex."

Taking her to bed had never crossed Rod's mind. He'd met girls during the occasional road trip or, when he could make himself go, an infrequent mixer, but none of those casual encounters had led to a one-night stand, much less to an intimate romance. ". . . So, Nataliya . . . where do you live?" he sputtered, thrown off by her response.

Caught off guard by his question, she faltered, too. "With my parents . . . even with the stipend the Institute gives me, it's all we can afford."

Rod hadn't meant to embarrass her. "Nataliya, I know what it's like not to have money. After my dad died, things got so tough that my mom and I had to move back to a hick town to live at my grandparents'. If it weren't for my stepfather, I couldn't swing Edwards. Right after he married my mother, he became a partner in a large law firm that made him an offer after he won a big case against them. So now that you know something about me, tell me a little about you—where does your family call home?"

"For me, it's always been Queens, but Mama and Papa are originally from Ukraine—"

"Some of my family came from there, too!" Rod broke in, pleased to have stumbled on something they had in common. "They left after a Cossack murdered my great-grandfather—"

Nataliya cut him off. "Several members of my father's family were Cossacks—most of them were killed by the Nazis and Soviets . . ."

As Nataliya's voice tailed off, Rod thought of how quiet Cantor Pinsky had become when he'd spoken of the Germans and Russians. ". . . Sorry, Nataliya, I didn't know."

"There's no way you could have," Nataliya said gently. "The main thing is that Mama and Papa survived. After the war was over, one of Papa's aunts, an old maid who'd emigrated to New York years before the fighting started, helped him and Mama come to the States. They moved into her little flat, and when she died, it went to Papa. Awhile later, my parents had me, and we've never lived anywhere else. —Now it's your turn again. Where does your family live?"

"In the Midwest, in Excelsior—my stepfather and mom just built a house in one of its suburbs. My grandparents live in a town called Huppertsville, which is about forty miles east of there."

"But your family's so far away! If there's one good thing about living in my apartment in Queens, it's that my parents—especially Mama—are there if I need them."

The couple lingered until the café closed, and Rod drove Nataliya to the station. Waiting for the train on the platform, she told him, "I asked you to dance, because I thought you were nice looking. But since then, the way you've treated me has attracted me even more. —Listen, I have a performance tomorrow. Would you like to come to it, Rod?"

"Sure! What time should I be at the Institute?"

"Meet me at my place instead. We need to leave by noon for the city." Before she boarded the train, she exchanged addresses and phone numbers with him, and that night, he fell asleep with images of her pirouetting through his dreams.

Sunday morning, he tried on three different outfits: blazer, tie, and wool slacks (too formal, he thought), jeans and denim jacket (too casual, he concluded), bell-bottoms and black, cotton turtleneck (perfect, he figured, for something "artsy"). As he combed his longish hair in the mirror, Louis walked in and said, "What are you getting so dolled up for?"

"I guess you didn't notice my taking off from the mixer last night. I met a girl there named Nataliya, and we really hit it off. She's a dancer, and she invited me to her ballet recital this afternoon in New York."

"A ballet recital, Zieglitz? How bourgeois can you get!"

Rod ignored Louis's jibe, intent on getting to Nataliya's on time. Once he had a quick breakfast at the commons, he drove down to the city, passing intersection after intersection of numbered avenues along Queens Boulevard, before turning left on one and parking near Nataliya's building, which was virtually identical to all the other red-brick boxes lining her street. Walking to it, he stopped at a bodega to buy her a small bouquet of roses. When he stepped beneath the faded brown awning with her address on it, he pushed the button marked "Lubyatko" and was immediately buzzed in, as though someone upstairs had been waiting to admit him. Taking the sluggish elevator to Nataliya's floor, he walked down a long hallway permeated by the smells of beans, cabbage, and curry. Near the corridor's end, he came to her apartment where, before he could knock, a diminutive woman opened the door. She had Nataliya's blonde hair, though with a few gray streaks, and, but for some crow's feet, the same sea-green eyes. Seeing Rod's flowers, she smiled and called out, "Nataliya, your young man is here!"

"Coming!" Rod heard Nataliya answer. When she got to the door, she burst out, "Mama, isn't it sweet what Rod's done?"

Mama nodded as she ushered Rod in. "Nataliya, quick, put the roses in water. We don't want to be late!" she said.

Nataliya motioned Rod to follow her to a kitchenette in the rear where she got down a cloudy glass vase from a cabinet whose shelves were lined with yellowed contact paper and beige Melmac dishware. Arranging the stems, she told Rod, "As long as you're here, you should meet Papa, too." She waved him into an adjoining cramped room in which a gaunt, ashen figure with a cigarette butt squeezed between the stubs of his right hand's middle and index fingers sat hunched over a transistor radio crackling classical music. Above his frayed armchair hung a badly flaked wooden miniature depicting a mother and infant with golden halos around their heads.

"Papa, this is Rod. He's coming to my recital," said Nataliya.

Papa put the transistor closer to his ear.

Leading Rod away, Nataliya whispered, "Don't mind Papa—he doesn't mean to be unfriendly. We better get going, though. It's a long subway ride to the Institute."

"We can take my car if you want."

"The subway's faster, and there won't be any problems parking."

Once they'd arrived, Rod and Mama took their seats down front in the auditorium while Nataliya went to dress for her lead role in Tchaikovsky's *Sleeping Beauty*. After the curtain went up, she danced the part of Aurora, the slumbering princess; watching her whirl across the stage, Rod had never been more awake. When the ballet ended, he leapt to his feet and led the audience in a wild ovation. A while later, having changed out of her costume,

Nataliya rejoined him and Mama. "So, Rod, what did you think of the performance?" she asked.

"It was sensational!"

Mama winked at Nataliya. "Your young man isn't only thoughtful, but he's also quite refined."

Nataliya was beaming. "I knew he was sensitive the first time I met him!" As they left the auditorium, she made a series of *piqué* turns down the aisle. Back in Queens, she told Rod when they got to his car, "I'm so glad you came."

"I'm glad you invited me, and I really liked meeting your mother, too." Realizing he'd left out Papa, he was about to correct himself when Nataliya hugged him before turning away to catch up with Mama.

Tuesday night, as Rod was struggling again with his Spinoza paper, the phone rang. He picked up the receiver, and Nataliya said at the other end, "Hello, Rod, I hope it's not too late."

"No, I've been up trying to write a term paper."

"Maybe I should call you back at a better time."

"No, now's perfect—a break would do me good."

"Could you come down tomorrow around five? I need to talk to you in person. Don't ask me about what—I'll tell you when I see you. We'll have an hour between my last afternoon class and an early evening rehearsal for my next performance."

Even with the Spinoza paper's looming deadline, Rod couldn't refuse her, especially if she'd planned on dumping him, telling himself he could talk her out of it if given half a chance. Wednesday afternoon, he caught a train to Grand Central, then took the subway to Times Square, where he transferred to another line that deposited him near the Institute. Nataliya was waiting for him in front. "There's a cozy bistro near here," she said.

After they'd been seated, they ordered a *salade Lyonnaise* to share, though Rod didn't feel like eating and Nataliya only nibbled around the edges. "So what's so important that you had to see me?" he finally asked her.

Nataliya took a few moments before she answered. "I didn't want to talk about it over the phone, because I wouldn't have been able to see the reaction on your face once I told you. I need to speak to you about Papa."

Rod became defensive; one Judge Hammond in his life had been enough. "Look, Nataliya, if he's got something against me personally, then you need to tell me now before this relationship goes any further."

"No, Rod, it's not that. Instead, it's about what happened to Papa in Russia during the war. Before the fighting broke out, Mama and Papa both attended the conservatory in Odessa, where she took ballet, and he trained as a classical violinist. They fell in love and dreamed of going to Paris and becoming great artists. The war put an end to those plans. In the battle against Hitler, the Soviets saw Papa's family as potential traitors, since they were Ukrainian nationalists who belonged to the dissident Old Believers Church. Papa's parents and two sisters were exiled to Siberia while he was conscripted into the Red Army as a mechanic. A year later, he was discharged after a tank tread slipped off its track and mangled his hand."

Wide-eyed, Rod said, "That's terrible, Nataliya! No wonder he's the way he is, so quiet and withdrawn."

"But he's not angry, Rod—not at you or anybody else. You saw the icon nailed above his easy chair? Papa says his injury was Jesus watching over him, because otherwise, he wouldn't have been able to rescue Mama from the Nazis, who would have killed her for being a Jew. As a sign of his gratitude, Papa named me 'Nataliya,' which in Ukrainian refers to Christ's birth. Anyhow, after the war, Russia didn't want either my Christian father or my Jewish mother. They're the reason I'm an atheist: it's safer."

Rod had held back telling her he was Jewish; her mention of her family's Cossack past had stopped him, and he hadn't wanted to risk losing her. "After all the Jew-haters I've had in my life, I could use something safer," he said with a sigh of relief.

Nataliya looked visibly relaxed, too, as she pecked at the salad and chatted with Rod until the time came for her to leave. Outside on the sidewalk, Rod pulled her close, and she whispered in his ear, "I hope you have sweet dreams tonight."

"They will be, Nataliya—you'll be in them," he said softly.

Rod wasn't ready to go to sleep, though. He knew how he'd finish his Van den Enden paper, now that Nataliya had shown him where human freedom resided in Spinoza's world of pure necessity. Rod entitled his essay "Spinoza, Atheism, and Tolerance," stating at its outset that for Spinoza, the world was governed solely by the ironclad laws of nature, thus rendering worship of the biblical God absurd. What point was there in praying to gravity? And what was the point of persecuting others who engaged in different, yet equally nonsensical rites? Little wonder then, Rod commented, that when Amsterdam's Jews expelled Spinoza as a heretic, he didn't become a practicing Christian, but a secular saint living famously in peace with those around him, preaching unrestricted freedom of thought even for, and especially for, people with opposing ideas. With echoes of Nataliya, Rod concluded by declaring that Spinoza's atheism led to an open-mindedness that made everyone safer. The next morning he turned in his paper a day early; Van den Enden returned it a week later, marked at the top with an A+.

Rod called Nataliya right after class, catching her around noon as she was leaving for the Institute. "Nataliya, can you come up tonight? I aced my paper because of you, and I want to show you how grateful I am."

"Oooh . . . sounds intriguing. I'll be on the six o'clock train."

After Rod met her at the station, he drove them to a high-end French restaurant off campus. "I guess I ought to help you with your homework more often," Nataliya remarked as a tuxedoed waiter pulled out her chair at a candlelit table covered by a white starched cloth with settings for multiple courses and glasses of wine.

Once the waiter took their orders and left, Rod said, "I owe you a lot more than the grade on my paper, Nataliya. Remember when you said it's safer being an atheist? Well, that really got me thinking. The way I see it, being an atheist means you don't pin your hopes on some otherworldly power to make things work out. As an atheist, you realize you're on your own, and recognizing that, you become more tolerant of others. You come to appreciate they're poor slobs like you, ultimately alone in the universe, just trying to make sense of life. So if we all became atheists, we couldn't help but be more broad-minded!"

"Oh yes, Rod, just like those extremely broad-minded atheists, Hitler and Stalin."

Rod reddened. He didn't mind her disagreeing with him—argument was philosophy's bread and butter—but he didn't like being made to feel foolish. "Okay, Nataliya, then explain to me how atheism makes *you* safer!"

"It's simple—I don't get caught between Mama and Papa when they fight about me. Sometimes, I think the whole building can hear them, with him ranting, 'If Nataliya doesn't get baptized, she won't go to heaven!' and with her railing, 'Isn't it enough I let you give her that name?!' And that's why being an atheist is safer for me—I don't have to take sides! But what about you, Rod? I know you're Jewish, but not whether you believe in God."

"When I was a little kid, I did in a tit-for-tat way—if you please God, He's good to you, but if you don't, He isn't. Then something happened. I told you my dad died, but I didn't say how. He killed himself, and that killed any belief I had in a just God. I guess that makes me an atheist, too."

Nataliya shook her head. "Hardly, Rod. It's not like you don't believe in Zeus or Thor or Vishnu. The only god you reject is the one in the Bible who doles out blessings and curses. So logically, my dear philosopher, if everything in your life seemed blessed, you'd have to be committed to worshipping Him again." Before Rod could answer, Nataliya put two fingers to his lips and said, "Let's enjoy the rest of our evening."

They tarried at the restaurant until Rod took her to the station to make the late train. As Nataliya was about to board it, he pulled her to him and kissed her for the first time. From her seat by the window, she blew him a kiss back as the train departed. Driving to the dorm, he reveled in how magical the evening had been. It would have been perfect, he thought, except for Nataliya's conclusion concerning his conception of God—with all the philosophical training he'd had, he considered himself more sophisticated than that. When he got to his room, he opened up to Louis, who'd ditched Judaism as "reactionary claptrap" (though without informing his family—God's wrath was one thing, his father's another).

"Louis," Rod confessed, taking a deep breath, "I had dinner tonight with Nataliya, and she said something that's really bothering me. She told me that while she's an atheist I'm not, because I'm still hung up on Judaism's God."

Louis unexpectedly replied with the same kindheartedness as when he'd offered eight-year-old Ricky a pencil in elementary school. "Belief in some deity isn't a problem in itself. Lots of people have a relationship with God like the one they have with the number pi: they believe that it exists, even that it's infinite, but that it makes absolutely no difference to their lives on a day-to-day basis. It's only when somebody's theism gets mixed up with a commitment to some religion or tribe that it runs into trouble. Remember that Judaism baloney they fed us in Hebrew school about God giving the Holy Land to Abraham and his descendants? Look what that led to when Jews drove out and murdered thousands of Palestinians to establish the state of Israel."

Rod didn't know how to respond, supposing that Louis's leftist thinking had gotten the better of him again. Still, he had no rebuttal to Louis's portrayal of Israel's founding or to Nataliya's characterization of his notion of God. After a restless night, he got up early and almost ran to the plaza outside the administration building where the Edwards Students for Israel had an information table. No one had yet manned it, but Rod saw a lone flyer left from the previous day:

Operation Legacy: Discover Your Heritage!
United Jewish Fund Undergrad Summer Tour of Europe and Israel
Space Limited, Scholarships Available

Rod grabbed the leaflet and raced back to his dorm to phone the number on it. He'd take a pleasure trip to Europe—Who knew? Maybe he'd get to see Spinoza's old house!—and then he'd journey to Israel, where a pilgrimage to the promised land might lead to the truth about it, God, and himself.

XII

He came back from Israel all Jewed up.
. . . Which was exactly what Gil Gorn wanted. The trip was his brainchild, and when he'd conceived it, he hadn't planned it as a sightseeing tour. Instead, he'd mapped it out as a *mission*. "Welcome to boot camp, gentlemen!" he greeted Rod and the other nineteen recruits. "By the time I'm finished with you, you'll be prepared to spearhead campus fundraising campaigns on behalf of the Jewish people's survival. Your training will consist of my leading you along a route that retraces the course of Jews' recent history, from the Holocaust to the Six-Day War. It's a transit commencing with terror and culminating in triumph. —*Questions*?" Not a hand went up. Even if Gil's bombast hadn't intimidated the inductees, they were too cowed to call him "Rabbi," a title he detested as he explained late one night in his Amsterdam hotel room to Rod and a few of the others.

"In 1942, I had a pulpit, and by that time, news of the Nazis' mass killings of Jews had leaked out. At that month's meeting of the Board of Rabbis, I urged the assembled *rebbe'im* to issue a joint statement from our pulpits the next *Shabbos* calling on our congregants to write and phone their representatives in Congress as well as the president to stop the genocide. And how did my so-called colleagues respond? They continued *noshing* on their tuna fish sandwiches—God forbid they should violate *kashrus*!—and unanimously rejected my proposal. 'What would our synagogue boards and membership think?' they *geschreied*. 'It might look as if Jews were disloyal by criticizing our country's leaders during wartime!' The next day I resigned from my congregation and enlisted in the US Army. First as a grunt and then through a battlefield commission, I did more to lick Hitler than all the sermons delivered by those American Jewish vicars! Three years after the war ended, I re-enlisted, but this time with the *Haganah* to fight for Israel's

independence. Later, I joined the United Jewish Fund, and in the fall of 1967,
I created these missions to produce future generations of American Jewish
leaders who would never again sit by while Jews were being slaughtered. I
believe that's my destiny, gentlemen, and now it's yours, too." Inspired by
a newly released movie, Rod and the rest of the squad started calling Gil
"Patton" behind his back—though Gil likely wouldn't have minded if they'd
addressed him like that to his face.

The mission's first stop was the Netherlands, and Rod supposed he'd
set out for Spinoza's house; instead, he got taken to Anne Frank's. Inside
it, Gil told the group, "The Franks fled to Amsterdam from Frankfurt, and
for seven years, they were safe—*until* the Nazis invaded the Netherlands.
So the Franks moved to the secret room we're standing in now, where they
remained safe for another few years—*until* the SS broke down the door.
So what's the moral of the story? Hiding's not an option for Jews!" When
Rod recalled how, from the Kyrchyks to Judge Hammond, anti-Semites had
singled him out, he had to agree.

From Holland, the mission's participants, like Anne Frank and so
many other Dutch Jews, were transported by train to Auschwitz—albeit
not jammed in an airless boxcar. At the camp's gates, Gil pointed to a sign
above them that said, "*Arbeit Macht Frei.*" Surveying his band of leaders-
in-training, he asked, "Any of you know what that means?" Mitchell, a guy
in the outfit who'd majored in German, piped up, "Work makes you free!"

"Yeah—you were free when the work killed you," Gil said.

After that, Rod and the others filed in silence along the camp's rows of
barbed wire, between its tiers of rotting prisoner bunks, and finally, like the
millions of Jews who'd preceded them there, into one of its series of deathly
still gas chambers. "Look at where the walls meet the ceiling," Gil ordered
them. "See those scratches in the concrete? They're where the victims tried
to claw their way out when the Zyklon-B began pouring in." While the
group stared at the gouges, Gil slipped out and slammed the chamber's steel
door behind him. Its clang made the boys shudder.

Moments later, Gil reentered and, like a general exhorting his troops
before battle, paced back and forth in front of them while his voice grew
louder and louder. "Did the Gentiles make a peep when the Nuremberg
Laws were passed? No!" he growled. "Did they raise a squawk when the
Franks and the six million were slaughtered? No!" he snarled. "Did the
sainted Franklin Roosevelt even spare a few planes to bomb the tracks to
this abattoir to slow down the trains shipping Jews here like cattle? *No!*" he
bellowed. "Today, though, we don't have to rely on the *goyim*'s good graces!"
he roared as he shoved the gas chamber door open. "Unlike the victims,
we've got an Israel to go to!"

Up to that point, Rod had felt, at best, like an American tourist escorted from one place of interest to another and, at worst, like a Holocaust victim dragged from one horror to the next. Now, as he prepared for his arrival in Israel, he felt he was on the verge of conducting himself into the Jews' story as a figure who'd significantly affect it. He peppered Gil with questions about Israel and devoured books about it that other students had brought with them. When the mission finally landed at Ben-Gurion Airport, he led it in singing *Hatikvah*, as if he'd at last reached the homeland he'd yearned for. When he stepped onto the tarmac, the light seemed brighter and the Uzi-armed Jews braver than any he'd ever beheld. When he was lodged at an outlying Tel Aviv hostel, its Spartan furnishings and meals gave Rod visions of an army barracks in which he could picture himself as an IDF soldier. After dinner that night, he went out for a stroll and walked straight into the racket of honking horns in the streets and ear-piercing newsboys on the sidewalks. One sound, though, was missing: the low, background thrum of the anti-Semitism he'd grown up with, like when his father finally shelled out for a new car, and he'd notice the old clunker's faint, familiar rattle suddenly gone. On his way back, Rod passed by a dimly lit alley and glimpsed Mitchell butt-fucking an Arab prostitute. What was shocking to Rod was how little it shocked him. Before he'd left on the mission, he would have stopped dead in his tracks, transfixed by a mixture of surprise and disgust. Now, he took it in stride. Here, things were different; here, Jews were the majority; here, Jews were *in charge*.

From Tel Aviv, the mission embarked for Jericho, site of the ancient Israelites' first beachhead in the promised land and within whose squalid environs cowering Palestinian refugees attested to present-day Israel's power. From there, the contingent headed out for Masada, the Jews' own Alamo where every man, woman, and child died valiantly rather than surrender. Next, the company advanced north along the Bet She'an Valley before decamping at a kibbutz whose founders had intentionally chosen a malarial swamp, the very place in their eyes to bring forth a hardier strain of Jew, one able to fight off much more than disease-bearing mosquitoes. An old-timer recounted how during the settlement's early days, one of its girls had been raped on her way home from town. "When we caught the Arab who did it, we gave him our own kind of *bris*, and that was it for his love life!" The unit continued through the Galilee to the Golan and a burnt-out Syrian tank from the Six-Day War that Rod and his cohorts got off the bus to piss on. Then, like countless pilgrims before them, they set forth on the last leg of their journey, ascending the winding road to Jerusalem. With its antique walls, arched gates, and immense gold dome rising like a shimmering bubble toward heaven, Rod understood why the city had been repeatedly destroyed: who could possibly want to share it?

Marching at the front of the column, Gil led it through each of Jerusalem's ancient quarters, from the Armenian with its black-robed priests to the Christian and its candlelit altars to the Muslim, whose spice stalls' sweet fragrances mingled with butcher shops' putrid odors of camel heads decaying on hooks. Eventually, the detachment emerged onto a broad, sun-splashed plaza immediately below two massive mosques, the Dome of the Rock cradling the gold cupola Rod had spied from afar and beside it, the silver-vaulted Al-Aqsa.

"All this used to be *ours!*" Gil declared with a sweep of his arm. "Hundreds of thousands of Jews brought their sacrifices to the temples that stood here, and hundreds of thousands of Jews died defending them both times they were razed. Nothing remained but what the *goyim* spent the past twenty centuries calling 'The Wailing Wall.' But thanks to a reborn Israel, it's got its rightful name back. 'The *Western* Wall' is how it's known today, no longer a byword for Jews' weakness, but a sign of their strength. Run to that wall, men," bawled their commander, "and lay hands on your history!"

Everyone rushed off except Rod.

"What are you waiting for, Zieglitz?!" Gil barked.

Even if it was Gil who was giving the order, Rod wouldn't obey—neither Spinoza nor his own life would let him. A moment before, he couldn't have imagined raising his voice to Gil; now, the fury in it seemed natural. "I'm not going up to that Jewish Lourdes! I don't believe in that fairy-tale garbage, and I'm not about to go there and pray—there's no God to connect with!"

Gil stood his ground. "I'm not religious either, Zieglitz. But that's not the point. Israelis fought and died to retake that piece of real estate. You owe it to them and the Jewish people to honor their heroism. Now get going!"

As Rod trudged across the plaza, an elderly Chassid thrust a black cardboard *yarmulke* at him. He grudgingly took it and gazed up at the mammoth stones, wondering how many other unwilling human beings had been dragged there to stack them. "*Well, Zieglitz?!*" he heard Gil's voice boom from behind him. Not merely reluctant now, but resentful, he reached out and touched the Wall.

And something touched him back. Less than a jolt and more than a shiver, a kind of tug pulled at his fingertips, then his hand, forearm, and shoulder until it caught hold of his whole body. He didn't know what it was; he only knew his life would never be the same.

Within days of returning to Edwards, Rod began fulfilling Gil's charge on the mission's first day by starting work on a campaign dedicated to the survival of Jews in Israel and any place else Jewish lives were in peril. He initially considered having a kickoff event, where he'd give one of Gil's patented stemwinder pitches. He quickly scrapped the idea, though, figuring that the bulk of Edwards's Jews were either too assimilated or too apathetic to show up. The most they'd managed to collect previously had been a measly two hundred dollars, and then, only by employing a gimmick—make a donation, get a kazoo. Rod by contrast used handpicked lieutenants to solicit commitments door-to-door. By the campaign's second week, it had raised over $15,000 with only a few students refusing to give. Schwartz, who lived a flight above Rod, was among those who'd said no. Hearing about it outside commons at lunch from the volunteer Schwartz had stiffed, Rod responded, "I'll get a pledge card from my room and hit up that shithead myself!"

As a senior, Rod had rated a single room, which was just as well since, after his visit to Israel, Louis had stopped speaking to him, because Rod couldn't keep himself from talking about the mission, and Louis couldn't stand any more "Zionist propaganda." Rod had just fished a card from his desk and was about to waylay Schwartz when Nataliya showed up at his door.

"What's going on, Rod?" she demanded.

While he'd launched the campaign as soon as he could, he'd postponed calling her. The niceties of Jewish law and matrilineal descent aside, she was a half-breed at best, a traitor at worst, and either way, somebody with no allegiance to the Jewish people. It had taken the life-changing experiences of that summer to make him care about Jews' fate. How could he expect her to? "It's complicated," he told her.

"Fine, invite me in—I've got all the time in the world," she said.

After she sat down, Rod began rehashing where the mission had gone, but he'd only gotten as far as Auschwitz when Nataliya interrupted, "But what's any of this have to do with us—*with me*? Remember? I believe in God even less than you do!"

Rod responded, "*So what*? The gas chambers didn't have a separate line for Jewish theists and another for Jewish nonbelievers. When it came to killing Jews, the Nazis only had one line! Even if you don't think of yourself as Jewish, Nataliya, it doesn't matter. The Jew-haters always will! Look, I've got to go hit up some jerk before he gets away."

Nataliya only smiled. "Good, I'll go with you. Maybe you'll make more sense."

As they went upstairs, Rod ran through his *spiel* in his head: Jews in Eastern Europe need money to ransom their way out; Jews in Israel need funds to resettle them; Jews at Edwards need to come to the rescue with fifty bucks apiece.

Schwartz cut Rod off before he could get through his first sentence. "Hold on there, Superyid—I've got a lab to go to. Here's a sawbuck. Keep the change."

"And you keep your damn conscience money!" Rod rebuffed him as he grabbed the ten, tore it in half, and flung the pieces in Schwartz's face.

Nataliya cringed, expecting a fistfight. To her astonishment, Schwartz went to his dresser, slid open the top drawer, and took out some more bills. "I didn't realize it was so important," he said sheepishly, offering Rod five crisp twenties.

"If you can give a hundred in cash, you can afford a pledge that's a lot more," Rod replied coolly.

Schwartz meekly took the pledge card Rod gave him and filled it out for three hundred dollars. Rod snatched the card back and muttered an ungenerous "Thanks." Going downstairs with Nataliya, he said, "And *that's* how it's done!"

"But weren't you worried you'd lose the money he originally offered you?" Nataliya asked.

Rod grinned and shook his head. "It was only ten bucks, Nataliya. I'd have replaced it with a ten of my own if that's how things had ended."

"I've never seen you like this before, Rod."

"Like how?"

"So single-minded . . . so . . . unbending."

"When it comes to Jewish survival, Nataliya, there's no way to be anything *but* unbending! You know what bending over has gotten Jews in the past? Nothing but getting fucked up the ass!"

"Nice language, Zieglitz!" he heard Louis call up.

Rod answered Louis's sarcasm with his own. "Haven't heard from you in a while, Chazen—Come to make a contribution?"

"Come to deliver a message. Your mom's been trying to reach you all morning, and when she couldn't, she had the dean call me."

"What's this about?" Rod asked.

"How should I know, Zieglitz? —Pick up the phone and find out," Louis said, holding out a slip of paper with a number written on it

The only thing Rod recognized about the number was its Excelsior area code. After following him into his room, Nataliya and Louis looked on as he dialed it.

"This is Leah at Congregation Beth Shalom," a voice answered.

"My name's Zieglitz. I got a message to call you."

"Oh, yes. Rabbi Mishkin's been waiting to hear from you. Let me connect you."

Seconds later, another voice came on the line. "Hello, Rick, this is Sam Mishkin."

"First of all, it's Rod, not Rick. —Why are you having me call you?"

Correcting himself, Rabbi Mishkin went on, "Forgive me, Rod. I was just going by what your mother told me."

". . . Is she okay?" Rod asked apprehensively.

"She's fine, but she needs you to fly back here."

"Why—what's wrong?" Rod said, increasingly anxious.

"I'll tell you when I meet you at the airport, Rod. I'll be wearing a *kippah*."

"What's the matter, Rod?" Nataliya asked, seeing how his hand trembled as he put down the receiver.

"They wouldn't tell me—just that I have to catch the first flight home."

"Do you want me to go with you?" she said.

"How can you do that? What would you do for clothes? Besides, what would your parents say?"

"Let me handle that. I just need to drop by my place on the way to the airport."

"I'll get my car," Rod replied.

"No, I'll drive you in mine," Louis said to Rod, his animus towards Israel overpowered by their friendship. While Louis went for his car, Rod booked a flight, phoned Leah with its arrival time, and hurriedly stuffed a suitcase with everything from jeans to a blazer.

"Thanks for this, Louis," he said as he threw his bag in the trunk. "You'd do the same for me," Louis replied before taking off like a maniac for Queens. "I won't be gone long," Nataliya said when they got there. A little later, she returned with a small grip, telling Rod as she got in, "Mama and Papa both helped me pack—they want you to know they hope everything's all right." At the airport drop-off, Louis unlocked the trunk, saying, "Just let me know when you're coming back, Rod. Whenever it is, I'll be here."

After their plane touched down in Excelsior around six, Rod and Nataliya were among the first to get off. Awaiting them at the gate was a plump, balding man with a salt-and-pepper moustache and a multicolored knit *kippah*. Running up to him, Rod said, "So now that I'm home, will you tell me what's going on?"

Rabbi Mishkin turned to Nataliya. "I'm sorry, but I didn't get your name—"

"It's Nataliya Lubyatko," Rod broke in. "For the last time, what's happened?"

Rabbi Mishkin put his arm around Rod's shoulders. "I have some news that's best delivered in person. Your mother's not here to tell you herself, because she's in Huppertsville comforting your grandmother. I'm afraid that your grandfather Jack has died—"

"But Jack's never sick!" Rod cried.

Rabbi Mishkin's voice grew much softer. "It wasn't an illness—it was an accident. From what your mother told me, he was out early this morning making a wall on his property higher. They had a heavy rain last night, and his ladder slipped in the mud. Apparently, a stone he was mounting on the wall fell on his head and killed him."

Any sophisticated philosophical statement Rod might have uttered about God, life, and death was instantly strangled by tentacles of grief that seized him from a previous sudden loss of somebody close. "So where's your God now, Rabbi? Goddammit, Jack didn't deserve this!" Rod howled as tears rolled down his face.

Rabbi Mishkin held him closer. "Your mother's asked me to take you to Huppertsville. She said she called me because one of the synagogue's past rabbis had married her and your father, and she couldn't think of anyone else in town to come meet you. I told her I didn't mind—that's what I'm there for."

When they got to *Casa Futura* shortly past eight, Gene embraced Rod at the door. "Jack was such a good man," he said before turning to Rabbi Mishkin and introducing himself. "Hello, Rabbi, I'm Gene Williams, Madge's husband. We're so grateful for everything you've done."

"Compared to Rod's friend here, Nataliya Lubyatko, I haven't done anything. She's come all the way from New York to support him."

"Where's Mom, Gene?" Rod asked, letting go of Nataliya's hand so he could take their luggage from the rabbi.

"Upstairs trying to comfort your grandmother. I'll tell them you're here. Why don't you take everyone to the atrium? They'll be more comfortable there."

As Gene left, Rod escorted Rabbi Mishkin and Nataliya to the mansion's two-story glassed-in courtyard where a half dozen potted palms surrounded a central fountain whose pale yellow tiles were etched with green and blue arabesques. The three of them took seats on the atrium's padded, wicker couch, and after a while, Gene appeared on the balcony above them with Madge. The second she saw Rod, she darted down the terrazzo steps to him.

"Daddy's gone!" she said, drawing him close before spotting Nataliya and pulling away.

Echoing Rabbi Mishkin, Rod said, "This is my friend from New York, Nataliya Lubyatko. Without her support, I don't know how I would've made it through today."

Madge clasped Nataliya to her. "Thank you for looking after my boy."

"And let's not forget Rabbi Mishkin," Gene interjected.

"Rabbi, I can't tell you how much I appreciate all the trouble you've gone to," Madge responded.

Rabbi Mishkin shrugged, saying, "If you can't call a rabbi at a time like this, Madge, when would you ever call one?"

Madge let out a long sigh. "I've got another favor to ask you. Mother's in terrible shape. She won't stop crying, and she won't eat or drink anything. But she's a diabetic—she at least needs some juice. Would you please go up and speak to her?"

"Of course," Rabbi Mishkin answered.

Rod hadn't come all this way to be a bystander—he had to do *something*; he owed it to Mom, to Dee-Dee, but most of all, to Jack. "I'll bring the orange juice!" he burst out.

Rabbi Mishkin nodded and said, "After you get it, you, your mother, and I will go up to your grandmother's room, and maybe together, we can get her to calm down. For now, it's probably best if Gene and Nataliya stayed here. There'll be a bit less commotion that way."

Once Rod came back from the kitchen with the juice, he, Mom, and Rabbi Mishkin climbed the atrium's staircase to Dina's bedroom.

"Go away!" Dina screamed when Madge knocked on the door.

"Please, Mother . . ." Madge implored her.

"Stay out, Madge!" Dina shrieked.

Ignoring her, Madge let herself in with Rod and the rabbi by her side. When Dina saw Rabbi Mishkin's *kippah*, she said, "I don't want no damn holy Joe! Get him out of here!"

Undeterred, Rabbi Mishkin came nearer Dina's bed and said quietly, "I'm Sam Mishkin, Mrs. Apter, and I'll make a deal with you. Drink some juice, and if, after that, you still want me to go, I will."

Dina defiantly swiped the glass away from Rod and swigged down the juice, indifferent to spilling any on the bed or the rug. "I kept my part of the bargain—now keep yours and get out!" she said to Rabbi Mishkin, who furtively motioned Madge and Rod to leave them. An hour later, he descended the stairway with Dina on his arm. Halfway down, she called out to Rod, "Who's that with you?"

This time, the words were Rod's own. "This is my girlfriend, Nataliya Lubyatko," he called back.

Dina waved Nataliya to her. "Let's have a look at you, honey," she said from the foot of the stairs.

More nervous than she'd ever been for a performance, Nataliya walked over trying to muster all the poise she'd garnered from years of ballet. "Mrs.

Apter, I'm so sorry about your husband. Rod's told me what he meant to you and how much you've both meant to him."

"This one's a keeper," Dina winked to Rod. "And little girl, none of this 'Mrs. Apter' stuff. You call me Dina like everyone else." Taking Rabbi Mishkin's hand, she went on, "So, everybody, this is what me and Rabbi Sam have decided. Jack's funeral will be at the rabbi's temple the day after tomorrow—the funeral parlor in town where Jack's at now ain't big enough for all the folks who'll want to come. After the service, we'll bury Jack in a cemetery that Rabbi Sam says has a section just for Jews. As far as I'm concerned, anywhere's okay so long as it's not the damn graveyard here!"

Rabbi Mishkin looked at his watch and said, "I think Dina's given me enough for Jack's eulogy, but if anyone else thinks of something you'd like me to say, feel free to give me a call at the synagogue tomorrow. Seeing as how late it is, I probably ought to get going if I want to get any sleep before then."

After everyone showed the rabbi out and thanked him again, Madge turned to Dina and asked, "What did the rabbi say to you, Mother? You seem so much better."

"That's between the rabbi and me. Part of it, though, you all need to hear. Rabbi Sam asked what advice Jack would give me at a tough time like this. I said it'd probably be something Jack picked up from his prizefighting days. 'When you get knocked down,' he always told me, 'you gotta get up off the mat and keep pluggin.'"

Two days later, a hearse transported Jack's body to Excelsior. Dina had been right about holding his funeral there—Rod couldn't believe all the friends that Jack had. Besides Oscar from the diner and Sol from the sporting goods store as well as the dozens of customers Rod had waited on at the grocery or seen at the bars, scores of others attended whom he'd never laid eyes on. He assumed that a close pal of Jack's had sent the enormous garland of white gladiolus draped over his coffin.

The instant Dina saw the card accompanying the wreath, she knew better. "Get that SOB's flowers away from my Jack! That bastard of a liquor distributor did my Jack dirty, and no damn bouquet is going to make it right now." While Gene hustled the arrangement out of sight, Rabbi Mishkin whispered something in Dina's ear. After she'd settled down, he produced two small, black ribbons, pinning one on her dress and the other on Madge's. Recalling Dad's funeral, Rod stood up for his. "Grandchildren don't get one," Rabbi Mishkin said gently as he withdrew a pocketknife and made a rip in each ribbon. "It symbolizes how grief's rent your heart," he explained to Dina and Madge, afterwards asking them to recite with him, "The Lord giveth and the Lord taketh away," a verse, he told them, from Job.

Rod thought back to *Mar* Galston's class when he'd first heard the story of Job and then to a philosophy of religion course in college when he'd reread it. "Instead of that milquetoast verse surrendering to God," Rod murmured under his breath, "they should have chosen one that challenges Him like 'He wounds me for no reason!'" Seething, Rod didn't pay any attention to the service until Rabbi Mishkin mentioned his name at the start of Jack's eulogy.

"When I told Rod that his grandfather had died," Rabbi Mishkin began, "he responded in ways that were deeply Jewish. Like Abraham, who questioned the fairness of God's destroying Sodom and Gomorrah's righteous along with their wicked, Rod challenged the justice of Jack's death by protesting that he didn't deserve it. And who could argue with that? Jack was someone who loved life and couldn't get enough of it. More important, he loved sharing it with others. He loved driving Madge and her friends to movie grand openings. He loved teaching Rod how to play baseball. Most of all, he loved being in love with Dina in a marriage that spanned fifty years. And the sad, somber faces filling this sanctuary now are a testament to how many people likewise loved him. No wonder Rod reacted to Jack's death by bursting out, '*Goddammit!*'

"I know, I know—a word like that isn't supposed to be used in a place like this. But remember what I said earlier about Rod's responses being deeply Jewish? 'Goddammit,' it turns out, hearkens back to the kind of utterance so ancient we hear strains of it in the Bible. It comes from a curse that was originally 'God doom it,' and it's what people used to say when they'd reached the limits of their power to overcome something awful in their lives. Then, they'd call on God's power for aid and comfort. Now, with Jack's death, we've come to the limits of our power. And yet, it's precisely at those limits where Jewish tradition has a response whose depth matches Rod's when he cried out to me, 'So, Rabbi, where's your God now?'

"'Right here among us!' Judaism answers. As Jews, we're taught that it's in the presence of the community of the Jewish people that we encounter God's presence, too. It's why we require a minyan, the quorum of ten signifying community, to recite Mourner's Kaddish when, after a loved one's death, we find ourselves at life's limits, bereft and powerless. So as we rise now for Kaddish, let those who loved Jack call on the power of this community and this community's God to mend their broken hearts and give them the strength to go on—or as Jack would have put it, to 'get up off the mat and keep pluggin.'"

As Rod got to his feet, wiping his eyes, he knew he'd found a rabbi unlike the feckless ones Gil despised or the windbag in Medina. For the first time in his life, he'd met a rabbi he could call by that Jewish title for teacher and mean it.

XIII

———

"**I**t sure ain't like it used to be," Dina sighed.

"No, Dee-Dee, it sure isn't," Rod replied wistfully as he gazed out at the parking lot where the only vehicle to be seen was theirs.

It was Thanksgiving vacation, and with Jack gone and Mom and Gene off on a cruise, he'd returned to Huppertsville so Dee-Dee wouldn't be alone her first holiday since Jack's death. She'd sent a stock boy named Wayne to fetch him at the Excelsior airport in the Imperial Jack had bought the month before he'd died. Still, even with Rod there, she couldn't bear having Thanksgiving dinner at *Casa Futura*. "Let's eat at the Vagabond Inn outside town," she told him as she handed him the keys to the car.

The motel's dining room was empty, save for a surly adolescent who met them at its entrance. "Meal's $14.95, self-service," she said, listlessly tilting her head toward the stack of cardboard trays, paper plates, and plastic utensils. After Dina and Rod each took a set, they moved down the line of the restaurant's festive offerings: processed sliced turkey, instant mashed potatoes, reconstituted gravy, canned cranberries, refrigerator biscuits, and, for dessert, Jell-O chocolate pudding.

"I wish your girl could've come with you," Dina said as she and Rod set down their near-empty trays on a table.

"I invited her, Dee-Dee, but she said she'd miss too many rehearsals for a big performance she has around Christmas."

"At least you'll be seeing her again . . ." Dee-Dee exhaled, her voice trailing off. "The way I've been feeling lately, I've been thinking maybe I should go see Rabbi Sam. Services tomorrow night might be just what I need."

They weren't, though, because Rabbi Mishkin didn't lead them or give the sermon. That evening turned out to be "Sisterhood Shabbat," during which a string of blue-haired matrons came to the *bimah*, mechanically repeating, "We continue on the next page with the English responsive reading." After the congregation's third half-hearted effort, Rod leaned over to Dee-Dee and whispered, "Sounds more like a *despondent* reading to me!"

Even so, Rabbi Mishkin made the trip worth it, going to welcome them before he went over to anybody else once the service ended. "Dina and Rod, what a nice surprise! If you can stay a while, I'd love to catch up."

"I got no place to be—" Dina answered as the Sisterhood officers hustled the rabbi off to the pastries they'd baked.

When Rabbi Mishkin at last slipped away, he found a gaggle of *yentas* pressing Dina to come to their meetings and pestering Rod to call up their granddaughters. Wading through the cluster of women, the rabbi told them, "As usual, ladies, your babka and strudel were out of this world! Now, though, if you don't mind, I'd like to spend some time with our guests."

"But Rabbi . . ." the women protested with more fervor than the congregation had mustered in all its responsive readings combined.

"So, how's Nataliya?" Rabbi Mishkin asked Rod once he'd whisked him and Dina into his office.

"She's fine, thanks."

"What about Madge and Gene?"

"Seems like they're fine, too," Dina answered.

"And what about *you*?" Rabbi Mishkin asked her.

"I keep thinking of how you said at Jack's funeral . . . ," Dina faltered, beginning to weep, "that he'd want us to keep pluggin'. I try, but it's hard!"

Handing her a tissue from a box on his desk, Rabbi Mishkin said softly, "I know it is, Dina, and so does Jewish tradition. The Talmud recounts how after a two-year debate, the Sages decided it would have been better for us not to have been born. But then they added an important caveat: given that we *have* been born, all we can do is go forward!"

As Dina dabbed her eyes, Rabbi Mishkin turned to Rod and inquired, "Have you made any plans about what you'll do after you graduate?"

"I've applied to Edwards's philosophy PhD program. It's one of the only places that focuses on big questions like the meaning of life instead of on narrow ones like the meaning of words. I could care less about the theoretical implications of 'ought'! That Talmud story of yours really hits the nail on the head. To me, it's the issues having to do with our existence that matter."

"In that case, have you thought about rabbinical school?" asked Rabbi Mishkin.

"I'm not religious!" Rod answered, reprising the objection he'd given Gil at the Wall.

Rabbi Mishkin shook his head and replied, "Neither was I when I started seminary. I went for another reason—to learn about Judaism. Let me ask you a question: if anti-Semitism disappeared tomorrow, what explanation would you give for being a Jew then?"

Rod realized he didn't have an answer. From the Kyrchyks of his boyhood, to the Courtney and Tom of his adolescence, to the Cossacks, Nazis, and Arabs of his history, his Jewish identity was nothing more than a scar left by malevolent others, whether real or imagined. Even what most literally marked him as a Jew, his circumcision, was the work of somebody else.

Rabbi Mishkin opened a desk drawer and tore off a page from a notepad inside. "Here's the seminary's phone number in New York—even with all the years that have gone by, I still know it by heart. Call and have the registrar send you an application and set you up with an interview. Obviously, I'd be happy to serve as a reference."

"And I thought I knew how to make a pitch!" Rod laughed.

"Whatever you settle on, Rod, I want you to know you can always call me. That goes for you, too, Dina."

Breaking into a smile, she said to the rabbi, "I just knew that seeing you would do us good!"

The next day Rod phoned Nataliya.

"Is something wrong? —Is Dina okay?" she asked him.

"Everything's fine, Nataliya. It's just that last night, I saw Rabbi Mishkin, and we talked about my going to rabbinical school. I called to get your opinion."

"I think you'd make an excellent rabbi! You're smart and sensitive, and on top of that, if you go to the seminary, you'll be in New York with me!"

Rod flew back to Edwards Sunday afternoon, and before going to class Monday morning, he called the seminary.

"We've already begun reviewing candidates," Irmgard Fitcher, the registrar, told him.

"Have I missed the deadline?" Rod asked her.

"We have rolling admissions. Just spell your name, and give me your address, and I'll send you an application."

"But your deadline?"

"We keep going until the entering class is filled."

"How much longer do you think that will be?"

"No idea. —Do you want me to take your information or not?"

After Rod gave it to her, Mrs. Fitcher hung up, leaving him in the dark about how much time he had to apply.

Dismayed, Rod dialed Rabbi Mishkin, who told him, "Don't let Irmgard throw you. She's been around so long, she could have been Methuselah's prom date! Just make certain that when you go for your interview, you wear a *kippah*."

The seminary application finally arrived three weeks later. To Rod's relief, completing its few pages took virtually no time, let alone thought, and he mailed it back Special Delivery. A week passed before he heard from Mrs. Fitcher. "Be here tomorrow morning at eight o'clock sharp. You'll meet with the Admissions Committee and a psychiatrist."

Rod wasn't sure he'd heard her correctly. "A psychiatrist?" he repeated as Mrs. Fitcher hung up on him once more.

By the time he found a parking space on the street and had hiked the six blocks to the seminary's gated entrance the next morning, Rod was so rattled he had trouble holding his hand steady enough to keep his knitted *kippah* from Israel firmly in place. Glancing at his watch, he saw it was 7:50. "Pardon me, I have an appointment—" he told the security guard on duty, who, spotting the *kippah*, yawned and waved him on through.

"If they had *yarmulke*s on, he'd probably let the whole SS in," Rod thought to himself.

As he wandered the corridors in search of the right office, he couldn't find anyone to help him—the building seemed empty except for the occasional strains of the same adenoidal *davening* he'd grown up with in Medina. When he finally stumbled on the door that said "Registrar," it was eight on the dot.

"Cutting it a little close, aren't we?" said Mrs. Fitcher as she opened the door to answer Rod's knock. After she'd gestured him to a low metal stool wedged between two file cabinets, she got up and left, only to return a half hour later sipping a cup of coffee. Even if she'd brought one for Rod, he wouldn't have been able to drink it: his butterflies had become wildebeests. At nine, just as he was going to ask Mrs. Fitcher where a men's room was, a goateed man with thick, owlish glasses walked in.

"I'm Dr. Demshets," he introduced himself tersely to Rod, stuffing the *yarmulke* he'd been wearing into his three-piece suit's vest pocket while afterwards telling Mrs. Fitcher just as curtly to wait outside. Removing a pen and notebook from his jacket and flipping to the page where he'd scrawled Rod's name, Dr. Demshets said, "So, Mr. Zieglitz, why don't you tell me something about yourself?"

"What would you like to know?" Rod answered.

Dr. Demshets jotted down Rod's response and mumbled, "Hmm . . . evasive." Looking up, he asked, "And how, Mr. Zieglitz, would you describe your relationship with your mother?"

At first, Rod was glad he hadn't been asked about Dad, but as question after question focused on his feelings toward Mom, he grew increasingly annoyed. He'd taken Psych 101, knew all about Oedipus, and could guess where the shrink was headed.

"So you've attended an all-male college?" Dr. Demshets commented.

"That's right," Rod said.

"And now you're applying to an institution that's all-male, too?"

"Looks like it."

"And according to your application, Mr. Zieglitz, I see that last summer you went on an all-male trip . . ." Dr. Demshets paused, put down his pen down, hunched forward, and asked in a low voice, "Have some sex?"

"No thanks—I just ate."

"I think I've got all that I need!" Dr. Demshets snapped, shoving the pen and notebook back in his jacket before stalking out. When Mrs. Fitcher still hadn't come back forty-five minutes later, Rod started walking around her office, and as he paced past her desk, he noticed an entry in her open daily planner: "Zieglitz, Admissions Committee, 9:30, Room 210." Rod panicked—it was already well past ten! He sprinted up the stairs to the second floor where he ran back and forth until he finally decided to knock on an unmarked door between Rooms 209 and 211. A voice answered, "Enter!" and inside, he came upon a graybeard with a black rayon *yarmulke* and an equally elderly woman sitting next to a platter of cookies.

"Since you're late, most of our interview panel has already left," said the old man.

Rod replied, "I'm sorry, but nobody told me the time to be here, and then I had trouble finding—"

"Excuses don't make for a good first impression, Mr. Zieglitz. I'm Rabbi Dr. Crannack, the seminary's rector, and this is Mrs. Lutz, President of the Board of Trustees."

"Would you like a cookie?" Mrs. Lutz asked Rod.

Before Rod could answer, Rabbi Dr. Crannack broke in, "While we await the arrival of another interviewer, a rabbi whom I believe you know, I have some questions for you."

Feeling more confident now that Rabbi Mishkin would be there for support, Rod replied, "Please, ask anything you want."

"Let's start with questions about your observance of Sabbath prohibitions. Do you refrain from driving or riding on *Shabbat*?"

"No."

"Do you refrain from spending money?"

"No."

"Do you refrain from using electricity?"

"No," Rod answered again. Frustrated by Crannack's questions about all the *mitzvot* he hadn't observed, he tried to change the subject by citing one he thought he'd performed. "I led a fundraising campaign for Israel," he said.

"Raising money for the seminary is what matters most to us, Mr. Zieglitz. —Isn't that right, Mrs. Lutz?"

"Would you like a cookie?" Mrs. Lutz asked Rod.

Just then, the door opened, and Crannack said, "Ah! Our guest rabbi has joined us."

Rod turned around, expecting Rabbi Mishkin. Instead, he saw the Medina rabbi.

"Good to see you again . . . Rick, isn't it?"

Stunned, Rod didn't correct him.

Taking a seat at the far end of the table, the Medina rabbi went on, "I still remember your *bar mitzvah* speech. You were right about one thing— your grandfather Irv, of blessed memory, was a religious, learned Jew. Unfortunately, his knowledge seems not to have been passed on, as evidenced by how Jewishly ignorant you and your mother both were. So, to be fair, I'll ask you a question I generally reserve for Hebrew school children: What's your favorite Bible story?"

Rod could brush off how he'd been mistreated all morning, but he couldn't disregard the insult to Mom. He looked the Medina rabbi in the eye and answered, "Well, if you really want to know the story I like best in the Bible, I guess it's the one where the guy gets the nails in his hands."

"I see you haven't changed a bit," said the Medina rabbi.

"Neither have you, asshole," said Rod under his breath.

"You're excused, Mr. Zieglitz!" said Crannack, who, sitting closer to Rod, heard him.

"Would you like a cookie?" Mrs. Lutz asked Rod on his way out.

As soon as Rod got back to Edwards, he phoned Rabbi Mishkin and told him what had happened, concluding his report by saying, "I'm sorry, Rabbi. I hope you're not too disappointed."

"Whatever for, Rod? How many people do you think want to be rabbis these days? A century ago, bright Jewish boys aspired to be heads of *yeshivas*, but now they strive to be doctors, lawyers, and CEOs. You have to understand that the seminary's not Edwards—it's not like they have so many applicants they can afford to be choosy. Believe me, they take everybody!"

Despite Rabbi Mishkin's counsel, Rod immediately called Edwards's grad school after he received its acceptance letter to say he'd be enrolling in its philosophy doctoral program. When he told Nataliya the news, she was overjoyed since he'd still be nearby.

His family's reaction, though, was much less enthusiastic, because they were concerned about his economic future as a philosophy professor.

Hoping to sway him to think about law school, Gene offered Rod a summer job helping out with various office tasks at his law firm. It didn't change Rod's mind, though; from what Rod could see, lawyers' day-to-day work was fairly boring. He nevertheless appreciated the opportunity to drive to Huppertsville every weekend to try and cheer up Dee-Dee, who was still struggling with Jack's death. Some days, he'd cajole her into a ride to Oscar's for dinner, while on others he'd wrangle her into a late afternoon stroll in the park where they'd gone when he was a toddler. One early evening, she told him she wanted to walk down to the meadow. He was amazed she'd go anywhere near the flagstone wall, but he was dumbstruck when she made for the woods.

"Where are you going, Dee-Dee?" he called after her, afraid that between the uneven terrain and her neuropathied toes, she'd stumble. Ignoring him, she kept moving down the slope until she stopped at the Star of David mosaic in the gazebo at the bottom. After Rod caught up with her, she told him, "Now that you're going off to philosophy school, you need to know a couple of things in case I'm not around."

"Don't talk like that, Dee-Dee," Rod said gently.

"Why not? —I'm not getting any younger! If my diabetes don't get me, something else will. I want you to hear what I've got to say before I'm not here anymore to tell you. See this Jewish star? Go ahead and feel around its edges."

Crouching down, Rod pried under the star's notches and cried, "They're loose!" After he tugged harder, the *Magen David* slid open to reveal wads upon wads of hundred-dollar bills. "Where did all this money come from?" he burst out.

Dee-Dee chuckled and said, "Funny, the IRS kept asking Jack the same question. He told me that he'd socked it away here not only to avoid paying more taxes, but in case we had to get hold of some cash fast. From now on if you need any, consider it yours."

Rod merely nodded. He'd never seen so much money in one place.

"As long as we're here, you should know about this gazebo's other big secret," said Dee-Dee.

"You mean about how *Casa Futura*'s previous owner built it for his Jewish wife so she'd have somewhere to pray? Jack said that after she died, her husband—Mackey, I think his name was—sold the place, because he loved her so much he couldn't stand living here without her."

"Mackey wasn't the only man who loved her," said Dee-Dee.

Rod wanted her to stop, suddenly feeling like the little boy who had believed in an all-perfect God, only to have his faith shattered. He didn't want his belief in an infallible Jack destroyed, too. Before he could say anything, though, Dee-Dee continued, "I was so stupid thinking that Jack would change when we got married. Oh, I knew about his girlfriends in all the towns where he'd played ball. I just reckoned that once we got hitched, he'd quit fooling around. In the beginning, he did. Nobody could have asked for a better husband. But almost right after he went into business with that good-for-nothing Mackey, he got involved with Mackey's wife Rose. It's not hard to figure out what Jack saw in her. She was so high-class and educated I couldn't compete, what with my having to drop out of school at eleven to take care of my two little brothers. So what did Rose see in Jack? The same thing I did: *a man*! Sure, Rose may have fallen for Mackey's money, but that didn't last long after he planted her out here in the sticks, and she started to wither on the vine. Then my Jack came along like a ray of sunshine, and she blossomed again until during a cold snap one winter when the temperature hit fifteen below, she got pneumonia and died. Mackey wanted her laid to rest in the graveyard by the meadow, but the ground was froze so hard they couldn't break it up. When it still hadn't gotten above zero by the next week, Mackey took Rose's body back to New Orleans for the funeral. I think Jack kept his treasure buried here under this star because it made him feel closer to the other one lying in the ground down south. It's why I haven't been back here since Jack died—it only makes me wish I'd had his grave dug nearer to home."

Rod envied how Dee-Dee could tell her story without any rancor, since he knew he could never again speak of Jack devoid of a sense of betrayal. Part of him didn't want any of Jack's loot: unearthing it had robbed him of the Jack he'd worshipped. Still, he was getting too old to keep taking Gene's money, and although he hated admitting it, his family's misgivings about a philosopher's prospects weren't unwarranted—Spinoza had been reduced to grinding lenses, and it had led him to an early death. Rod bent over and scooped out several bundles of Jack's cash to pay the grad school tuition.

Two months into the program, Rod wondered whether he'd have been better off joining Louis after their commencement as a *compañero* harvesting sugarcane in Cuba. Between the grad school's Gothic architecture and its students' all-consuming devotion to their research, he felt like he'd entered a monastery with a vow of silence. His coursework left him cold, too. For a compulsory class in symbolic logic, he had to master the forty-one steps of Gödel's Theorem. Try as he might, he couldn't deduce Step 23 from 22, and so, for the exam, he memorized them all. His test came back marked 100. As he ripped it in two, he groused to himself, "Big deal—I've proved I'm as smart as a Xerox machine!"

His search for a dissertation director was equally frustrating. In the year since he'd applied to the department, its younger faculty had staged a coup, emboldened by all the other places that had enthroned semantics while banishing every rival school of thought. Staff responses to Rod's proposed thesis on Spinoza ranged from muffled snickers to outright disdain as one professor he approached smirked, "*Philosophy of religion?* You ought to try the English Department—they specialize in folklore!"

Fed up, Rod met with the grad school dean about quitting.

The dean tried to persuade him to give the program more time by saying, "I sympathize with you, Mr. Zieglitz. Being a graduate student can be quite lonely and certainly at the outset when you haven't yet immersed yourself in your thesis topic."

"That's the problem, sir. Nobody in the department is interested in my topic."

Smiling, the dean answered patiently, "I can understand your frustration. I had a devil of a time finding an advisor for my work in avant-garde dance. In the end, however, things couldn't have turned out better—I got a degree in administration!"

Rod hadn't dipped into Jack's hoard so he could be a paper pusher, and so he made the kind of assertion his logic class had taught him was beyond empirical refutation. "To be truthful, dean, for the past several nights, I've had a recurring dream where God commands me, 'Get thee out of this place to one that I will show thee.'"

The dean hastily grabbed a piece of letterhead and scribbled a note. "Take this to the bursar, and have him remit the remainder of your tuition."

Telling Mom and Gene he'd dropped out was hard enough for Rod—"What will you do now?" they fussed—and telling Nataliya was even harder—"When will I ever see you?" she moaned—but he dreaded telling Dee-Dee he'd squandered some of Jack's stash. He needn't have worried. When he walked into *Casa Futura* after Wayne drove him there from the airport, she merely shrugged at his news and said, "You got here just in time. Rabbi Sam's temple sent a card to remind me Jack's *yahrzeit* is this Friday night. You can take me to say *Kaddish*."

In the receiving line following the service, Rabbi Mishkin was just as welcoming to Rod as the previous time he'd seen him. "So, how's grad school going?" he asked.

"It didn't work out," Rod answered, blushing.

"What will you do now?"

"I haven't made up my mind yet—maybe look for another philosophy program. I still have my questions about God, religion, and the meaning of life."

"Well, then, how about reconsidering the seminary?"

"I called them to withdraw my application when I got accepted into the Edwards PhD curriculum. Besides, after the interview I had, they'd never take me."

Rabbi Mishkin grinned. "Remember, Rod? They take *everybody!*"

XIV

———

"Could you guys go over that again?" Haggai (formerly "Huey") asked Rod and the other soon-to-be rabbis in their weekly Bible class study group. Haggai's fellow students had already tried to explain the passage to him twice, but like always, it hadn't helped. Looking back, Rod saw Rabbi Mishkin had been right—the seminary *did* take everybody.

Rabbi Mishkin had been wrong about something else, though. The seminary wasn't a place where questions about God, religion, and life might find answers, because as Rod had learned yet again via a liturgy course earlier that day, such questions at the seminary simply weren't welcome.

"In this prayer, we implore *HaShem* to wield His might to crush our enemies," propounded Pupke, the course's instructor.

"But weren't the rabbis who composed that prayer referring to Jews who had different beliefs than they did?" Rod asked.

"And your point, Zieglitz?" Pupke replied.

"Well, do you think that Jews nowadays ought to use it to curse other Jews they disagree with?"

Pupke leaned over Rod's desk and glowered as though he'd been disrespectfully challenged. "Forget about me, Zieglitz. Do *you* think we ought to say it?"

"Invoking some deity's wrath reminds me of when my friends and I ganged up on another little kid our age, and he ran home crying to get his big brother to get even."

"If that's your attitude, Zieglitz, you've got no business being a rabbi!"

"And who made you God to decide that?"

"The same people, Zieglitz, who made me the guy to give you your grade."

When the semester ended, Rod couldn't believe the D- he got from Pupke; from elementary school on, he'd never gotten anything lower than a B+. He thought again about quitting when just as it had every year he'd attended the seminary, something he couldn't name but couldn't shake either, stopped him from leaving.

As an ordination requirement, the seminary made him and his final-year classmates take a High Holy Day pulpit. By playing matchmaker between students lacking rabbinic experience and synagogues short on rabbinic prospects, the school courted future financial contributions from clergy as well as laity, should their brief holy day encounter blossom into a permanent union. The closer the seminary placed a budding rabbi to the New York metropolitan area, the more highly it thought of him. Rod got sent to the Deep South.

"Here's something y'all will appreciate, Rabbi," drawled Morris Nudelman, President of Temple Israel in Rifton, when he spoke with Rod during their first phone call.

"I'm not really a rabbi yet, Mr. Nudelman, since I won't be ordained until the end of the year," Rod said.

Morris gave a little laugh, then replied, "As far as the folks down here are concerned, if you're going to be our rabbi for *yontif*, it's just good manners to address you that way. It'll be different, though, with my nephew Buddy Jacobs, who'll be leading the chanting. Nobody would think of calling him 'Cantor'—he doesn't have the schooling to be one. But what Buddy's got going for him is his daddy Nate, who's married to my wife Harriet's sister, Edna, and in these parts, having my brother-in-law on your side counts for a lot, since Nate's the biggest wheeler-dealer around here. To hear Nate tell it, Buddy's gotten real Jewish at college, and Nate thinks that having him do the cantorial parts will save us a bundle. The congregation's so strapped for cash that we couldn't say 'No.' I suspect Buddy couldn't say 'No,' either. Everybody in Rifton knows that once Nate sets his sights on something, he won't let go till he gets what he wants. I guess that's why he's been so successful in going from the junk business to becoming a real estate tycoon. Anyway, Rabbi, having Buddy as cantor will sure take a load off you, what with me tooting the *shofar* like I always do and one of our old-timers doing the Torah and *Haftarah* readings. —Oh, and get this, Rabbi! Every fall, Rifton has a crayfish festival, and this year it's on the second day of *Rosh Hashanah*, which means we won't be holding any services then—people will be so busy eating crawdaddies, nobody'd come even if we did! Bottom line, Rabbi, that's one less sermon you got to write."

Rod felt anything but relieved when he hung up. Knowing how lengthy and complex the High Holy Day liturgy was, he would have gladly taken on another day of *yontif* rather than being saddled with an untrained and untested rookie for his cantor. Even so, he knew his own voice wasn't nearly good enough to carry the load by himself. His struggles with carrying even the simplest tune, which dated back to his *bar mitzvah* preparation with Cantor Pinsky and Dad, hadn't troubled him before, because in spite of his philosophy grad school experience, he still pictured himself as someday leading seminars rather than services. The more Rod thought about the holidays with Buddy, the more jittery he got.

"I could come with you for moral support," Nataliya volunteered after Rod confessed his fears to her one night over coffee.

"That'd be wonderful, Nataliya—I'll buy you a plane ticket tomorrow!"

"Don't be silly, Rod! I'll pay my own way. But I can only go with you for *Rosh Hashanah*. If I went for *Yom Kippur* as well, I'd miss too many rehearsals."

Morris couldn't have been more gracious when Rod said Nataliya would be flying down with him. "Why, we'd be tickled to extend some Southern hospitality to you and your lady friend! By the way, Rabbi, how are things coming along with Buddy?"

". . . Oh, just fine," Rod lied.

His sole conversation with Buddy hadn't bolstered Rod's confidence in him. After Buddy had hemmed and hawed for a while, he'd reluctantly admitted, "I ain't never led no service except for one Friday night at summer camp. But once Daddy gets hold of a notion, he don't turn it loose. When it came to my doing services for the holidays, he made it mighty appealing by tempting me with a new Corvette, telling me to consider it kind of like a *bar mitzvah* present. And that got me thinking—I got a tape from the temple to help me with what I needed to know for my *bar mitzvah*, and so I thought I'd get the campus rabbi to make me one for the holidays."

A knot formed in the pit of Rod's stomach. Learning a bare-boned *bar mitzvah* service compared with mastering the intricacies of the entire High Holy Day liturgy was like the difference between flying a kite and piloting a jet. "Sounds like a plan," Rod said half-heartedly.

Eight weeks later, a puddle jumper carrying him and Nataliya touched down in Rifton at what was more of a landing strip than an airport. "Glad you all made it!" Morris hailed them as they approached his dinged-up Mercury Comet parked at the curb. As they got in the back, Morris gestured toward the front seat and a delicately built woman wearing a pink summer dress and only a trace of makeup to highlight her soft brown eyes and ash-blonde hair. "This here is Harriet, my missus," said Morris.

Harriet's greeting was as warm as her husband's. "We're delighted to have you staying with us! Now that both of our children are grown and have moved out, we have two empty bedrooms."

Caught by surprise, Rod fumbled, ". . . Thank you . . . but I'd assumed we'd be staying at a motel."

Harriet responded, "Goodness no, Rabbi! That would start the Rifton gossip mill working overtime."

Jumping in, Morris said, "And even if it was just you, Rabbi, we'd still want you to stay at our place. Like I told you—'Southern hospitality!' That includes my giving you all the fifty-cent tour of Rifton—it takes more time now that we're growing. There's plans for expanding the airport, what with all the newcomers moving in down here and bringing more business with them. We aim to keep our small-town charm, though. This'd be one fine place for you to settle down and raise a family."

Feeling Nataliya's sudden clutch of his hand, Rod changed the subject. "I think that might be getting a little ahead of ourselves. For now, let's just focus on the High Holy Days."

Harriet looked at Morris and remarked, "The rabbi's right, dear. We don't want to be late for services tonight. Perhaps we should head home."

"Whatever you say, sugar," Morris replied.

As Morris drove back to the house, Harriet told Rod and Nataliya, "The Jacobses will be joining us for dinner. I thought it might be good for you, Rabbi, to meet Buddy before services. He's a sweet boy, but to be truthful, his reputation in Rifton stems from his football exploits and not from his classroom achievements. I do hope he doesn't let everyone down."

After they arrived home, Harriet showed Rod and Nataliya to their bedrooms. "Let me know if there's anything you need. Meanwhile, I have some dishes I need to finish cooking for dinner, and Morris has some last-minute synagogue matters to tend to."

When Harriet had gone back downstairs, Nataliya said to Rod, "Looks like we'll get at least a little time to be together."

Rod shook his head. "Not now, Nataliya. I'm so jumpy about Buddy, I just want to be alone. It'll give me a chance to go over my sermons again and take my mind off of him."

"I understand, Rod. I need to be by myself so I can collect my thoughts before I go on for a performance."

Having Nataliya liken his leading services to "a performance" only made Rod more uneasy. When he heard Morris holler, "Supper, y'all!" eating was the last thing on his mind. Walking down with Nataliya, Rod spotted a wiry man with mottled skin, a protruding jaw, and close-set, pale green eyes, who said, "I'm Nate Jacobs" as he coiled his arms around the couple at the foot of the stairs. With a slight twist of his body, Nate introduced the rest of his family. "These here are my son Buddy and my wife Edna." While Buddy's head amiably waggled atop his beefy neck and torso, an icy stare emanated from Edna, whose only shared features with Harriet seemed to be the shade of her eyes and hair.

Once in the dining room waiting for the meal to begin, Rod thought he'd be polite by engaging in small talk. "So, Mr. Nudelman and Mr. Jacobs, how did you two end up marrying sisters?"

Morris giggled and said, "I expect up North, you hear stories about how down here we're all inbred with close kin marrying one another. In our case, nothing could be further from the truth. Before we took Harriet and Edna under the *chuppah*, Nate and I weren't related to either of them or each other. Harriet and I got married, then later, he wed Edna and—"

"Interesting story about that," Nate cut him short. "I started out courting Harriet first, but her pa never cottoned to me. After she got hitched to Morris, though, he gave me and Edna the go-ahead, figuring he wouldn't be stuck with a spinster older daughter and reckoning I'd be a step up from his other son-in-law who worked as a manager at a five-and-dime."

Visibly embarrassed, her face flushed, Harriet placed two candles in front of Nataliya. ". . . I thought you might like to lead us in *lichtbenschen*," she said.

Knowing Nataliya had no idea what Harriet meant, Rod interjected, "—Thank you, Harriet, but since it's your home, you ought to have the honor of lighting the *Shabbos* candles."

"Oh, for goodness sake, *I'll* light them!" said Edna as she perfunctorily took a match to each wick, cupped her palms over her face, and smothered the benediction's words in her hands.

Next came the *Kiddush*, and following Rod's lead, everyone looked to Morris as head of the household to chant the *Kiddush*, but Morris looked away toward his nephew and stammered, ". . . Why don't you do *Kiddush* for us, Buddy? It'd . . . help you . . . warm up for tonight."

"Gee, Unc, my prayer book—Dang, what's it called? The *machzor*?—is out in the car."

"My dinner's getting cold!" Edna interrupted again. "I'm sure Mr. Zieglitz must know the *Kiddush* by heart."

Given his voice, Rod would have preferred Buddy sing it—*he* was supposed to be cantor, after all. Still, he couldn't let Edna undermine whatever rabbinic credibility he had before he'd ever ascended Rifton's *bimah*. He picked up his wine cup and began chanting. By the time he finished, Morris and Harriet were staring at their laps, Nate and Buddy were fiddling with their silverware, and Edna was covering her face with her hands once again. Only Nataliya's eyes weren't averted.

When dinner was over, and the Jacobses had peeled away in Nate's jade-green Caddy, Morris pulled Rod aside and said, "The *shul* ain't Orthodox, but we've got some members who feel the rabbi and *rebbitzen* oughtn't be riding to services on *yontif*. The synagogue's a good four miles from here, and it still being so warm this time of year doesn't make it any easier. So what would you prefer, Rabbi? —I'm okay either way."

During his years at the seminary, Rod had always walked to *shul*—it was either that or risk getting thrown out if he was caught in a car. Yet looking at Nataliya in her high heels, he couldn't imagine forcing her to make a trek reminiscent of the stifling death march he'd taken years before to Louis's for *Shabbos* lunch. "We'll go with you, Mr. Nudelman," Rod answered.

Morris drove to a small, yellow-brick building fronted by a row of bas-relief plaster columns. After he'd parked, he explained for Rod's benefit, "This used to be a funeral parlor, but now it's our *shul*. For the High Holy Days, we not only built a stage with curtains on both sides, but we rented you and Buddy each a podium with an attached mic. We even got you white robes! They're on loan from the choir of the Baptist church down the street. —You being a Northerner, Rabbi, I don't want you getting the wrong idea about where they came from."

"I brought my *kittel*," Rod replied, thankful he had a light, linen garment instead of a heavy polyester gown as he went inside and saw that the *shul*'s cooling system consisted of a few paltry open windows in its pine-paneled walls and a sluggish overhead fan. While Buddy strained to stuff his shoulders into the choir robe and then struggled to stretch his skimpy *bar mitzvah tallis* around them, Rod draped himself in the folds of the large *tallit* he'd ordered from Jerusalem at the same time he'd sent away for the *kittel*.

After putting his own prayer shawl on and checking his watch, Morris said to Rod, "Well, I guess we ought to get going. Unless we begin punctually tonight, we won't have a snowball's chance of starting the other services on time. So, Rabbi, I'll tell you what I told Buddy like I was his coach giving him a pregame pep talk: Go out there, and put up a W for the home team!"

Rod took a moment to glance down at Nataliya in the front row. He was thrown off to see that she wasn't seated beside Harriet but wedged between Edna and Nate. After waiting several minutes for absolute silence, Rod finally announced, "The service starts on page 26." A shudder ran through him—he sounded like the Medina rabbi.

Buddy, though, sounded nothing like Cantor Pinsky. Despite the tape he'd acquired, he hadn't got the hang of the service's plainest refrains, much less its Hebrew, as he mangled even the easiest words. Rod was glad when it came time for his sermon. Back in New York, he'd made several false starts with various topics—"the shofar's call to repentance"; "the true meaning of fasting"; "prayer as self-reflection"—until he finally came up with something that clicked. He coupled the theme of *Rosh Hashanah*'s marking the birth of the world with his old fundraising pitch of Israel's signifying the Jewish people's rebirth.

"Grand slam, Rabbi!" Morris said when the sermon ended. After the service concluded, he escorted Rod off the *bimah* and over to Nate, exclaiming, "I told you we got ourselves an all-star!"

Lavished with so much praise, Rod was in a magnanimous mood to share some with Buddy. "You know, Mr. Jacobs, I couldn't have done it without your son."

"When I get him home, I'll tend to what needs fixing," Nate replied tersely.

Rod was about to ask Nataliya her opinion of how he'd done, when Edna broke in, "I wouldn't let tonight go to your head Mr. Zieglitz—even a student rabbi can have one good sermon in him."

Back at the Nudelmans', Harriet said to Rod and Nataliya, "Tomorrow morning, we'll have breakfast around 7:30—that ought to give us plenty of time before services start at nine. Is there anything either of you need before you turn in? I've laid out everything I can think of in your bedrooms, though Morris and I would certainly understand if only one of the beds were slept in."

Nataliya blushed, and as she walked upstairs with Rod, she told him, "It was nice of Harriet to say that, but I feel too self-conscious right now, like I'm on display in a fishbowl, especially after being with Edna all night."

"Me too," Rod said before he kissed her good night.

Over a breakfast of poached eggs and grits the next morning, Morris asked Rod, "So, Rabbi, ready for another at-bat today?"

"Raring to go!" Rod answered. The previous evening, he'd appealed to people's emotions, but this morning he'd aim for their intellects by posing the question, "If there's no God, how might Jewish ritual be justified nonetheless?" Before last night, Rod had obsessed about whether services could be a success even if Buddy's *davening* wasn't. Now he knew the sermon was all that mattered—he couldn't wait to get to *shul*.

Once there, he quickly got garbed with Buddy, stepped to his podium, and, calling out the page number, signaled Buddy to begin at his lectern. Predictably, Buddy hadn't magically improved overnight; if anything, he'd gotten worse with even more flubbed Hebrew and flawed chanting. Rod longed for the moment he could save another service with his sermon. First, though, came the *Amidah*, one of the day's two lengthy standing prayers, which the congregation would initially recite silently and which Buddy would subsequently sing aloud. Morris opened the ark and took his place facing it on Rod's left while Buddy positioned himself to Rod's right. While everyone else slowly worked their way through their devotions, Rod hopscotched through his, too preoccupied with his sermon to attend to the words in the *machzor*. Finished, he looked to his right to cue the repetition. No Buddy. Instead, Rod spied him offstage in the wings, hunched over, vomiting down the front of his no longer white robe.

"*What are we going to do, Rabbi*?!" gasped Morris in Rod's ear.

"I guess I'll just have to chant it myself," Rod answered.

"*Oy!*" came Morris's reply.

Before his *bar mitzvah*, Rod had had a recurring bad dream of having to lead services before he was ready; what was happening to him now was a nightmare he couldn't wake up from. For the next hour and a half, he croaked out one off-key note after another. As he paused for a sip of water after he'd slogged through to the end, Morris snatched at his sleeve and said, "Rabbi, nobody knows where Buddy's gone to—Nate's drove off to find him!"

Rod leapt at the chance to redeem himself, exclaiming, almost too loudly, "I'll buy some time with my sermon!"

"Good idea, Rabbi! That talk you gave last night is why folks came back today."

But within minutes after Rod started speaking, many of the congregants had left, either literally departing the premises or figuratively exiting the service by dozing off in their seats. The sermon ground on for another three quarters of an hour without any sign of Buddy or his father. When the service finally wrapped up after Rod had given the congregation a taste of what eternity might be like, there wasn't even a *minyan* for *Kaddish*. As Rod walked over to Nataliya for solace, Edna intercepted him and said, "I wouldn't consider your sermon a total failure, Mr. Zieglitz—it saved my son from being today's chief disgrace."

That night, Rod had trouble getting to sleep, because he couldn't stop thinking about having to return for *Yom Kippur* in little more than a week. All of a sudden, he heard the door creak open followed by a series of muffled footfalls coming toward him. As he bolted upright in bed, Nataliya slipped in beside him, placed her fingers on his lips, and whispered, "I've decided to fly down for *Yom Kippur*, too. You're more important to me than my rehearsals."

"Thanks, but with any luck, they won't want me to come back," Rod sighed. Soon, he was asleep in her arms.

The next evening, after he and Nataliya had flown home, he got a call from Morris.

"I saw lots of our members at the crawdaddy fest today, Rabbi, and most of them chewed my ear off about what happened yesterday."

Rod decided to resign before Morris could fire him. "I'm sorry. I hope you find someone else—"

Before he could finish, Morris cut him off. "Buddy shouldn't have jumped ship like that, Rabbi. But I got it all taken care of. One of the folks I spoke to is offering to be cantor! He's a new arrival down here, and he says he's *davened* the holidays before. Oh, and before I forget, Rabbi, don't go fussing with a sermon for *Yom Kippur* morning—that's when Nate always gives his 'State of the *Shul*' address. You get what I'm saying, Rabbi? You only have to give a sermon *Kol Nidre* night."

Granted a reprieve, Rod bought Nataliya a plane ticket the next morning and then skipped his classes to go to the seminary's library in search of sermon material. Yet despite all the pages of commentary he pored through the succeeding week, those in his notebook stayed blank. Exhausted, and with *Kol Nidre* only a day away, he gave up—when the time came for his *drasha*, he'd just have to wing it. Rationalizing an ad-libbed sermon was easy: once *Yom Kippur* was over, he'd be gone from Rifton forever.

During dinner the following evening with the Nudelmans and Nataliya, Rod excused himself before the meal was over. "If nobody minds, I'd like to walk to *shul* by myself to think over services some more." As he plodded to the synagogue, Rod kept hoping lighting would strike him with a sermon idea, but when he got there, he still didn't have even a glimmer of one. When Morris arrived with Harriet and Nataliya to open the building, he told Rod, "Now that's what I want—a rabbi who's gone and gotten himself spiritually prepared for *Kol Nidre*."

"Good luck, Rod," said Nataliya, kissing his cheek as they entered. She thought she'd sit by Harriet that night, but as she walked down the aisle, Edna swooped in and led her away to be sandwiched once more between herself and Nate, their demoted son alongside him.

Meanwhile, Rod climbed the steps of the stage behind Morris, feeling like a condemned man being led to the gallows. Once on the *bimah*, Morris introduced him to a powerfully built man with an irresistible smile. "Meet Bob Nelson, Rabbi. He's volunteered to be your *chazzan* tonight and tomorrow."

Adjusting his *kittel* and *tallit*, Bob said, "Honored to do it, Rabbi—I'll try my best to meet your standards."

"*What* standards?" Rod silently castigated himself, the rabbi who'd come to services without a sermon on the holiest night of the year. He shook Bob's hand and mumbled, "I'm sure you'll do fine."

As Rod gazed out on the crowd, he saw Nataliya stuck again between Edna and Nate. In a few minutes, the chanting of *Kol Nidre* would commence with an Aramaic declaration that in addition to giving the evening's service its name, absolved those assembled of any vows they might break. Rod nevertheless made a pledge he had every intention of keeping: even if he flopped with everyone else that evening, there'd be one soul whose spirits he'd raise.

Bounding off the stage, he called out to Nataliya, "What are you doing down here in front? You know you always sit way in the rear so you can concentrate when you *daven*! Pardon us, Mr. and Mrs. Jacobs, while we find a seat in back before they're all gone."

"Thank you," Nataliya said softly to Rod as he took her hand and ushered her away.

When they got to the last row, Rod told her, "You'll be more comfortable here. It's where I always sat as a boy to help me get through the service." He gave her a hug and was about to return to the *bimah* when a tap from behind made him stop. "*Shanah Tovah!*" said a wisp of a woman whose liveliness belied her years.

Taken by surprise Rod responded, ". . . And . . . a good year to you—I'm sorry, but I don't know your name . . ."

"It's Lilly Marx. I appreciate your coming to be with us for the *yom tovim*, Rabbi. I don't mean to intrude, but I'd be happy to keep the young lady company during services. I know what it's like to be by yourself—my Edgar's been gone five years now."

Nataliya thanked Lilly and then said to Rod, "Looks like I'll be in good hands."

Rod wished he could say the same for himself. After the debacle with Buddy, he didn't look forward to depending on yet another layman—even Morris's "*shofar* tooting" on *Rosh Hashanah* had been dismal, more like sporadic honks than mighty blasts, while the geezer who'd done the Torah and Haftarah was so frail he could scarcely be heard. "I'll keep it simple," Rod assured Bob before he started the service.

"You're the rabbi!" Bob answered.

Rod had the congregation rise as Morris opened the ark, took out the Torah, and held it while everyone stood stock-still for Bob to begin chanting the *Kol Nidre*, which for many of them was the holy days' high point. Bob quickly dispelled Rod's misgivings; his voice was resonant yet sweet, his Hebrew both effortless and impeccable. Shortly after he started singing, Rod, like everybody else, had shivers running down his spine as the *Kol Nidre's* ancient melody engulfed him. At its conclusion, Rod rushed over to Bob, clasped his hand, and exclaimed, "Beautiful, just beautiful!"

Beaming, Bob said, "Good to know that all those years in *yeshiva* weren't wasted, Rabbi! But chanting's the easy part—it's just a matter of practicing what somebody else has composed. Having to compose something of my own like a sermon, now that's what I call tough!"

Reminded of what came next in the service, Rod plummeted from the *Kol Nidre's* heights to the low he'd been at before Bob sang it. He shuffled to his podium, where for several moments he stood speechless while below him, people fidgeted. Unable to stall any longer, he at last began, "You know . . . *Yom Kippur's* the day for making up . . . and . . . since we didn't meet for the second day of *Rosh Hashanah* . . . tonight's sermon could count—if you want, that is—as a kind of 'make-up' talk in more ways than one!" When his wordplay failed to elicit so much as a chuckle from his audience, Rod cleared his throat and started over. "What I meant to say is that since we skipped the second day's Torah reading about the *Akedah*—where Abraham comes close to sacrificing Isaac—I'd like to talk about it now. It's one of the best-known stories in the Torah. Most of us first heard it in *shul* or Hebrew school when we were children. Honestly, though, if I were a parent, I'd never tell it to my kid!"

Rod's voice wavered a bit as he told the congregation, ". . . My own dad . . . was anything but perfect. . . . He was pursued by disaster and depression for most of his life, and sometimes, he took it out on me and my mom. But compared with Abraham, my dad was father of the year! Just stop and think for a minute about the man our tradition calls 'Abraham our Father.' What kind of father takes a blade to the penises of his two boys, merely because some voice in the middle of the night tells him to do it? And go on, ask yourself, what kind of father banishes his firstborn to the wilderness, maybe even to his death, simply because some voice in the middle of the night tells him to do it? And can anyone tell me what kind of father then sets out to butcher his sole surviving child, Isaac, all because, you guessed it, some midnight voice tells him to do it? In his own time, Abraham might have been considered a man of faith. In ours, he'd be called a schizo."

Looking down, Rod saw Edna scowling.

He was just warming up.

"No wonder, then, that after the *Akedah*, Isaac never speaks to his dad again. And you know what? He doesn't speak to God either, that midnight voice his father followed."

Rod paused, then spoke louder to drive home his point. "But that doesn't mean we're through with Isaac! For while he's still splayed out on the altar, we learn something crucial to his story—a story that's also ours as Jews. It's Isaac, we're told, who will sustain Abraham's legacy; it's Isaac, we hear, who'll bear the blessing Abraham carries! Who'd ever have expected that kind of plot twist in the story? While Abraham's a man of action, Isaac's passive his whole life long. He gets circumcised as a newborn when he can't possibly have any say about it, he's later led away to be sacrificed without a peep of protest, and even on his deathbed, his last wishes aren't heeded. Isaac seems like such a *nebbish*!"

With his voice increasingly stronger, Rod continued, "Now don't get me wrong!—It's not as if Isaac never does anything important in his life. Right after the *Akedah*, Genesis relates something remarkable he did, for as the text tells us, 'Isaac took Rebecca for his wife, and he loved her.' Hear that? '*And he loved her*!' The Torah doesn't say that about Adam when it comes to Eve, about Noah when it comes to Mrs. Noah, not even about Abraham when it comes to Sarah. But it says that about Isaac!"

The tug at the Wall had Rod in its grip—the words poured out of him now. "Think about what that means! Despite everything Isaac endured in his life, he somehow overcame it all to fall in love with someone else. Despite all the terror and trauma he'd suffered, Isaac's still able to go on and love another person. To be a Jew, you don't have to be an Abraham who distances yourself from others. Instead, you have to be an Isaac who draws another to you. To be a Jew, you don't have to be an Abraham, who puts somebody on an altar. Instead, you have to be an Isaac who puts your heart in the hands of another human being.

"That's what tonight and tomorrow are really all about—the attempt, *the need*, to draw closer to our loved ones! It's what this Day of Atonement in essence holds out to us—*At-one-ment*! We can become *at one* again by drawing close to the loved ones whom we've estranged. We can bridge the breaches between us with love that's unbroken."

Lifting his arms, Rod exhorted the congregation with everything in him, "So rise now, be at one, you Isaacs! Rise now, draw close, you blessing bearers! Rise now, and embrace one another in love, *you Jews*!"

Throughout the sanctuary, people stood, hugged, and wept. Once the service ended, the congregation raced to the *bimah* to mob Rod with congratulations. After Nataliya had at last made her way onto the stage, Rod took her in his arms and was on the verge of kissing her when Nate pressed between them and said, "That's the finest sermon I've ever heard! Why don't you two come by my place tomorrow night for our break-the-fast?"

"Sure . . . of course . . . thanks, Mr. Jacobs," Rod said.

Breaking in, Nataliya asked Nate, "How's Buddy? Nobody deserves what happened to him."

Nate dismissed her question with a flick of his wrist. "He'll get over it—I'll count on seeing you two tomorrow."

"Are you ready to go?" Morris called over to Rod and Nataliya.

"I think we'll just walk home," Nataliya answered.

"What about your high heels?" Rod asked her quietly.

"We'll take it slow. It'll give us some time to be alone with each other."

On the long walk to the Nudelmans', Nataliya told Rod how much she enjoyed the service. "Even though I can't follow the Hebrew, the music was marvelous. More than that, though, I was moved by your sermon. Instead of drawing on peoples' worst fears, you appealed to their best instincts. For the first time, you made me feel good about being Jewish."

Rod halted and said, "That means a lot to me, Nataliya, but there's something else I need to tell you tonight about being Jewish—I hope it doesn't make you feel different. On *Yom Kippur*, sex, like eating, is forbidden, and I'm so hungry for you, I don't think I could control myself if you came into my bedroom again."

Nataliya nuzzled Rod's chin. "If you put it that way, Rabbi, I'll be a good little Jewish girl and wait till we get back to New York to pay you another visit."

The service the next morning initially went as smoothly as it had the previous night. When it had gone on a while, though, with no trace of Nate for his speech and with Rod having none of his own on hand, he started worrying that the Jacobs family would once more be leaving him holding the bag. Well past the service's halfway point, Nate sauntered down the aisle with Edna and Buddy. Dropping them off next to Harriet, he strode up on the *bimah* uninvited and commandeered Rod's lectern and microphone. "Good *yontif*, everybody! I'm downright thrilled to say that financially, the *shul's* fit as a fiddle. I'm the one person here who *can* say that on account of the sizable donation I made after last night's service."

None of the other congregants looked nearly as pleased by the news as Nate did.

Unfazed, Nate went on, "Things in Israel aren't nearly so good, though, and I'm not just talking about its economy—I'm talking about its overall situation. Some folks here get their pants in a bunch over whether this synagogue will make it. Well, suppose it doesn't. Big deal! You and me and our families will still survive—nobody's going to come kill us. But you know what'll happen if Israel doesn't survive? After the Arabs have killed the last Israeli, the other Jew-haters out there will come for each one of us. Jews everywhere will be fair game—just like we were in the Holocaust!

"Yeah, I know there's lots wrong with Israel. I've been there so many times and met with so many high officials there, I can't help but know it. But you know something? It doesn't matter a hill of beans to me, and it shouldn't to you, either. How come? The answer's simple—*it's the only Israel we've got!*"

Nate stopped and motioned to Buddy to stand up. "So now, like I do every year, I'm having Buddy walk through each row to collect the pledge cards I had him put in your *machzors* before you got here this morning. If you haven't filled out your card already, go ahead and take a minute to write down a number—a *large* one—that'll help Israel buy weapons. For make no mistake about it: Israel needs your pledge today lots more than it needs your prayers!"

As Nate walked away from the microphone and down off the stage, Rod didn't know what to do. There was *Yom Kippur's* additional ban on writing, but what then of "at-one-ment" if he raised a stink that split the congregation? He kept his mouth shut. Even so, he didn't like it. Here was Nate's call for weapons instead of worship, and yet there were the day's repeated public confessions of sins against God with blasphemy and violence high on the list.

Bob started up his *davening* again, and before long, Rod and the congregation had eased back into the service's slow, steady rhythms. Nobody drifted off or schmoozed, and, except for Nate and his family, no one got up to leave. At first, Rod assumed they'd just gone outside for a breather, but as the service continued through the afternoon and on toward sunset without their return, he grew increasingly concerned: he'd heard Nate had a bad heart. Just as services drew to a close, Edna and Buddy reappeared to drive him and Nataliya to dinner at their house, where Nate greeted them at the front door. "Well, if it isn't my rabbi and his sweetheart! —So good to see you!"

Rod replied, "Good to see you, too, Mr. Jacobs! I thought something might have happened to you when you weren't in services after your talk."

"Sorry about that. Today was the big game at my alma mater, and we had to hightail it there on my Cessna to make the kickoff in time."

Once again, Rod didn't speak his mind. "Thank you for making room for Nataliya and me to be with you and your other guests tonight."

"*What other guests?*" Nate responded.

Taken aback by Nate's harshness, Rod stumbled, ". . . I . . . guess I meant . . . the Nudelmans . . . or Bob Nelson, our cantor."

"I see Morris and Harriet enough as it is! And what's this about the cantor? *You're* the celebrity around here now! Enough of this chitchat—you must be starving!" Nate led Rod and Nataliya into the imposing dining room, and after Edna rang a tiny silver bell by her place setting, two black women appeared, the first portly and older, bringing rolls, the other slender, carrying salads, whom Edna introduced as Eula and her daughter, Cassie.

"They've been with us for years," she said. As the meal progressed, she kept ringing her bell to summon them, but nothing they did satisfied her. After they cleared the dessert plates, Nate said to her, "Why don't you and Buddy go to the kitchen and help Eula and Cassie clean up?"

"What's the point of having them then?" rejoined Edna.

"Just do what I say, woman!" Nate answered.

Once Edna and Buddy had gone, Nate fixed his gaze on Rod and said, "You know, I can spot a winner a mile off, and you, my friend, are a winner! I haven't breathed a word of this to anybody, not even Edna, but I've had a plan in mind for a long time now. I just had to find the right person, *the right piece*, to make it happen!"

Nate slid his chair closer to Rod's before going on, "You know how I made my money as a developer? I did it by seeing opportunities other people missed for putting up tract homes, parking lots, and shopping malls. And now, I see an opportunity to build a new *shul* north of town. Why there? Because young professionals are moving in up there, that's why! Those people have money, and they spend it. Otherwise, my new mall out there wouldn't be making such a killing. I gave my brother-in-law a chance to lease a space from me with a below-market rate and open a discount store of his own. I even told him I'd float him a loan with the kind of interest that would match any bank's. But did he take me up on my offer? Of course not—he's a small-timer! Like the rest of them in that synagogue, he hasn't got a lick of imagination!"

Only days before, Rod had relished the thought of being rid of Temple Israel's Jews once and for all. Now, though, he found himself sticking up for them as well as for the mortuary they'd made into their *shul*. "But, Mr. Jacobs, what if you renovated the current building and attracted newcomers that way?"

Nate glared at him with barely concealed contempt. "With all due respect, you may know the religion business, but I know the real estate business. And you know the main thing those young people care about when they pick a temple to go to? It's the same thing they care about when they pick a place to go shop—how long it takes to drive there. That's true whether they're picking a dry cleaner to drop off their clothes or picking a Hebrew school to drop off their kids! That funeral home we've got now for a *shul* could be fixed up like Buckingham Palace, and those young people still wouldn't come—it's too damn far from where they live!"

Nate all at once turned chummy again as he curled his arm around Rod's shoulders. "Just the same, even if I build a brand new *shul*, it'll stay empty if I don't put the proper man in its pulpit, and, Rod, that man is *you*!"

Rod tried to move his chair away and work loose of Nate's grasp. "I really appreciate the compliment, Mr. Jacobs, but—"

"But nothin'!" Nate cut in, holding Rod faster. "You come down to be my rabbi, and I'll build you a temple just the way you want it, from the layout of the sanctuary, to the number of classrooms, to the size of your office. I'll be straight with you—I'm so set on your being my man that I'll beat any other offer you've got!"

"I'm grateful, Mr. Jacobs, but it's a little premature—I'm not even ordained yet. On top of that, there are placement rules that candidates and synagogues have to follow."

"Those placement folks are more concerned with their pocketbooks than their principles—there's nothing a well-placed contribution can't fix! Meanwhile, Rod, how's a starting salary of six figures sound?"

Nate's offer was so unexpected, Rod didn't know what to say. Apparently having mistaken his silence for resistance, Nate upped the ante. "Tell you what, Rod. One of my north side houses is about to go on the market. It's got five bedrooms, a three-car garage, and a swimming pool. You just say the word, and it's yours! I'll even throw in the use of my plane if you want to get away every now and then—"

"We really need to talk it over, Mr. Jacobs," Nataliya intervened to free Rod from the bind he was in.

"I was speaking to your boyfriend, missy!" Nate answered.

Rod had had enough of Nate's lording it over everyone including the Lord Himself. "If you honestly think I'm the right man, Mr. Jacobs, you'll just have to wait."

Nate's eyes narrowed to mere slits. "And you'll just have to see if my offer's still standing." Uncoiling his arm from Rod, Nate yelled toward the kitchen, "Buddy, come drive these two back to your aunt and uncle's!"

Flying home the next day, Rod couldn't have been happier. He'd met every High Holy Day challenge, and as he looked at Nataliya beside him, the year ahead seemed ripe with blessing.

XV

———

It soured a few months later.

When an ice storm hit New York in mid-January, it downed power lines, snarled traffic, and delayed Nataliya's train for her audition with the prestigious Manhattan Ballet. Rushing from the station, she slipped on the sidewalk, broke her hip, and, despite (or because of) multiple surgeries, was left with a permanent limp. By midsummer, her dreams of a luminous globe-trotting career were replaced by visions of a dreary existence in Queens, made even bleaker by her lacking so much as a high school typing course, let alone a college degree that might provide her with enough income to move out on her own. Before her accident, Rod had started applying to philosophy grad school again, intent on enrolling once he'd been ordained in June with what little remained of Jack's cache, but Nataliya's altered plans changed his. To rescue their hopes of a future together, Rod and Nataliya reached for the most available lifeline: the pulpit in Rifton. When Rod started to call Morris, though, Nataliya stopped him. "Morris Nudelman might be the synagogue's president, but Nate Jacobs controls its purse strings."

"Why, we'd love to have you for our rabbi!" Nate responded when Rod phoned.

"Great, Mr. Jacobs, just clear it with the placement committee and send me a contract!" Rod answered.

"None of that Mr. Jacobs stuff, Rod, now that we're going to be working together! Like I told you before, don't pay no never mind to that committee. I'll handle them. As for something in writing, strangers might need that, but the two of us don't, especially since we outlined the broad strokes of a contract not all that long ago."

Although Rod would have preferred to have received a written agreement, he was in no position to argue. Relieved that he'd at least come away with a deal, he replied, "Thanks, Nate. I'll let you know when to expect me and Natal—"

"About that," Nate cut in, "for us to even have a gentleman's agreement, you two will need to take a walk down the aisle. Around here, folks want their rabbis *respectable*. With it coming up on August already, and the High Holy Days starting the first week in September, there's not a minute to lose for you and your girl to tie the knot."

Ever since they'd returned from Rifton the previous autumn, Rod and Nataliya had talked about marriage, but they'd put it off until he got a teaching position and she'd landed a place with a ballet company. After Rod told her about his conversation with Nate, Nataliya could barely contain her excitement. "Let's find a justice of the peace, Rod, and get married today!" she exclaimed.

"You know I want to be married as much as you do, Nataliya, but the congregation would never accept a secular ceremony, and they'd be right not to. What kind of rabbi would I be if I set such an example?"

"All right then, what about having Rabbi Mishkin marry us?"

"That'd be terrific! We'll fly him in for the ceremony."

"Rod, what would you think of having him marry us at *Casa Futura*? It'd be easier for him and your family, and we can fly out Mama and Papa. Besides, Rod, how many friends do either of us have in New York who we'd want at our wedding? You certainly haven't made any at the seminary, and since I've left the Institute, I've lost touch with the ones I had there."

Opting for Huppertsville wasn't hard for Rod. His grandmother had lost both her legs to diabetes, and flying wheelchair-bound to New York would have been an ordeal for her. Rod thought that Mom and Gene would also be pleased with a Huppertsville wedding, since they'd recently returned to Excelsior from Palm Springs after an abbreviated sojourn there following Gene's retirement. The desert landscape combined with the wizened population had given them the sense that their lives were becoming desiccated, too, as the early-bird-special conversation invariably withered into gossip about this one's decline and that one's demise. Or as they'd quipped to their Excelsior chums, "We moved for our health."

Dina initially favored the mansion's atrium for the ceremony—"I'll get it made up real nice!"—but Rod persuaded her to hold it in the meadow by saying, "I've got so many good memories of playing ball there with Jack that it'd almost be like he'd be with us." Scheduling a time when the Excelsior caterer and Rabbi Mishkin could both come to Huppertsville was much tougher, and as a result, the marriage didn't take place until the last day of

August, on an increasingly overcast Sunday afternoon. As his wedding present to Nataliya, Rod had bought her parents plane tickets, which won him
Papa's approval at last. Mom and Gene came with an Excelsior contingent of
their old pals and his former clients while a cohort of Dina's Huppertsville
friends and employees assembled as an honor guard of sorts to escort her
down the driveway to the meadow. Rabbi Mishkin arrived after everyone
else because of some *bar mitzvah* tutoring he'd had to cover due to his cantor's being away on vacation. Once he got to the meadow, he told Nataliya
and Rod, "I don't have anywhere near my *chazzan*'s ability, so I'm going to
keep the ceremony simple—it'll be short and sweet."

Getting the ceremony underway, however, was anything but simple.
Out in the open, people milled around, kibitzing in groups of threes and
fours, deaf to Rabbi Mishkin's requests, unaided by microphones or ushers,
to take their seats so the service could start. As Rod scurried about trying to
corral the guests, a cluster of thunderheads formed to the west.

"Maybe we ought to move back to the house," Rabbi Mishkin suggested.

Shaking her head, Dina answered him, "No dice, Rabbi Sam. It'd be a
mess—the caterer isn't through setting up for the reception."

A lightning bolt skittered across the sky, followed almost simultane-
ously by a booming thunderclap. "We can't stay *here*!" cried Nataliya as
raindrops started pelting her brocaded silk wedding dress.

After one gust of wind had billowed the marriage canopy's velvet cover
upward, another toppled the *chuppah* altogether. Rod cupped his hands to
his mouth and yelled, "This way, everybody!" Placing the bottle of wine
and crystal goblet for the ceremony in Dina's lap, he began pushing her
chair across the meadow with one hand while with the other, he steadied
Nataliya, whose limp was exacerbated as she hobbled as fast as she could
across the rain-muddied ground and the slippery wet grass. An impromptu
procession quickly formed behind them—first Rabbi Mishkin, then both
sets of parents, trailed by the bulk of the guests. At Rod's direction, some
men ran ahead to help him navigate Dina through the woods and down the
slope to the gazebo at the bottom. As the wedding party packed inside the
long-abandoned chapel, the others squeezed in around it, seeking shelter
from the winds and the deluge. "Now's the time for 'short and sweet'!" Rod
prompted Rabbi Mishkin, who began reciting the prayers at a pace rivaling
Grandpa Irv's seder Hebrew, until he ended by shouting into the tempest
at the bride and groom, "Drink the wine and break the glass!" After they'd
each had a sip, Nataliya placed the goblet inside the chapel's Star of David,
where Rod's foot stamped the spot witnessing to both love and deception.

Just as suddenly as the storm had blown in, it blew over, and everyone
trudged back up the slope toward the house and reception. Rod looked at

his drenched wife in her soaked gown and sopping wet hair. Seeing Nataliya was about to cry, he drew her close and whispered, "All that matters is that we're with each other."

Whispering back, Nataliya answered him, "I know the sacrifice you're making for me, darling, and I can't tell you how much I love you for that. I'll do whatever I can to be the *rebbetzin* you need."

In keeping with Rod's Rifton starting date, he and Nataliya had to fly there that evening. So after putting in a brief appearance at the reception and thanking their families and saying their goodbyes to their guests, they made for the Excelsior airport to catch the last flight out. When Nate met them at the at the other end, he said, "Too bad about your honeymoon, but with *Rosh Hashannah* beginning less than seventy-two hours from now, there's not a minute to lose."

"With Bob Nelson's being cantor again, services should go a lot smoother this year," replied Rod.

Nataliya chimed in, telling Nate, "I really don't mind having to fly down now. I'll still be spending my wedding night in a hotel."

"What hotel?" Nate responded as he pulled up in front of an apartment building that looked like it had seen better days. Leading Rod and Nataliya inside, he said, "It's the only vacant property I've got just now—damn shame you didn't take that house I offered you last year."

Apart from the flat's bathroom whose shocking-pink tiles were cross-hatched with green, moldy grout, it couldn't have been drabber, a mixture of scuffed, gray linoleum and chipping, beige paint. When Nataliya stopped to use the toilet, the flush from its lowing pipes could be heard throughout the entire apartment, from the adjoining dinky bedroom, which would have to double as Rod's study, to the cubbyhole of a living room, where they'd be forced to eat their meals. Coming back from the bathroom, Nataliya fanned herself and asked Nate, "How do I turn on the air conditioning in here?"

"There isn't any," Nate said. "It doesn't help that the windows are nailed shut, but the neighborhood's kind of iffy. You probably ought to get yourself some fans. Eventually, you'll get used to our near year-round heat and humidity. For now, you should be downright cozy with the cot, card table, and folding chairs I put here you until you can buy your own furniture."

Speaking to Nataliya as much as to Nate, Rod answered, "We won't be in this place very long—we'll be leaving once I get my first paycheck."

"That'd be the end of the month, but your salary will be considerably less than what I mentioned before. The bank's got its hooks in most of my real estate. If and when things start looking up again, maybe we can revisit the matter of your compensation."

Around ten the next morning, after a sweltering, sleepless night, Rod and Nataliya were preparing to grab a bite out when they heard a knock at the door. Answering it, Rod found Morris and Harriet standing in the hallway, each armed with two sacks of groceries. "Remember what I said about Southern hospitality, Rabbi?" said Morris.

"You'd never know it from this place!" Harriet said, stepping inside. After putting away the groceries in the apartment's tiny kitchen, which consisted of a hot plate with a frayed cord and a mini-fridge with a half-drunk can of beer left by the last tenant, the Nudelmans treated the Zieglitzes to breakfast at a restaurant where Rod and Nataliya enjoyed the air conditioning as much as the food.

Near the end of the meal, Harriet went over to the cashier to ask if she could use the phone. When she and Morris delivered Rod and Nataliya back to the apartment, Bob Nelson and Lilly Marx were waiting out front.

Smiling as always, Bob said, "I've got a window air conditioner in my trunk that's been sitting in my basement ever since I installed central air."

Lilly fished some keys from her purse, gave them to Rod, and nodded toward a Buick parked behind Bob's Olds. "It's yours for as long as you need it. My eyesight's gotten so bad, my doctor doesn't want me driving anymore. If I need to do errands, Harriet has told me she'll take me."

In less than half an hour, Bob had pried open a window and got the air conditioner going, which cooled down the small set of rooms within minutes. "We'll never forget your kindness," Nataliya said to him and the others on their way out.

Once she'd closed the door, though, Rod told her, "Don't get me wrong—I'm grateful for their help. I just don't want it to become a habit where people feel they can simply drop in on us and then have everything about our life become public knowledge."

Nataliya took his hands in hers and said, "Don't you see, Rod? Right now, we can use it to our advantage! We'll invite the congregation over for *Rosh Hashanah* afternoon."

That year, in the week between New Year's and the Day of Atonement, the talk of the temple wasn't about its *Rosh Hashannah* services or sermons, but about the lodgings where Nate Jacobson had dumped the rabbi and *rebbetzin*. On *Yom Kippur* morning, as Nate was on his way to the *bimah* for his annual Israel solicitation, Bob stood up and got to the microphone before him. After waiting for Nate to sit back down again, Bob addressed his fellow congregants, saying, "Like many of you, I attended the open house at the Zieglitzes. Afterwards, some of us started discussing how we could improve their current living arrangements, and together, we came up with a solution. So, with Morris's consent as President, I'm asking you to take the pledge card at your seat, and instead of giving to Israel this year, contribute to moving our rabbi and *rebbetzin* somewhere that better reflects how much we appreciate their being here with us in Rifton."

Nate tore his pledge card in half, but Rod and Nataliya never had to spend another night stuck in his rathole. When *Yom Kippur* ended, they packed their bags for a hotel, and the next morning, they signed the rental agreement on a furnished, all-equipped apartment and still had enough money remaining from Bob's appeal to buy Lilly's car. Nataliya's inviting the congregation's members to the open house and her charming them once they arrived laid the groundwork for her gaining a following far greater than any she'd had as a dancer. Her progress as the *shul's rebbetzin* outpaced that of its rabbi, whose inexperience repeatedly hindered his.

"I'm so glad to meet you, Stuart!" Rod greeted the first *bar mitzvah* student of his career. Stuart's chubby, freckled face made Rod think of two others: his at that age and the pompous dolt's who'd ruined his earliest interaction with a rabbi. He resolved that Stuart's time with him would be different—they'd work through Stuart's Torah portion together in English and engage in deep, meaningful exchanges.

"So, Stuart, since this is our first meeting, is there anything you'd like to ask me?" Rod said affably.

"Uh-uh," Stuart grunted.

"Have you had a chance to look at your portion?"

"Uh-uh."

"Well, then, let's open a *chumash*—you know what that is, don't you, Stuart?"

"Uh-uh."

Bent on forming a rapport with Stuart, Rod continued, "Not to worry! '*Chumash*' comes from the Hebrew word for 'five,' and it's alluding to the Torah's first five books, which we Jews call 'The Five Books of Moses.' The fancy term other people sometimes use is 'Pentateuch.' It's this thick, blue and white book on my desk. You and your family must have seen one at services."

"Uh-uh—we don't go," Stuart mumbled.

Rod started wondering who was the tutor and who the tutee attending his initial *bar mitzvah* lesson. He opened a Jewish calendar on his desk and said, "Okay, Stuart, let's see which *sedrah* is slated for your thirteenth birthday." After sliding his finger down one column of dates and then another, Rod precipitously brought it to a stop. Stuart's portion was *Tazria-Metzorah*, a compendium of all manner of bodily irruptions, including seminal emissions and menstrual flows. Now Rod was the one who didn't have much to say.

"Uh . . . Stuart . . . have your parents talked to you about . . . I mean . . . do you know where . . . . What I'm getting at, Stuart, is . . ." Rod stammered, fumbling for an erudite philosophical circumlocution. Several moments later, all he could say was, ". . . Stuart, what do you know about the birds and the bees?"

Stuart blushed. Rod blushed. He handed Stuart the *chumash* and told him, "For next time, learn verses 1 and 2 of Leviticus 12—in Hebrew."

During those early days, Rod's sermons scarcely fared better, as they lurched between being overly cerebral and, at the other extreme, over-wrought. Nataliya proved to be his most perceptive critic; nobody knew him better, and nobody cared more than she did, not only about him, but increasingly about Judaism, too. "Rod, stop trying to sound like you're either Spinoza or Gil Gorn—There's nobody without a head *and* a heart, and you need to speak to them both. From what I've read, Judaism has never been like Christianity where there's a split between body and spirit." When Rod managed to follow her counsel, another voice seemed to be speaking through his, so that what he'd first experienced as a touch, then a grip, felt like an embrace. Little by little, his sermons increased service attendance as his own members' numbers were augmented by other Rifton Jews. More and more, Rod delighted in having come there to be its rabbi, amazed he could have ever considered doing anything else.

One *Shabbat* morning, a worshipper started coming whose age, at twenty or so, was far younger than everyone else's and whose complexion, so black it bordered on onyx, was much darker. Spare but sinewy, he slipped in five or ten minutes after the Torah service began and slipped out again as it ended. Rod would have liked to introduce himself, but he was otherwise occupied on the *bimah*. He finally got his chance on a Saturday when Bob, who was just back from another week on the road, took his usual place as *Shabbos gabbai* and said, "Rabbi, today's the anniversary of my *bar mitzvah*—I can spell you with the Torah reading and *Haftarah*." As Bob began chanting the first *aliyah*, the mysterious visitor walked in as if on cue and sat down in the back by himself. Rod immediately stepped down from the *bimah* to go sit beside him. "Shabbat Shalom, I'm Rabbi Zieglitz," he said, extending his hand.

". . . Dawit," the man murmured without taking the hand.

Unsure whether he'd heard the man's name correctly, or whether it was his first name or last, Rod responded, "Why don't you stay for *Kiddush*? It'd give you and the congregation the opportunity to get acquainted."

Dawit shook his head no.

"Perhaps some other time . . ." Rod said getting up, disappointed he hadn't made Dawit feel more welcome.

Monday around noon, Rod's secretary Christine burst into his office and told him in a hushed, urgent voice, "There's a man outside who wants to see you."

"Turns out I'm free now—go ahead and send him in," Rod replied.

"But . . . Rabbi, he's a . . . stranger—I've never seen him before," Christine spluttered.

"I think that's the definition of 'stranger,'" Rod gently teased her.

"But we don't know a thing about him!"

Rod grinned. "That makes you two for two defining 'stranger.' Would you like to try for the grand prize, and go for three in a row? Christine, please show our guest in."

As Dawit walked past her, Christine asked, "Rabbi, would you like me to leave the door open in case you need me?"

"Close it on your way out," Rod responded, shooing her away. Once she'd left, he turned to Dawit and said, "I'm so glad to see you! At services, people couldn't really get to know you."

With his eyes fixed on the floor, Dawit answered, "That's what I've come about. . . . It's better they don't."

"Why's that?" Rod asked.

Looking up, Dawit told him, "It goes back to my boyhood in Ethiopia. Perhaps you can hear that my name sounds like 'David.' It is because I, too, am a Jew. My parents were *Beta Israel*, though our enemies called us *Falashas*—it's Amharic for 'strangers.'"

Fearing Dawit might have heard Christine's comments, Rod proceeded as delicately as possible. "Stop me, Dawit, if I'm prying, but how did you wind up in Rifton? Whatever you tell me won't leave this office."

Dawit averted his eyes once again and replied quietly, "It has been a long journey, and there are many parts of it I cannot remember. The doctors say it is because of the violence I have suffered—which they also say is why I sometimes act violently toward others and must remain in a psychiatric group home for now. Coming to the synagogue settles me. Although I cannot read or understand Hebrew, being here with other Jews makes me feel there is somewhere I belong."

Smiling, Rod answered, "That's exactly what's supposed to happen. I can still remember feeling that way as a boy when the Torah was carried through the congregation. If you'd stay after services, I could introduce you to a few of our members whom I know would be discreet about anything you felt like sharing with them."

"Staying longer isn't possible for me, because I'd miss my bus back to the group home—it's that same one that brings me here."

"I could arrange rides for you if you'd like."

Rising to leave, Dawit said, "Thank you, no. Then people would see where I live."

Dawit continued coming to the Torah service on Sabbaths, and from time to time, he'd even put in an appearance on festivals as the bus schedule permitted. Raising a *minyan* for a holiday's conclusion wasn't a problem as attendance swelled thanks to the addition of the *Yizkor* service when people thronged to commemorate their departed. Rounding up ten congregants for a festival's beginning was always a struggle, though, and particularly if it occurred on a weekday when even devoted members like Bob had to go to work instead. At those times, everything depended on the *shul's* cadre of stalwarts composed of seniors like Lilly, along with some of its middle-aged members such as Morris and Harriet, complemented by its young rabbi and *rebbetzin*, who welcomed every opportunity she had to practice the Hebrew her husband had taught her.

Midway through Rod's second year at the synagogue, the first day of Passover fell on a Tuesday, and mustering a *minyan* seemed more daunting than usual. To begin with, Nataliya was forced to stay home, laid low by a bug she'd picked up from one of the families she'd asked over for seder the previous evening. When Rod walked into the sanctuary the next morning, he learned that Nataliya wasn't the only regular who was ailing. "Plotnik's out with kidney stones!" Fritz Caen, the *shul's* self-appointed festival *gabbai*, announced to Rod and anyone else within earshot. Decked out in a peacock blue polyester sports coat, canary yellow shirt, jade green tie, and cranberry slacks with a white, patent leather belt and loafers to match—the same finery he wore to his other dressy venue, the track—Fritz told Rod as though he'd consulted a betting sheet for services, "With your Frau a scratch, too, the odds of our getting a *minyan* are one hundred to one."

Fritz, who'd fled Nazi Germany as a teenager, held his presence at a festival's commencement like a sword over the other attendees' heads, and yet, he wanted a *minyan* much as they did, because in his eyes, a service without one was as much a personal slight as an affront to God. With no Torah reading, he'd get no honors, neither the first *aliyah* as the synagogue's sole *Kohen* whose titular priesthood purportedly stretched back unbroken to Aaron, nor the second that Jewish law let him have absent a Levite, the priest's traditional lieutenant. Irrespective of *halacha*, though, Fritz would also claim the *aliyah* of any congregant who, by his lights, couldn't properly recite its Hebrew. Fritz nonetheless never poached *maftir*. "How can I sing the *haftarah* with joy when my heart still grieves for the six million?" he'd lament as he predictably sloughed it off on Rod, who these days took it in stride. While as a boy, he'd spent the better part of a year mastering his *haftarah*, the rabbi he'd become could flawlessly chant any text cold with a much improved voice, due to Bob's coaching. Still, without a *minyan* that morning, the *haftarah*'s cantillation would be rendered moot, since there'd be no Torah reading to precede it.

"Post time!" Fritz hollered his call to worship, indifferent as ever to how it made Rod grimace. Forty minutes later, Rod silently took another head count; including himself, the *minyan* was still short by one. Resigned, he flipped to the *siddur*'s closing hymns and was about to call out the page number when Dawit walked in through the doors in the back. Shouldering the scroll, Rod jubilantly proclaimed, "The Torah service begins on 117!" As he carried the Torah through the congregation, he paused to wish Dawit an especially hearty "*Gut Yontif!*" When he'd looped around to the *bimah* again, he laid down the sacred parchment and removed its crown, pointer, and cover. Afterwards, Fritz called up each of the day's five *aliyot*—himself first (and second), then Morris, Harriet and Edna (whom Harriet had cajoled into coming), followed by Rod as *maftir*. Before the *haftarah* could be chanted, however, the Torah had to be lifted so it could be rewrapped.

"Who should I call to hoist it?" Fritz asked Rod.

Scanning the sparse, aged assembly for someone strong enough to heave the thirty-five-pound scroll overhead, Rod's eyes came to rest on Dawit. He and the honor seemed made for each other: Dawit didn't have any physical debility, and the *aliyah* didn't have any Hebrew. Answering Fritz, Rod pointed at Dawit and said, "What about him? If he hadn't come, none of us would have gotten an *aliyah* today." When Fritz didn't respond, Rod invited Dawit himself, calling out to him, "Please come up for the honor of *hagbah*."

Dawit hesitantly rose from his seat and slowly made his way down the aisle, but the moment he stepped on the *bimah*, Fritz stomped off it. Before exiting the sanctuary, he spun around and, even more loudly than when he'd called the service to order, cried, "*Neger!*"

Two years earlier, Rod hadn't made a peep following Nate's blasphemous Israel fundraising pitch, but the intervening time had done more than bolster his confidence when it came to speaking out—it had also honed his judgment about when to do it. There'd be changes, he decided, but he'd wait until the next *Shabbos* to make them public.

"—Rabbi," Lilly's voice brought Rod's thoughts back to the service, "shouldn't we rewrap the Torah so it's not lying uncovered?"

"You're right . . . thank you," Rod replied and motioned her to come to the *bimah*. After she dressed the scroll in all its trappings, he placed it inside the ark, afterwards telling everyone how appreciative he was for their having come. As the sanctuary emptied out, he went over to Dawit and said, "I'm so sorry about what happened. Why don't I give you a ride home?"

"Thank you, but I will take the bus," Dawit answered almost inaudibly before he, too, disappeared through the doors in the back.

The next Saturday morning Fritz unexpectedly turned up, having temporarily relinquished his pride of place as first in line at the betting window to reassert his priestly prerogatives as first in line for the Torah honors. By contrast, Dawit was missing, and so was Rod's customary sermon. As Fritz opened his mouth to recite the blessing, Rod cut him short, telling the congregation, "While we're still in the midst of *Pesach*, I'm instituting a change that's based on the only thing I learned in Hebrew school worth remembering. My teacher Mr. Weinstock drilled into us that we must never become 'good Egyptians.' He was referring to the kind of people who witness wrongdoing and don't speak out against it, and he warned us that a good Egyptian is as bad in God's eyes as Pharaoh. So this *Shabbos*, I'm going to right the wrong done here Tuesday morning. As of this moment, the *aliyot* in this synagogue won't be distributed according to honorific titles like *Kohen* and *Levi*. Instead, they'll be awarded to those who *deserve to be honored* for acts they've performed during the past week. Therefore, this *Shabbat's* first *aliyah* goes to Lilly Marx, who spoke up to remind us of the Torah's holiness after it had been profaned."

As Lilly walked toward the *bimah*, her cheeks flushed from all the attention, Fritz stormed out past her, crimson with rage once again. He never returned—nor did Dawit.

At *Kiddush*, after news spread of Fritz's previous conduct, several congregants told Rod that that if he ever needed them for a *minyan* on *yontif*, all he had to do was give them a call. That afternoon, though, he discovered that not everyone agreed with his handling of Fritz's outburst.

"I've heard about the ruckus you stirred up this morning," Nate said when he phoned.

"*Heard from whom*?" Rod demanded as if he couldn't have guessed.

"Fritz Caen. He got on the horn to gripe to me about how you insulted him in front of the whole congregation."

"And did he happen to mention how *he* publicly insulted somebody a few days ago?"

"Cool down, Rod—I know all about it. Listen, I don't give a tinker's damn about Fritz Caen. He might be a *Kohen*, but he ain't got no cash, and no matter what he happens to think of that friend of yours, the only color I care about is green . . . which brings me to the reason I was going to give you a jingle tonight anyway. Even though the *shul's* been getting some more members, at the rate it's going, they'll be saying *Yizkor* for both of us before it gets enough of those newcomers to join up. So I've decided it's high time for me to go ahead and build my north side temple!"

"I thought all your finances had been tied up by the bank!" Rod said.

"No, not for sometime now."

"—So where's my increased salary, Nate?"

"All in due time, Rod, all in due time. As for now, though, how about my showing you the new synagogue's plans tomorrow morning?"

"What time should I meet you at the *shul*?" Rod asked.

"I'll pop by around eight to pick you up at your place," Nate said before he hung up.

Rod put down the receiver and said to Nataliya, "This is exactly the kind of thing that's bothered me since we got here—there's no boundaries, no respect for our privacy. Remember that first *Rosh Hashannah* at the Nudelmans' when you said you felt like we were in a fishbowl?"

Nataliya told him to calm down. "It's only Nate, Rod, not the whole congregation. Everything will be just fine."

Nate's Caddy rolled up half an hour early on Sunday and summoned Rod with three sharp honks of its horn. As Rod got in, Nate said, "I'll show you the blueprints later, but first, we're going on a little excursion." Nearly an hour went by before he turned into a housing development in north Rifton, and as he drove past the thirty or so homes in various stages of construction, he stated proudly, "All these are mine." Finally stopping in front of one of the houses, he stuck his forefinger out the window and declared, "But that one, Rod, is *yours*."

Rod craned his head to look through Nate's window at the development's lone finished dwelling, one which didn't sit on a barren lot like the others, but on a lush, sodded lawn made all the more verdant by a shimmering grove of live oaks that abutted it. Once Nate had retrieved the blueprints from the trunk, he walked around to Rod's side, opened the door, and asked puckishly, "Interested in having a look-see?" Following Nate in, Rod gaped at the house's spaciousness. "It's the model home I described at my *Yom Kippur* break-the-fast," Nate explained, seeing the expression on Rod's face. "Just like I told you, it's got five bedrooms, four baths, large living and dining rooms, a comfy den and state-of-the-art kitchen, not to mention a three-car garage and Olympic-size pool. So what do you think?"

"It's impressive, Nate, but I doubt I could even scrape together the down payment."

"Whatever it costs, Rod, I've got it covered. It's to my benefit as much as yours for you to move in here. Having a rabbi and his temple in the neighborhood will give me an edge over my competitors—it'll attract more Jews to my houses in this part of town rather than to theirs in other parts of Rifton. Of course, if that happens, it means a bigger package for you."

"Meanwhile, I'd still like to know what my monthly mortgage obligation would be," Rod responded warily, as uncomfortable with being bait to lure Jews to Nate's project as with congregants' proximity to his and Nataliya's home if they bit.

With a wave of his hand, Nate dismissed Rod's reservations. "You leave your housing to me! Now, though, let's take a look at the *shul*'s blueprints. Remember what I told you—the synagogue is going to have my backing, but it'll still have your input. Is there anything you want to add?"

Examining the plans Nate had laid out on the countertop, Rod had to admit they incorporated practically every item which, if he'd had the talent, he would have diagrammed himself. The architect had included numerous classrooms and ample office space, not merely for a current synagogue, but for a future one if it flourished. Rod's focal point, though, was the sanctuary, where the drawings depicted a high, peaked ceiling overlooking a semicircular *bimah* nestled among crescents of pews, a design that evoked a sense of intimacy amid transcendence. And yet as much as Rod admired what the architect had achieved, he thought one key element had been omitted. "Where are the windows?" he asked Nate.

"We put in a ton of lighting instead—Otherwise, the AC bills would kill us."

"Can't be helped, Nate—Jewish law requires them."

"And just why is that?" Nate retorted.

Rod took a deep breath and reminded himself that as a rabbi, his essential task was teaching Torah, regardless of how uninterested—or hostile—a student might be. "While the Talmud never gives an explicit rationale, I suspect it's because windows connect us to the world outside of the sanctuary, where the words of the service have to be put into practice. It's why I couldn't ignore what Fritz did Tues—"

"Will you let it go already?" Nate broke in. "I'll have my guy ink in some windows for you. But here's what *I* want—a groundbreaking ASAP. Does that Talmud of yours have anything to say about that?"

"Well, *Shavuot* is coming up in a few months. The rabbis of the Talmud taught that it marks when Israel received the Torah and came into existence as a people. So in a way, the holiday's about a community's starting out fresh. Don't you think it'd be the perfect occasion to break ground for the new *shul*?"

"Just so it's sooner rather than later," Nate replied.

"And where will the synagogue be built?" Rod asked.

Nate opened the kitchen window. "See those oak trees at the edge of your backyard? Once they're cleared and the temple goes up, it'll only be a hop, skip, and a jump between your work and your home."

XVI

———

Twelve Passovers later, Rabbi Roderick Zieglitz, his wife, and their child were on the five-minute walk home from *shul* after morning services for the festival's first day. While attendance hadn't rivaled the three hundred congregants he typically drew *Shabbos* mornings, let alone the six hundred he attracted Friday nights, the dozens of worshippers present were proof he didn't have to worry anymore about getting a *minyan* for a Jewish holiday that began during the work week. Between his rabbinic skills and Nate's real estate savvy, the synagogue had flourished. So many more households had joined that they'd justified the Board's expanding the staff so that Rod didn't ever again have to serve as *chazzan*, since he now had a guitar-playing, crowd-rousing cantor. The Torah and *haftarah* readings had likewise ceased being his responsibility. The augmented religious school included a cadre of tutors who ensured a *bar* or *bat mitzvah* would ascend the *bimah* every week to chant from a scroll and red primer. In addition to its new members and building, the synagogue even had a new name, thanks to another of Nate's marketing ideas. Leaving the groundbreaking, he'd said to Rod, "You remember how you told me we'd be making a fresh start? Let's do it up right, then, and call ourselves something different, not just from what we've been until now, but from what any other temple's been known as."

Rod considered—and rejected—several possibilities: "*Anshei Kavod*" meaning "People of Honor" (too self-satisfied, he thought); "*Pitchei Shemayim*" or "Gates of Heaven" (too pretentious, he concluded); "*Ramot Simcha*"—"Heights of Joy" (just plain too too-too, he reckoned). With the fallout from the Fritz and Dawit fracas still fresh in his mind, he wanted a name that would do more than move the congregation's ranks forward—he wanted one that would move them forward *together*. As he ended services in the old converted funeral parlor for the last time, he recalled his initial *Kol Nidre* there when he'd appealed for reconciliation. At the new *shul's* dedication a week later, he unveiled the name he'd cleared with Nate and the Board only a few days before. Looking out over the assembly, he said, "From now on, we're *B'ikvot Hoshea*, which means 'In Hosea's Footsteps.' It's as much aspiration as designation, because through the prophet Hosea's marriage, God manifests what we'll need to remain close to one another. Hosea and God both had wayward partners—Hosea's wife Gomer cavorted with other men while Israel consorted with other gods. No less anguished than angered by its unfaithfulness, God had Hosea divorce Gomer to signify He'd cast us out. But then, God had a stunning change of heart. He has Hosea take back Gomer as a symbol He's re-embraced us, vowing never to spurn us again by pledging, 'I betroth Myself to you forever.' Let the Jews of this synagogue follow the path God set for Hosea by always displaying such forgiving love toward each other!"

In retrospect, Rod thought the book of Hosea could just have as easily have been about God's enduring devotion to him, despite all the times he'd disavowed Him, from his blasphemy at Jack's death to his idolatry with Israel to his heresy in rabbinical school. And yet, apart from his rocky start at the *shul*, Rod's tenure there had met with nothing but triumph. Hosea aside, Rabbi Kimmelman's latter-day prophecy had come true—Rod's Hebrew name hadn't been a curse but a blessing; rather than voicing an idle plea for divine intervention, "Yerachmiel" had heralded God's steadfast support.

Even so, nobody at *shul* called him "Yerachmiel," much less "Rod." The younger members came closest with "Rabbi Rod" while their teens preferred the shorter—and in their eyes, cooler—"Rabbi Z." For their part, the AKs favored what they saw as the more respectful "Rabbi Zieglitz." In the end, his name got swallowed up by his title, reducing his identity to "Rabbi."

The name that mattered most to him, though, belonged to the nine-year-old skipping ahead of him and Nataliya on the path home that first day of *Pesach*. Agreeing on the child's name hadn't been easy, however. After Nataliya's sonogram indicated she was carrying a boy, Rod had asked her, "What do you think of 'Yitzchak'? In Hebrew, it means 'laughter.' What better thing could we wish for our son?"

Nataliya winced and replied, "That he shouldn't be a laughingstock—we live in Rifton, not New York!"

"So what name do you want to give him, Nataliya?"

"I like 'Ilya.'"

"Oh, I'm sure a Russki name like that would go down big in these parts!"

"But it's a connection to my family's roots. And besides, I didn't do so bad when I named you, Rod."

"No, you didn't. Just promise me 'Ilya' isn't Cossack for 'Jew-killer,'" he said with a smile.

Smiling back, Nataliya responded, "I already looked it up, Rabbi. 'Ilya' in Russian is like 'Elijah' in Hebrew—it means 'My God is the Lord.'"

Rod laughed and said, "Well, look who's done her homework! I still like 'Yitzchak' for his Hebrew name, though. God only knows, I could have used a lot more laughter in the house where I grew up."

As the three Zieglitzes got ready for *yontif* lunch in their own house, Rod had no doubt it was a far happier one than his had been, for unlike Dad, he'd prospered. That prosperity had nonetheless come at the cost of the very thing he and Nataliya had fretted about after Rod's inaugural *Rosh Hashannah* service in Rifton: their privacy. In the beginning, Nataliya had downplayed his fears, but not anymore. Unlike a ballet performance that was over in a few hours, her role as *rebbetzin* had her constantly onstage, and she resented being subject to the critical review of one congregant after another. More important, ever since Ilya's birth, she'd increasingly begrudged the congregation's intrusiveness into her home life. Although Rod shared her concerns, he often had trouble balancing his family obligations with those to his membership. As he gave Ilya a little grape juice and *matzah*, Nataliya said to him, "Maybe since it's a workday instead of *Shabbos*, we'll be spared having some congregant come by uninvited with the same flimsy excuse—'Pardon me, Rabbi, but as long as I was at the *shul* anyway, I thought I'd pop over for a minute of your time.' Why can't they just catch you at *Kiddush* or your office? It's bad enough that Nate holds our mortgage, but a lot of them act like they're our co-tenants! Even our supposedly unlisted number doesn't stop them. It was one thing for the Nudelmans or Bob and Lilly to have it, but now it seems like the whole congregation's got it—"

Nataliya had scarcely finished speaking when the telephone rang. "I'll get it—I promise I won't be long!" Rod said, seeing the irritation on her face.

"But *Abba*," Ilya protested to his father, "you said you'd play catch with me!"

"Just let the answering machine take it!" Nataliya told Rod.

"But then, it'll be hanging over us all afternoon," he answered.

He went to his study, picked up the phone, and heard one of his congregants say on the other end, "Hello, Rabbi, this is Arnie Golub. I apologize for calling you at home. I would have approached you at *shul* this morning, but there were always too many people around."

"What can I do for you, Arnie?" Rod said softly so Nataliya wouldn't overhear him.

"It's about my niece, Kitty, and it's a long, sad story, Rabbi. About six years ago, she married a local Jewish boy, Mickey Bledsoe, who was a Navy flier. They had a romance straight out of Cinderella with Mickey being the Prince Charming who rescued Kitty from an absolutely wretched existence. My sister and brother-in-law both died when Kitty was small, and by the time she was twelve, she'd been in and out of so many foster homes, I lost count. As God is my witness, Rabbi, I wanted to adopt her myself! But with my being a bachelor, the courts and social-work agencies wouldn't hear of it. Anyhow, once Kitty got old enough, she moved out on her own, going from one lousy job to another until she wound up as a stockgirl at the base PX. Mickey stopped in one day for some aftershave, saw her, and then kept coming back day after day, pretending to need something or other until he finally mustered the courage to ask her out. Pretty incredible for a guy with the guts to fly in combat missions and air shows! Well, after they'd been dating for close to a year, Kitty took the initiative and popped the question. Rabbi, you've never seen such a happy couple."

". . . You said it was a sad story, Arnie," Rod prodded him, suddenly conscious of Nataliya tapping her foot behind him.

"I think it's best if Kitty tells you, Rabbi. She's not a member of the congregation, but would you be willing to meet with her anyway?"

"Of course, Arnie, but on one condition—Kitty has to call me herself. Otherwise, she might feel like I was meddling."

"Agreed. I'll drop her a hint and leave it at that. Thanks for your help, Rabbi." The line went dead before Rod could say, "Have Kitty call me at my office!"

Weeks went by with no word from Kitty, and Rod forgot all about her. He was getting his briefcase to head home one late afternoon when Christine buzzed him on the intercom. "There's a woman named Kitty Bledsoe on the phone for you, and she sounds upset."

Once Christine put Kitty through, Rod said, "It's so good to speak with you at last! What can I do for you?

". . . I think I need to see you."

Rod had promised he'd hit Ilya some fungoes, a game he enjoyed, too, as he played Jack to his boy's Ricky. Still, since Kitty had taken so long to call him, Rod hesitated putting her off until the next day, afraid he might put her off altogether. "I could see you first thing tomorrow," he told her, pausing, ". . . unless you feel it's urgent, in which case I could see you today."

"No, tomorrow's fine," she replied.

When Kitty walked into Rod's office the next morning, she looked every inch the grief-shrouded widow with her black dress, stockings, and shoes as well her sooty eyeshadow, sable lipstick, and raven hair. Around

Kitty's neck was a heavy chain dangling some sort of pendant Rod couldn't quite make out, but given the rest of her appearance, he wouldn't have been surprised if it was a lump of coal.

After Kitty sat down across from Rod at his desk, she said, "When Uncle Arnie broached my coming to talk with you, I told him I could handle things by myself. But now, I've discovered I can't. I'm still not sure, though, how you can help."

"Why don't you just say what's troubling you? Arnie thought it best if you told me yourself."

After taking a deep breath, Kitty went on, "As horrible as my life had been before I met Mickey, I should have known that what we had couldn't last. We were about to celebrate our first anniversary when Mickey was practicing a new stunt near the coast. As he was going into a dive, his engine stalled . . . and his plane crashed in flames on the beach." As Kitty leaned forward to take a tissue from the box on his desk, Rod got a closer look at the necklace hanging around her throat: it was the likeness of a flight-helmeted pilot. In that instant, Rod understood why Kitty had come—she was enchained by her dead husband's memory.

Kitty mopped her eyes with the Kleenex. "There wasn't enough left of Mickey for a proper burial, so we only had a brief memorial service. Ever since then, it's been like I've been dead, too. Despite what everybody keeps telling me, I just can't move on . . ."

Handing Kitty another tissue, Rod said, "Sometimes, people think that things should simply return to normal once the *shivah*'s over."

"What *shivah*, Rabbi? As soon as the memorial service ended, every-one started pushing me to get on with my life."

"That's just awful, Kitty—I'm so sorry you didn't get to have a *shivah* and the chance to mourn Mickey."

"What do you mean? It seems like all I've been doing is mourning!"

"No, Kitty, what you've been doing is grieving, which is different from mourning. There's a verse in Proverbs that says, 'The heart knows its own pain,' and its point is that grieving is subjective, varying from one individual to the next. By contrast, mourning consists of a set of shared practices a community observes so its bereaved can cope with their grief. If anyone's bereaved, you are, Kitty. The word's root meaning is 'robbed,' and you've been robbed twice—first of the man you loved and then of the opportunity to mourn him. But that's not all that's been stolen from you. How'd you put it? 'Ever since Mickey's death, it's like I've been dead, too.' Holding a *shivah* for him could start you getting your life back again."

"You mean Judaism allows that?"

"In instances like yours, it does."

"I'm not sure I could stand it . . . it would mean turning back the clock to when Mickey died."

"Isn't that where you're at now anyway?" Rod asked.

"Would it be all right, Rabbi, if I took some time to make my mind up?"

"Take as much as you need. If and when you decide a *shivah*'s what you want, just let me know, and I'll arrange it. Meanwhile, I think it would be a good idea if you got in touch with a therapist. There are several in Rifton I could recommend."

Kitty shook her head. "Maybe later. For now, I've got my hands full figuring out whether I want a *shivah*."

A week passed before she phoned Rod again at his office. "I'd like to go ahead with the *shivah*—I'll do anything to turn my life around!"

"I think you've made the right choice, Kitty. After we hang up, I'll call some folks to line up a *minyan*."

"Before you do that, I have another favor to ask you. Uncle Arnie told me that a *minyan*'s held both evenings and early mornings. Could we just skip the morning service, though? With all the sedatives I take to get to sleep, I'm afraid I'll never get up in time."

"Whatever you need, Kitty. The *shivah* is supposed to ease your suffering, not add to it. By the way, have you given any thought yet to seeing a therapist?"

There was a long pause before Kitty said, "Not really. The *shivah*'s taken all my attention."

"Perhaps once it's over, you'll feel like reaching out to one," Rod replied, telling Kitty goodbye. Next, he called several of the *shul*'s stalwarts to have them attend her *minyan*, and as a little added insurance there'd be one, he asked Nataliya to go with him. Ordinarily, she would have resisted being in the *rebbetzin* spotlight again, but after Rod told her of Kitty's plight, she relented, saying, "How could I refuse a poor woman like that?" She found a sitter for Ilya and arrived at Kitty's early with Rod, who introduced her as he carried in *siddurim* he'd brought from the *shul*. While Nataliya distributed them among the semicircle of chairs set up in the living room, Kitty confided to Rod, "I'm not sure I understand how this works. I thought the goal was to get me out of the house to live my life the way I did before Mickey died. I just don't see how sitting at home for a week will make me feel better."

"That's part of the wisdom of *shivah*, Kitty. You ought to appreciate more than anyone what can happen when death strikes, and we still go on as though it's business as usual. In all kinds of ways, *shivah* makes us acknowledge it isn't. So when you sit *shivah*, you don't use an easy chair, but a footstool to represent how you've been brought low by a loved one's loss.

Another thing you do in a house of mourning is to cover all the mirrors, because when you're face-to-face with death, what difference does it make how you look? That's also the reason why women in mourning don't wear makeup."

Kitty flushed and put her hands to her cheeks. "Let me go to the bathroom and wipe this stuff off!"

"Would you like me to help you?" Nataliya asked as she put down the last prayer book.

"Please," said Kitty.

When she and Nataliya returned, her funereal cosmetics were gone. "Am I okay now?" she asked Rod.

"You look positively beautiful!" Nataliya jumped in before he could answer.

Kitty looked at her and said quietly, "I'm lucky to have such a rabbi, but you're lucky to have such a husband."

"I know," Nataliya replied.

While Rod was grateful for Kitty's praise, Nataliya's meant much more, especially given the strain on their marriage his position had caused. He pressed her hand gently before saying to Kitty, "There's one more thing we need to do to get ready. Traditionally, you'd symbolize how death has rent your heart in two by tearing your garment's collar opposite it. Nowadays, though, most people just have me pin a little ribbon there and cut it halfway through." As Rod sliced the ribbon, Kitty whimpered and reached for his arm for support.

Once Kitty had her *minyan*, Rod conducted a brief service that climaxed with the Mourner's *Kaddish*. Although he said it as slowly as possible so Kitty could follow along in the transliteration, he could see she still had trouble reciting it. After everyone else had left, she confessed to him and Nataliya, "Tonight's the first time I've even tried saying *Kaddish* for Mickey. At his memorial service, I was so angry I couldn't bring myself to do it, and later on, I didn't want to, because it would have meant actually admitting that he'd died. Maybe now, though, I've finally begun to accept it."

By the time Rod and Nataliya saw Kitty again, another layer of her widowhood had been stripped off: she'd rinsed away the jet-black dye from her hair, revealing herself to be a brunette. After welcoming the rabbi and *rebbetzin* inside, she told them, "The *shivah* seems to be helping. I don't want to be a bother to anybody, but do you think we could also have a morning *minyan*? —Or is that silly, like thinking that if one dose of medicine is good, two must be better?"

Once more, Nataliya responded before Rod could. "No, it's not silly at all, Kitty. Remember—two *minyanim* per day are what's prescribed by Jewish tradition."

"So do you think I'll be okay once the *shivah*'s over?"

"Now *that's* a question for the rabbi," Nataliya said, winking at Rod.

Taking the cue, Rod explained to Kitty, "*Shivah* doesn't magically make everything swell. It's been five years since my grandmother Dina died, and unlike Mickey's death, hers wasn't the result of a sudden, tragic mishap—she'd had diabetes for years. But there are times even now when I instinctively reach for the phone to call her for some advice, and out of nowhere, a fresh stab of pain reminds me she's gone. It's not as bad now as it was right after she died, but though those pangs aren't nearly as frequent, I expect they'll be with me for the rest of my life."

Kitty replied, "I should have known that, I suppose. Thank you for always being so patient with me."

"Just doing my job as a rabbi," Rod said.

"And you're really good at it, darling," Nataliya whispered in Rod's ear.

The last morning of the *shivah* Rod showed up at Kitty's by himself. "Is your wife okay?" she asked.

"She just had to take our son to school early to help with his show-and-tell. They're both disappointed I won't be there, and while I am, too, my being here for your *shivah*'s conclusion takes priority. At the end of today's service, I'll ask people to collect the prayer books, uncover the mirrors, and put your stool and chairs back where they belong. Meantime, you'll go with me for a walk around the block. When you return, this won't be a house of mourning anymore, but hopefully, a home where you can start living again."

Once the *shivah*'s final *Kaddish* had been said, Rod and Kitty took a stroll outside, ambling past the crepe myrtles and magnolias that lined her street. They rounded a corner and came to a park where Rod had them sit down on one of its benches as he told her, "Rabbinic literature has all kinds of stories about the question God puts to us when we come before Him to be judged. In one of them, God asks whether we routinely gave *tzedakah* to the needy. In another, He asks whether we regularly studied Torah. But there's a version of the story, Kitty, with a question I think God might ask you."

". . . What is it, Rabbi?"

"Of all the pleasures forbidden Jews, like eating pork for example, which of those still permitted to us have you nevertheless denied yourself? In other words, Kitty, by continuing to grieve for Mickey, which of life's joys have you wrongly said no to?"

Kitty slowly loosed Mickey's chain and let it fall to the grass. "Will you take me home now, Rabbi?" she said so low Rod could barely hear her.

When they'd made the circuit back to Kitty's front porch, Rod took her hands in his and recited the customary verse from Isaiah foretelling death's destruction and an end to all grieving. As he started to let go of her hands, Kitty clasped his and kissed his cheek. He flinched, and she blushed. Pulling away, Rod lied, "I have to get back to the synagogue for an appointment."

On the next *Shabbos* morning a few days later, Rod wasn't entirely surprised—and more than a little relieved—that Kitty wasn't at services to say *Kaddish* for Mickey; she hadn't been a *shul*goer previously, and the *shivah*'s goal had been to have her start up her life again. On Monday, though, he'd barely sat down in his office ahead of Christine's getting there when Kitty walked in wearing a sleeveless, gauzy pink shift.

". . . Is something wrong, Kitty?" Rod asked nervously.

"No—everything's great! Over the weekend, I did a lot of thinking about the question you asked me, and now, I have the answer. The pleasure I want, Rod, is you! —I haven't felt this way about a man since Mickey."

Rod didn't want to hurt her, but he didn't want to encourage her, either. "Kitty, what you're experiencing is transference. It's not uncommon in counseling."

"*Transference*—you think that's all there is to it! Don't you feel something, too?"

"Not in the way you mean, I don't. Besides, I'm a married man, Kitty, which makes me one of those pleasures that's off-limits."

"Mickey was shy, too, Rod. Is it that hard for you to admit I'm attractive? Even your wife said I'm beautiful!"

"Do you also remember what *I* said about your needing a good therapist? Like I told you, there are several around town I'd be glad to—"

Before he could finish, Kitty stalked out of his office, slamming the door behind her.

"Thank goodness you're done with that woman," Nataliya said later after they'd put Ilya to bed and Rod related what had happened. "Anybody who goes around wearing a bust of her dead husband for a necklace has to be a little *meshugah* to begin with."

At 2:30 that night, Rod was awakened by the phone on his nightstand. ". . . This is Rabbi," he answered groggily, bracing himself for the news that somebody in the congregation had died.

"It's me."

"Who?"

"Me, Kitty. . . . Don't you recognize my voice?"

"Why are you calling?" Rod muttered, rubbing his eyes.

"I miss our time alone together!" Kitty cried so loudly through the receiver that she woke Nataliya.

Rod propped himself up on his pillow and said, "I don't know what you're talking about, Kitty. We always had lots of other people around at the *shivah*."

"Not when I kissed you!"

"But I didn't kiss you back!"

"Maybe if you weren't married, you would have."

"Go back to sleep, Kitty. I'm going to hang up now. Good night."

The next night at three, the phone rang again.

"What is it with that Kitty Bledsoe?!" Nataliya groaned even before Rod answered.

"Kitty, you've got to stop calling me like this," Rod said after hearing her voice.

"But I really need to be with you!"

"Kitty, you know that's impossible."

"I know, I know . . . I just want to see you, that's all."

"Then call Christine to make a time to meet me at my office," Rod responded as he set the receiver down on its cradle and tried to get back to sleep.

Nataliya rolled over toward him and said, "We need a new number, and this time, you've got to keep it to yourself."

"But what if somebody genuinely needs me?"

"Have the *shul* get an answering service to screen your calls."

"I'll take it up with the Board, though I doubt how much good having one would do. What if Kitty called and sounded really desperate? How could I tell the service, 'Don't put her through'? I've already had one suicide in my life—I don't want another one here." Hearing himself, he paused and said, "My God, Nataliya—listen to me! Wasn't I the guy who brooded about the congregation's not having boundaries? Turns out I'm the problem, not them."

"Just try to get some sleep, Rod, before Ilya gets up . . ." Nataliya said as she dozed off.

The next night, Kitty rang even later. "I can't go on without you, Rod— I'll kill myself if we can't be together!"

"Tell her to just get it over with," Nataliya mumbled into her pillow.

"For the last time, Kitty, you need professional help."

"I don't want a shrink! I want you!"

"Please, Kitty, don't call here anymore—it's not fair to my family," Rod said, putting the receiver down on its cradle and then quickly taking it off so the phone wouldn't ring again that night.

Later that morning, when Rod joined Nataliya and Ilya for breakfast, he told them, "I'm glad it's my day off—I'm really tired."

"But can we still play ball?" Ilya asked.

Pouring Rod's coffee, Nataliya replied, "*Abba* needs some rest, Ilya, and so do I. You'll just have to amuse yourself with something else like—"

A rap on the kitchen door cut her off. Looking through its window-pane, Rod saw Kitty standing outside wearing a low-cut blouse and short skirt and holding a leather clutch with a slight bulge at the bottom. After he cracked the door open a bit, she told him, "I went to your office to ask your forgiveness for the way I've behaved. When your secretary said you wouldn't be in today, I decided I'd take a little walk over here to tell you how sorry I am."

Rod didn't want to provoke Kitty and inflame the situation, so he said as calmly as he could, "I forgive you, Kitty. Now please leave. It's my day off, and because of your phone calls, I can definitely use it."

"I was under the impression that hospitality's a *mitzvah*," Kitty answered.

Concerned about Kitty's making a scene in front of Ilya, Rod had Nataliya take him to his room. Once they'd left, he told Kitty through the crack in the door, "You're right about the *mitzvah*, but today, it's one I'm going to have to ignore. If you want to see me, you'll have to do it at the *shul*."

"No, Rod, don't say that—just let me in!" Kitty shrieked as she reached for her bag and pulled out a snub-nosed .38 Special.

When Rod tried to shut the door, it hit Kitty's hand, and the pistol went off. Hearing the discharge, Nataliya told Ilya to stay put where he was and then came hobbling into the kitchen as fast as her limp would allow. By then, Kitty had forced her way in and flung herself on Rod.

"Get off my husband, you psycho!" Nataliya yelled as she yanked Kitty loose.

Kitty pointed her weapon at Nataliya and screamed, "Get back—Mickey taught me how to use this! Don't you realize it's me Rod should be with?"

With her eyes on Nataliya, Kitty didn't see Rod lunge for the firearm. As they struggled, he smacked her hand against the kitchen counter, and Kitty dropped the revolver, which struck the floor and fired again, grazing her shoulder. Nataliya grabbed the gun and held it on Kitty while Rod phoned 911 for the paramedics and the police.

After the paramedics had tended to Kitty and the cops had taken her away, Nataliya came back to the kitchen with Ilya and an ultimatum for Rod: "This family's moving—or else!"

XVII

———

"Where, Nataliya, where should we move to? —And what do you mean, 'Or else'?" Rod said, no less distressed than she was.

"I don't know, Rod—just somewhere that's not Rifton!"

"But there's another year to go on my contract, and if I break it, no other congregation will touch me."

"Then at least find us a house that's farther away from the *shul*."

"How would that have helped with a stalker like Kitty? She still could have tracked me down."

"Maybe, but it wouldn't have been such a short walk for her. Even if there's never another Kitty, getting more breathing space between your job and our home might help you make more room in your life for Ilya and me."

"All right, but where would the money come from to buy us another house? Between Nate charging the congregation rent for this place and the Board's deducting it from my salary, you know as well as I do what our bank account looks like. I doubt we could even scrape together a down payment! Would you settle for an apartment?"

"What choice do we have?" Nataliya sighed.

The Zieglitzes moved to a flat on the other side of town, but what the family gained in location, it lost in size. "This apartment's almost as small as where Nate dumped us the first night we got here," Nataliya said to Rod after they'd lived there a few weeks.

"And there weren't three of us then," Rod added, looking down at Ilya, whom they'd just put to bed. "I promise you, Nataliya, when my contract comes up again at the end of the year, I won't rest until I get a deal that pays enough for us to buy our own house."

Months later, as the contract talks approached, Rod kept rehearsing his *spiel* to the Board for a hefty raise. "Just look at the spike in revenue from all the members who've joined in the years that I've been here," he repeated over and over in front of the mirror.

Once the negotiations started, though, his pitch fell flat when Sid Robbins, the *shul*'s new president, told him, "No can do, Rabbi—the numbers don't pan out. Yes, it's true that we've been growing, but it's also true that most of those fresh faces are twentysomethings with small kids. It's why a number of us younger members ran for the Board—we didn't feel represented! With you in your mid-forties, we've decided to look for an assistant rabbi who's closer to our age and can relate to us better. Financially, the only way we can swing it is to find somebody who's so musically talented that we can axe the cantor. Bottom line, Rabbi, we're in no position to raise your pay."

Rod dreaded reporting Sid's response to Nataliya, but he needn't have worried: when she heard it, she was ecstatic. "So much for Rifton! If we have to move, I'd rather do it now while Ilya's still in grade school."

Relieved, Rod let out a deep breath and said, "Maybe this is good news after all. The last time I checked the Rabbinic Federation's listings, there was a congregation with an open pulpit in California. I'll send it my résumé first thing tomorrow."

Two weeks later, Rod was on a conference call with the West Coast synagogue's president, Stacy Vogel, and her search committee, to determine whether they'd take the next step of flying him in to meet face-to-face. "Good evening, Rabbi. If you're ready, I've got a question I'd like to begin with," said Stacy.

"Fire away!" Rod answered.

"So, Rabbi, what keeps you up at night?"

Although he knew it'd be risky, Rod told her the truth, because he didn't see the point of winding up in another Rifton. "It's the nagging feeling that despite all my efforts, I've failed to make the congregation any more Jewish."

"So Rabbi, do you know why we named our synagogue *Ruach Chadasha*?" Stacy asked.

"'New Spirit,' you mean?—I know that it's what Ezekiel prophesizes God will give the Jewish people."

"Exactly! When we founded this synagogue, we wanted a congregation that would perpetually renew our spirit to make Judaism thrive."

After that, the interview became a freewheeling give-and-take as each committee member asked Rod a few questions while he followed up with questions of his own: What would the *shul* think of his training congregants as lay rabbis who could officiate at life-cycle ceremonies for their families and friends?; How would parents feel about his implementing a pre-and-post *b'nai mitzvah* curriculum where they'd study side by side with their youngsters?; Where would the Board stand on his instituting "Jewry duty" that twice a year obliged each household to help form a *minyan*?

"How have these programs worked in Rifton?" said Stacy.

"Frankly, they never gained traction," Rod admitted.

"Well, they've captured our interest, Rabbi! You should see all the heads nodding at my end. I think it's safe to say that we'd love for you and your family to come out here so we can get better acquainted."

When Rod relayed the invitation to Nataliya, she burst out, "Just say the word, and we're packed!"

"Listen, Nataliya, let's keep the trip under wraps for now. I don't want it getting out that I'm looking for another pulpit and have it undermine what little influence I still have with Sid and the Board. If anybody asks, we're just taking a short vacation."

Stacy called Rod the next day about his upcoming visit. Besides logistics like flights—"We can reimburse you for your tickets or purchase them for you"—and hotel accommodations—"Your family's entitled to its privacy!"—she included some crucial background about the congregation. "Up to now, we couldn't afford a rabbi, and so, we took turns giving sermons and leading services. We don't want to lose that sense of shared responsibility when we bring a rabbi onboard, and the programs you outlined last night sold us on having you out. Consequently, rather than have you give a sermon during services, we'd like you to offer a couple of classes while you're here, since what we're mainly looking for in a rabbi is a teacher. Because one of our members will also be conducting services, you won't have to. Our rabbi, whoever it is, should be able to come *daven* like everybody else."

When the Zieglitzes landed in California, Stacy and the search committee were waiting for them at the gate. "*Shalom!*" they called out together.

"If you're hungry, we can stop by the local deli," said Stacy.

"Or if your little boy needs a nap, we can go straight to your hotel," the committee's nominal chair, Hal Tisch, chimed in.

Smiling, Nataliya responded, "We're just fine, but I would like to see the parts of town where we might be living."

"By all means!" Stacy replied as they walked from the concourse to her car. "If you're going to be part of our community, you should be able to live wherever you want, just like the rest of us do."

As the weekend unfolded, Rod came to think of it as more of a spiritual retreat than a job interview. Between the stirring lay-led services, the enthusiastic response to his classes, and the *haimish* embrace of him and his family, he felt reinspired as a rabbi as well as a Jew. "Your *shul* sure lives up to its name!" he raved to Stacy as she delivered him, Nataliya, and Ilya to the airport for their flight back to Rifton.

"And your résumé, Rabbi, doesn't do you justice. I've received nothing but positive feedback about you, and that goes for Nataliya and Ilya, too. All I need now are three references from your *shul*—our search committee rules require that one be a board member."

Morris and Bob, both of whom had been replaced by Sid and his insurgents, were easy picks for Rod, and taking a pen and notepad from Stacy, he promptly jotted down their phone numbers, which he knew by heart. But he had to think twice about the serving board member he'd choose, since if it weren't for the Board shake-up, he wouldn't have been out looking for another position. With no alternative, he listed the only officer who'd held on to his seat. "This last name and number belong to Nate Jacobs, who's been on the Board forever," he reluctantly told Stacy.

"Thank you, Rabbi. I'm sure you'll be hearing from me soon," she said.

The five-hour, cross-country flight passed quickly for Rod as he lost himself in one California daydream after another. He thought he'd probably get a call from Stacy by midweek, and when he didn't, he simply assumed she'd experienced a delay contacting his references. But when he still hadn't heard from her by Sunday evening, he began to get nervous. On Tuesday night, the California call came at last.

"Good evening, Rabbi, this is Hal Tisch."

". . . Oh, . . . Hal . . . hi . . . I guess I thought Stacy would be phoning me," Rod said, taken aback.

Hal responded with an unfamiliar chill in his voice. "She asked me to do it. . . . Unfortunately, we won't be making you an offer."

". . . May I ask why?" Rod replied, stunned.

"On advice of counsel, I'm not at liberty to say. We wish you the best," Hal said as he abruptly hung up.

"This *shul*, this town! We'll never get out of here!" Nataliya cried after Rod told her what had happened.

Moments later the phone rang again, but neither she nor Rod felt like talking. "I'll get it!" Ilya hollered before they could stop him. "It's Mr. Jacobs, Abba," he yelled from the kitchen.

"Yes, Nate?" Rod said, picking up.

"Just checking to see how you're doing after you got the thumbs down from out west."

"How'd you know about that?"

"C'mon now—why do you think you got rejected?"

"What are you talking about, Nate?"

"When they asked me how you were at counseling congregants, I just told them how well things worked out between you and Kitty Bledsoe."

Rod was about to say "I quit!" but Nate kept on speaking. "See, I might have lost some of my clout what with all these young upstarts on the Board, but as long as you're here and I'm still footing the bill for a chunk of your salary, they can't afford to ignore me completely. So a word of friendly advice—get used to staying right where you are."

"Even if I never give you as a reference again?" Rod responded.

Nate snickered and said, "You really think that'll make a nickel's worth of difference? Nobody so much as farts around here without my knowing it."

Out of options, Rod signed a new three-year contract, which left him so despondent that he began missing office appointments, neglecting hospital visits, and losing track of page numbers during services. The congregation hardly noticed, though, because it had fallen head over heels for his recently arrived youthful assistant, Brett Bloom.

"'Rabbi Brett's so dynamic! Rabbi Brett's so creative! And he's so good with children!'" Rod mimicked how his congregants had gone gaga for Bloom as he and Nataliya drove home one night after services.

"'And Rabbi Brett's so good looking!'" Nataliya joined in, mocking the *shul*'s love affair with Bloom.

In scarcely three months' time, whenever congregants spoke of "the Rabbi," everyone understood they were referring to Bloom rather than Rod. Parents relished Bloom's free-spirited approach to religious school education, which resulted in their not having to hear their offspring whine anymore about going to class. Bloom's most ardent following, though, stemmed from the novel ditties he sang to the *shul*'s teens at each *bar* or *bat mitzvah*. "Why's all our music have to come from nineteenth-century Polish cantors?" he asked from the *bimah* before crooning his first ballad parody. "We need to *re-Jewvenate* the tradition with contemporary *chazzanim* like Bob Dylan!" To the delight of the adoring adolescent's family and friends, he then serenaded her with his reworked version of the folk troubadour's "Forever Young":

> May you bless and keep the Torah,
> May your wishes all come true,
> May you never be a *schnorrer*,
> Who lets others do for you,
> Forever Jew, forever Jew,
> May you be forever Jew.

Seething inside, Rod could only sit and watch as the mantle of "cool" passed to Bloom, leaving him exposed to members carping that he was, by comparison, "cold."

Bloom's rising star reached its zenith during the High Holy Days. Over Rod's objections, he'd persuaded the Board to make them more "with it" by trimming *Rosh Hashannah* from two days to one along with paring every service to no more than an hour and eliminating formal sermons altogether. After he gave what he called "an interactive *Rosh Hashannah* show-and-tell," complete with puppets, posters, and piano, several congregants asked Rod what he'd be doing for *Yom Kippur* morning, aware that under Bloom's revised format, there'd be no rabbinic address, informal or otherwise, on *Kol Nidre* evening. "You'll just have to wait and see," Rod answered evasively, since owing to his growing bitterness over his tightfisted contract, dashed California dreams, and smoldering resentment of Bloom, he hadn't even begun preparing what he'd say. He ultimately fell back on his old standby about the looming threats to Jewish survival. He'd scored with it his first High Holy Day outing in Rifton, and he figured it would be a hit now with the synagogue's scores of newcomers who hadn't yet heard it.

His talk touched all the bases—bloodthirsty Arabs in the Middle East, suicide bombers in Europe, Holocaust deniers in the US, anti-Semites everywhere Jews looked. When he finished, he turned around and saw Sid coming toward him with what he presumed would be a hearty "Well done!" Instead, he got a stern "You got to be joking!" Exasperated, Sid said, "Who do you think you're scaring with that Hitler bogeyman *bubbe meise*? Not our younger new members, that's for sure! They're comfortable here in Rifton—the Klan hasn't been around for years, and there hasn't so much as a peep from any neo-Nazis. Even Nate's fearmongering doesn't work anymore—why do you think we've dropped his Israel appeal?"

Once they got home, Nataliya's critique of Rod's sermon was only slightly more charitable. "That wasn't the rabbi I know up there—just an Edwards undergrad haranguing a crowd."

Wounded, Rod cried, "Don't you get it, Nataliya? Look how they treat Bloom, and look how they treat me! Do you think they care what sermon I give?"

"But I do!" she called after Rod as he stalked off toward the bedroom.

In the year that followed, what at its best had felt to Rod like he'd been tapped by God for a sacred calling seemed increasingly like a lonely, pointless chore, an unending cycle of daily appearances at the office, weekly ones on the *bimah*, and monthly ones with the Board, where he'd be scolded yet again for his shortcomings, real or imagined, with the *shul*'s younger members. His toxic relationship with the congregation spilled over to his family as he began coming home every bit as bad-tempered as Dad on his worst days. Eventually, to avoid Rod's explosions at dinner, Nataliya would feed Ilya early, get him a sitter, and go out with one of the few friends she'd made in Rifton outside the *shul*.

"I don't know what to tell you," Mom said after Rod called her for solace, depressed by his job, his marriage, and his life's downward spiral. Fearing that her son might end up like his father, Madge told him, "Staying in Huppertsville when you were small didn't help me, and moving to Medina certainly didn't help your dad. In retrospect, I'd say that it wasn't where we lived that mattered as much as what lived inside us—I'm talking about the feelings we had for one another. Speak to Nataliya, listen to what she has to say, and see if there's still some of that love that originally brought you together."

At breakfast the next morning, Nataliya told Rod that Ilya was going for a sleepover that night and she'd made plans for a movie with some of her girlfriends. Rod decided he'd come home early and surprise her by taking her out to dinner at her favorite restaurant. As he entered the apartment late that afternoon, he heard the almost-forgotten sound of Nataliya laughing coming from the bedroom and assumed she was playing with Ilya. He bounded in from the hallway, only to find her and Bloom on the bed, Nataliya refastening her bra and Bloom zipping his pants.

Making the kind of fist Jack had taught him, Rod drew it back, poised to break Bloom's perfect nose.

"No!" screamed Nataliya.

"Shut up, you slut!" Rod roared back.

"What do you expect with how you treat me?"

Stung, Rod lowered his fist, left the apartment, and drove to a motel on the outskirts of town, where he spent a largely sleepless night. Wide awake an hour before sunup, he nevertheless stayed in bed till midmorning, unable to go in to work and anxious about returning home lest he encounter Nataliya there and possibly Bloom as well. In the end, he realized he had no choice but to drive back to the apartment, since in his haste to flee it, he hadn't brought so much as a toothbrush or razor with him, let alone a fresh change of clothes. When he finally arrived around noon, he was relieved to find the place empty—until he discovered that so were Nataliya and Ilya's closets and dressers. His knees buckled, and he collapsed on the floor. Part of him wanted to talk to someone about what had happened, but he felt too raw to call Mom and Gene, and too mortified to tell anyone inside the congregation, much less outside it. He considered retreating into the obscurity of a movie theater's shadows, but quickly dismissed the idea, recognizing he'd have no convincing answer if somebody spotted him and asked, "Why,

Rabbi, what are you doing at a weekday matinee?" Giving into routine, he went to the office.

"I suppose you've already heard the news," Christine said as he walked in.

"What news?" he replied, feigning total ignorance.

"Rabbi Brett's given his notice, effective immediately. No one knows why, though."

By the next day, all Rifton knew why Bloom had left *B'ikvot Hoshea* and why Nataliya and Ilya had left with him. Yet Rod knew something that the others in town didn't: the part he'd played in Nataliya's forsaking him. All the same, what wouldn't leave him were his anger and self-pity. "At least when Hosea got married," he brooded, "God told him he was going to get a whore for a spouse. But what did I get? A tramp who's gone off with my son! A lot of good Hosea's done me. While he was a prophet God spoke to, I've got a God who's gone silent and betrayed me as much as my wife!" That moment, he vowed he'd never again answer to "Rod," the name Nataliya had given him, nor to the others he'd been saddled with—not "Ricky," not "Rabbi," and sure as hell not "Yerachmiel," the one he now loathed most of all. He pledged to himself that until the day he died, he'd only go by the name which had stuck with him since the day he'd been born: *Zieglitz.*

Bloom, he later learned, had swept a congregation in Manhattan off its feet, seducing it with the winning ways he had with its children, and not incidentally, its women. Not long afterwards, he jettisoned Nataliya, who, along with Ilya, wound up back in Queens at Mama and Papa's, where one day, she received a letter that Bloom had forwarded to her from Zieglitz's lawyer. "Be hereby advised," the document stated, "that my client is initiating divorce proceedings against you. He has instructed me to inform you that although he will provide child support and not seek custody at this time, he will under no circumstances grant you a Jewish bill of divorce, otherwise known as a *get.*"

"Why are you doing this to Ilya and me?" Nataliya asked Zieglitz when she reached him by phone. "You know I can't marry a Jew again if I don't have a *get.*"

"So marry a *goy!*"

"Do you really want a Gentile bringing up Ilya? Look, Rod, I can still obtain my *get* without you—I can go to a rabbinic court to have our marriage annulled. And didn't you teach in an adult education class on marriage that with infidelity, the Talmud dictates that the unfaithful party is forbidden to stay married to their spouse or to be married to their paramour?"

"Go ahead, Nataliya—go to a rabbinic court! That takes time and money. From what I gather, you've got a lot of one, but not much of the other."

"Aren't you the rabbi who had a *shul* identify itself with the God who commanded a husband to forgive the wife who'd wronged him?"

"You should read Hosea more closely. God never commanded him to forgive Gomer, only to stay married to her . . . which is why you'll never willingly get a *get* from me."

What Zieglitz intended as a rebuke, Nataliya took as an opening. "Does that mean we might get back together like Hosea and Gomer?"

Hearing her, Zieglitz softened, caught off guard by the suggestion they might still repair the breach between them. "So you'd be willing to come back to be with me in Rifton?"

"When Hosea's wife came home, it was a sign of God's pardon of His people, but my coming back would just be a piece of juicy gossip for the *shul*. Can't you do something else? Can't you go somewhere else?"

"I've talked to some local ministers as well as a few of my former seminary classmates around the country, and they all told me the same thing: despite our communications, counseling, and management skills, the business world sees most clergymen as well-meaning simps. That's when I decided that if I couldn't change professions, I'd at least change pulpits. Every time I tried, though, I got stopped cold, not only by Nate but by Sid and the rest of the Board who know what a bargain they've got in me now that I've had to take on all of Bloom's duties without their giving me one red cent more. So whenever another congregation calls to inquire about hiring me, they're threatened with a lawsuit for interfering with my contract, which still has a year to go."

There was a long silence before Nataliya spoke again. "I'm genuinely sorry for how I've hurt you, but I just can't go back to Rifton and the rabbinate."

"Don't you see I'm suffering, too, Nataliya? I'm not happy about being stuck in this job and town, either. But what choice do I have?"

"I don't know—I only know I need my freedom!" she sobbed.

"So have a rabbinic court give you a *get*, because I'll never grant one!" Zieglitz cried heartbroken, unable to let go of what they once had together.

"And you'll never see or speak to Ilya again!" Nataliya said, slamming down the phone.

That night, Zieglitz resolved that he'd redouble his efforts to find another congregation. While he might not be able to leave the rabbinate, he knew he had to leave Rifton: it was too rich with pain, and its pay was too meager. For the next several weeks, he kept scanning the open pulpits until one day, a listing leapt off the page, although more because of the search committee's chair than on account of the synagogue itself.

"What a surprise!" Louis said when Zieglitz called him. "Who would have thought when we were at Edwards that you'd want to end up back here at our old *shul* in Medina?"

"Talk about a surprise, Louis! Last time we spoke, you were a Trotsky-ite who didn't want anything to do with Jews or Judaism. What made you return home and become a pillar of the Jewish community, no less?"

"A lot of things have changed for me since college. After graduation, I spent a year in Cuba, and that was enough of any 'Workers' Paradise' for me. Who wants to drive a '57 Chevy all their life? Don't get me wrong—I still believe in workers' rights. Only now, instead of being a revolutionary fighting to overthrow the system, I'm a labor lawyer plugging away in it on the workingman's behalf."

"But *in Medina?*" Zieglitz repeated in disbelief.

"I suppose that after being away so long, I was ready to come home. Choosing to attend law school here was simple; they gave me a scholarship, and my folks offered me free room and board. Once I passed the bar, my dad took me into his practice."

"Speaking of your parents, how are they these days? I'll never forget their kindness," said Zieglitz.

"They couldn't be better! They're still at services every *Shabbos* and *yontif.*"

"But you still haven't told me, Louis—how did you, of all people, get so Jewish?"

"Unlike you, it didn't have anything to do with the survival of the Jew-ish people. It had to do with my own."

"What do you mean?"

"I needed something to sustain me. By Friday night, I'd feel so beat up and worn out that I needed a place where I could find some peace and quiet, and little by little, I made my way back to services. After a while and almost despite myself, I started following in my dad's footsteps by lending a hand around the *shul.* About a year later, I met my wife there. Actually, she was somebody you and I both knew from decades before—I'm talking about Emily Funkelbush! After almost fifteen years together, Em and I have three great kids. But *nu?* Tell me what's been going on with you. Anything ever happen between you and that girl you were dating at Edwards?"

". . . We got married . . . and had a son." Somehow, talking to Louis made it easier for Zieglitz to add, "But we aren't together anymore." Before he knew it, he was confiding to his oldest friend what else had gone awry in Rifton, from the Kitty Bledsoe disaster to his difficulties with Sid and the Board.

Louis chortled and said, "That's it? Compared to some of the *shnooks* I've heard from, you're Moses! While most of those *yutzes* were zeroes their *shuls* had let go, a few were outright crooks who'd resigned one step ahead of the law after their congregations caught them with their hand in the till. I'll just deal with my board like it's a jury I'm facing when I've got a client with a few blots on his record—I'll bring up your issues *before* the good citizens of Rifton can use them against you. That said, I'm still going to need to make a case for what you've accomplished down there."

Taking extensive notes on a legal pad, Louis listened intently as Zieglitz recounted how he'd help transform the congregation from a tiny gathering of Jews in a funeral parlor to a large synagogue with a new building. When he'd finished, Louis said, "I've got all I need to get you an audition! The *shul*'s as hidebound as ever. Even though I've tried to get them to rethink their process, our leadership still won't do telephone interviews—the membership's so flush with dough, the cost of flying a candidate in for a tryout is chump change to them. And get this! Once somebody's here, the Board doesn't give a rat's ass about how they give a sermon. Think of the snoozers we had to sit through as kids! That old windbag was still putting us to sleep until he finally retired last year. Died a week later—I guess he just ran out of hot air! Trust me, the only thing the Board will care about is how you get along with *machers*, though I bet you wouldn't have lasted this long in Rifton if you hadn't been able to play along with your *shul*'s muckety-mucks. And don't sweat them spoiling your chances by bringing up your contract." As Zieglitz started to ask Louis why not, the boy who'd always spoiled for a fight cackled, "Just let them try to come after us!"

Before the week was out, Zieglitz was on a plane bound for Medina. On Saturday morning as he ascended the *bimah*, a veteran *gabbai* shook his hand and told him, "I still remember your *bar mitzvah* speech. It's the only time I paid attention to something said from up here." But Zieglitz's mind wasn't on the sermon he'd give after the Torah reading but on how he'd sweet-talk the Board after the *Kiddush*. Heeding Louis's counsel, he answered their questions not as a man of the cloth speaking for God but as a yes-man echoing them. As the interview wore on, Zieglitz realized that the old rabbi hadn't merely stupefied his congregants with his preaching, he'd anesthetized them to having any higher aspirations, and it bothered Zieglitz—*briefly*. The place was no *Ruach Chadasha* in California, but it wasn't any Rifton, either. In Medina, he'd get all the help he needed, including an old-school cantor like Cantor Pinsky (who'd left for Hungary some years earlier to assist with his boyhood *shul*'s revival), religious school teachers like *Mar* Galston (who'd been retained without any regard for how they got on with children), and, utterly unlike Bloom, an uncharismatic assistant (who'd been handpicked by the former rabbi precisely because of his blandness).

Thanks to Louis, the Board presented Zieglitz with a generous package and turned a blind eye to his past problems in Rifton as well as to the time remaining on his contract. Near the end of the meeting, the synagogue's treasurer told him, "There's a house that we've got, but if you'd prefer your own place, we'll rent ours out and have a real estate agent show you around." Zieglitz wasn't about to repeat the mistake he'd made in Rifton with congregation-owned housing, and he welcomed the realtor's assistance in locating a home easily within his price range yet comfortably away from the *shul*.

"Before we go back to my hotel," Zieglitz said to the broker after they'd put in a bid, "would you mind driving me over to the neighborhood where I grew up?" When she asked its name, and he answered "Graceland," she replied, "If you insist, but you should know it's been taken over by blacks." When he followed up with a question about Grandpa Irv and Grandma Thelma's suburb of Greenlawn, she responded, "I'm afraid it's gone downhill for the same reason." Where Zieglitz once would have upbraided the realtor for her racist slurs, after Rifton he'd become such a moral cynic that he let them pass without comment. As they rolled past Zieglitz's old house, he thought it looked even grimmer than he'd recollected—its gray paint was peeling, its driveway was crumbling, and its yard was overgrown with weeds. Riding away, he thought back to when he'd first seen it with Mom and Dad. Then, as now, it was set against Medina's low, leaden skies, which, it occurred to him, had been overcast ever since his plane had touched down. During the return flight to Rifton, he vacillated about living in Medina again. Nevertheless, when Medina's draft contract arrived on his desk, he signed it, skipped out to the post office, and overnighted it back. "I can't tell you how much everything you've done means to me," he phoned Louis afterward. ". . . And I can't tell you how much it means to me that you're going to be my rabbi," Louis replied with a tenderness in his voice Zieglitz hadn't ever heard in all the years he'd known him.

As word spread through the Rifton *shul* about Zieglitz's imminent departure, some congregants, like Sid, sniped at him, "Some rabbi you are for ditching us!" A few, like Morris, sympathized with him, "Some synagogue we are for deserting you!" Most, though, like Nate Jacobs, never spoke to him again.

On his last *Shabbos* morning in Rifton, Zieglitz took to his pulpit in a near-empty sanctuary for one final sermon. "I'm not going to enumerate my reasons for leaving. That's all in the past, and it's the future that counts," he began.

"Of course, when it comes to the future, there's the old Yiddish adage, '*Mirtzashem,*' or in English, 'God willing.' But what kind of guidance is that? For what human being can say at any particular moment in his or her life what God truly wants? Standing here now, I know I can't.

"For that matter, I can't even say that God exists, and besides, supposing for the moment that He does, I still can't say for certain what kind of god He is. Just think of the beginning of the Twenty-Third Psalm where it says, 'The Lord is my shepherd.' There, God's portrayed as His flock's protector against any predator lying in wait. Now think about when that psalm's most often recited. It's at funerals, when that deity, like some ravenous beast, has snatched a loved one away!

"So when you're questioning what kind of god exists, or whether God exists in the first place, for God's sake, don't look to me or some other rabbi for answers. Instead, look to your own life to find them. If you want, you can do it day by day like a sports fan; some days you win, some days you lose, some days God's on your team, and some days He's on your opponent's. But if tracking, let alone enduring, those daily ups and downs is too tough for you, you can be like a stock analyst who follows God's performance over the long-term course of your life. Maybe you'll see that it's been nothing but upticks, and that you'd do well to buy into the tenet that there's a benign God who's blessed you. On the other hand, if it appears your life's been cursed with nothing but losses, you'd be smart to invest in a belief with more cash value like God's really the devil—*if*, that is, you buy there's an Almighty at all."

With that, Zieglitz stepped down from the *bimah*. He had no more words about God for Rifton, and as he headed off to Medina that evening, he reckoned he had none for anyone else.

XVIII

———

The Medina *shul's* view of Zieglitz's function was reflected in the name it gave to the event marking his ascension to its pulpit: installation. Like some valve that had been popped into place, Zieglitz's job was to discharge the synagogue's flotsam of ritual and to shut off any congregational backwash before it spilled over on the Board. In keeping with his predecessor's practice, though, emergencies got funneled to his assistant, leaving Zieglitz's evenings free, especially since the old rabbi had conditioned the Board and its committees never to expect him at their meetings. Yet despite Zieglitz's availability, even parishioners like Louis and Emily knew better (once again, thanks to their former rabbi) than to invite him to dinner. As a result, when his unlisted home phone rang one night, Zieglitz assumed it was a wrong number.

"Hello?" he answered tersely.

"Is this the Zieglitz residence?" a distantly familiar voice asked.

"Yes — *Who's this?*"

"Your Aunt Aileen. I—"

Of the all the calls Zieglitz might have gotten, hers was the one he'd least expected. "How'd you get my number?" he said, cutting her off.

"Your secretary gave it to me when I explained who I was. Ever since I heard that you'd come back here, I've thought about contacting you."

Zieglitz pictured her family's row of empty seats at his *bar mitzvah* following Dad's death. "Take the four years I've been here, add on thirty more since my father's funeral, and not so much as a peep out of you except for a couple of obits."

"I was ashamed. While I may have blamed your mother for Bernie's death, I shouldn't have punished you."

"You just figured that out? It's late, and I'm going to bed, so good—"

"Wait!" Aileen stopped him. "Soon after your father died, your Uncle Ernest did, too. Now, all your cousins except Jimmy have moved away. When the last of them left a few months ago, I finally realized how fragile family ties are. What I'm saying is that I'd like to see you and try to make up."

Unmoved, Zieglitz said, "Call the *shul*, and make an appointment like everyone else."

Aileen was as unflinching as her nephew. "I'd love it if you'd come over Sunday for a bite to eat. I'd meet you somewhere else, but my vision's so bad, I can't drive anymore. I'm in a senior community—our house in Greenlawn was too much to manage."

"Sundays are busy days for me," Zieglitz lied.

"Regardless of how early or late you'd get here, I just want you to come."

"All right, but I can't spend all day," Zieglitz relented.

When he knocked on Aileen's apartment Sunday at noon, she rushed out and hugged him. "Great to see you!" someone yelled behind her.

"Hello, Jimmy. . . . Your mother didn't tell me you'd be here," Zieglitz greeted his youngest cousin coolly.

Jimmy pushed forward the scrawny, scowling schoolboy standing beside him. "This is my son Stevie. I guess that makes him your first cousin, once removed. He's a—"

"Can I go watch TV?" Stevie broke in.

As Stevie walked away, Jimmy smiled wanly and said to Zieglitz, "You'll have to pardon him, but he's like that around new people."

"Forget it," Zieglitz replied, suspecting Stevie was like that around everybody, whether he'd just met them or not.

"I hope you guys are hungry!" Aileen said, gesturing toward the dining room.

Shaking his head, Jimmy responded, "Don't count on Stevie's eating much, Ma—you know how he is."

Aileen laughed, answering, "Wait till he starts growing! At his age, you weren't much of an eater, either. But once you and your brothers hit your teens, you practically ate us out of house and home. All of you loved *kosher* deli, which is what we're having today, the same as your Grandma Thelma and Grandpa Irv always did when they had the rabbi over."

". . . Too bad they didn't lace his lox with cyanide," Zieglitz mumbled to himself.

As Aileen plied her nephew's plate with cold cuts, she asked him, "So did you ever marry or have children?"

"I had a wife and son . . . but not anymore . . ." Zieglitz stumbled, unexpectedly taken aback by how much a brunch with his long-lost relatives could make him miss the meals with the family he once had. He felt lonelier than he had in years.

As Aileen started serving dessert, Stevie magically reappeared. "See, Ma?" said Jimmy, "There's nobody who can turn down a piece of Grandma Thelma's sponge cake! It was the only thing I liked about those god-awful seders Grandpa Irv ran." Catching himself, Jimmy quickly added for the benefit of his cousin, the rabbi, "No offense meant!"

"None taken. I couldn't stand them, either," Zieglitz replied.

Aileen exhaled and said, "They did tend to go on and on. Still, it was wonderful having us all together. It would have been nice, Jimmy, if your Ashley could have joined us today."

"My wife sends her regrets, but like I told you, Ma, she's covering a weekend nursing shift at her hospital's ICU."

Zieglitz looked at Stevie attacking his cake and thought of how Ilya had wolfed down Nataliya's *vatrushkas*, whose recipe she'd gotten from *her* mother. "So, Stevie, what do you like doing?" Zieglitz asked, attempting to engage him in the sort of conversation he used to have with his little boy.

"Stuff," Stevie muttered.

"Like what?"

"*Stuff!*"

Seeing another opportunity to repair the damage she'd caused, Aileen said to Zieglitz, "I remember your being crazy about baseball when you were Stevie's age. It'd be marvelous if you could take him to a Medina Blues game. With Jimmy so busy running Ernest's business since his brothers have gone, he just hasn't had the time. It'd give me so much *naches* knowing my nephew and my grandson were getting better acquainted."

As Stevie shoveled another wad of cake into his mouth, Zieglitz recalled the pleasure baseball had given him, first with Jack, then later with Ilya, and reckoned it might do the same for him with Stevie. Turning to Jimmy, he said, "Wednesday would work best for me. It's my day off, and with the Blues in first place, it'll probably be easier to get seats then than if we went on a weekend. I read in the paper that they have an early evening game, so I could pick Stevie up at your house around five."

Wednesday afternoon Ashley was waiting at the curb with Stevie when Zieglitz pulled up. As she opened the car door, she told Zieglitz while she bundled Stevie inside, "I really appreciate your doing this—I only hope he behaves himself."

". . . I'm sure he'll be fine," Zieglitz responded, having second thoughts about an outing with Stevie.

At the ballpark, an usher showed him and Stevie to the minor-league team's still-pricey box seats he'd purchased, the same kind he imagined Jack would have bought if he'd been taking Stevie to the game.

"It's too hot here! I wanna move up where there's shade," Stevie whined.

"But you can't see the players as well from up in the grandstand," Zieglitz answered patiently.

"I'm hot! I want a Coke!"

Zieglitz waved over a vendor and asked for a medium-sized drink. "No! A big one!" Stevie insisted. After gulping it down, he told Zieglitz, "I'm still hot! I want another!"

"Why don't we wait a little? Maybe in an inning or—"

"Another!" Stevie shouted. Cowed, Zieglitz hailed another vendor and watched as Stevie slurped down his second pop in less time than his first one.

"I gotta pee!" Stevie screeched, flinging his empty cup on the field. With his avuncular veneer wearing thinner by the moment, Zieglitz escorted Stevie to a men's room, where one of the urinals finally became free. Relieved that Stevie hadn't had an accident in the meantime, Zieglitz pondered relocating to the grandstand to put an end to the brat's *kevetching*. He never got that far, though, because as Stevie flushed his urinal and stepped away, he shoved the burly man at the one beside him up against its porcelain basin. Before the hapless fan could zip the fly of his splattered Bermudas and give them a piece of his mind, Zieglitz had seized the little hooligan by the scruff of his neck and hustled him out to the car. Once Zieglitz got Stevie home, he frog-marched him to the front door, rang the bell, and hurriedly drove off. That night, Ashley called him, gushing, "Stevie can't stop talking about what a good time he had! It's like Aileen always says—family means everything." Where Stevie was involved, Zieglitz told himself hanging up, family meant being as distant a relative as possible. He was about to relax and watch the evening news when family much closer to him upended his plans. The phone rang, and after he lifted the receiver, he hadn't even said "Hello" when he heard Mom's voice. "You need to speak to Nataliya!"

"And just why should I do that?" Zieglitz responded. The last he'd heard about Nataliya from his mother was that she'd married a non-Jewish investment banker. A registered letter from his lawyer subsequently informed him that while he'd been released from paying her alimony, she'd oppose ever having Ilya released to his custody.

"Nataliya's sick—very sick," Mom answered him.

"What difference does that make?" said Zieglitz.

"If not for Nataliya's sake, then call for your boy's!" Mom told him.

Zieglitz couldn't refuse: after the lengths he'd gone to for Jimmy and Ashley's son, how could he do anything less for his own? "All right, Mom, I'll do what you ask, but it won't be easy. I haven't spoken to Nataliya for years, and besides, what will her husband think if I reach out to her now?"

"Don't worry about him—he died six months ago of a coronary. He left Nataliya and Ilya so little that they had to move back in with her parents."

Zieglitz still knew Nataliya's number in Queens by heart. Reminded of the night they'd first met at Edwards, his anger gave way to concern as he hung up with Mom and dialed the Lubyatkos.

"Hello, who's calling, please?" a teenager answered.

"Itzhik? It's Abba," Zieglitz replied to his son, who sounded nothing like the youngster he'd last spoken with in Rifton.

"Who?" Ilya responded.

"Your father. Don't you remember what we used to call each other?"

"Why should I? —When's the last time I heard from you?"

For Zieglitz, it was like Aunt Aileen's call to him except that he was now the party whose initial overtures the other had spurned. "But what about all those letters, cards, and presents I sent you?" he asked Ilya.

"What are you talking about? I never got them!"

Zieglitz struggled to refocus himself on Nataliya's condition. "Your Grandma Madge told me your mother's not feeling well, and I just want to speak to her and see how she's doing."

"So *now* you're interested in her welfare? Where were you when my stepfather was beating her? Where were you when she started drinking?"

"Ilya, believe me, I didn't know. Please, would you tell your Imma— your mom—I'm on the phone?"

"I don't know why it'd even matter to her," Ilya replied as he put down the receiver and went to get his mother. While Zieglitz stood by for Nataliya, he comforted himself with the thought that even if she wouldn't speak to him, he'd at least tried to do the right thing by calling her.

"What . . . do you . . . want?" Nataliya said when she got on the line, her voice was so feeble that Zieglitz barely recognized it. He'd spoken with hundreds of severely ill congregants over the years, but none of that helped him now—he hadn't loved any of them; he hadn't had a child with any of them; he hadn't lost any of them to somebody else.

"Mom told me your health hasn't been great lately," Zieglitz answered delicately.

"So you phoned out of pity for me?"

"No, because I care."

"If you care so much, what are you going to do about it? Give me my *get*? —It's a little late for that."

"What are you talking about, Nataliya? Just tell me what's wrong!"

"It's my liver. All the doctors say that it's failing, and there's nothing they can do."

Stunned, Zieglitz flailed for a way to mend the rift in his family by becoming an involved partner and parent again. "Nataliya, I know lots of doctors—we'll find you the best specialists we can! And don't fret about Ilya. I'll look after him while you're recovering."

Nataliya's voice suddenly got stronger. "Don't even think about it! Remember what I told you when you wouldn't give my *get*? —Nothing's changed. I made Ilya promise me that after I'm gone, he'll never let you near him again!"

Zieglitz had left himself vulnerable to Nataliya, and what had it gotten him but fresh salt in old wounds? After she hung up on him, he wondered if he were as depressed as his father had been before he committed suicide. Bereft of the wife, son, and life he'd once had, Zieglitz felt like reciting *Kaddish* for himself.

He hadn't eaten anything since breakfast, not even, due to Stevie's antics, some popcorn at the game. Because he was too tired to cook and his fridge and cupboards were virtually empty, he drove to the nearby Get 'n Go to pick up a *nosh*. After rambling from one aisle to the next, vacantly tossing snacks in his cart, he rounded the last corner to make his way to the register and nearly collided with another shopper coming from the opposite direction.

"Oh, my goodness, excuse me," said Emily Chazen.

"No harm done," Zieglitz replied. Regardless of how many times he'd seen Emily in the years since he'd moved back to Medina, he still couldn't get over how different she looked from when they'd been in Hebrew school. She was no longer the bucktoothed girl with the thick glasses—orthodontia and contact lenses had fixed all of that while nature had taken care of the rest, transforming the string bean with short, mousy-brown hair into a shapely woman with long, chestnut tresses.

"This is my daughter, Becca," Emily introduced the squat preteen peeking around her shoulder.

". . . I don't think . . . we've ever met," Zieglitz faltered, certain that if he had, he would have remembered the child's slanted, wide-set eyes, flat nostrils, and protruding tongue.

"Becca, can you say 'hello'?" Emily prompted her.

"Hello," Becca parroted as she thrust her stubby hand forward to Zieglitz.

"And . . . hello to you, too . . ." he sputtered.

"—We've got to be going," Emily said brusquely. She paid for her groceries, Zieglitz paid for his, and they went their separate ways.

The next morning when Zieglitz arrived at the synagogue, Emily was waiting for him in the lobby. "I saw how you reacted to my Becca last night—we need to talk," she told him.

Zieglitz already had an early morning appointment scheduled, but following a fitful night after his phone call with Nataliya, he didn't have the strength to start the day squabbling with Emily. He showed her into his office and said, "So what I can I do for you?"

"My Becca has Down syndrome. There's a reason you hadn't seen her until last night. Years ago, way before you got here, Louis and I enrolled her in the synagogue's Sunday school, but the other children made fun of her. On top of that, when we took her to services, people gawked. Because we couldn't stand seeing her hurt, we kept Becca away from the *shul*."

"It's unfortunate your family had to go through that," Zieglitz commented with practiced professional empathy.

"That's why I need your help," Emily replied.

". . . And just what that might be?" Zieglitz asked guardedly.

"You met our two older children, Deborah and Judah, when they came home for college vacation. As you no doubt gathered last night, Becca's considerably younger—having her was something we hadn't planned on. After she was born, my OB said that my age at the time might have contributed to her birth defect. Don't get me wrong! Louis and I both love her, but Becca's presented us with a series of challenges, including the one that's brought me here today. Even though Becca was only a small child at Deborah's *bat mitzvah*, she still remembers it, and now, at ten and a half, she keeps asking me when she can begin getting ready for one of her own. Because I saw this day coming, I brought up the subject with our old rabbi a while ago, but he said it was out of the question. He told me that since Jewish law doesn't regard Becca as somebody who can be held accountable for her actions, she couldn't possibly have a ceremony that celebrates a Jew's becoming responsible for performing the *mitzvot*. I'll never forget how he put it—'In the eyes of *halacha*, your daughter's an idiot.'"

How the old rabbi had dealt with Becca triggered memories in Zieglitz of how the insensitive *putz* had mistreated him at her age. "*He* was the idiot, Emily! The *halacha*'s talking about insane people who can't be held responsible for what they do, not ones like Becca, who might be a little slow. Tell me, Emily, is Becca responsible when it comes to doing chores she's been given?"

"Always! She sets and clears the table every evening, and each morning, she makes her bed and packs her lunch for school, which, by the way, isn't a special one for children like her, but the public one in our district. In all the years she's gone there, she's never missed turning in her homework on time."

"I only wish this congregation had been as welcoming as her school! In any case, though, it sounds to me like Becca's plenty responsible. I can't see why she shouldn't have her *bat mitzvah*. We'll have the cantor begin working with her as soon as she's old enough."

Emily slumped in her chair. "I'm afraid that's a dead end. Our cantor thinks the same way as our ex-rabbi—it's the reason the rabbi chose him."

Zieglitz had seen enough of the pain his predecessor had inflicted. "Emily, bring Becca here in six months, and I'll start training her myself!"

"I can't thank you enough," Emily responded. As she wiped the tears from her eyes, she stirred Zieglitz's memories of another long-forgotten rabbi, one who at his best had touched others' lives as deeply as God had once touched his own.

"Glad to be able to do it, Emily," Zieglitz replied. He was about to escort her out of his office when she stopped him by saying, "I hate to ask, but there's another favor I need from you."

Zieglitz's guard went up again. "—What is it?"

"As you know, I'm Sisterhood President, and the children of some of our members have been approached by a group of their Christian classmates out to convert them by claiming that while Christianity has a gracious, loving God, Judaism's is vengeful and unforgiving. Several of our ladies have therefore requested that you give a presentation on the Jewish concept of forgiveness."

For Zieglitz, Emily had instantly reverted to the preening little teacher's pet in *Mar* Galston's class, ever eager to portray herself as more-Jewish-than-thou. While moments before Zieglitz had bent over backwards to accommodate Emily's wishes, now he was equally bent on impeding them. "I've got so much on my plate at this point, Emily, that I couldn't possibly meet with the Sisterhood until sometime this summer."

"But most of my ladies will be off on family vacations by then! They won't return until the new school year begins."

Zieglitz held his ground. "So we'll aim for the last week of August. With their kids returning to class, the session will be more timely then, particularly with the High Holy Days and their emphasis on repentance coming so soon after that."

Zieglitz put off preparing his talk until the afternoon of the Sisterhood meeting that evening. "Despite what Christian evangelists preach, Judaism's always taught there's a God who loves and forgives us," he scribbled on his notepad. "Unlike Christians, however, we Jews don't believe in a God who forgives you if you haven't repented beforehand. So if, for example, you've stolen some money, you have to repay it, or if you've said something hateful, you have to retract it, and only *after* the people you've wronged forgive you, will God forgive you, too. Consequently, no Nazi murderer can ever be granted atonement by God—his victims aren't around to forgive him." After Zieglitz scrawled out a few more points, he penned his closing, writing in all caps: "Some things are simply unforgivable—even by God Himself!"

Zieglitz was suddenly struck by the irony, the *hypocrisy*, of what he'd just written compared with how he'd behaved years earlier. Although Nataliya had apologized to him for her transgression, he'd been mercilessly implacable, profaning not only the Torah by holding a grudge, but worse still, the love they'd once shared. Putting his notes aside, he rang her number seeking to make amends.

"Who's calling?" a woman answered.

"Nataliya?" said Zieglitz.

"No, this is her mother. Who's this?"

". . . It's me . . . her ex-husband. I guess it's been a while since you and I have spoken, and—"

"I'll get the boy," Mrs. Lubyatko said before Zieglitz could finish.

Several minutes later, Zieglitz heard muffled sobs at the other end. "Ilya, is that you? . . . What's wrong? . . . How's your mother?"

"She . . . died . . . this morning . . ." Ilya said, his voice cracking with emotion. "It's all your fault . . . I won't *ever* break my promise to Mama. Don't try to see or call me again!"

The receiver fell from Zieglitz's hand. Before, he'd dreaded speaking with Nataliya; now he regretted that he'd never have the chance. Reconciling with her would have been hard enough while she was alive, but with Ilya's words still in his ears, he felt like a Nazi killer who'd carry his guilt forever. If only he'd made up with Nataliya in Rifton, if only he'd gone to be with her in New York, if only . . .

He dragged himself to the Sisterhood class that night and, three weeks later, through the High Holy Days, all the while mouthing pieties about repentance and pardon right up until *Simchat Torah*, the joyous festival denoting the holidays' end. As he walked into his office the next morning, his secretary told him, "Emily Chazen called to say she'll be here at four to arrange her daughter's *bat mitzvah*. She said you'd already set the appointment."

After leading a Jewish holy month's worth of worship, Zieglitz could have used the afternoon off, but he couldn't back out of the commitment he'd made a half year before. After Emily and Louis had sat down with Becca on the sofa in his office, Zieglitz asked the girl, "So why do you think your mom and dad have brought you to see me today?"

"So I can be a grown-up!" Becca chortled.

Chuckling, Zieglitz replied, "Well, for that to happen, I need to know more about you. For instance, what are you good at?"

"Singing and drawing!"

"When it comes to music and art, my Becca's the best!" said Louis.

Echoing her husband, Emily chimed in, "Listen to what happened with Becca when we brought her to services over the holidays. Despite people's stares when we'd come with her before, Louis and I thought that if Becca's going to have a *bat mitzvah*, she needs to get used to going to *shul*. Her response, if I say so myself, was nothing short of amazing! After hearing the congregation sing a prayer only once or twice, she'd join in the next time and have its tune and Hebrew down perfect. I suppose I really shouldn't be so surprised. At three, she could already sing the Friday night *Kiddush* with me and Louis when we made *Shabbos* at home."

A grin spread over Zieglitz's face. "Becca's picking up melodies so quickly should make practicing for her *bat mitzvah* lots easier. The service's music gives most kids fits."

"Becca, say what else you liked about services," Louis prodded her.

"The story where God made the world!" Becca answered, referring to the opening verses of Genesis which had been read on *Simchat Torah*. "I could picture it all in my head."

Zieglitz sighed, "That's more than I can do! There are parts of God's creating the universe that seem so mysterious I just draw a blank, such as when—"

"It's settled then!" Emily interrupted. "We'll schedule Becca's *bat mitzvah* for this time next year when that section comes up again. I don't mean on *Simchat Torah*—people are so *shul*ed out by then, the attendance always drops way off. We'll slate it instead for the *Shabbos* when that portion's normally chanted. We'll have a bigger audience!"

Zieglitz had heard rumors that Emily had been promoting herself to be the *shul*'s new president, leapfrogging over its current vice president, the next in line for the post. A synagogue president in Rifton had made Zieglitz's life miserable, and he wasn't about to go through that again in Medina if he could help it. "No problem, Emily. We'll reserve *Shabbat Bereshit* for Becca," he acquiesced.

Triumphant, Emily declared, "Excellent! I'll start working on the invita—"

"Before we end today," Zieglitz interrupted her this time, "I'd like to spend some time alone with Becca."

"Is that all right with you, honey?" Emily asked protectively.

"Why wouldn't it be, Mommy?" Becca asked in return.

After Emily and Louis stepped out, Zieglitz said, "So, Becca, let's take a look at that creation story you mentioned." Pulling up his chair beside her, he opened a *chumash*, leafed to its beginning, and pointed to Genesis's first verse. "Would you please start reading here, Becca?"

"When . . . God . . . began to . . . cre . . . cre . . ."

Seeing how much Becca was struggling, Zieglitz tried another approach. "What if I just told you the story, Becca? That's how Jews did it in olden times when most people had trouble reading."

Visibly relaxing, Becca listened intently as Zieglitz recounted the world's inception from its origins in chaos and darkness while a wind from God blew over the primordial waters to God's creation of light on the first day. "Any questions about the story so far, Becca?" Zieglitz asked.

"Just one—where did the water come from? Did God make it, too?"

Slapping his forehead, Zieglitz responded, "Wow, nobody's ever asked me that before! The story doesn't say, and I don't think anyone actually knows the answer. For next time, though, I want you to draw me a picture of how you see that part of the story in your mind. Unless there's anything else, I think that's enough for today. Let's call your parents back in."

When Emily and Louis had rejoined them, Zieglitz had Becca recap her assignment. "Could you also repeat for your mom and dad that great question you had for me?" he asked her afterwards.

". . . I forget . . ." Becca replied almost inaudibly.

Putting his arm around her shoulder, Louis said, "It's okay, sweetie. You've had a long day."

Zieglitz wasn't willing to give up on Becca so easily. "Remember? It was that question I said nobody had ever asked me before."

Becca lit up and answered, "Oh now I've got it! I'll tell it to Mommy and Daddy on our way home." As the Chazens walked out of his office, Zieglitz marveled at Becca's perceptiveness—while she may have been mentally impaired, she wasn't by any means dimwitted. Despite her *chutzpadik* mother, Zieglitz looked forward to working with Becca.

As soon as Becca walked into Zieglitz's office a week later, she pulled out the picture she'd drawn him. "See, here's the sunshine—I colored it yellow with lots of black behind it for the darkness, and blue along the bottom for the water, and then above it, white streaks for the wind."

"There's just one thing wrong, Becca," Zieglitz told her.

"I'm so stupid!" she said, throwing her picture down on the floor.

"No, you're not!" Zieglitz corrected her, upset with himself for having so stupidly worded his response to her drawing. Picking it up, he told her,

"When I originally read the story, I pictured it just like you did, which is the way lots of other people have, too. We all missed the same thing, though. While the story says God created light on the first day, it's not until the fourth day that it mentions His making the sun, moon, and stars. You and I didn't get nearly that far last time."

"So where did the light on the first day come from?" Becca perked up.

"That's another great question, Becca. Like before, though, there's no easy answer. All we know for sure is that the story says it was some kind of light from God."

"Like a light beam?"

Zieglitz shrugged and replied, "Why not? We'll look at the story again at our next meeting, but for the rest of today, I want to go over one of the blessings you'll chant when you're called to the Torah."

"What's it about?" Becca asked.

"It thanks God for choosing to give us Jews the Torah with all its wonderful teachings," Zieglitz answered. Having seen how much trouble Becca had sounding out even the simplest words, he'd scrapped the idea of resorting to an English transliteration of the prayers and decided to rely on her musical aptitude instead. "Would you mind if I sang you the blessing?" he asked her.

"I'd like that," Becca responded.

After Zieglitz sang the benediction's opening words, Becca effortlessly chanted them back, and by half an hour later, she'd mastered the entire blessing. When she came for her next lesson, she told Zieglitz she'd learned the blessing after the Torah reading as well. "Mommy helped me with the tune. I've got a question about what the prayer means, though. Daddy said you'd know the answer."

"We'll see . . ." Zieglitz said, bracing himself to be challenged again.

"You said the first blessing thanks God for the Torah."

"That's right."

"The second blessing says that, too."

"Right again, Becca."

"But then it adds something else."

"And what might that be?"

Becca unfolded a scrap of paper she'd brought with her. "That . . . God's . . . put . . ." she read slowly, "'e . . . ter . . . nal . . . life in our . . . midst.' That's the part I don't get."

Zieglitz took a moment before he replied, "That's another tough passage to make sense of, Becca. Here's what it means to me, though. The blessing's saying that if the Jewish people keeps the Torah God's given us, it'll never die. Does that make things clearer for you?" As Becca nodded,

Zieglitz was awed once again by her knack for posing questions that were anything but simpleminded.

Over the next several months, Zieglitz's lesson plan with Becca never varied: she'd hand him a picture of the Torah verses they'd gone over the previous week, he'd move on to the next section, she'd sing the latest portion of the liturgy she'd learned, and he'd record the subsequent two or three lines. Using his tapes, she eventually memorized her *haftarah* from Isaiah, in which God commanded Jews, Zieglitz taught her, to be "a light unto the nations." Although she hadn't been asked for one, Becca came the following week with a rendering of a Jewish star whose rays encircled the earth. Placing the drawing on Zieglitz's desk, she said, "It's like what my family's been doing at the community center. Mommy can tell you all about it when she gets me today."

Later, after the session was over and Emily had arrived, she explained to Zieglitz, "We've been volunteering to help other Down syndrome children with everything from getting their scout badges to finding after-school jobs. We've also formed a support group to encourage their parents, like you've done with Becca, to focus on what they *can* do instead of on what they can't. We've gotten so much out of it—I can't count the new friends that we've made!"

Near the end of Becca's last lesson with Zieglitz, she said to him, "There's one more thing I want to ask you. In my Torah portion, it says we're created 'in God's image.' So does that mean God looks like I do?"

". . . What makes you ask that?" Zieglitz replied, uncertain how to answer.

"I look funny, and so do other kids like me . . ." she said so faintly he had to strain to hear her.

Zieglitz put her hands in his and responded, "Not to me you don't. When the Torah says we're created in God's image, Becca, it doesn't mean we're little 'God statues.' What the Torah's teaching us is that we're like God in what we can do."

"But God can do everything, and I can't!" said Becca.

"Look at your Torah portion again, Becca. What is it that God keeps doing over and over at the world's beginning?"

". . . Making things?"

"And what kind of things does God keep making?"

"Bright things in the sky, and everywhere else, things that are alive."

"Just like your pictures—things that are bright and full of life! And that's how we're all in God's image, Becca. It's when we create something new that brightens up the world by making it more lively." Gazing at Becca's face to see if she'd understood what he'd said, Zieglitz realized that he'd never seen her so happy—nor been so happy himself in a very long time.

At Becca's ceremony *Shabbos* morning, every seat in the sanctuary was filled. Her mother-the-president's board members and supporters were there alongside her father-the-lawyer's colleagues and clients, interspersed among the Chazens' Down syndrome contingent of well-wishers. But Zieglitz knew there were also more than a few cynics in the pews questioning what a person like Becca was even doing on the *bimah*. Her performance at the podium, though, from the impeccable caliber of her chanting to the irrefutable logic of her *bat mitzvah* speech, left every naysayer dumb.

Becca set up an easel with a large portrait of assorted flora and fauna around the edges and various heavenly bodies at the top. "These are all things the rabbi taught me my Torah portion says God made," she told the congregation. Then pointing to the center of the canvas where she'd painted an orange heart with sparks shooting out, she said, "But I learned this part all by myself. At the end of each day, God looks at what He's created and sees that it's good. On the last day, though, when God's finished making everything, He says, 'It's all *very good.*' That means me, too!"

While Zieglitz's *bar mitzvah* address from that same podium had impressed people, Becca's speech *moved* them. Hardly any eyes in the sanctuary remained dry, Zieglitz's least of all. The claim that God's whole creation was faultless, when Becca said it, sounded so persuasive.

But when Zieglitz's oncologist, Y. H., informed him a year later, "Your penis's cancer has spread—it's got to be severed," he was convinced more than ever that only an imbecile could believe in either the world's goodness—or God's.

XIX

———

Even so, Zieglitz couldn't blame God for his cancer. He could only blame himself.

And Emily.

It had all started so innocently, so virtuously, so *religiously*. In the afterglow of Becca's *bat mitzvah*, Emily became Zieglitz's biggest booster. Once she'd persuaded him to start attending board meetings, she backed his proposals for deepening members' commitment through a series of initiatives from requiring periodic "Jewry duty" for *shivah minyan*s to postponing *b'nai mitzvah* until age sixteen. "It'd buy us more time," she argued on Zieglitz's behalf, "to teach our kids what it means to be Jewish." When the synagogue's treasurer objected, "But think about the hit we'd take from people leaving us for *shul*s where thirteen-year-olds can still have their parties," Emily dismissed his protest as though she were shooing a fly. "If head counts were all that mattered," she said drily, "Jews might as well become Christians—there's lots more of them than us!"

Fueled by Emily and Zieglitz's enthusiasm, participation skyrocketed. Even though some of the old-timers initially squawked, most signed on for their new *minyan* duties while more and more families signed up for a "Sweet Sixteen *simcha*," as those *bar* and *bat mitzvah* ceremonies affectionately came to be known. Much to the treasurer's surprise, the congregation's size increased, too. As one newcomer put it, "This *shul*'s not like where I used to belong—it's anything but vanilla!"

The growth in membership, programming, and budget meant that Zieglitz spoke with Emily almost daily. While at first he viewed it as a chore to be dispensed with as quickly as possible, he gradually came to look forward to their conversations, which often went well beyond the time needed to address the matter at hand. Near the end of one lengthy phone call, Emily

said, "I can't remember this congregation's ever being so alive—what a blessing you've been!"

No woman since Nataliya had talked to Zieglitz that way, and after
that, the mere sound of Emily's voice gave him as much pleasure as any
of their projects' success. Eventually, though, simply hearing her wasn't
enough. During their next afternoon chat, Zieglitz got up the nerve to say,
"I think we'd get more done if we started meeting face-to-face. How about
coming by my office tomorrow night at eight?"

"I'll be there!" Emily responded like a woman who needed no
convincing.

When she arrived at the synagogue the next evening, the building was
empty but for Zieglitz, who, after they'd gone into his office, took a seat opposite her behind his desk. Within minutes, they'd concluded the business
that had ostensibly necessitated their getting together.

Zieglitz fished for a reason to have Emily stay. "Since we're already
both here, why don't we discuss some longer-term issues the *shul* will be
facing?"

"Good idea!" Emily answered, relieved that he'd spared her having to
concoct her own rationale for protracting their session.

Zieglitz's next words could have come from the mouth of a gawky
teenage boy. "If you want to, Emily, . . . we might be more comfortable . . .
on my sofa."

Emily, nervous herself, slowly walked over to the couch, where she
wedged her body tight against one of its armrests while Zieglitz squeezed
himself up against the other as though the yard of upholstery between
them were a mile-wide barrier to any physical contact. Soon, though, they'd
inched close to one another, and the tête-à-tête turned from the synagogue's
future to their pasts. Emily knew about Zieglitz's father's suicide, but nothing at all of Zieglitz's estrangement from his wife and son. He knew even
less about the hardships she'd suffered until, lowering her guard as well as
her voice, she confided to him, "My dad walked out when I was six, and my
mother never got over it, constantly worrying that I'd run out on her, too.
So she'd never let me go to play at other kids' houses—they always had to
come over to ours. The older I got, the more rules she laid down to try to
keep me with her. I think it's why she sent me to Hebrew school. Judaism's
nothing if not rules!"

. . . As were Emily and Zieglitz. To abide by the *halacha*'s rules on
sexual propriety, they relocated their nighttime encounters from the seclu-
sion of Zieglitz's office to the more public venues of well-lit coffee shops
and diners. Before long, though, they'd adjourned to dimly lit cafés and
bars, where they'd moved on from tapping fingertips over a cup of decaf

to caressing thighs under a cocktail table as their inhibitions went down with their drinks. Emily had no worries about leaving her responsible Becca alone at their house, and neither she nor Zieglitz had any reservations about being discovered by Louis, whose work always kept him later at the office than before Emily returned home, allowing Zieglitz to continue wishing his old pal "Shabbat Shalom" at services as though nothing had happened.

Something had happened much earlier, though, in Emily and Louis's marriage that she eventually divulged to Zieglitz after she'd met him again for martinis. "I hate to admit it, but like Louis, I left my Jewish upbringing behind when I went off to college. Sorry to say, I became quite promiscuous before finally finding my way back to Judaism. It makes my situation now kind of ironic. After our second child, Judah, was born, Louis started using condoms while I took the pill, since we didn't want any more additions to our family. So Becca's birth came as a surprise, and after that, Louis and I stopped being intimate altogether, because we were afraid of having another child with a birth defect. I can't remember the last time I had sex."

Zieglitz sighed, "Same here. After what went on with Nataliya, sex lost its appeal, and even if it hadn't, what could I have done about it anyway? Look at us! What would the *yenta*s say if they found out? Shit, Emily—screw 'em! Let's go to my place."

"No," she answered.

A wave of shame washed over Zieglitz, thinking he'd overstepped. He was about to apologize when Emily continued, "We'll go to my house instead. It'll be safer there, because it's farther away from the *shul*, and we'll have it all to ourselves. Louis and Becca are gone for the week visiting his folks in Florida."

When Zieglitz ended up in Emily's bed, their coupling was more exciting than either had fantasized, a fusion of their sexual ardor for one another and their spiritual passion for Judaism that neither had experienced since early on in their marriages. After Louis and Becca returned home, the lovers moved their trysts to a motel on Medina's outskirts, where two sawbucks could get them a room for two hours without any raised eyebrows at the front desk. Still, to avoid suspicion from either Louis or the *shul*, the pair planned their rendezvous with all the attention to detail with which Emily drafted board meeting agendas and Zieglitz prepared High Holy Day services. Month after month, their affair went undetected—until the day when Emily couldn't keep secret her genital warts caused by the human papillomavirus, which had lain dormant in her for years.

Not that Louis noticed: he'd long since given up seeing her naked. Emily put off telling Zieglitz, though, hoping the blisters would just disappear as she, his paramour, gave him some theologically dubious reason for not having intercourse—"It's my time of month, and you know as well as I do that the Torah forbids it"—or, less doctrinally, "I've got a headache." But as the lesions kept spreading, she finally called him as much out of panic as out of concern for his welfare. "I've got sores all over my vagina!" she cried on the line.

"I've started breaking out, too!" he said, as alarmed as she was. Yet neither of them went to see a doctor, dreading word of their illness leaking out more than they feared their sickness. By the time they sought medical assistance, Emily had advanced cervical cancer, and Zieglitz had cancer of the penis. His circumcision hadn't protected him, since his HPV wasn't due to any *dreck* trapped beneath his foreskin, but to the filth of the betrayal he'd committed with the wife of the man who'd once been his best friend.

In time, Emily had to give up her office at the *shul*, succumbing at last with her husband and heartbroken children gathered around her bed, all of them still unsuspecting of what had transpired in it, even when an emaciated, ashen Zieglitz performed her funeral. Whether or not, though, anybody spotted him with Emily's symptoms, no one caught sight of his grief over losing her or his fear of sharing her fate. Later, when he, too, grew so ill he had to relinquish his post, not a whiff of scandal tailed him any more than it had her. Despite all the hospital visits he'd made in Medina, the sicker he got, the fewer congregants came by, treating him as more of a castoff than shut-in. Nevertheless, when his family tried to see him after he'd been hospitalized, he shunned them like a recluse.

"No need to come all the way from Huppertsville, Mom," he told his mother when she phoned him from *Casa Futura*, where she'd moved with Gene after they couldn't find anyone in the small town well off enough to buy it. Nor did the hospital's ICU charge nurse, Cousin Jimmy's wife Ashley, fare much better in her attempt to provide Zieglitz with family support. After she told her husband that Zieglitz was on her ward, Jimmy came with Aileen and Stevie, who kept pestering Zieglitz for a peek under the covers. "I bet it's gross!" said Stevie. "I need to rest now," said Zieglitz. From then on, his only visitors were staff.

"What do you mean 'sever it'?" a stunned Zieglitz asked Dr. Blustein as he cursorily made the rounds of his oncology patients. Although Y. H. had aged—his shoulders stooped, and his belly sagged—his tongue was every bit as sharp as when he'd been a boy. "What word don't you understand, Zieglitz? I mean cut it off! —Or are you ready to die?"

Always, always, it had been the same choice for Zieglitz from when he'd first gone to his internist through all his radiation treatments: "Do X or you'll die." Through it all, he'd opted for X, but now he wondered if he'd be picking death anyhow. "What kind of man wants to live mangled like that?" he mused bitterly about the choice Y. H. had left him. Six months earlier at his diagnosis in January, he'd done what believers and unbelievers alike invariably do—he bargained with God. Though he'd stopped praying a long time before, he petitioned God then, "If You give me another half year, I'll stop being angry with You and do anything You say." But in July, as he lay in the hospital and hadn't yet died, his anger hadn't either. "God's such a chump, there's no deal He'll turn down," he fumed to himself as Y. H. departed.

His next staff visitor only made Zieglitz madder.

"*Nu*? They tell me you're a Jew," said the Orthodox rabbi who, Zieglitz recalled from an article in the local Jewish press, had been hired by the Medina Federation as the new "Community Chaplain."

"*Who*? Who told you that?" Zieglitz demanded, offended by the sight of what he'd once been, an agent of the God of Israel.

Pushing back the black fedora on his head, the other rabbi replied, "The *shiksa* downstairs—she gives me the names of all the Jews here."

Zieglitz decided if he couldn't take his rage out on God, he'd unload on His stand-in. He wasn't about to divulge, though, that he wasn't a simple Yid. "So what do you want to talk about?"

"To start with, how you got here," said Rabbi Black Hat, fingering his side curls.

"I've got penile cancer."

"You've got me wrong! Tell me what you did to end up in this bed."

Emily's bed was the last thing Zieglitz was going to confess to the Jew at the foot of his. "Not sure. It just happened."

Raising his voice, the Voice of Tradition answered, "Nothing ever just happens! Everything's caused by *HaShem* as a reward or punishment for the things that we've done. But, *baruch HaShem*, even if you don't know why you got sick, there's still a way for you to get well."

Zieglitz raised his voice, too. "Don't you get it? I wouldn't be having an operation if things didn't look so hopeless!"

Orthodoxy's spokesman looked genuinely surprised. "What, you never heard of miracles like Chanukah?"

"So what did people do to have God come to their rescue?" Zieglitz asked, feigning ignorance.

Once again, Rabbi Black Hat seemed taken aback that anyone could ask such a question, let alone not know its answer. Fiddling with his *payis*, he told Zieglitz, "The Jews back then showed their faith by doing *mitzvahs*. The temple's menorah was supposed to stay lit all the time, but the Maccabees only had enough oil to keep it lit for one day. They went ahead and lighted it anyway, because they put their trust in *HaShem*. And it paid off! Their little bit of oil lasted eight days, giving them the time to make more."

"So what's any of that got to do with me?" Zieglitz said defiantly.

"Maybe, if you started doing a *mitzvah* or two, *HaShem* would cure your cancer. What about going to *shul* on *Shabbos*, for instance?"

Zieglitz turned apoplectic. "What kind of *schmendrick* do you take me for? I fell for that *narishkeit* when I was a kid. What crap! You do good, God's good to you, you do bad, He isn't. Get the hell out of here before I call the nurse!"

The Defender of the Faith wouldn't give up. "So you won't try doing a *mitzvah*? Then I will! I'll say a *misheberach* praying for *Hashem* to heal you."

Zieglitz had had enough. "I'd rather have a prayer said for me by Hitler! At least his beliefs got results!" As Rabbi Black Hat started for the door, Zieglitz couldn't resist one last shot. "You want I should do a *mitzvah*? Okay, I'll teach you some Torah. I learned it a long time ago from a great *rebbe* of mine, Mr. Cochran—he wasn't Jewish, but what he taught me is still the honest-to-God truth. He said that religion is about what people wished had occurred instead of what actually took place. That goes for your Chanukah miracle. Never happened. Just a story made up by religious Pollyannas like you."

Rushing out, God's Servant paused long enough to turn around and spit at the godforsaken patient, whose furor gave way to tears. "Forget about Jewish history—what about mine?" Zieglitz thought to himself between sobs. "Has it just been a string of inane wishes, too—a series of pipe dreams about sanctifying Jews' lives and magnifying God's name? Maybe I've spent my life as much of a holy fool as that pious clown!"

Zieglitz had his surgery soon afterwards, and early one morning a few days after that, Y. H. appeared in the doorway with Mom, who said, "I know you told me not to come, but—"

"I had your mother come here today," Y. H. said, cutting her off, "so I wouldn't to have to repeat myself."

Zieglitz's response was a clipped as Y. H.'s. "I suppose I ought to feel flattered you've made an appearance! I haven't seen you since you sliced off my dick."

Ignoring Zieglitz's sarcasm, Y. H. glanced down at his watch. "Let me get right to the point. There's nothing more we can do for you here. That means hospice. I can discharge you to a nursing home or send you back to your own, provided you get a full-time caregiver. Which will it be?"

Before Zieglitz could answer Y. H., Mom did. "Neither! He's coming to Huppertsville with me."

"Do they even have hospice care out in the boonies?" Y. H. said.

Mom looked past him at her son. "How do you feel about going to *Casa Futura*?"

"What difference does it make where I die?" Zieglitz said with an air of indifference, too proud to let Y. H. see him start blubbering from the solace of knowing that when the end came, he'd be at the one place he'd loved in his life with the one person in his life he knew still loved him.

Mom arranged with an ambulance service to transport him, and as he lay strapped to a gurney, each bump in the road sent a jolt of pain surging through him. When the van finally reached *Casa Futura* and rolled up the serpentine driveway, he looked out a rear window and glimpsed the meadow and its wall bordering the graveyard. The ambulance attendants lugged him up the stairs on a stretcher to the old bedroom where, as a young boy, he'd found refuge from his father's temper.

Nurses and aides came twice a week from the Henry County Hospice. "Our goal is to make you as comfortable as possible," they told Zieglitz at the start of each visit. "We're leaving behind some morphine—take as much as you need for your pain," they'd always remind him at its conclusion. Regardless of the amount Zieglitz took, though, he couldn't numb the agonizing memories of where his life had gone wrong.

"What do you want?" Y. H. barked when Zieglitz phoned him. "If you've got a medical issue, call hospice!"

". . . It's something else. . . . You're the only one I can talk to about it," Zieglitz said hesitantly.

"Well, make it fast! You wouldn't believe how many people want something from me."

". . . It's about . . . something Jewish."

"Who do you think you're talking to, Zieglitz—my *zeyde*?"

"No, . . . but you might be the one person who can explain something he told me. . . . It's about my Hebrew name, Yerachmiel. . . . He made it sound like some kind of blessing."

"So?"

In anguish, Zieglitz broke out, "So where's the blessing been in my life? With the wife who cuckolded me? With the son who won't speak to me? And where the hell's the blessing with what I'm going through now—dying, like my father, before I reach fifty?"

"You want to know what my *zeyde* had to say about blessing, Zieglitz? Pay attention, I'm only saying it once!

"Being blessed doesn't mean your life's going to be happy-go-lucky. Look at Abraham, Isaac, and Jacob! They all got God's blessing, but none of them had a life that was exactly a day at the beach. Abraham had to banish one of his sons and almost butcher the other, Isaac got duped by his wife and his kid on his deathbed, and Jacob's life was no bowl of cherries after eleven of his boys sold the twelfth, his favorite, into bondage. So being blessed doesn't mean you'll have a life where nothing bad ever happens. Instead, it means that whatever good you've gotten in life, *the godsends*, won't die with you. That's the way blessing's worked from Abraham's time down till today with his descendants, the Children of Israel, where every generation has had its mixed blessings of *goyim* admiring or hating it. But even when the Jew-haters have tried to exterminate it, Zieglitz, this God-blessit people's lived on and flourished."

"But where's the blessing in my life, Y. H.? What's flourished in it for me?"

"What am I—your rabbi?" Y. H. thundered. Done speaking, he left Zieglitz to figure out his life for himself.

A week or so later, a hospice nurse told Madge, "It won't be long now." After thanking the nurse and showing her out, Madge phoned Ilya at the college where he was enrolled as a junior. After he picked up, she told him, "There's not much time left for you to come and make up with your dad. If you don't, you could regret it for the rest of your life."

"I doubt it, Nana, but I'll do it for you. I haven't forgotten how you stood by Mama when he wouldn't."

When Mom told Zieglitz his son was coming, he wished Ilya wasn't: he didn't have the *koyach* to endure another of his tirades. Apologizing to Ilya for not being a better father, he thought to himself, would probably turn out as badly as when he'd tried to make amends with Nataliya; even mentioning the effort, Zieglitz figured, would probably strike Ilya as self-serving and, by inflaming him further, ultimately prove self-defeating. In the end, Zieglitz settled on speaking to Ilya about something innocuous when he got there. "Do you know why your mother named you what she did?" he asked the strapping twenty-year-old looming over his bed once they were by themselves.

"It's obvious, isn't it? Because it's Russian," Ilya responded.

"There was more to it than that, Ilya. She wanted a name that sounded almost exactly the same in Hebrew."

"I couldn't care less," Ilya said as he walked away to stare out the window.

"But wouldn't you like me to tell you what your name means?" Zieglitz persisted.

Ilya exhaled and replied, "Can I stop you?"

As if he hadn't heard Ilya's barb, Zieglitz continued, "'Ilya' in Russian comes from the Hebrew 'El Yah.' Hear the resemblance? Either way, they mean 'God is Lord.'"

"And why should I give a damn about that?"

"Because your mother did! Get a chair and sit down!"

Chastened, Ilya walked back and took a seat by the bed, where Zieglitz went on, "As long as we're at it, you should know your Hebrew name, too. It's 'Yitzchak.'"

"Who the hell can even say it?" said Ilya.

"It's the equivalent of 'Isaac' in English," Zieglitz answered, undeterred.

"Like the guy whose old man nearly killed him?" Ilya responded.

Zieglitz lacked the strength to push back. "That's true, Ilya. The reason we called you Yitzchak, though, was because it comes from the Hebrew word for laughter. As a boy, I had so little of it, I desperately wanted it for you. When you were a baby, I'd look down in your crib and poke your tummy with my pinky and say 'Itzhik'—the pet name I gave you—and then point my finger at myself and say 'Abba'—the name I hoped you'd call me. You'd let loose big, throaty chortles, and I'd think to myself, 'Itzhik, your Abba doesn't laugh as much in a month as you do in a day!'"

"Yeah, my life's been a yuk a minute," Ilya replied.

Zieglitz looked away. "I failed you, Itzhik, . . . even more than my father failed me."

"So now that you're dying, you're asking my forgiveness?"

"Not that—I don't deserve it, I just want to tell you I love you," Zieglitz said, clasping Ilya's wrist, which, when Ilya tried to wrench it away, he only gripped tighter.

"I need something to eat," Ilya mumbled as he pulled his hand loose, wiped his eyes, and hurried toward the door.

Over the next three days as Zieglitz required more morphine, he spent less time alert and conscious as Mom, Gene, and Ilya took shifts at his bedside. When Zieglitz awoke near dawn on the fourth day and found Ilya beside him, he whispered weakly, ". . . Could you . . . read to me?"

"What would you like?"

"In the nightstand . . . there's a *chumash*—the Five Books of Moses. I got it for my *bar mitzvah*. . . . My portion's marked . . . with a ribbon. . . . Start there."

Ilya got the book, opened it, and began reading aloud the story of Abraham's circumcising all the males in his household.

"That's the last thing I want to hear about now," Zieglitz moaned. "Turn to the *haftarah*—the section from the prophets that comes next."

As Ilya recited the first few verses, Zieglitz stayed quiet until Ilya came to the passage:

But you, Israel, are My servant,

The offspring of Jacob, whom I have chosen,
The seed of Abraham, My friend—

"Who in the hell would want God for a friend?" Zieglitz broke in. "Just look how He treats them!"

"So what should God do for His friends?" Ilya asked gently.

"Be God! *Protect them!*" Zieglitz burst out.

"But doesn't that make God like a fairy godmother who grants our wishes with a wave of her wand?" Ilya asked even softer. "Besides, what real friend gives us what we ask for when they know there's something else we need more?" Receiving no answer to either of his questions, Ilya kept on reading:

> You whom I drew from the ends of the earth
> And called from its far corners,
> To whom I said, "You are my servant;
> I chose you, I have not rejected you—
> Fear not, for I am with you,
> Be not frightened, for I am your God."

Ilya put down the *chumash* and said as he moved closer to his father, "That's the kind of friend I'd want—somebody who wouldn't abandon me, no matter what, even when I was dying."

"I'm sorry how I abandoned you, Ilya! I'm sorry how I abandoned your mother! Please, I don't want to be alone!" Zieglitz cried, reaching out to his son.

"I won't leave you, I promise," Ilya responded, reaching back.

Later that night after he'd spelled Gene, Ilya had nearly drifted off when he heard, "Itzhik, where are you?"

"I'm here," he answered.

"I want . . . to talk about . . . my funeral," Zieglitz rasped.

"Wait, I'll get Nana and—"

"No, Itzhik, just you!"

"I don't even know where you want to be buried. Do you want to go back to Medina, or do you want to be in Excelsior with Nana's side of the family?"

"Just beyond the meadow . . . is a cemetery. Put me there . . . where I'll be near this house . . . a place that's always felt like home."

"But don't you want a cemetery that's got Jews buried in it? While we didn't have enough money for me to have a *bar mitzvah*, and as angry as Mama was at you, she made sure that's where she was buried."

"So I'll be the first Jew in this one," Zieglitz said with a feeble laugh.

"Where do I get a rabbi for the service and your eulogy?" Ilya asked him.

Zieglitz's voice grew fainter. "On the dresser, there's a prayer book . . . with the service. You can say it in English, and . . . you can give my eulogy, too."

"Me? —I've never done anything like that."

"Just talk about the blessings in my life, Itzhik . . . the good I've gotten from others. Do you remember how much you loved throwing a ball around with me? That's one of the good things my grandpa, Jack, gave me, and now it's lived on in you. And I know how good you are with words. That's from my father whose Hebrew name was Baruch, which means blessed and whose gifts blessed me as a rabbi so I could do good and bless others' lives, like a girl named Becca. And then there's your Nana, my mother, and hers, my grandma, Dina, who gave me the greatest blessing of all—their love. Don't become a man like me, Ilya, somebody so fixated on what he's lost he's been blinded to what he's been given, someone who's grown too stingy in giving what goodness he has—his blessings—to others."

Ilya broke down weeping, "But what about Mama? Was there anything good she gave you?"

"You—and you're the blessing . . . that'll live on after us."

Kissing his Abba's hand, Yitzchak smiled.

"Get the . . . prayer book . . ." said Abba, and after Yitzchak got it from the dresser, he told him, "there's something in the back . . . for somebody who's dying. . . . Read it for me. . . . Use the translation."

"I can't Abba . . ." Yitzchak answered, choking back tears.

"Please, Itzhik, don't desert me now when I need you most."

"'Our God and God of our ancestors,'" Yitzchak began reading, "'God of Abraham and Isaac and Jacob, bless . . .'—the prayer wants your Hebrew name, Abba."

"Yerachmiel ben Baruch," he answered, invoking his father. With his own son at his side, he finally had his proof that his name wasn't a curse but a blessing, the confirmation of God's promised compassion for him.

"'Bless Yerachmiel ben Baruch,'" continued Yitzchak ben Yerachmiel. "'O God, full of compassion, free him of all pain and suffering as he leaves this world and enters the next. May he rest in peace, and may his memory be a blessing.'"

The dying took the hand of the living who'd survive him, and in that moment, the grasp he'd felt at a far different wall from the graveyard's took hold of him once more.

And Ricky, safe in his old bed, shut his eyes and slept.

CPSIA information can be obtained
at www.ICGtesting.com
Printed in the USA
LVHW100132151222
735091LV00001B/13